PRAISE FOR THE ANTHONY AWARD–NOMINATED
ISAAC OF GIRONA NOVELS

"Isaac of Girona, a good man in a bad time,
should delight readers."
—Bruce Alexander,
author of *Experiment in Treason*

"Finely written, well-plotted."
—*The Washington Times*

"Richly eventful, deftly plotted, and notable
also for a believable sweetness . . . A delight."
—*The Drood Review of Mystery*

A POULTICE FOR A HEALER

"The best. In the past, Roe has been favorably compared to
the late Ellis Peters, but Isaac is a finer character than
Brother Cadfael. Roe's medieval Spain offers more plot possibilities than Shrewsbury Abbey, and her full use of Isaac's
extended family keeps everything fresh."
—*The Toronto Globe and Mail*

"Wills, poisons, false identities, and fortified walls meet
their match in that 14th-century Sherlock Holmes, blind
healer Isaac of Girona." —*Kirkus Reviews*

"Isaac of Girona is a refreshingly different contender in the
field of medieval mysteries. The historical and cultural
details add flavor to the tales without overwhelming the
characters or plot." —*Hamilton Spectator* (Ontario, Canada)

continued . . .

A DRAUGHT FOR A DEAD MAN

"Roe offers an intriguing glimpse of another time and place which fans of Ellis Peters's Brother Cadfael might enjoy visiting."
— *St. Petersburg Times*

"The action arrives with a breathless rush [and] the ending will leave readers feeling as warmly content as the members of the joyous wedding party."
— *Publishers Weekly*

"Isaac is a credible and likable character . . . readers will forget for long periods of time that he is sightless, because he doesn't let his lack of seeing stop him from being an excellent healer, sleuth, husband, and father . . . an excellent historical mystery that gives readers insight into an era long gone but not forgotten due to works like this."
— *Midwest Book Review*

A POTION FOR A WIDOW

"A strong series . . . The setting and atmosphere are both exceedingly authentic."
— *The Mystery Reader*

"It is very obvious that Caroline Roe has done in-depth research on late Medieval Spain . . . A colorful and appealing historical mystery."
— *BookBrowser*

SOLACE FOR A SINNER

"I love this excellent series set in Medieval Spain . . . a wonderful ongoing character . . . the mix of Christian, Jewish and Muslim faiths affords plenty of good plot lines."
— *The Toronto Globe and Mail*

"An exceptional medieval murder mystery . . . The plot is mind boggling. Just when you think you know the murderer, you run into a dead end."
— *Rendezvous*

AN ANTIDOTE FOR AVARICE
An Anthony Finalist for Best Paperback Original

"The story weaves its way through history and gives you an insight of what life would be like in the Middle Ages . . . If you like history, you will be fascinated with this story."
—*Rendezvous*

CURE FOR A CHARLATAN

"Caroline Roe is the real deal . . . The story is filled with detail and action that paints a panorama of Medieval Spain, especially the Jewish quarter. The medical mystery is absolutely awesome, but it is the depth to all the characters that turns this into one of the best historical mystery entries . . . the Chronicles of Isaac are first-rate reads."
—*Painted Rock Reviews*

REMEDY FOR TREASON
An Anthony Finalist for Best Paperback Original
Nominated for the Arthur Ellis Award for Best Novel

"Intelligent, beautifully written and superbly researched . . . Roe gives us genuinely interesting characters, chief of whom is her detective, Blind Isaac." —*The Toronto Globe and Mail*

"Isaac of Girona, a good man in a bad time, should delight readers in this tale of court intrigue and religious tension in Medieval Spain—a rich, spicy paella of a book."
—Bruce Alexander, author of *Blind Justice*

"Not only a good mystery, it is a window into a time and place not usually approached by anyone but the dedicated scholar." —*The Washington Times*

"Blind Isaac and Yusuf are a delightfully incongruous pair . . . A deliciously nasty brew of fanatics and scheming royals." —Candace Robb, author of *The King's Bishop*

"A clever mystery, unusual setting and lashings of historical
     ial detail." —*The Toronto Star*

A POULTICE
for a
HEALER

Caroline Roe

BERKLEY PRIME CRIME, NEW YORK

A POULTICE FOR A HEALER

A Berkley Prime Crime book / published by arrangement with the author

PRINTING HISTORY
Berkley Prime Crime hardcover edition / November 2003
Berkley Prime Crime mass-market edition / November 2004

For information address: The Berkley Publishing Group,
a division of Penguin Group (USA) Inc.,
375 Hudson Street, New York, New York 10014.

Visit our website at www.penguin.com

ISBN: 0-425-19866-9

Berkley Prime Crime Books are published by The Berkley Publishing Group, a division of Penguin Group (USA) Inc., 375 Hudson Street, New York, New York 10014. The name BERKLEY PRIME CRIME and the BERKLEY PRIME CRIME design are trademarks belonging to Penguin Group (USA) Inc.

PRINTED IN THE UNITED STATES OF AMERICA

10 9 8 7 6 5 4 3 2 1

*This book is affectionately dedicated to
Alain Duffieux and Thong Ling
whose wisdom about life, travel, and everything that grows
has been of inestimable value*

LIST OF CHARACTERS

From Girona

ISAAC, physician of Girona
JUDITH, his wife
RAQUEL, their daughter
REBECCA, their eldest daughter, estranged
NATHAN AND MIRIAM, their twin children
YUSUF, a Muslim boy, ward of the King, student to Isaac
IBRAHIM, JACINTA, LEAH, NAOMI, their servants
DANIEL, Raquel's suitor
EPHRAIM, Daniel's uncle, a glover
DOLSA, his wife
MORDECAI BEN AARON, a businessman
AARON, his servant

BERENGUER DE CRUÏLLES, Bishop of Girona
BERNAT SA FRIGOLA, his secretary, a Franciscan
DOMINGO, sergeant of the Bishop's Guard
JORDI, Berenguer's servant since childhood
GABRIEL, a handsome guard
BLANCA, a housemaid, his friend

JAUME XAVIER, notary
PAU, his clerk

LUCÀ, a herbalist
MAGDALENA, an elderly widow, his patient
NARCÍS BELLFONT, his patient
ANNA, Narcís Bellfont's maid
ROMEU, a joiner
REGINA, his daughter
TOMAS, nine, a boy from the streets

On the road

ANTONI, a shipping agent in Sant Feliu de Guíxols
JOAN CRISTIÀ, an herbalist

In Mallorca

MAIMÓ, a wealthy businessman
PERLA, widow of Ezra ben Rubèn, Mordecai's uncle
FANETA, her daughter
RUBÈN, Faneta's son
SARA, Perla's laundress
JOSEP, Sara's son
MIQUEL, ten, an unemployed messenger boy

HISTORICAL NOTE

FROM the fall of 1354 to the summer of 1355, Pere (Pedro) the Ceremonious, King of the Aragonese empire, and Eleanora of Sicily, his Queen, were on the strategically crucial island of Sardinia, dealing with the aftermath of insurrection. The political landscape there was a kaleidoscope of shifting alliances and uncertain loyalties, with yesterday's foe suddenly turning himself into today's friend and loyal ally.

On the Iberian peninsula, the provinces of Catalonia and Valencia were being called upon to foot the heavy expenses of the war, with all the resentments and difficulties that such levies bring along with them.

The provinces had their own expenses. The coast of Catalonia was being harassed by pirate ships from various Mediterranean states; raiders attacked the smaller ports, which lacked the defensive works of larger cities, like Barcelona, in search of slaves and other valuable, easily sold items. Many of these ports, if taken by enemy troops, afforded a pathway into the rich, easily traversed countryside of the Empordà, which over the course of recorded history was one of the most fought-over plains in all of Europe. Within its green hills and around its ruins and ancient structures lie the remains of Celts, Greeks, Romans, several groups of Muslims, and a variety of later Europeans, all of whom—for longer and shorter periods of time—passed over, fought, lived, and died there.

To protect it, the hills of the Empordà are dotted with a network of defensive castles. The best overland route to it is blocked by the city of Girona, with its high, solid walls.

But Sant Feliu de Guíxols had long been an easy target for raiders and invaders, as were other seaports, including Palamós. Girona was outgrowing its fortifications. With the possibility of a war with Castile on the horizon, defensive strategies were on people's minds. The fortifying of Sant Feliu and Palamós, and the extension of fortifications to the city of Girona—monumental tasks in terms of time, effort, and money—were a contentious issue.

PART I

THE STORM

❖

ONE

Quan plau a Déu que la fusta peresca
En segur port romp àncores i ormeig

When it please God that the ship perish
In a safe port He breaks anchors and rigging

October 21, 1354

THE bells started to ring sometime between sext and nones, just at the end of a hard morning's work for the citizens—or at least many of the citizens—of the port town of Sant Feliu de Guíxols. The bells in the tower of the Benedictine Abbey were the first to sound the alarm. They were followed by bells from all the churches in the vicinity, until the clamor drowned out the shrieks of the terrified as well as the curses of the angry.

Down by the port, a tired-looking mother snatched her tiny infant from its cradle and headed for any place more strongly fortified than her makeshift hovel. She turned to her two other children, boys of seven and nine. "Take a blanket," she said. "Get out and hide yourselves."

The older one snatched up a thin bedcovering, took his younger brother by the hand, and ran without hesitation toward a small niche in the rocky coastline that marked the end of the beach. They wriggled into the niche and settled down on their stomachs, their heads resting on their folded arms. Making themselves as comfortable as they could, they watched silently as the spectacle unfolded before them.

A wind was rising, adding its own noise and confusion to the harsh discord of the bells; then in one tower after another, the bells gave up their task, as the ringers sought safety for themselves.

"I don't have enough room," the younger boy whispered.

"That's because you're growing," the older replied in a soft but worried voice. "And so am I. We'll have to find another place to hide."

"Where?"

"Don't know. We'll look once they've gone away. Look over there. If we move now they'll see us."

Five ships, square-rigged galleys, were lying out in the bay, appearing small and harmless in the distance. Ten boats with four to six sets of oars each sliced rapidly through the tossing water. When they were almost at the shore, the rowers jumped into the surf and towed the boats onto dry land. Without a pause they took out their weapons and began to yell at the top of their lungs, the essence of unbridled destructive fury, caring nothing for what they damaged or whom they destroyed. Then two on the edge of the crowd, armed with what looked like clubs, raced out of the boys' line of vision. They heard the sound of smashing wood, and the younger one asked, "Why are they doing that?"

A second later they appeared again, brandishing their clubs, now turned into flaming torches. "Fire," said his brother. "That was what they were after. They're going to burn down the town."

From their hiding place farther down the coast, they hadn't seen their door being broken down and the torches lit by their fire, but they heard the screams, and saw the smoke, and smelled the burning. The little one had begun to cry. "Stop that," his brother had whispered, "before someone hears you."

With some difficulty, he stopped. "What's that?" he had asked, pointing to the ships waiting out in the deep water.

"Don't be stupid. It's their ships," his brother said impatiently.

"No, that little one." The smaller boy had pointed toward the water directly in front of them.

There, bobbing about in the increasingly rough water, was a

tiny ship's boat, barely large enough for the two men it was holding. One of them was rowing and the other sitting in the stern. "There's someone else in there," said the older boy.

"No." The younger had the sharper eyes. "The one in the stern is carrying a bundle in his arms. Something big."

The wind suddenly picked up strength again and began to push the little boat toward the harbor at Sant Feliu de Gúixols. The boys were able to see the man at the oars straining to control its path, pulling hard on his left oar to compensate for the wind, trying to direct the tiny vessel toward them. Then a good-sized wave carried it upward and dropped it again, leaving a heavy cargo of seawater behind. Ungainly with the weight of water as well as its two-man crew, the boat wallowed clumsily, riding low in the heavy seas. At every pull of the oar, more water washed over its gunwales.

Then an erratic blast of wind hit the port side of the tiny craft. At the same moment, a large wave struck and the oarsman took a heavy pull on his left oar. "There she goes," the older boy said.

The boat disappeared from sight. After a short while, it bobbed up again, capsized, with no sign of its occupants. Shortly after that it hit a sandbar some small distance out and appeared again, in pieces. "There's someone hanging on to that wood," the younger boy said.

"You're right," said the older boy.

A huge wave broke over the sandbar, picking up man and wood and tossing them onto the wet sand where sea and earth met.

"Let's go see what happened," said the little brother.

"You're crazy," the older boy said to the younger. "Look at them over there. They're coming down for their boats, and they haven't got much with them. They'd be over here for us in a minute. Do you want to go to Genoa or Venice or maybe even Egypt and be sold? We'd never see each other again. Wait and don't move."

THEY waited until the last man climbed into the last boat and rowed halfway back to the ships. "Now," said the older boy. "As soon as that boat gets far enough away that they can't see us—"

"When's that?" asked the younger.

"When *you* can't see them. When they're just a black mark on the sea moving toward the ships."

Silent, the younger boy followed the movement of the last boat. "Now," he said. "I can't see people in the boat."

And the two boys walked very carefully over the sand to where the smashed remains of the little boat sat beside the wet man. "Señor," said the older boy. "Can you hear me? Are you alive?"

The man was lying on his stomach, his head turned toward the sea, and his arm over the segment of boat that had, apparently, brought him this far. A small bundle was tied over his shoulder. He neither moved nor spoke.

The older boy gave him a delicate push with his bare foot. This elicited no more reaction than the spoken word had.

"What's wrong with him?" asked the younger boy.

"He's dead," said the older one. "I think. We had better go and tell someone about him."

+=— —=+

A few hours earlier in the morning, three men were riding at a moderate pace on muleback, falling from time to time into desultory conversation. "Did you take this road when you came to Girona?" asked the serious-looking young man desperately. He had been asked to be kind to his companion, but his store of friendly conversational openings with the unresponsive stranger beside him had been used up long since. The silence was growing oppressive.

The stranger glanced up at his surroundings. "It doesn't seem familiar," he said abruptly. He was little more than a slight and beardless boy, who seemed to embody all the capricious sulkiness that often accompanies that age. He also possessed a quantity of curling, reddish hair that defied all attempts to keep it in control. He irritated his companion by pushing it constantly away from his face, with the self-consciousness of a girl. "But it was a rainy day. Everything looks different in the sun," he added.

"How did you travel from Seville?" asked the serious-looking young man, whose name was Daniel. The boy looked at him as if he were a judge, examining him for some suspected hideous offence. "Over land? By sea?" added Daniel.

"By sea," said the boy quickly. "It's a wearisome journey by land, they say, and not too safe."

"How long did it take you? By sea, I mean."

"You mean to sail to Barcelona? It took—What is that?" he asked suddenly, pointing up ahead.

"It's an oxcart," said Daniel. "Have you never seen an oxcart before?"

But Rubèn seemed to feel that this question did not deserve an answer and fell back into his previous silence. "Why do you travel to this seaport?" asked Rubèn after a long pause, apparently feeling that he had been discourteous.

"I go for my uncle Ephraim," said Daniel. "The glovemaker. His agent at Sant Feliu de Guíxols received a delivery of merchandise he wants me to look at. Not a very interesting reason unless you are also a glover, as I am."

Rubèn returned to studying the scenery as they rode.

"What brought you to Girona?" asked Daniel, silently vowing that this would be his last attempt to begin a conversation. "It's a long way, isn't it?"

"It is," said Rubèn, pausing ominously before continuing. "My mother is cousin to Mordecai. Her father and Mordecai's father were brothers. My mother went to Seville to marry, but when my father died, we left to live with my grandmother in Mallorca. My mother urged me to visit my kin in Girona. She hoped, I think, that I might stay to learn a trade."

"You have no trade?" said Daniel, surprised.

"Trade?" said Rubèn thoughtfully. "Not really. I was raised to be a scholar, but my father decided that he wanted me to go into his business—"

"What was that?"

Rubèn paused again. "He was an agent," he said, "like the man we go to see. Much trade comes through Seville, you know."

"I know little about Seville," confessed Daniel.

"It's a pleasant city," said Rubèn vaguely. "There are many things to do there." He wiped his forehead with the sleeve of his tunic and looked up at the sky. "It's very hot today."

"But you must be well accustomed to the heat," said Daniel. "Coming from Seville."

"Of course," said the boy. "But here the air is still," he added fretfully. As if the boy had summoned it, a light breeze sprang up from the south, enough to flutter the leaves. "How much longer will this journey take? I do not wish to miss the ship that is to bring me home."

"It is Aaron who has the responsibility for the journey," said Daniel, smiling. "When will we arrive, Aaron?" he asked.

The burly servant riding along with them turned toward Daniel. "It's not a long journey, Master Daniel. Even at this pace, it's no more than five hours in all."

"Then why don't we ride faster?" asked Rubèn.

"We'll be in Sant Feliu in time for us to enjoy a leisurely dinner before your ship sails," said Daniel. "Uncle Ephraim said that it planned to sail in the afternoon, I believe. We're making good time, aren't we, Aaron?"

"Very good time, Master Daniel. But we might consider hastening our pace. There's a smell of rain in the air. I suspect the weather is bad on the coast."

"The wind is changing," said young Rubèn suddenly. "I can feel it. If we don't hurry, my ship may decide to leave early without me."

"You're over-young to feel the weather in your bones," said Aaron, laughing. "But look at those trees, Master Daniel. Young Master Rubèn is right. The wind has changed."

⊹━━ ━━⊹

AND at the same hour in the morning, the Bishop of Girona, Berenguer de Cruïlles, walked into the great hall in the Benedictine Abbey at Sant Feliu de Guíxols. He shivered. The sun had disappeared behind a mass of dark cloud; the room was chilly. The bells for terce still seemed to be ringing in his head and rebounding off the vaulted ceiling; he blinked and sat down at the head of a long table. Its dark polished surface gleamed like cold, wet marble and he closed his eyes as if that could shut out the cold. His secretary, Father Bernat, and his confessor, Father Francesc, were on either side of him; Francesc

Pou, the Abbot of Sant Feliu and four brothers sat next to them. All had the air of men prepared to sit and argue their positions for hours.

"The situation is impossible, Your Excellency," said the Abbot, determined to strike the first blow. "We cannot do it."

"His Majesty has expressed his great concern over attacks on towns along this coast, Father," said Berenguer firmly. His voice was hoarse, and he pitched it low to emphasis his point. "Sant Feliu de Guíxols and Palamós in particular," he added. "Both towns have more shipping and other endeavors than they have fortifications to protect them."

"We are aware of that, Your Excellency," said the Abbot, "but—"

"The towns are as vulnerable to raids from enemies of the crown as they were in the time of our noble lord, King Pedro the Magnificent, when the French most cruelly destroyed the town and most of its inhabitants."

"Those were events that we are unlikely to forget, Your Excellency. They greatly affected our predecessors here."

"Because of this," said the Bishop, ignoring the Abbot, "the Genoese, pirates, and others who have a mind to help themselves to our wealth and our citizens are free to do so. This cannot continue." Berenguer shivered and rubbed his hands together in a fruitless effort to stay warm.

Father Bernat summoned a servant and murmured something to him.

The Abbot shook his head, whether in agreement or frustration was difficult to tell. "The towns do not have the resources to build major fortifications, Your Excellency. In fact, at the moment, the town of Sant Feliu cannot even pay the rent it owes us. I need not remind you that the responsibility for the town's safety lies as much with Girona as it does with the abbey or the town. His Majesty's demands put us in a very difficult position."

"And why is this?" asked the Bishop.

"Have you not received my letters, Your Excellency?" asked the Abbot.

"I have," said Berenguer. "But not all explanations are fit to be put into a letter that will then be saved for all to see. Tell me

frankly and honestly why the financial resources of such an apparently lively and prosperous town have not been and are not
now sufficient to pay their annual rent to the abbey, which
therefore does not have the financial resources to help protect
the coast from raiders."

"The reasons go back many years. Some of them are honest
ones, and others, perhaps, have more to do with the greed of
men," said the Abbot with a sigh. He bundled together the
documents in front of him and began a lengthy exposition of
just what those reasons were. Berenguer looked down the table
at the powerful Abbot, noticed that his eyes were focused
somewhere on the vaulted ceiling of the Great Hall, and realized that he was prepared to speak until nightfall, if necessary.

A servant set a cup of hot mulled wine in front of Berenguer.
The Bishop clutched the silver goblet tightly in his hands in an
effort to warm them and then took a sip of wine to clear the
discomfort in his throat.

The Benedictine's voice boomed and faded away in a series
of meaningless waves, but Berenguer scarcely heard a distin-
guishable word of it. He only wanted to leave this cold and
echoing hall and ride to La Bisbal, where he had his own chamber at the residence there. La Bisbal. It was not far from here.
His thoughts drifted. At La Bisbal he would be a few miles
away from the castle at Cruïlles where he had spent some of the
happiest moments of his boyhood. At Cruïlles he could huddle
by a blazing fire, wrapped in warm fur covers, in a tapestry-
hung room behind a tightly shut door.

"Does Your Excellency not see the situation that we are in?"
asked the Abbot.

When Berenguer finally recognized that the words had been
spoken to him, it also occurred to him that the Abbot had said
them more than once. And that he was pink with anger. The
Bishop turned helplessly to Father Bernat, who paled and then
quickly drew some papers from the leather wallet he had set in
front of him.

"His Excellency drew up some proposals that he felt might
ease your difficulties, my lord," murmured the secretary to the
Abbot. "Perhaps I could leave them for you to study at your

leisure before we continue discussions on the topic. And perhaps, if Your Excellency does not object," he said, with a worried look at the Bishop, "I could bring up a few minor points on other issues on which the assistance and wise counsel of His Excellency, the Abbot, would be most valued."

Berenguer sat huddled over his cup, breathing in the spices from the hot wine while the business that had brought him to this place was efficiently and ruthlessly dealt with by Father Bernat.

Before the Abbot had time to raise the multitude of issues he had been hoarding up for this meeting, Berenguer stood, leaning with his hands on the edge of the table. "My most noble lord," he said to his host, "I fear we must excuse ourselves. We must continue on our way as soon as possible. If you will be so kind as to send me that formidable list you have in front of you, everything on it will be dealt with. Bernat, Francesc, we are riding out at once. Quick, man. Send for my warm cloak and my horse and prepare yourselves. Everything else can be sent on later."

The abbey was suddenly in a state of turmoil. "Your Excellency," murmured Father Francesc, "what ails you?"

"A fever is coming on me, and I must leave while I can still ride," said the Bishop, his voice cracking from hoarseness. He turned and walked as steadily as he could for the door. "Send for my physician to meet us at the castle at Cruïlles, and let us leave at once," he whispered. "I refuse to end my days shivering in this cold and drafty place."

Minutes later the Bishop, his personal servant, the two priests and four guards rode out into the gray, shifting, uneasy wind that presages a storm.

They were a third of the way toward their destination when the bells began to ring for sext. Berenguer, by nature a bold and daring rider, was hunched forward over his horse, allowing it to set the pace that carried them all forward. Two of the guards rode next to him, one on either side, their anxious glances more on the Bishop than on their surroundings. As the road began to swing inland, the first drops of rain fell lightly on the small procession.

‡══ ══‡

AN hour later, Daniel, Rubèn, and Aaron rode into the town of Sant Feliu de Guíxols. "Master Antoni, the shipping agent, has his house on this street," said Aaron. "His warehouse is directly behind it. I will take you there first, for I have letters and other business documents to deliver to him. He should be able to tell you about ships sailing to Mallorca."

"Where are we dining?" asked Rubèn.

"With Master Benjuha. You will be very comfortable as his guest, Master Daniel," said Aaron.

"Is he a rich man that we should be so comfortable?" asked Rubèn with more interest than he had shown so far in any part of their travel.

"No, he is not," said Aaron with a disapproving glance at the young man. The attitude of Mordecai's servant toward his master's kin amused Daniel considerably. No doubt there was a story there. "But he is a good man, and hospitable."

Aaron dismounted, unfastened his mule's saddlebags, and took them with him to Master Antoni's door.

‡══ ══‡

WHEN the maidservant ushered them through the door into the hall, Master Antoni was standing in the doorway to his office, filling the frame. He stepped out, smiling broadly, a big, powerful-looking man with brown hair bleached by the sun and skin as bronzed as a sailor's. "Aaron," he said. "I am most heartily glad to see you. But who are these that you bring with you?"

"I am Daniel, nephew to Ephraim the glovemaker of Girona," said Daniel, stepping forward with a bow. "Being much occupied with business, my uncle sent me to look over the new merchandise you gave him notice of."

"You are most welcome, Daniel," said Antoni. "Your uncle has spoken highly of you. And this young man?"

"This is Rubèn, kinsman of Mordecai the bootmaker," said Daniel. "We were fortunate to have him as traveling companion on the trip."

"I carry letters from Master Mordecai," said the servant.

"Letters that outline his requirements and introduce the young master."

"Thank you, Aaron. You come at an excellent hour. You will, I trust, dine with me? My cook has prepared an abundant dinner, and I am sure that you can find something on the table that you would enjoy."

"But I believe that we are expected by Master Benjuha," said Daniel.

"It is raining now, and Master Benjuha stays close to his fire today with a feverish cold. I will send a message that you are dining here."

"Thank you," said Daniel.

"Good. Now I suggest that you wash away the dust of travel and refresh yourselves a little while I read the letters. Then we will go into the warehouse to inspect what has come in."

TWO

Per molt amor ma vida és en dubte

Through much love my life is in peril

"AND what do you believe is the root of her illness?" Isaac the physician asked his daughter. They were strolling through the streets of the *call*, the Jewish Quarter of Girona, heading slowly for home. His hand lay lightly on her shoulder for guidance, although in such familiar surroundings, he had no real need of it.

"The root?" asked his daughter, Raquel. "In such a case should we not be treating the symptoms before concerning ourselves with the roots?"

"You do well to counter with my own advice," said her father, laughing. "But that does not mean the root should fail to interest us, and since Regina is closer to your age than mine, I value your insight into the matter."

"It does not take much insight, Papa," said Raquel. "She has been in love with young Marc since she was little more than a child, and now he has abandoned her. She is in despair, Papa, and cares not if she lives or dies." Raquel pulled at the gate to their house and found it locked. "If Ibrahim insists on locking the gate while we are out, I wish he would stay somewhere close by to open it," she snapped. "Ibrahim!" she called. "Open the gate!"

"And what is the remedy?" asked her father, once the porter

and houseman Ibrahim had arrived and slowly unbarred and unlocked the gate that led into the courtyard.

The October sun was pouring its late warmth into the courtyard, as if to deny the existence of the approaching winter. The dinner table had been set up in a sunny corner, and the family was already gathered around it.

"The mistress is waiting dinner, Master Isaac," said Ibrahim reproachfully.

"So early, Mama?" said Raquel.

"Nonsense," said Judith. "We are enjoying the sun while it lasts. Mistress Dolsa tells me we are to have a storm soon."

"I think Ibrahim is trying to tell us that we are keeping him from his dinner," said Isaac dryly. "And he may go. But what do you suggest?" he said to his daughter.

"We must get her to eat and drink something, so that she will feel better, and then we must convince her that at seventeen she can still look forward to a happy and useful life."

"And how do you propose to do that?" asked Isaac, as they took places at the table. "Her family has had no success. How can we, who have much less importance in her life than they have, do better?"

"I told her that there were other things in life besides love," said Raquel. "Although it is important."

"You know, my dear," said her father, turning his face with its blind eyes toward her as if seeking to see her once more. "I doubt if you are right. If you have the means to live, however poorly, everything else is a matter of what you love."

"Don't you mean who, Papa?"

"No. A man—or a woman—may love family, a lover, his religion, country, money, or even food and wine. Deprive him of the object or objects of his love and he will despair. And love, like many herbs, can feed us and make us whole, but can also poison us. Where it poisons, we must seek its contrary and use it as a poultice to draw the poison out."

"Hatred? Are you saying we must make her hate Marc? That's not possible, Papa. We must look for some remedy."

"That is what we have been talking about," said her father mildly.

"But you were talking of poultices," said Raquel.

There were already four people around the table. Judith, Isaac's wife, their eight-year-old twins, Nathan and Miriam, and a Muslim boy of twelve, Yusuf, who had permission from the king to live with the family.

"Who needs a poultice?" asked Judith, "Romeu's daughter?"

"Not yet, Mama," said Raquel.

"And how is Regina?" asked Judith. "It is this sad business of young Marc that has caused it, is it not? Her parents should never have allowed her to fall in love at such an age."

"But Mama, how could they stop her?" asked Raquel.

"They could have found a way. But once the war is over, surely young Marc will come back. He cannot have fixed on a soldier's life forever."

"She has heard from the castellan," said Raquel. "Do you remember him? He was Marc's officer in Sardinia and was sent back when he caught the fever."

"I may have lost my waist, but I have not as yet lost my wits," said Judith. "Of course I remember."

"Well, now that the castellan is beginning to recover, he has sent poor Regina a message that her Marc, instead of coming back with his companions, has joined a regiment of Almogàvers and is off to Athens or some such place. He wants to be rich and thinks it worth dying for. Also the castellan said that he likes the soldier's life."

"That's not very hopeful," remarked Judith. "For as I understand it, Marc is poor, and although Regina has a respectable dowry, he'll not get rich marrying her."

"She is sick with crying, Mama," said Raquel, "and refuses to eat. She swears she wants to die, or dress as a soldier and go to join him."

"They sound like much the same thing to me," said Judith. "What an idea for a respectable girl with a dowry!"

"That seems to have been her father's thought," said Isaac. "Romeu said that he never heard anything so mad in his life."

"But Isaac," said Judith. "I think you're making too much of her grief. At that age all sorrows, even tiny ones, are mountains to climb over. Wait a week or two and she will be the same as she was before."

"Yes," said Yusuf. The boy was learning the arts of medicine from Isaac, and of arms and horsemanship from the captain of the Bishop's guard. Very recently, the Bishop had added philosophy to his studies, and twice a week he sat with one or another of the priests at the cathedral to read passages from Augustine or Jerome or Gregory, depending on the tastes and learning of his tutor for that day. "For the philosophers tell us that no woman can hold to one idea for long," he said.

"And when did you become expert on women, Yusuf?" asked Raquel tartly. "And I could ask the same of your philosophers. Which philosophers are you talking about, and what reasons do they give?"

"What is a philosopher?" asked Miriam, one of the eight-year-old twins.

"I am a woman as well," said Raquel, heatedly. "And I think I have held to many ideas and principles for as long as I can remember. And I know more about what it is to be betrothed than you do, Yusuf. I saw Regina and talked to her, and she is truly in despair. In the same circumstances I would be, too."

"But you and Regina are two very different people," said Isaac. "As different as two young women can be. And now, if you will excuse me, I shall wash and prepare myself for dinner."

"She will get over her despair and sorrow," said Judith, "just as soon as someone else comes along."

"Mama," said Raquel, "that is cruel. She truly suffers."

"Of course she does. All I am saying is that she will recover." She paused to watch her husband walk across the courtyard and open the door into his study. When it had closed again, she turned back to her daughter. "Raquel, now that your father is away from the table, there is something I must ask you."

"What is that, Mama?"

"Postpone your wedding for a few more months. By the time the rabbi comes back from the meeting in Barcelona we are sure to have cold, wet weather. Please, for the sake of your father, stay here and help him deal with the winter's serious illnesses."

Raquel stared at her mother, her face stiff with anger and astonishment. "Mama, I can't," she said at last. "I have waited so long already. And Daniel will be furious. What am I to tell him? What excuse do you want me to give now?"

"Tell him the truth," said Judith. "If he is as good as we believe he is, he will understand. But not a word to your father."

Isaac crossed the courtyard once more, moving silently over the stones, and sat down in the ensuing silence. Raquel stared mutinously at her empty plate. Judith was looking with vague, unfocused eyes at Miriam and Nathan, who were laughing over a private game and ignoring the differences between adults.

"Have you lost your appetite like poor little Regina, my love?" asked Isaac. "But surely not for the same reason."

"Dinner is not yet on the table," said Judith, horrified. "Whatever was I thinking of?" she added and hurried off to the kitchen to see what was going on.

"Raquel," said her father quietly, "when your wedding takes place, is it possible that you might stay at home until your mother's baby is born? She is more tired than she is willing to admit. I can hear it in her voice and in the movement of her feet; they are neither of them so light and sure as they should be."

"But, Papa, we found her Jacinta to help Naomi, and she is able to do so many things in the kitchen that Mama no longer has to concern herself with them. Don't you understand what a great difference the child has made?"

"But your mother will always concern herself, my dear," said Isaac. "It is in her nature."

"And she is now heavy with child. It is only normal that she should be tired and slower on her feet."

"It was not so when she was carrying the twins," said Isaac.

Raquel recognized defeat when it faced her. "Perhaps it would be better if we were to marry in the spring," she said with a sigh.

THREE

Bullirà la mar com la cassola en forn

The sea shall boil like the pot in an oven

THE shipping agent pushed aside the remains of a fine baked fish, stuffed with herbs and rice, that they had dined on. His maidservant put a large bowl of dried fruits and nuts on the table and left the three men to talk. "Is Master Ephraim well?" Antoni asked. "It is unlike him to miss an opportunity to come down here and inspect our wares. And listen to the latest news and gossip."

"He is very well," said Daniel. "But much too busy to travel, he claims. I don't believe him. I fear it is my fault that he stays at home."

"How can that be?"

"It is a long tale."

"After dining is the best time for hearing a long tale," said Antoni. "For then, if it is too wearying, one may combine it with an afternoon sleep."

"I shall attempt not to be that long," said Daniel, laughing. "Last month I was to be married to the cleverest and most beautiful woman in all of Catalonia," said Daniel. "Her name is Raquel, and she is the daughter of a most respected and well-known physician, Isaac."

"I know of him," said Antoni. "Her father is the blind physician who healed the young Duke of Girona, is he not?"

"Yes, and because of his blindness, his daughter, who is almost as skilled as he is, assists him. Unfortunately for me, shortly before our wedding was to take place, Master Isaac was called away to the north to help a friend, and it seemed that he must take his daughter with him. She has only recently returned, and begged for a few weeks to make her wedding preparations."

"I can understand her reasons," said Antoni. "And so instead of a greatly desired marriage, you have been given a trip to our fine seaport of Sant Feliu de Guíxols to see what you fancy among the rarities in my warehouse."

"I have, and I am greatly enjoying it. I was particularly interested in some of those rare dyes and beads. Such quality is almost unheard of in our city."

"Or anywhere else in this part of the world," said Antoni with satisfaction. "They come from a port on the Black Sea."

"Recently we have had a great demand for new or unusual furs for trimmings. My uncle will be very annoyed that he did not come with me when he hears of the skins that you have brought in. But to have joined me would have spoiled his excuse for sending me, I suppose."

"That is the penalty he pays for being too subtle," said Antoni. "And too kind. But tell me where you have sprung from, young sir," he continued, turning to Rubèn.

Rubèn reddened slightly at the sudden assault and turned to his host. "Sprung from, sir?"

"Mordecai said that you are his cousin Faneta's child and this was your first visit to Girona," said Antoni. "A brief visit, it seems."

"Only a week," said Rubèn. "I was born and grew up in Seville, but now we live with my grandmother in Mallorca. And this afternoon, if all goes well, I shall board a ship to return."

"Indeed," said Antoni. "With whom are you sailing?"

"A small vessel you would not have heard of," said Rubèn. "My grandmother knows the captain. But Master Mordecai pointed out that if the ship failed to arrive, there was no man on the coast who knew more about shipping than you, Master Antoni. I had been depending on your good counsel."

"Whatever counsel I can give you, you are welcome to," said Antoni, observing him with growing interest.

"It was for my mother's sake" said Rubèn, "that I made this journey. She greatly wished me to meet her family."

"And what did you think of your eastern cousins?" asked Antoni.

"I was greatly astonished to meet Master Mordecai. I had thought that he was a simple bootmaker and discovered that he is a man of great wealth and distinction. I felt most uncomfortable, fearing that he might believe I came to seek advantage with him, but he has been most kind to me, and hospitable."

Antoni studied him all the time he was speaking, as if he were a doubtful commodity that he was considering buying. "When did you go to Mallorca with your mother?"

"Almost three years ago," he said.

"You know," he said, "if you hadn't told me you were from Seville, I would have thought you had lived all your life in the islands."

"What do you mean?" asked Rubèn, looking puzzled.

"I have many friends and acquaintances from Mallorca," said Antoni. "And some relations. Already you sound like a true Mallorcan."

"Thank you," said Rubèn. "But I fear that in exchange I can no longer speak like one from Seville."

"You'll have little call to do that around here," said Antoni with a malicious wink in Daniel's direction.

"I do not know," said Rubèn shyly.

Something slammed with a loud crack and ended the interrogation. "What was that?" asked Daniel.

"I'm afraid that was the wind," said Antoni. "It does that. I think we may be in for a storm."

❖──── ────❖

A dish piled with small grilled fish, a fat braised duck with a sauce of bitter orange and dried apricots, rice, and lentils were set on the table by a youthful maidservant. "I smell something delicious," said Isaac. "Tell me what you brought us, Jacinta."

"Grilled fish and duck and rice, master," said the girl.

"And Jacinta has prepared the sauce for the duck," said Judith of the servant her husband had recently brought back from Perpignan. "She is good little cook already. I must—"

But whatever Judith had been intending, it was interrupted by a loud clanging of the bell at the gate. Nathan peered over at the gate to see who was making all the noise. "It looks like a soldier, Papa," said the boy.

Alarmed, Raquel rose and went over to see. "It is one of the Bishop's guard, Papa."

"What can the man want now?" said Judith. "Must you be hunted down every day in the midst of dinner?"

"Not every day, my love," said Isaac. "I will see what he wants."

Raquel tugged at the gate to get it open and let in a young and awkward-looking guard. He bowed to all, murmured something apologetic, and fell into a longer, quiet conversation with the physician.

Isaac turned toward the family again. "I have received an urgent summons, my dear, from His Excellency. He is most unwell and I am to meet him in Cruïlles at the castle as soon as possible. But in the meantime, our messenger has had nothing to eat since early this morning. I am sure there is enough food in the kitchen . . ."

"Of course," said Judith. "Jacinta. Bring a plate for the guard."

"Raquel, Yusuf, as soon as you have eaten, put together what I will need to carry with me."

"We'll do it now, Papa," said his daughter, "and eat later. Come along, Yusuf."

Yusuf snatched up some bread, dipped it into the sauce, and stuffed it in his mouth before following Raquel to the study.

"Who are you taking with you?" asked Judith.

"His Excellency has sent his guard to escort me," said her husband.

"Nonsense," said Judith. "You must take Yusuf as well."

"I would be better off with Raquel, if I am to take someone else," said Isaac sharply. "His Excellency is very ill."

"Then take both of them. But Raquel will need Leah to go with her."

At the end of a frenzied quarter of an hour, the guard had finished his hasty meal and was headed for the Bishop's stables to fetch mounts for Isaac and his assistants. The rest ate, packed what they needed, and by the time he returned with three mules and Yusuf's horse, they were ready to mount and ride out of the city gates. As they left, the first drops of water from a threatening sky fell on their heads.

THEY started out at a walk, hampered by the fact that Isaac's mule was on a lead. "The sky looks very black, Papa," said Raquel. "I fear that we are heading into a storm."

"Then why are we traveling so slowly?" asked Isaac.

"I did not wish you to be in danger of being unseated, master," said the guard, turning scarlet in embarrassment. "Can you ride more quickly? It would be a great help."

"I can try. And if I tumble from this docile creature, I suspect that at the worse, I will be covered in mud. And we shall be that in any case."

"I will take the lead rein," said Yusuf, with all the confidence of his twelve or thirteen years. "I know my horse better than you know that mule."

Since what he said was true, there were no objections; Yusuf took the rein and spurred his horse to a fast trot. The mule balked for a moment then sped up and fell in with the bay mare's pace.

The road was still dry, despite the sprinkling of rain. "We must keep this pace up as long as we can," said the guard. "There is heavy rain ahead that must be turning the roads to mud, and once it is dark, neither man nor beast will be able to see in this weather."

"Can we not stop if the road becomes too bad?"

"Please, no, mistress. His Excellency was very bad when he left Sant Feliu, and after riding to the castle he can only be worse," said guard, panic-stricken. "What could I say if I brought you too late to help?"

"We will not stop," said Isaac.

THE road followed the plain of the river Ter, skirting the hills and mountains on their right hand. The rain was intermittent and scanty, accompanied by gusts of wind, but hardly troublesome. Ahead of them, however, heavy black clouds loomed. Yusuf spoke something to his master and protector, then gave a warning pull on the lead rein and spurred his mare into a gentle canter.

Leah, Raquel's maid, gave a little shriek as her mule followed suit. White with terror, she concentrated on clinging to the beast with all her strength. Raquel caught up to her without difficulty and the whole group kept up the pace for several miles. All the while, thunder rumbled in the distance, and across the sky ahead of them were occasional flashes of lightning.

The road climbed and curved around the side of the mountain, a steady rain began to fall, and the mules slowed down. They lurched and scrambled over the hilly, slippery roads at a slower and slower pace. The guard looked back at his followers and waved them to follow him to a stand of trees beside the road.

"I think we should rest the animals a little," said the guard. "And there's a stream over there as soon as they cool down."

"My mare could go on for hours," said Yusuf.

"I'm sure, young master," said the guard, glaring at him and nodding in the direction of the two women. He walked over to the blind physician and fell into earnest conversation with him.

THE young guard did not let them rest long enough to cool down or for their tired limbs to stiffen. "The weather ahead will only get worse, I think," he said nervously, not being used to giving orders to anyone, much less to people of more consequence than he was.

"Then let us carry on at once," said Isaac.

They started out at a gentle trot. The rising wind drove into their faces, and the rain grew heavier.

"We've come out from behind the mountains," called the guard over the noise of the wind. "It'll be like this for a while," he added.

The horses and mules slowed even more, carrying their heads down into the wind. The slashing rain turned the road into a river of treacherous mud; the small stream that tumbled down the slope close to the road, already swollen to three or four times its usual depth, met an obstruction in its bed and overflowed.

The guard slowed to a careful walk, allowing his horse to pick its own way, followed by the rest of the party. From that point on, every low spot on the road was covered with water of varying depths. Somewhere behind the clouds, the sun was setting and the light, already dim, darkened until it was difficult to see the road ahead. It had been a long time since they had met another traveler on the road. Even couriers and others with urgent business had stopped somewhere to wait out the storm.

Raquel began to wonder if they would perish in it, should it grow worse, and if the risk to the five of them was worth a chance of saving the Bishop whose condition must be quite grave. She wanted to talk to her father, but riding side by side under these conditions seemed folly. It was better to allow the mule to pick her own path than to try to force her.

—◆◆———◆◆—

IT was dark when they reached the road to Cruïlles, but the rain had begun to ease and the wind to die down. Some of the water drained off the road, leaving a wet, but almost visible surface. Raquel pushed back her hood, glad to have the water off her face, and peered around her, looking for signs of a town. She found nothing. The guard, who seemed to have the eyes of a cat or an owl, doggedly continued along the way. "It's right over there," he said, pointing up.

Raquel looked in the direction of his hand and discerned a hill that rose out of the plain, standing alone. The road they were on turned and twisted as it searched out the easiest route up the steep slope. Water still raced down the paths and ruts in the road, but the beasts picked their way up slowly, stumbling from time to time as they climbed through the darkness.

"Surely we should be walking," said Isaac.

"They will climb up the hill more certainly than we would on foot, and they're not heavily laden," said the guard firmly, not adding that he wouldn't allow them to waste the extra time it would take to dismount and walk.

THE castle sat on the very top of the hill, its well-built, soaring tower just barely visible against the night sky. The houses that made up the little town clustered around it in the shape of a horseshoe, and the solid walls of the town served to protect both castle and townspeople. The guard called out as they drew near the outer gate, and someone began at once to open it. Torches flared up, lighting their way up a short street lined with houses and into a square in front of the castle. The courtyard was ablaze with light when they arrived and filled with voices.

The gate stood open at its widest. As Raquel prepared to dismount, strong hands lifted her off the mule and she was hastened off into the hall with the others.

They were a bedraggled group. Water dripped from their clothing and pooled on the stone tiles. They were muddy and tired and cold. Raquel looked around and saw that she was being stared at with great curiosity by a crowd of servants; there was not a familiar face in the great vaulted room. "Where is my patient?" asked Isaac quietly.

Light, quick footsteps sounded on the stone steps leading down from the upper chambers, and Father Bernat appeared, followed a few moments later by Father Francesc.

"Master Isaac," he said, "I am most pleased to see you. You have come with great dispatch."

"How is His Excellency?"

"Poor, Master Isaac. Very poor. I beg you to hurry. He has been feverish and very ill since this morning."

"Then why did you bring him here?" said Isaac. "Are you mad? In all this wind and rain? The guard you sent tells me he was not even on a litter, but riding his own horse. It was foolish, perhaps fatal."

"I could not stop him, Master Isaac," said Bernat, his voice cracking with emotion. "He gave the orders and they were obeyed. He would not listen to us. We tried to convince him that he would be better off staying where he was, but he insisted on coming here right away. Then he insisted on riding. 'I am dying, Bernat,' he said, when I tried to stop him, 'and I will not recover anywhere else. Would you kill me? And if I must end my life now, let me do so in the country where I was born.' I could not deny him that," said Bernat, his voice thick with tears. "Shortly after we left, the rain started, and by the time we arrived he was very wet and cold. I fear my obedience has killed him."

"If you will allow me to take off my wet cloak and wash away a little of this mud, we will see. Let us hope his condition is not as grave as you fear," said the physician. "I will need my daughter as well. Perhaps someone could take her to a room where she may do the same. The road here was very dirty."

+=——— ———=+

"TELL me what you can of his condition," said Isaac to Jordi, the Bishop's manservant. He had been in Berenguer's service since they were boys together, and knew his master better than anyone living.

"He has kept nothing in his stomach since he arrived here," said Jordi. "And has suffered much from a watery flux from his bowels."

"Bloody?"

"No."

"What has he been given since he arrived?" Isaac asked.

"He asked for spiced wine, but only touched a little of it," said Jordi carefully. "Someone sent for a physician who prescribed a poultice for the throat and some sort of drink, but His Excellency would not touch it. Father Bernat suggested that I try to keep him comfortable and wait for you. I have been bathing his face and trying to get him to drink a little."

"You have done well," said Isaac, as he felt Berenguer's throat and neck, and then put his ear down to his chest and listened. "How do you feel, Your Excellency?" he asked.

"Cold," said the Bishop. "So cold. My hands are cold, and my feet." He moved his head irritably. "The dog frightened my pony and he threw me in the pond. I am cold."

"How long has he been raving?" said Isaac, his hands moving back to Berenguer's throat and feeling it delicately.

"Off and on since before nones," said Jordi. "And it must be close to compline now."

"Some six hours," murmured Isaac.

"Sometimes he is himself and complains of thirst, and yet he is in too much pain to swallow anything."

"Tell me what you see, Raquel," said her father.

"I see the swelling about the neck that you have felt, Papa. Even in this light, I can see that he is very gray in the face and sicker than I have ever seen him."

"Rashes, spots, or sores that I did not feel?"

"No, Papa."

"That is good. What would you give him?"

"Something for the fever and vomiting and the pain in his throat, then warm broth every few minutes until he can sleep," she said.

"Did you hear that, Jordi? Is there broth?"

"I will have a kettle of it brought up and placed on the fire here. And stones wrapped in linen to warm his feet, if I may," he added.

"Yes, indeed. Make him as comfortable as possible. Is there a kettle of water on the hob, Raquel?"

"Yes, Papa."

"Then steep a good quantity of willow bark and herbs. As soon as it is cool enough, we must see about getting it into him. Where is Yusuf?"

"I will do it, Papa."

"Yes, my dear, I know you will, but he should be here. Part of his training is to learn not only the skills but also the patience."

While Raquel poured boiling water over a small bundle of herbs and set it to one side to steep and cool, Isaac opened up a small wooden casket of already prepared medications. "Have you finished?" he asked.

"Yes, Papa," she said.

"Then put a spoonful each of wine and water into a cup," said Isaac.

She looked around her. One candle and the fire provided the room's only light. But over on a dresser, she saw a tray with two jugs on it and two cups. She sniffed them. Wine and water. She splashed a tiny amount of the contents of each in a cup and brought it over to the bed. "Here it is, Papa."

"One drop, no more, in the mixture," said her father, handing her a vial he had taken from the box.

Raquel tipped one drop into the cup and swirled it around to mix it. Taking a square of clean linen from the box, she dipped it into the mixture and brushed it over the sick man's lips. His tongue touched it and he shuddered. She dipped it in again, this time squeezing a little into his slightly open mouth. Again he shuddered. After repeating this three or four times, she held the cup up to his lips and let a little trickle into his mouth. With great difficulty, he tried to swallow. Some of it dribbled out of the side of his mouth and she mopped it away carefully. Two more repetitions of the same and the cup was empty. "I don't know how much he actually swallowed, Papa," she said.

"Even if he didn't swallow any, the essence will numb his throat a little," said Isaac. "Enough to enable him to swallow some of the other, and then take a little broth. He can have another dose, exactly the same, after the bells have rung once more. Are you dry and comfortable?"

"No, Papa. I am wet and cold."

"Go and change, have something warm to drink, and come back with Leah. Then I will change and make myself comfortable as well. He cannot be left until the fever breaks. Go quickly."

WHEN Raquel came back with a reluctant Leah in tow, Jordi had returned with broth that simmered on the fire, warm rocks for His Excellency's feet, and two boys bringing a heartening collation of hot soup, bread, and cold chicken as supper for those in the sickroom. Father Bernat had the room next to their patient prepared with a good fire in it, as a place where those who were not sitting with the Bishop could rest a while.

Once Isaac was satisfied that all was as well as it could be, one of the serving boys conducted him next door. Yusuf was already there, warming his hands at the fire. "Excuse me, lord," he said. "I did not know where you were."

"And where have you been?" asked Isaac, sharply. "You were

not brought here to acquaint yourself with the amusements of the town, but to help with the Bishop in his illness."

"I was seeing to the beasts, lord," said Yusuf. "My horse and His Excellency's mules. I am sorry, lord. I will be ready to sit up all night if I am needed."

"Take care, lad, or some day I will take you at your word," said Isaac. "And did you take care of the beasts?"

"I did, lord."

"Then we will change into dry garments and return to our patient."

FOUR

Oh, mort, que est de molts mals medicina
e lo remei contra mala fortuna

*Oh, death, that is medicine for many ills
and the remedy against bad fortune*

THE crack of the shutters was followed by a profound silence. Everyone at Antoni's table waited, tense and expectant, for something to happen. Then, like the cry of doom, bells began to ring, loud, chaotic bells, drowning out the normal sounds of life.

"Why do they ring those bells everywhere here?" said Rubèn irritably. "We had not such things at home. Not like that. Your churches must have a great desire to be noticed."

"They are not calling anyone to prayer," said Antoni. "Those are the warning bells." He clapped his hands loudly and listened for a moment. "Mateu, Pere," he yelled. "At once."

A half-dressed manservant ran in, obviously just awakened from a nap. "The gates and the doors, Mateu," said Antoni.

"They are fastened."

"Check them again. They must all be barred, including the warehouse. Come with me," he said to his two guests.

They ran through the rear of the house, collecting a train of five servants, through a small courtyard, and into the warehouse. "Everything from here back," said Antoni. "Into the house."

Master and servants moved the most valuable items from

the warehouse into a cellar of the house with speed and precision, and some help from the guests.

As soon as they were finished, the servants disappeared again.

"If you are nervous of pirates," said Antoni, "you are free to join the servants in the cellar. If you are curious to see what they will do this time, you may join me on the roof."

"Then we will join you on the roof," said Daniel. "Are you coming, Rubèn?"

<hr />

"WHAT are they after?" asked Rubèn.

"Anything that is easy to carry and that can be sold," said Antoni. "That is why I take the trouble to move my high-priced goods out of the warehouse when the alarms go. Otherwise, they are after slaves."

"You are very calm about it, Master Antoni," said Daniel.

"There is no advantage in panic," said the agent. "I have worked hard and spent good money to make my house as safe from marauders as I can. Having done that, I come up and watch."

As they talked, Rubèn walked over to the edge of the roof, crouched down behind a small parapet and watched intently.

"Seville has no pirates, I assume," said Antoni, raising his eyebrows in mock astonishment. "So a young man brought up there must be unacquainted with them."

"I would think he would have heard of them in Mallorca," said Daniel.

"Look at him, Master Daniel. Hola, Rubèn!" said Antoni. "Who are you waving at? Do you have the same pirates in Seville? Or in Mallorca."

"Was he waving?" said Daniel.

"How could he have been?" said Antoni. "But he seemed to be looking for someone and I startled him, didn't I?"

Rubèn jumped to his feet, and with an incoherent mumble, ran from the roof. The heels of his boots clattered on the stone stairs as he went.

"Where are you going?" called Antoni and set out after him. "You may stay up here and watch the entertainment," he said to Daniel. "The lad is my guest here—I must make sure he stays safely inside my walls."

Daniel heard the agent call for Mateu and moved over to the other edge of the roof in time to see Rubèn cross the courtyard, unbar the heavy wooden gate, and run out. Two servants rushed to the gate after him, not to bring him back, but to lock the house up again. By the time Daniel moved back to the side of the roof closest to the harbor, the attackers had fired two houses and were dragging a small group of frightened children over to the boats. Every once in a while, Daniel caught sight of Rubèn, or thought he did, in among the few people who were milling distractedly around in the streets.

In less than an hour from the first clamor of the bells, the pirates were in their boats, rowing quickly back to their waiting ships.

AS the ships disappeared from the horizon, the rain that had been spitting down in intermittent bursts started in earnest. The townspeople ignored it, pouring into the streets to assess the damage. Some children had disappeared, some goods were stolen, two one-room wooden houses were destroyed, and Rubèn was nowhere to be found. While neighbors consoled the weeping parents of the lost children, Antoni, Daniel, and two of the servants went up and down the streets, searching for him. One woman said she thought she saw a young stranger, nicely dressed, run toward the strand south of the town, but she wasn't sure. Someone else swore she saw the pirates seize him and carry him off to one of their boats.

"Are you certain, woman?" said Antoni. "He's not a child."

"It was a stranger," she said. "I know that."

Irritably, he brushed the rain off his face. "Come, Master Daniel," he said. "We grow wet to no purpose."

As he turned back to his house, a hand plucked at his sleeve; he shrugged it away and it pulled harder. Two ragged children stood beside him, determined to attract his attention.

"Master Antoni," said the older boy, "there is a dead man on the beach."

"That is all that I need," muttered Antoni. "The cousin of an excellent client dying while under the protection of my house."

"It cannot be considered your fault, Master Antoni," said Daniel.

"Do you want us to show you?" asked the older boy.

"Yes, lad. I thank you for bringing me the news. This penny is yours if you will take us to where you found him, and quickly. It's confoundedly wet out here and, who knows, perhaps he is not beyond help."

Antoni, Daniel, and in spite of the rain, two or three bystanders headed out. As they trudged along the sandy, rocky surface, the rain was growing heavier by the minute, lashing the coast, driven by even higher winds.

"Now where is this dead man?" asked Antoni.

"Over there, señor," said the older boy. "Right beside the gray rocks."

They trudged over, bending into the wind, their heads ducked to protect them from the driving rain. "Where, lad?" asked Antoni when he reached the rock.

"There, señor," said the boy and pointed. The beach was deserted. "He was right there, señor."

"The body's been washed out to sea," said one of the bystanders, a fisherman. "The water's coming up pretty far at its worst." He nodded at the sea-drenched sand. It was sculpted into wave patterns that were flattened by the pounding of the rain and then reshaped by the next surging wave.

"No," said the boy, raising his voice to be heard above the noise of the wind and the surf. "We pulled him onto dry sand so that wouldn't happen. See. That is where we left him."

Just above the waterline, there was a depression in the rain-dampened sand. It was surrounded by a confusion of footprints superimposed on other footprints, very much as if two children had struggled to drag a body to the spot and leave in a hurry.

"Tell me," said Antoni, bending down and speaking into their ears, "did he look my client's kinsman? Just a lad, of medium size, taller than you, but not so tall as I am. With pale red hair, worn almost to his shoulders. And—"

"No, señor," said the older boy. "He was very long in the legs and the arms and had dark hair. And he looked much older than I am."

"Are you sure, boy?"

"Yes, I'm sure," said the boy firmly.

Antoni reached for his purse and fished out two coins. "These are for you, lads," he said. "Run home and get out of the rain. It's safe now."

"There's no sign of a dead man or even a live one," said one of the neighbors. "I'm going home, that's what I'm going to do. Do you realize how wet it is out here?"

"You're right," said Antoni. "We can't solve these riddles out here in the wind and the rain."

"YOU found nothing either, then?" asked the agent, once he and Daniel put on dry clothing. They had gathered once more at the table, where a blazing fire on the hearth warmed them and beat back the gathering darkness.

"We looked everywhere for him, Master Antoni," said Daniel. "A few more people said they thought they saw him running through the streets, but they were all so intent on their own safety that they couldn't be sure."

"That is to be expected," said Antoni, finishing off a plate of good hot soup. "I would say he is not dead," said the agent. "He certainly is not the man who died on the beach, if there was a man dead on the beach."

"When I was up on the roof I saw something on the beach," said Daniel. "It looked like a man. And someone was bending over him."

"That could have been the little boys bending over the stranger. Would Rubèn have left so hastily because he saw what the boys saw? A body down on the beach?"

"I don't think so," said Daniel. "I would not have recognized my own father at that distance, much less a stranger lying on the sand. If there was a stranger lying on the sand," he added. "Perhaps he saw the captain of his ship coming to get him."

"The only ships that have come in today were with that raiding party," said Antoni. "Of course it is possible that he was planning to leave with them."

"With the pirates?" said Daniel.

"It doesn't seem possible," said Antoni. "I have never heard of pirates who planned out their raiding so carefully they could afford to promise passage to casual voyagers."

"I agree," said Daniel. "But why flee in the middle of a storm?"

"People can be strange creatures. Who knows?" said Antoni, with a wry smile. "Master Daniel, I notice that the rain is still pounding on the shutters," he added. "May I suggest you stay here for the night? You will be soaked yet again going across the town, and I would be delighted to entertain you. I took the liberty of warning your host not to expect you unless the weather improved."

BERENGUER lay in his bed, shivering, in a state between sleep and waking, consciousness and unconsciousness, all the night. Jordi never left him, fetching hot stones for the foot of his bed, making up the fire, chafing his hands to warm them. Raquel and Leah, and Isaac and Yusuf alternated sitting with him, coaxing broth and mixtures against pain and fever down his swollen, painful throat, and sponging his forehead. Sometimes he muttered and then cried out in a hoarse voice for people only Jordi had ever heard of; the rest of the time he lay still, dozing occasionally. All this time his fever raged, in spite of the expertly concocted potions he swallowed, drop by painful drop.

In the morning, Leah went off to bed, complaining sorely of exhaustion. Yusuf and Jordi sat alone with the Bishop for a quarter of an hour, while Raquel and her father ate a breakfast together of fresh bread, cheese, fruits, and eggs. Raquel was pale with exhaustion and discouragement. "I tried so hard, Papa," she said. "Things that usually work. Keeping his mouth moistened, and placing the drug one drop at a time on his tongue, so he cannot choke and yet will get it in his belly. And still he is in agony."

"Between the sixth hour of the night and the first hour of the morning, my dear, and especially between the ninth hour and the first, nothing seems to work. If you can keep someone alive during that dangerous time then you have hope. You have done well. Now, go to bed and sleep for a little while. Yusuf and I will take over. He becomes more useful these days—not as useful as you are, but not in my way any longer."

"Papa, you are unkind. He is better than that."

"Perhaps. Now go to bed."

WHEN Isaac returned to his patient, the Bishop was sleeping. His sleep was uneasy, to be sure, but sounder than it had been. "How long has he been like this?" asked Isaac.

"Since the bells finished ringing for prime, Master Isaac," murmured Jordi. "He was agitated by the bells, but when they stopped he swallowed a little broth and fell asleep."

"Excellent. We can let him sleep for a while, but he must not go too long without something to drink."

"I will sit by him, Master Isaac."

"No, Jordi, you must sleep for a while. You have been awake with him for a full day and a night. You cannot help if you fall ill from lack of sleep. Just for a few hours. I will wake you when I need you."

"I will be in there," said Jordi, pointing to a doorway with a curtain over it. "I have a bed in that alcove. Since there is only a curtain between us, I can hear if my master needs me."

Isaac sat down very quietly beside the bed. Judging by the absence of chatter from Yusuf, the boy had fallen asleep in some comfortable corner of the room. He listened for his light, regular breathing and nodded in satisfaction. He spent some time considering his patient's ailment and then meditated on other, and graver, matters.

All the while, without thinking of it, he was listening to the sounds within the chamber. Suddenly he sat upright and sniffed the air. He leaned closer to the bed and concentrated intently on the Bishop's breathing. He put his ear to his patient's chest and listened, and then held his hand lightly on his forehead. He shook his head and considered for a moment. At last, he murmured, "Yusuf."

Something stirred. A chair creaked, and finally a voice said, "Yes, lord?"

"Good. You are here."

"I am sorry, lord. I dozed off," said the boy.

"Since I was here, it is not of great matter, but I would like you come over here and look at him for me."

"Yes, lord," said the boy, walking quietly over. "He is very quiet, lord, quieter than he was. And—"

"His eyes, Yusuf. Are they sunken a little?"

"They look unlike him, lord."

"Raquel was worried. I should have taken her more seriously," said her father. "Wake Jordi. He is behind a curtain somewhere in the room."

"I see it, lord."

Jordi padded across the room, almost soundlessly in his soft slippers. "You wanted me, Master Isaac?" he said quietly.

"I am sorry to disturb you, Jordi, but we may have need of you. Now Yusuf, send someone to wake Raquel. Do not go yourself."

"Yes, lord."

"We must arouse him and force him to drink. It will be best if he is sitting up. We will start with the herbal mixture that should be steeping over there somewhere."

Yusuf fetched the cup while Jordi bent over his master and gently held him almost upright. "We must moisten his lips with the liquid," said Isaac. "Give me the cup and guide my hand to his lower lip." And Isaac gently forced the cup between the Bishop's teeth so that some ran into his mouth. He held out the cup, Yusuf took it, and Isaac closed the Bishop's mouth, feeling his throat. "He swallowed," said the physician.

"Let me do that, Papa," said Raquel, hurrying into the room. "I knew I should not go to bed," she said, taking the cup and repeating her father's actions.

"No, my dear, you thought perhaps you shouldn't. That is not the same, even though, as it turned out, your fears were correct. But I was here, and very little time has been lost. We must give him something stronger for the pain—less water than usual, a teaspoon of wine, and extra sugar. It must be stronger but not bitter or harsh on the throat. Two drops, this time, and he must drink all of it. If he cannot feel the pain in his throat, he will be willing to drink other things. It will also calm his stomach and stop the flux from recurring."

For the rest of the day and the next night they labored to keep the Bishop from dying of thirst and dehydration. At the darkest hour of the night, between Laud and Prime, Raquel was watching over him, battling with fatigue so overpowering that she seemed unable to keep herself awake. Her arms and legs were heavy and unresponsive; her eyes burned, and her head seemed thick with a woolly substance that dried her mouth and stifled rational thought. She got up, splashed water on her face, and began walking back and forth across the chamber to keep herself awake. Leah had fallen heavily asleep balanced precariously in a chair. She was snoring lightly, almost drowning out the Bishop's labored fight for breath. Except for them, the castle was eerily quiet. The rain had ceased in the afternoon, and now she realized that the wind too had died. She slipped behind the heavy tapestry that had been hung in front of the window. A trickle of moonlight penetrated the shutters here and there. She unfastened them quietly and opened them a handsbreadth to catch a few deep breaths of cold air.

Stars spread out across the blackness of the sky like pale seed broadcast in great fistfuls over the dark earth by a careless farmer. In their faint glimmer, Raquel could just make out the outline of the horizon. Across the flat plain below rose another hill. The two hills were like a pair of despairing lovers, thought Raquel, separated forever by so little, but so completely. On top of the other hill was the dark, squarish shape of a building. Through one of its windows she could just see the warm light from a single candle. She was tempted to lean out and call to the person who watched through the hours of the night as she did, across that magical space between them, and would not have been surprised to hear him answer. Then she shook her head. The cold night air could do her patient no good. She secured the shutters once more and slipped back into the room.

Something was different, and she stopped, uneasy, conscious that she had been neglecting her patient. The candle by the bed was guttering, burnt down to its last inch. She hastened to

fetch a fresh one and light it on the old. She mended the fire
that had burned down to embers and trimmed the stub of the
old candle.

The room seemed to be as bright as day. She bent over to
check her patient and was suddenly awakened by a jolt of excitement that sent the blood racing through her body. The
gray, sunken look to his face had smoothed out to a healthier
pallor, and it seemed to her that his breathing was less labored
than it had been. She put her hand on his forehead, and it still
seemed abnormally warm. She was about to slip next door and
awake her father, when doubt assailed her. The changes, if they
were changes, were slight. Her father was as tired as she, if not
more so. And she was loath to look like a fool.

"Jordi," she called softly, no longer trusting her judgment
in anything.

Jordi came into the room without a sound. Except for a look
of slight dishevelment, you would think he had been up for
hours, thought Raquel enviously.

"Yes, Mistress Raquel?" he whispered, looking anxiously in
the direction of his master.

"Look at him, Jordi," she said quietly. "What do you think?"

"I think he is better," said Jordi. "May the Lord be thanked."

"Will you sit with him while I fetch Papa, Jordi?" she
asked, and without waiting for an answer, left the room.

⊹══ ══⊹

"HE looks a little better, Papa," said Raquel, when her father
had straightened up from examining the Bishop.

"He does," said Isaac. "And does Jordi think so as well?" he
inquired courteously. "For he knows him better than we do."

"He looks much better, Master Isaac."

"Excellent," said Isaac. "I shall return to my couch for an
hour or two more, and then you may sleep the day away in a
quiet room, my dear."

"Shall I keep on with the same treatment?" she asked.

"Yes," said her father. "Until he can swallow with little pain.
It is not enough to stave off death. We must strive to bring him
back to health."

"I should hope so," said a croaking voice from the bed. "Else why do I pay you, my friend?"

"Do you know where you are, Your Excellency?" asked Isaac.

"I'm warm, Isaac. That means we can't be in the abbey. I dreamt we were at Cruïlles, but that seems impossible."

"You are at Cruïlles, Your Excellency. It was extremely unwise of you to ride here in your condition, but you arrived."

"He has fallen asleep, Papa."

"Let him sleep for a little while, and then start again."

THE light was filtering in around the tapestry when Isaac returned. He listened attentively to Raquel's report and nodded. "He is not safe yet," murmured the physician, "but now there is hope. You may go and sleep, my dear. If I need you, I will send for you. Where is Yusuf?"

"I think he has gone in search of breakfast, Papa. Shall I fetch him?"

"No. The excellent Jordi is as much use and more reliable than any boy."

A lanky man dressed like a poor merchant rode into the town of La Bisbal on a resentful-looking donkey. He looked pale and mortally tired, as well as being preoccupied with much more pressing matters than his trip. He hailed the first responsible-looking man he could find.

"*Hola*, señor," he said. "Are you of this place?"

"I am, sir," he said. "I am a clerk at the Bishop's palace. You are a stranger here," he added.

"Yes," said the man on the donkey. "tell me, is His Excellency, the Bishop, in residence?"

"No, sir," said the clerk. "But he is not far off, at Cruïlles. If you have a message for him, I can see that it is delivered."

"No," he said distractedly. "I must see him. Where is the road?"

"Just ahead on your left hand."

"Thank you for your courtesy," said the man on the donkey.

"If I may trouble you again—do you know a potter by the name of Baptista? I am returning the donkey his cousin borrowed from him."

"His shop lies on the road to Cruïlles, not far from here. But perhaps you should stop and rest. There is an inn a few steps away." He looked closely at him. "You seem ill."

"It is nothing," said the stranger. "How far is it to Cruïlles?"

"Not far at all," he said. "But I believe the Bishop has not been well. He might not be able to see you, and you will have wasted the trip. They sent for his physician the day before yesterday. All the way from Girona."

"It won't be wasted," said the stranger. "I thank you," he added and rode away.

FIVE

. . . aquells són decebuts

. . . those are deceived

ISAAC sat by the bedside of his patient, deep in thought, considering a number of practical matters and at the same time, paying close attention to the breathing of the man on the bed. Should His Excellency not recover, there would be more to wrestle with than a few practical matters, he feared.

A tap on the door interrupted his somber thoughts. He heard it open and Yusuf's footsteps move quietly across the room.

"Forgive me for the intrusion, lord," murmured Yusuf. "But there is a strange man in the chamber by the staircase. He came to the door this morning, and he seemed so very ill that they asked me to look at him. They did not wish to disturb you or Mistress Raquel."

"What is wrong with him, Yusuf?" asked the physician. "*Ill* tells me nothing."

"He is covered with scrapes and bruises, lord," said the boy, "and his skin is all reddened from it. I do not think that the injuries are serious enough to cause his condition. He is weak and in great pain. He insists that he must see you and His Excellency. I told him His Excellency was too ill himself to see anyone, and he begged me to fetch you."

"Did he ask for me by name?"

"He did, lord. Someone told him His Excellency's physician was here, and he asked for you by name. He seems very ill."

"Then I must see him," said Isaac. "Jordi, can you stay here and watch over your master? I think you may allow him to sleep until the bells sound again, but if there is any change for the worse in him, even the slightest, send someone for me."

"Certainly, Master Isaac."

"Yusuf, take me to the stranger."

"AND who are you, sir, who comes here and asks for me?" said Isaac. "I am tending a very sick man."

"I am a traveler, Master Isaac," said the man panting on the bed. "My name is Joan Cristià. I know something of medicine and herbs, and I assure you that my scrapes and bruises that so interested your young colleague are of no consequence."

"Are you certain? Yusuf tells me your face and head received a good share of the damage to you, wherever it came from."

"That is of no matter, Master Isaac. That was almost two days ago. I was stunned, but I have not been troubled by it since. But I fear I have little time if you will not help me," he said, his voice falling to a whisper. "Send everyone away, I beg you, sir."

"Yusuf is my eyes. I know he can be trusted, but, if you wish, the others may leave."

And the servant who had stripped away Joan Cristià's torn and muddy clothes and dressed him in a dry shirt went off, slamming the door.

"I have offended him, I know," said the man lying on the couch. "But it cannot be helped. Master Isaac, I beg you, can you or your assistant make up a strong preparation for me of herbs?"

"Which herbs?" said the physician, intrigued by the man who summoned a physician and then diagnosed and treated himself.

"Gentian, crushed berries of juniper, and the ground root of thistle. Steep them with fresh leaves of plantain and rue flowers."

"What do you think has poisoned you that you wish such a concoction?"

"There is no time to explain. I am sure of what was in the drink I was given."

"Would it not be better to clean out the stomach first?" asked Isaac. "I have a tincture of berries—"

"It is too late for that. I did what I could as soon as I perceived what was happening," he said.

"We have almost everything with us, lord," said Yusuf. "The rest can be found in the fields. I will send someone out right away."

"Make haste, lad, make haste," said the sick man.

"I must go to my patient for a short while, but I will return." Isaac sent the servant in, with instructions to keep the man warm and as comfortable as he could.

YUSUF came in with the mixture shortly after Isaac had returned.

"Is everything in it?" asked the sick man.

"It is, sir," said Yusuf.

"Then give it to me," he said desperately, grabbing at it. His hands were shaking so much that he couldn't bring the cup to his mouth, and Yusuf held it to his lips so that he could drink. Shuddering and gagging, he drank it all and fell back on the pillow. "God knows if that will help," he said. "I have concocted it for enough people in my life. Now I am fated to learn at first hand if it is of any use."

"Let us hope that it is," said Isaac. "Or that you are mistaken in your belief that you have been poisoned."

"I doubt that," said Joan Cristià. "The person responsible would think no more of poisoning someone than he does of offering him a cup of wine. I knew that, but I did not think that he would treat his master the same way—the traitor! The cold-hearted traitor."

"Where have you traveled from, sir?" asked Isaac, "that you have met such a welcome around here? For your speech is not of these parts."

"From?" he said vaguely and blinked. "I have traveled from—I have traveled from Genoa. I landed on the coast in the storm. Our ship anchored before it started, but the boat that brought me into shore ran into rough waters. It was then that I earned these bruises."

"Where did you land?" asked Isaac. "At Palamós?"

"Palamós," he said alarmed. "No, that is not where I landed. Mustn't go to Palamós. There is treachery there." He grasped Isaac's sleeve. "I must see the Bishop. There is something that I must talk to the Bishop about. Take me to see him. I am thirsty, so thirsty."

"It would do you no good," said Isaac. "He is too ill. Now he sleeps, but when he is awake he scarcely knows where he is."

"I must see him," said Joan Cristià. "I must see the king's officers. No matter what happens to me. I have heard such things and know such things—you could not believe the treachery, and he betrayed me."

"Yusuf," said Isaac. "Send for Father Bernat and ask him to bring a scribe. What this man is saying should be witnessed and copied down. Master Joan," he said, "you must make an effort. It is not enough to swallow something. You must help it."

"Yes. My limbs do not tremble any more, and I need to sleep."

"No. Not yet. You must stay awake. Talk to me. Tell me about yourself."

"My name is Joan Cristià."

"Are you a *converso* that you have that name?" asked Isaac.

"Why do you ask?" asked the sick man, suddenly alert for a moment. "You treat a bishop. Why not a *converso*?" he said.

"I inquire only out of interest. What name did you go by before your conversion? I may know your family."

"You don't. It used to be—but that is of no account. I have forgotten that life."

"You are a traveler, you said."

"I have traveled much—from Genoa to Venice, and from Sardinia to Constantinople—in pursuit of my calling, which is herbs and medicaments."

Bernat hurried in, as he always did, followed by a young

scribe bringing a writing desk, pen, and ink. "You summoned me, Master Isaac?" said the Bishop's secretary.

"Forgive me for that, Father Bernat," said Isaac, in clearly audible tones. "This man has come here to warn His Excellency of some danger." He rose and went in the direction of the priest, and when he spoke again, his voice had dropped to a whisper. "It is a matter of some urgency. He believes that he has been poisoned, and I fear that he is correct in that. We may not have much time. When His Excellency recovers, he will want to know what the stranger has said, for, although I will do everything I can, I do not believe he can recover. Death is hovering over this bed." He returned to his chair and continued on.

The door opened once more, and the sergeant of the Bishop's guard slipped in quietly. He stood in the dark shadows of the corner farthest from the couch and prepared to listen.

"Serious accusations should be witnessed, if at all possible," said Bernat prudently, nodding at the sergeant. "Does the man know he is dying?"

"I am sure he does," said Isaac somberly. "He is, in his way, also a healer."

"Has he asked for a priest?" asked Father Bernat.

Isaac shook his head and turned back to the man on the bed. "Master Joan," he said, "this is Father Bernat, the Bishop's secretary. He will make a note of what you say and tell the Bishop as soon as he is well enough to return to his duties."

"I was aboard a merchant vessel from Cagliari in Sardinia," said the sick man in composed tones. "We were making for Barcelona and less than a day's sail from harbor, when we were caught on the edge of the storm and driven off course. They put me ashore and I don't know what happened to them." He gasped with a spasm of pain. "Sant Feliu," he said, "I thought we'd never make Sant Feliu de Guíxols. They went off, but they said they'd put me ashore; dumped me in the sea in tiny boat and went to join the others. They laughed at me. I thought I'd die in all that sea. Never thought this would happen, never. Of all things, the treacherous little swine."

"Who is a treacherous swine?" asked Bernat. "Does he threaten His Excellency? Or His Majesty, perhaps?"

"Cast adrift," he muttered. "Me. I had given them so much. My lord had given them so much. I had messages to deliver from my lord. Important messages."

"Tell me how he looks," said Isaac, as his hands ran over that body, now rigid with pain. "Quickly."

"He is white with pain, lord," said Yusuf. "His body twists with spasms, but not like strychnine. I have seen that."

"He would be dead by now if that were what was given to him. Fetch a small cup of the pain medication prepared for His Excellency. Tell Raquel we must have more."

Not long after he had managed to swallow some of the preparation, his clenched jaw began to relax and he started speaking again. "It was the boy who did this. That stubborn wretch of a boy—I taught him everything I knew . . . all the skills . . . even the formula he has killed me with, that I learned from the greatest masters of the art in Genoa, I taught him that too, and he took it from me. He'll ruin it now. I told him. Poor men mustn't use such things. Only the rich can do that." He paused, opening his eyes wide. "The rich. His stupid, stubborn lordship isn't rich enough to win against the coldest, most grasping monarch in the world and his heartless wife. . . . She's a better general than he is. If she had been admiral, that would have been the end of us. But we escaped, my lord and me."

"He is referring to Their Majesties?" asked Bernat, primly seeking confirmation.

"I believe so," said Isaac.

"It is just as well that he is near death," said the priest. "But who is his lordship?"

"Who is your lord?" asked Isaac. "Does he live here, in the Empordà?"

He no longer seemed to respond to questioning. "We left his lordship, the great and craven Judge, to hide in his little tower while Rocabertí's daughter had to crawl on her knees to His Majesty, and remind him of her noble kin."

All this while the scratch of the scribe's pen continued, leaving line after line of fluid script behind it.

"He speaks of the Judge of Arborea," said Bernat, not so much shocked as intrigued. "For he is the one who married the Viscount Rocabertí's daughter, thus bringing together two great houses. I would guess that this man on the bed has been in Alghero. But he does not speak of him as his lord."

"Master Joan," said Isaac. "Who is your lord? Is the message for His Majesty from your lord?"

"My lord," he muttered. "Little does my lord care what happens to us, after all we have done for him. But he'll hear from us again; he already has heard. Beware, physician. Warn your Bishop to guard his back. He owes me a life. They stole my life from me, they owe it to me, all of them, chasing me from my life . . . take everything for themselves . . ." He struggled to sit up, but Isaac's hand was resting lightly on his chest. He eased the man back onto his pillow. "Guard his back, beware the apprentice," he cried in alarm, and subsided to a mutter. "Taught him everything. . . . No one else knows the things that I taught him. Thieves . . . they are all thieves. Stole half my gold, but they won't get the other half. He's not that clever."

"Who, Master Joan? Who is not that clever?" asked Isaac. "What is his name?"

"I am no thief. I only take what is owing to me. I am not a thief. It was the damned boy. He doesn't understand."

"What boy, Joan?" asked Isaac.

"If I hadn't, he couldn't have . . ." His voice drifted away. "Tell the Bishop . . . nowhere safe . . . nowhere safe . . . chased from port to port as kingdoms fall one after another."

The sick man stopped, panting for breath, and Yusuf bathed his face. The scribe finished writing and hastily mended a pen.

"Is your lord Mariano d'Arborea?" asked Bernat. "Have you come from Alghero?"

"My curse on all of them," he cried out again. "Thieves, liars, traitors, all of them! May they die in agony and rot in hell with those lying whores their mothers!"

"He is going quickly," murmured Isaac. "I can feel it."

"Joan, my son," said Bernat, quickly interposing himself be-

tween the questions and the soul on the bed. "Do not die with
curses on your lips." He turned to the others. "I must speak to
him alone," he said.

But before they could gather themselves up to leave, Joan
Cristià writhed in some final agony, cursing, and fell still.

Isaac bent over him, his ear to his chest, listening. He
straightened up, placing his fingers on the man's neck. "He is
dead," said the physician.

"Not an edifying end," remarked the scribe, breaking silence for the first time. "But then, if I had been poisoned I
would not be pleased either."

+‡=== ===‡+

"WHAT do we know about him?" asked Bernat, looking
down at the dead man with a puzzled frown. "We will bury
him, but if he has kin, they must be informed of his death. He
had a purse with six sous in it concealed in his clothing, and
then strapped to his person we found another purse with fifty
gold maravedís in it. The money must go to his heirs. I have
put it away safely."

"We know his name," said Isaac. "If that is his name. For
I fear, Father Bernat, that he is not as honest a man as you
are."

For the first time since he had entered the room, Sergeant
Domingo of the Bishop's Guard spoke. "If I understood what
he was saying, father," he said, "he was involved in something
that smells rotten to me. How did he get here? Was he alone?
Where has he been? We should try to lay our hands on his con-
federates, who must know the answers. I cannot ignore the
threats he spoke of against His Excellency. If there are men who
were with him and are now able to speak, we must search them
out."

"How do we do that?" said Bernat.

"I will take one of the lads and ask at the neighboring farms
and dwellings. Someone must have seen him come into the
area. When I find that person I will start searching for the one
who saw him before that."

"I must return to my patient," said Isaac, excusing himself.

"I have left my daughter in charge, and she is sorely in need of sleep."

⊷══ ══⊶

SERGEANT Domingo was accustomed to a life in which success came after frustrating endeavor—if it came at all. It did not surprise him that only one of the villagers seemed to have noticed Joan Cristià as he staggered up to the castle.

"Falling-down drunk he was," she said, giving a crying toddler a smack on the head and doubling the noise of its wails, "at that time of the morning. Should be ashamed of himself. Is that the man who died in the castle? Of drink, that's what. I keep telling my Roger that's what'll happen to him, and good riddance too." She snatched up the child and turned toward her tiny house.

"Which direction did he come from?" asked the sergeant. "The abbey or the town?"

"The town, of course," she said promptly. "As if the brothers would give a man like that enough wine to do that to him."

"Thank you, good woman," said the sergeant. "Where's everyone else?" he added, looking around the empty village.

"In the fields, of course," she said and slapped her swollen belly. "Can't stoop over, not like this, can I, so I've been staying back these last few days."

They headed in the direction of the town of La Bisbal, encountering two more people on the way; neither one had seen a stranger on the road. "Roads have been bad with mud," said one. "Heavy walking for man or beast until today."

When they came to Baptista the potter's modest establishment near the road to La Bisbal, he pulled up and dismounted. "Baptista's always in," he said to the young guard. "With any luck, he'll have noticed which direction our man came from, up there where the roads come together."

"A stranger?" said the potter. "What kind of stranger? None went by here, unless you mean the good man who returned my donkey to me."

"Don't know," said Domingo casually. "When was that?"

"Morning after—no—two, maybe three, mornings after the rain. Roads were still wet and dirty. The poor beast was covered with mud. I was glad to see her back. He paid me for the use of her, although by rights my cousin should have paid him for bringing her back. A very close man with his money, my cousin."

"Did he tell you anything about himself?"

"No. I asked if he would take something before he continued on, but he said he had an urgent message for the Bishop and headed off."

"On foot?"

The man nodded.

"Where had he come from that he had borrowed your donkey?" asked the sergeant as he was leaving.

"Palamós."

And armed with the cousin's name and occupation, the two returned to the castle to report and to prepare to ride out to Palamós in the morning.

<hr />

THE Bishop spent the afternoon in a state of torpor. He dozed uneasily, waking at intervals. Each time his eyes fluttered open, Yusuf, then Raquel, when she relieved him, pressed him to drink—water, broth, whatever he would take. Swallowing still caused him great pain, and he resisted after the first mouthful or two. But the fever seemed to have lessened somewhat this third afternoon, and Isaac was less gloomy about the outlook for his patient. "I do not expect to see a great change for a day or even two," he said to Bernat, "but he is no worse, and that is good."

"Do you mean that he is out of danger?" asked Bernat.

"By no means," said Isaac. "You will know when he is out of danger, I assure you. We have another difficult night before us."

<hr />

THAT night they shared the burden of watching, marking their watches by the bells. Yusuf took the first watch, from Compline to Matins, with one of the servants, since Berenguer seemed to have fallen into a sounder sleep. He had strict instructions to wake His Excellency and make him drink at least twice on his watch and to send for someone if there was any change. Raquel and Leah took over from them from Matins to Laud, but Jordi and Isaac sat with him during the most dangerous hours of the night, from Laud to Prime, when vitality drains away and hope dies.

"He seems much the same," said Raquel, as she left them, feeling that she had said the same thing over and over again.

"Take heart, my dear," said her father. "You have done well."

But as the first light stole around the shutters and fell on the floor, Berenguer awoke. "Are you still here, my friend?" he said. "Your wife will be coming to fetch you if you stay much longer."

"Can you tell me where we are now, Your Excellency?" asked Isaac.

"I had a dream that someone told me we were at Cruïlles," he said, "but that cannot be true."

"We are at Cruïlles, Your Excellency."

But the Bishop had closed his eyes again. "I am thirsty," he said. "And my throat is thick with phlegm."

Jordi raised him up and brought a cup to his lips. He drank, wincing as he swallowed, but finishing the cup.

"I am greatly in need of sleep," he murmured, and fell asleep at once.

◆━━━ ━━━◆

AT first light, the sergeant and the young guard set out for Palamós. The roads were almost dry again, the weather was clear and pleasant, and the distance between the castle and the port an easy couple of hours. As they descended the hill into the town, the guard began to inquire after the potter's cousin. The third person they encountered pointed them toward a narrow street leading down to the water. "You'll find him there," he said, "in his workroom, if he's not off at the tavern already. Not a great man for work," he added with a malicious grin.

"Go and see what you could find out from this cousin," said Domingo. "I'll drop in over there and get a feel for the neighborhood."

He headed for a conveniently placed tavern, watched enviously by his subordinate.

"I was to meet a man here this morning," said the sergeant when the landlord brought him a cup of his best wine and some bread and cheese. "But I don't see him. Tall fellow, thin as a pole. Planning to leave here yesterday, he said, but meaning to come back."

"Not he," said the landlord. "He was meaning to come back, and left a few things with me, but his friend took them later in the day, saying he had changed his mind."

"Can't be the same two," said the sergeant. "Very trustworthy both of them, I could have sworn it. Will you fetch a cup for yourself, landlord?"

When the landlord returned and sat down in the deserted tavern, he raised his cup and drained half of it. "Thank you, sir," he said. "But I fear you're wasting your time. If you're depending on them, you're doomed to disappointment. They look smooth and trustworthy enough, but what I could tell you about them . . . If they're friends of yours, I won't embarrass you with it. You seem a straightforward sort yourself."

"Not friends," said the sergeant. "More that it was a business deal we were going to talk about. They wanted another partner to come in with them—"

"I wouldn't do that," said the landlord. "They spent the night here, you know, and they were even cheating each other."

"I don't believe it," said sergeant. "Friends like that? Will you take another cup?"

The landlord was interrupted by the arrival of three men, thirsty and demanding his attention. Domingo waited patiently for him to satisfy their needs and return with a second cup of wine for himself. "The younger one accused the other of cheating him, and they spoke bitter words. Then your friend said he would make it all up to him after he came back, that he was to wait for him here. He paid the reckoning for the two of them and he left enough with me for two more nights for the younger one."

"That sounds like him," said the sergeant, stubbornly clinging to his belief in their honest dispositions.

"But when the older one left for a short time to go out to the back, he gave his purse to the younger one. He may look like one of God's angels, that boy, but he took a handful of gold out the purse—gold! Two men dressed like those two over there, only the older one's clothes were caked with salt from sea-water, carrying gold! You can draw your own conclusions from that, sir. Well, he replaced the gold with some pennies—to make up the weight, you see. He did it like an expert, but I saw it. In this trade you learn to look for things like that."

"Think of that," said the sergeant. "What a trick! What did my friend do when he found out?"

"Never noticed," said the landlord uneasily.

"He was too busy trying to find a donkey to take him to La Bisbal," said a man from the other table. "Looking for the Bishop," he added. "Although he didn't seem to me to be some-one much interested in his immortal soul." He laughed.

The guard came in, bursting with news and excitement. "Sergeant," he said. "I found—"

"Sergeant?" said the landlord nervously, picking up his cup and heading to his counter.

Domingo nodded and left three pence, a barely touched cup of wine, a piece of stale bread, and a chunk of moldy cheese on the table.

"From now on," said the sergeant, "when I am surrounded by people telling me what we have been sent to find out, do not storm in and address me by my rank."

Abashed, the young guard trailed after him out of the tavern.

✛══ ══✛

"WHAT did you discover?" asked Domingo. "And keep your voice down." They were seated in a more reputable tavern, with cups of excellent wine and the remains of a dinner of baked fish in front of them.

"He said that they had been sent over from the tavern and wanted to hire his donkey. When he found out they were going to La Bisbal, he said they could take her and return her to her own-er. The older one was called Joan. He described him perfectly."

"And the younger one?"

"He couldn't quite remember his name. He said it was something like Ramir, or Raul, maybe even Rafael. And he didn't get a good look at him outside in the light. The workroom is on the dark side. But he did notice that he had pale hair—yellow, maybe, or reddish—and looked young and smallish in size. But the landlord must have seen him closely."

"The landlord! He knows where his interests lie, lad, and they're not with us. As soon as he got the idea that we were seeking the partner, he turned pale and went back to his jugs and bottles. He didn't seem able to remember what they were calling themselves."

⋅⊱━━ ━━⊰⋅

WHEN the two men returned at dusk, the atmosphere in the castle had changed completely. His Excellency was free of fever and able to eat a little. For the castle servants, the Bishop's death would only affect those few who had known him well as a child and would mourn his death; for those who had come with him in his travels, it would have meant a complete disruption of their existence.

Bernat scarcely had time to listen to the sergeant's report and see that it was accurately transcribed. "All this will have to be put aside until His Excellency is able to approve our actions," he said. "How is His Excellency?" he said, catching sight of the physician leaving the Bishop's chamber.

"Improving still," said Isaac. "But weak and unable to withstand much. He wishes to return to Girona, but he cannot yet travel."

"Then I will not mention this incident until he is much stronger," said Bernat.

"Until then," said Isaac, "in all humility, for I know less than you do, I would suggest that my patient be shielded from all but those you most trust, no matter who they are. We have not worked night and day to keep him alive only to have him done away by poison or steel."

"Jordi will watch him," said Bernat.

"Yes," said Isaac. "I do not think Jordi would betray his master."

PART II

WINTER

✣

SIX

dins nos mateixs medicines trobam

within ourselves medicines we find

THE fall planting and harvesting were over; the city had had its fair and celebrated its saint's day, in honor of blessed Sant Narcís, who had rescued them from the French during that fearsome siege in the time of their grandfathers and great-grandfathers. Winter was closing in, and with it came weeks of heavy rains. Even when the rain stopped for a while, a miserable damp chill lingered in the air. The days grew short, and the sun—when it appeared—more feeble. Scribes complained that for days they could scarcely see well enough at midday to write. In the eternal struggle between the terrible black of the night and the merciful light of the day, night seemed to be winning.

The Bishop came back from Cruïlles on a day of cloud and pale sunshine, attended by his household guards and servants, his physician, Raquel, and Yusuf. In spite of being free of fever and insistent that he must return, he was still too weak to protest against the indignity of being carried back on a litter instead of riding his own horse or his comfortable mule.

ISAAC, Raquel, and Yusuf were greeted with warm fires, and a table laid with an abundance of savory dishes. Drawn by the inevitable noise and clatter of their return, Daniel set down his tools and declared to his uncle that he intended to grant himself a half-holiday. "Tell Master Isaac that we will visit before supper," said Ephraim peacefully, and Daniel ran out into the chilly afternoon sun. Another place was promptly laid at the table, and Daniel slid neatly in next to Raquel.

Once Judith had discovered exactly what the castle at Cruïlles looked like, and how many bedchambers it had, and how it was furnished, she shook her head. "It seems very small for a castle," she said. "I thought they were immensely rich."

"They have another, much larger castle close by," said Raquel. "But His Excellency likes this one and asked to be taken there. When did you return to Girona?" she asked, turning to Daniel. "We must have been very close to each other."

"In a way," he said.

"How did you enjoy traveling in the company of young Master Rubèn?" she went on, teasingly. "He didn't seem to me to be the ideal companion, but then, I've hardly spoken to him. Does he improve on longer acquaintance?"

Daniel choked on a bit of grilled fish. "You haven't heard?" he said. "About Rubèn's great escape into the arms of the pirates?"

"What are you talking about?" said Raquel.

"I shouldn't laugh," he said. "It is most unkind, but he was beginning to irritate me. Then as soon as we reached Sant Feliu, there was an attack—they've had several in the last few years—and he raced outside as if he were going to join them. We hunted all over the town and around it through all that rain and wind and didn't see a sign of him."

"What happened to him?" asked Isaac.

"No one really knows, but Master Mordecai received a letter from his agent saying that a body, much damaged by the sea, had washed up on the beach. It had brownish hair and was wearing boots that looked possibly like Rubèn's. He said that he wasn't sure, but he identified it as such, and that was that."

"Do you not think it was Rubèn's?" asked Isaac.

"I don't know. I find it difficult to believe that such a thing could have happened to him. But then I found it difficult to believe that he would run outside in the middle of a raid on the town. I'm sorry, but I didn't like him. If he's dead, that's a pity, but I cannot mourn for him."

And with that final elegy, the conversation turned to happier topics.

ONCE in the palace, the Bishop did nothing for the first few days but sleep in the comfort of his own bed, warmed by good fires and fur bed-coverings, and tempted by the best his excellent kitchen could produce. Then, little by little, he returned to work. One day he signed a few essential documents—licences and permissions that could not wait—that Bernat put in front of him. A few days later he insisted on reading the material he was signing. The day after he demanded changes in the wording of a document, and everyone breathed in relief again. His Excellency was returning to normal.

The following morning, he went into his study and summoned Bernat and the scribe.

"Where is everything?" he asked, looking at his desk. It was innocent of paper or parchment. "There isn't even a particle of dust to look at."

"I thought Your Excellency would not feel ready to deal with all the old business," said Bernat. "Not yet, and so I have kept it in my study."

"Perhaps not all of it today, Bernat," he said, "but if I do not start, it will soon be unmanageable."

Bernat refrained from saying that in his opinion, it was already more than unmanageable. "Yes, Your Excellency. What would you like me to bring in? The latest dispatches or the earliest?"

"All of them, Bernat. I like to know what I'm facing, not discover it in little daily shocks."

Bernat glared at the scribe, who scrambled to his feet and followed the secretary out of the room. They returned, each one carrying a formidable pile of documents. "Shall I put them on my desk?" asked Bernat.

"Certainly not," said Berenguer. "On mine. And let us see what we can accomplish before dinner. In deference to my physician, I shall work the first half of the day and no more."

==== ====

TWO days later a peremptory ring at Isaac's gate drew him
into the courtyard. A raw, cold wind from the mountains was
gusting down over the city walls and straight through to one's
bones. He shivered. "What is it, Ibrahim?" he asked.

"I have come from His Excellency," said a youthful voice before the porter had a chance to reply. "You are to come to the
palace at once, Master Isaac."

Isaac frowned slightly. He had four sick patients to visit that
morning and was only waiting for Raquel to return to the
house from a visit before setting out to see them.

"The Bishop requires your presence, Master Isaac," said the
boy, his voice rising in a panicky squeak.

Isaac considered this for a moment and decided that his four
patients could wait a little while. "Go back and tell His Excellency that I will be at the palace as soon as I have made some
necessary preparations," he said. "Ibrahim, fetch Yusuf from his
studies."

The physician returned to the comfortable, well-ordered
room that was his study, his herbarium, and when he returned
from a sickbed late into the night, his bedchamber. He put on
a warmer tunic and cloak, all the while considering what he
might need to treat all five patients.

At last, Yusuf stumbled in, yawning. "You sent for me,
lord?" he asked.

"Yes," said Isaac. "And I thought I was interrupting your
studies, not your sleep."

"I'm sorry, lord," he said, "but I . . ."

"Never mind," said Isaac. "I have set out what we will probably need. Pack it in that order and then put on a warm cloak,"
he added.

==== ====

"IS Your Excellency not well?" said Isaac. "I have had reports
that you were growing in strength and health by the hour. I
had hoped that they were true."

"Quite true, quite true," said Berenguer impatiently. "I do

very well, so well that I have now reached the portion of my work that my secretary considered unimportant."

"Not unimportant, Your Excellency," protested Bernat. "But not urgent."

"Truly?" said Berenguer. "You do not consider threats against me and against His Majesty and some of His Majesty's officials to be important?"

"Important, yes, Your Excellency," said Bernat stubbornly. "But likely to be carried out? No."

"You see, Isaac, they are all in revolt, even Bernat. One sign of weakness and . . ."

"Your Excellency!" said Bernat, horrified.

Berenguer began to laugh. "It is so long since I have laughed," he said, "that Bernat forgets that I know how. But in all seriousness, my good Father Bernat, I am inclined to agree with you, but I feel that we cannot keep this to ourselves. If the threat is genuine and can be dealt with, we cannot ignore it."

"The man was raving, Your Excellency," said Bernat. "One could scarcely make sense of his words."

"That is why I sent for Master Isaac. He heard those words as well. Isaac, I have the sergeant's report on the incident here. When I started to read it, Bernat, I decided that the physician might be able to help us if he is allowed to add his knowledge to that which the sergeant has given us."

"Perhaps he might," said the secretary in the tones of a man whose patience has been sorely tried.

"First of all," said Berenguer, "our good sergeant Domingo states that he described the man who died at Cruïlles to the innkeeper at Palamós, and that the innkeeper immediately recognized him as one of two men who stayed with him for a night. Our dead man was apparently calling himself Joan."

"Indeed," said Isaac. "He said to me when I first went into the room that his name was Joan Cristià. When I asked him if he were a *converso* to have such a name, he became quite angry. Why, I do not know. It is not a name often given to one who is born in your faith, Your Excellency. What else did the good sergeant discover?"

"Let Bernat read us the rest of it," said the Bishop.

"I have read the entire document," said Bernat, "twice. It will be simpler if I tell you what is in it, I think. When the dead man left Palamós he had every intention of coming back. He left his possessions, such as they were, with the landlord. They were collected by his friend later in the day."

"If our Joan Cristià was correct in his surmises," said Isaac, "his friend may have known by then that he would not be returning."

"That does seem likely," said Bernat. "The sergeant also discovered from the landlord that the young friend stole a considerable sum of gold from the dead man's purse. And that the dead man's clothes were soaked in seawater. I asked the servants who were looking after Joan Cristià, and they said that his tunic was stiff and discolored as if from salt."

"He said that he was thrown into the sea," said Isaac.

"That would explain it," said the secretary. "It puzzled me. The sergeant also discovered that although everyone described the dead man with accuracy, no one really seemed to notice his companion, except for the landlord, who said he looked like an angel, and the potter's cousin, who said he had pale hair—yellow or reddish in color."

"An angel!" said Berenguer. "And how are we to find him from that?" he asked. "The countryside is littered with boys who are considered by someone to 'look like an angel.' Who, in truth, knows what an angel looks like? If that is our only description, we know nothing at all about him. What concerns me even more, though," he added, "is the dying man's words as reported by Master Isaac and copied by your scribe, Bernat."

"Could we have them read out, Your Excellency?" said Isaac. "I would like to refresh my memory as to the exact wording of his final speeches."

"Certainly," said Bernat, nodding at his scribe, who read out his transcription in a clear, flat, colorless voice.

"Thank you," said Isaac. "That was very helpful."

"Helpful?" said Berenguer. "In what way?"

"I was uncertain of some of the details, and I now have a much clearer picture of what he said."

"I certainly do not," said the Bishop. "Tell me, Master Isaac, what meaning, if any, did you draw from what he said?"

"I think as he was speaking," said Isaac, "that he was slip-

ping back and forth between the truth and an innocent—
sounding tale he had manufactured for the occasion."

"Which was the innocent-sounding tale?" asked Berenguer.

"That he had bought passage on an honest merchant vessel
heading for Barcelona. His ship was hit by the storm, and when
it seemed likely to founder, the kindhearted sailors, taking no
heed for their own lives, put him in a boat so that he might
save himself."

"That seemed clear," said Bernat.

"No," said Isaac, "because he suffered at intervals from terrible spasms of pain caused by the poison he had been given.
Each time that happened, he became confused and spoke
wildly, but, I suspect, honestly. During those times, he said
that he had been on a ship whose master had been well paid by
his lord to take him, but instead of putting him ashore as
agreed, they threw him overboard."

"Surely the actions of unprincipled men, Master Isaac," said
Bernat primly.

"Pirates," said the Bishop.

"I think so, Your Excellency," said Isaac. "And I would also
suspect that the angelic boy and his apprentice to whom he
taught all he knew are the same person."

"What kind of man was he whom we attempted to succor?"
asked Berenguer.

"An expert in poisons, Your Excellency," said Isaac. "He
knew precisely what he had been given and ordered me to concoct a mixture of herbs and simples that might have helped
him if it had been given much earlier. I suspect that is what
made him useful to his lord, whoever he was."

"D'Arborea?" said Berenguer. "Did you not tell me,
Bernat, that he mentioned the Judge? And His Majesty is still
in Sardinia."

"We do not know that he was in the Judge's employ," said
Bernat. "He spoke of him with utmost contempt, but not as his
lord. However, since the diocese is now in possession of his effects, including that sum in gold, I took the liberty—because
Your Excellency was unwell—of writing to the Arboreas and
inquiring whether they knew of any kin possessed by this man.
We have not as yet heard from them."

"Well done, Bernat. But I must consider carefully what else is to be done," said Berenguer. "A rash accusation against a powerful noble can bring His Majesty more harm than good."

"I certainly had the impression," said the physician, "that he was—or had once been—employed by someone in the family of the Arboreas, and that he had been, no doubt with great justification, dismissed."

"One thing is clear," said Berenguer. "He was one of a pair of common scoundrels, and if the 'angelic-looking' boy, Rafael or Raul or Ramir, turns up, he will be seized. Although how we are to tell who he is, I do not know."

"Boys with names that sound something like Rafael are almost as common as angelic-looking boys," observed Bernat sourly.

◆━━ ━━◆

DINNER had been waiting for almost an hour when Isaac and Yusuf returned home. By the time they had left the house of Isaac's second patient that morning, the gusty, uncertain weather had turned into a ferocious rainstorm. The wind drove the water almost straight into their faces; the water hit the cobbles with such force that it splashed up, soaking the tops of boots and drenching the skirts of tunics and cloaks. When they reached the shelter of Isaac's substantial stone house with its warm fires, they were both sodden and shivering from the cold.

"What have you been doing, out in that rain?" asked Judith, getting up from the table where the rest of the family had gathered to wait for them to come back.

"It is just a little rain, my dear," said her husband. "We shall be fine as soon as we find dry clothing."

"Come with me," said Judith, "and I will dry you off and find you something warm to put on."

Isaac followed her with suspicious meekness as she pulled him into the sitting room and stood him near the fire.

"Stand there," she said, moving as quickly as she could into the bedchamber. She opened a large dresser and took a great pile of clothing off the shelves. She was back in a moment, draping the clothing over the stonework around the chimney where it could catch the heat of the fire. Then she hastily untied the laces that held together Isaac's hood and cloak, unbuttoned his tunic and untied his shirt. Each piece of clothing, from his hood to his stockings and boots, went into a wet pile on the floor near the fire. "You're shaking with the cold," she said crossly.

Naomi, the cook, hurried in with a large linen towel warm from the kitchen fire and dried him off briskly as she had done when she had been a nursery maid and he was a small child.

Judith picked up the shirt, warm from its contact with the hot stones and dropped it over his head. "It is madness for you to go out in that weather," she said, taking a warm stocking from Naomi and kneeling down awkwardly to pull it on him. "You should have come home as soon as that rain started. What will I do, and the baby, if you get ill and die?" she added, pulling on the other stocking.

Naomi slipped a warm tunic on him as Judith scrambled to her feet again. "I will fetch his furred slippers, Mistress," said the cook. "I have had them warming by the fire since I first heard the rain."

"There," said Judith, doing up the last button. "That's better. You must have some hot soup now. How are you feeling?"

"Better," said Isaac, "but still remarkably chilly."

"I will have a fire lit in the bedchamber. But you must come and eat something first."

Naomi brought a great pot of soup into the dining room and set it on the sideboard. The warm scent of chicken and herbs rose from it, aromatic with garlic, onion, pepper, and saffron. She placed a thick slice of bread toasted at the fire into Isaac's plate and ladled soup onto it. "There," she said, setting it in front of him. "A garlic soup with bread. It is the best thing for a day such as this one. And afterwards the chicken from the pot with a good, strengthening sauce."

"Thank you, Naomi," said Isaac. "I could not ask for anything better."

"Where is Yusuf?" asked Judith.

"I have set him down in the kitchen where I can keep an eye on him. He is in dry clothes and shivering like a puppy, but eating soup."

"They will all stay in, no matter who calls with what tales of illness, until I am sure they are well," said Judith firmly.

"I have patients in need of treatment," said Isaac.

"You are in need of rest," said Judith.

"I will go out, Papa," said Raquel. "You and Yusuf will stay by the fire."

"You cannot go out by yourself, my dear," said Isaac, sounding distressed, rather than angry.

"I won't. I will take Leah, who could use more exercise out of doors, and Ibrahim, who is big enough to look protective, even if he isn't very fierce," said Raquel. "I shall be both safe and respectable. If you're worried, I'll make Daniel come with us too, all four of us trailing our muddy boots into each of your patient's houses."

"I can tell when I am defeated," said Isaac. "I had best try to drink my soup."

<hr />

BUT in spite of the warm, dry clothes, in spite of the hot bread and garlic soup, and in spite of the warm bedchamber where Judith bundled him into bed with heated stones wrapped in soft linen to warm his feet, Isaac awoke the next morning with a fever and a sore throat.

So in addition to her father's patients, Raquel had him to look after, as well.

"It is not that I got wet yesterday, Raquel," he whispered hoarsely. "This is the same ailment that three of my patients are suffering from."

"Getting wet and freezing with the cold did not help, Papa," she said. "Now drink this, and then you must take a little hot broth. I expect you to be more cooperative as a patient than His Excellency."

<hr />

IT was two weeks before Judith permitted anyone to approach her husband with anything remotely connected to his work.

Friends arrived with delicate dishes that they vowed would slip easily down the sorest of throats. The Bishop's orchard and garden, so well protected from inclement weather, provided a bounty of late fruits and fresh herbs that won Naomi's grudging admiration.

Finally Judith relented. Her husband had been out of bed and roaming impatiently about the house for two or three days. The complaints from the servants that he was interrupting their work were becoming louder and louder. Judith allowed a messenger from His Excellency into the house.

"His Excellency said that he did not wish to take you from your warm fire if you were still feeling the effects of your illness," said the boy, like one reciting a difficult text that he despaired of getting right. "So if you can't, can you send some of the—the—whatever you give him?"

"What is His Excellency suffering from?" asked Isaac. "It makes a difference, you know."

"Oh. The gout. He said it was the gout."

"I really should go to see him," said Isaac. "I believe it is a sunny day, at last."

"Indeed it is, Master Isaac," said the boy. "When I came out of the palace I was dazzled by the sun, it was so bright. The *tramuntal* has blown all the storms and rain away and the sun has warmed the cobbles in the street. But it is not warm in the shade," he added in worried tones.

"Perhaps not," said Isaac. "But my warmest cloak should withstand a little chill."

"I will fetch it," said Judith. "And send Yusuf to you."

⊹⊱══ ══⊰⊹

"I have been well for a few days, Your Excellency, but my wife has kept me close to the fire, for fear that I would do something foolish and fall sick again. Your message was a welcome one. I do not withstand idleness well."

"And I do not withstand the gout very well, Isaac," said the Bishop in a discontented tone. "And those fools did not keep in an adequate supply of the mixture against the gout, so that when I fell a victim to it again, there was nothing. But you are kind to come."

"I have given Jordi another supply. He is brewing a cup of it for you now. May I examine the foot to see how far it has progressed?"

Jordi had come in with his silent step. He took out the stool that was level with the Bishop's footstool for Isaac to sit on and set it down. "Thank you, Jordi," said the physician, taking up the foot with great delicacy.

"I am amazed that you can tell it is Jordi. He moves so silently that if I did not see him I would think he didn't exist," said Berenguer.

"That is how I tell," said Isaac. "All of the other servants and Father Bernat and Father Francesc make noise of one kind or other. But Your Excellency, your foot is very hot and must be painful in the extreme. You should not have waited so long to summon me. You are too brave and determined, I fear."

"*Stubborn* is the word you seek, I believe, Isaac, my friend. I am that. But I did call at last."

"I have the mixture, Master Isaac," said a gentle voice in his ear. "How much of the other do you want in it?"

"A good spoonful, Jordi, please," said the physician. "And then the hot poultice to draw the inflammation and after a basin of cool water into which those salts have been stirred to soak the heat from the afflicted joints."

WHEN the treatment was finished and the Bishop had been made as comfortable as possible for the moment, he leaned back in his well-cushioned chair, his foot on the stool, the pain somewhat eased. "This is the worst possible time for the gout to strike me," he said irritably.

"It is unfortunate that you had scarcely recovered from one illness when this happened," said Isaac.

"That too," said Berenguer, "but I blame it on the cooks who are feeding me to excess because they feel that I have lost too much flesh, and that it reflects on their skills."

"I will speak to them again, Your Excellency," said Isaac.

"I have done so already, Master Isaac. No, the problem is that I have a delegation from Palamós here to lodge a com-

plaint concerning certain pirate attacks. They are emboldened
by the success of Sant Feliu de Guíxols in obtaining assistance
from His Majesty for fortifications and apparently were only
waiting for me to recover and for the rain to stop to descend on
me here in person. They arrived last night to the horror of the
kitchens, who hadn't been warned that five councillors would
be here with all their servants, expecting to be lodged and fed."

"Did they not write?" asked Isaac.

"It seems they did, but their messenger was an unreliable
fellow. They found him at an inn along the way, anticipating
his fee to the extent of numberless jugs of wine. So they
brought him, too, along with their letter. They expect to lay
out their complaints to me, having failed to obtain appoint-
ments with His Majesty's procurator, my Lord Vidal de Blanes.
Not that seeing him would have helped them. This is not a
matter of begging forgiveness of a fine of ten *sous*. This will
have to be decided by His Majesty himself, and I know that he
has already given great thought to it. When he wishes to hear
from the townspeople, he will let them know. But that is not
what they want to hear from me."

"What do they expect from you, Your Excellency?"

"I think they expect me to approach His Majesty and argue
most forcefully on their behalf. Perhaps they expect the diocese
to offer to build them some new walls, or to send a flotilla to
patrol their waters. It will be an unpleasant meeting, I fear."

"Such feelings do not help you to recover from an attack of
gout, Your Excellency. Sleep, tranquillity, and a good, cleans-
ing diet for the blood of herbs and foods that are not too rich
are what you need. In fact, they will help you as much as my
poor medicines can."

"I shall remember that when I meet these gentlemen. I shall
remain calm, smile, and promise to do what I can. Then I shall
remind them that these are decisions that have to do with the
defense of the realm, not just of their town, and that His
Majesty must make them. After that I might invite them to
join me to dine on bread, water, and a soup of herbs." At that
thought, the Bishop laughed and shook his head. "That would
surprise them. But I wonder whether there is any connection

between these latest attacks and our current difficulties with Sardinia. I would like to get my hands on some of those fellows from the marauding ships and find out exactly where these ships and their captains come from."

"Where do you think they come from?"

"I don't know," said the Bishop. "Genoa? North Africa? Somewhere farther afield? Those who have heard crew members speak, say that they come from everywhere. But it's the masters and owners that interest me."

"Do you think they are driven by a desire to bring down the kingdom, Your Excellency?"

"I do not believe so, Isaac my friend. Only by a desire to fill their own coffers with gold. Speaking of that, one of the delegation from Palamós told me that he was very sorry to hear of your death and asked me if I were still in need of another physician, since he had a young cousin who could fill the position most excellently."

"My death?" said Isaac.

"They will be pouring into the city to replace you," said the Bishop.

PART III

MARCH

✢

SEVEN

No em fall record del temps tan delitós

I have not forgotten such a delightful time

Sunday, March 1, 1355

THE late afternoon sun was warming the stone of the east wall of the courtyard and filling it with light. Judith and Raquel were sitting out of the wind, working quietly, as the twins played a complicated game involving sticks and a pile of small pebbles down on the flagstones. Judith suddenly set aside her needlework with a thump of the basket and looked around. "I cannot bear this any longer," she said.

"What's wrong, Mama?" asked Raquel. "Are you . . ."

"There is nothing wrong with me," said Judith. "It is this courtyard. As soon as the sun lights up those corners you can see how long it has been since they were swept. And who would want to sit by the fountain now? How are we possibly to prepare for Passover with the house in such a state? Fetch Ibrahim, Raquel. He must do something about all this."

"Now, Mama?" said Raquel. "First of all it is almost two full months until Passover, and look how far down the sun is in the sky. By the time you tell Ibrahim what it is you want him to do and he understands it, the sun will be set and he will be needed to help Naomi. Besides, Papa is going to be very disturbed if he discovered us scrubbing the courtyard when he comes home. We will give it a thorough cleaning tomorrow—all of us."

"I'm not cleaning the courtyard," said Nathan, mutinously.

"And I'm not cleaning it either," echoed his twin sister, Miriam.

"It might rain tomorrow," said Judith, getting to her feet with surprising speed, considering her awkward size.

"It might rain any day, Mama," said Raquel irritably. "If tomorrow is fine, we will clean the courtyard. Right now, you should be resting."

"I have rested all afternoon, at your insistence, Raquel. I do not feel like resting," said Judith. "I shall go for a walk in the evening sun. It is a pleasant day, and at this time of year, we cannot count on pleasant days all the time. Come along, Raquel. You look pale."

"If I do," said Raquel, "it is not for lack of exercise. But I will come for a short walk with you, if you like."

With common accord and without discussion, mother and daughter walked down a short street and over toward the house of Ephraim the glover—not seeking gloves, but his wife, Dolsa, and his nephew, Daniel. For Dolsa's lively conversation and Daniel's passionate intensity drew them in their different manners as water draws a thirsty beast.

But the courtyard was not destined to be cleaned the next day. Judith and Raquel paid their visit—an unsatisfactorily brief one, from Raquel's point of view—and as they took their leave heard Isaac's voice outside Ephraim's gate. The four of them—four Yusuf had been with his master—walked together up the short slope toward their gate. Halfway there, Judith stopped and leaned her outstretched left hand on the stone wall beside her. "Do wait a moment, Isaac," she said. "I must catch my breath."

He touched her right arm and felt that she was pressing her hand tight against her side. "Can you walk yet?" he asked softly.

"In a moment," she said.

"Brave girl," he said. "Raquel, go send for the midwife. I will take your mother home."

⊹═⊱ ⊰═⊹

BY the time darkness fell, the house has been taken over by women. The midwife, Raquel, and Naomi were all either in the bedchamber with Judith or moving back and forth between the kitchen and the chamber. Leah had swept the twins away into some corner of the house so remote that no one was aware of them. In spite of several suggestions that she go to her own bed, Jacinta, the little kitchenmaid, stayed up, preparing soup, keeping the fires going, and heating water for washing.

Isaac stayed in his study, murmuring prayers, and then meditating on birth and death. He knew that if his Judith were in a dangerous state, someone—Raquel or the midwife, who was a skilled and sensible woman—would come and fetch him. But when he heard the first bird stirring with a cheep or two, he rose to his feet in alarm. He washed in the basin of clean water that was always ready for him in his study, said his morning prayers, and set out to brave the female world inside the upper stories of the house. He almost tripped over the recumbent form of Yusuf who was sleeping on his doorstep, wrapped in a warm cloak.

"Pardon me, lord, but I couldn't sleep . . ."

"Nor could I, lad," said Isaac. "Let us go and find out if there is any news. How goes the dawn?"

"The sky begins to lighten in the east, lord. Otherwise a full moon still lights the sky and the courtyard. It has not begun to pale yet."

As they mounted the staircase toward the bedchamber Yusuf heard a loud cry. "The poor mistress," he said with a shiver. "What pain is in that cry, lord."

"No, Yusuf," said Isaac. "I hear no pain. That is a cry of triumph. Listen."

The next sound they heard was the outraged complaint of a vigorous newborn.

Raquel came out into the passage to bring her father the news and almost ran into him. "Papa," she said. "Mama is well, and my brother is big and lively already. There never was such a baby."

"Your brother?"

"Yes, Papa. I have another brother. Go and speak to Mama. She is asking for you."

⊷≡⊶ ⊷≡⊶

"ISAAC," said Judith. "He is beautiful. He looks just like you."

The physician held out his arms, and the midwife placed his newborn son in them. "He is indeed a good healthy size," said Isaac. "What a clever woman you are, my dear."

"Mama's right," said Raquel. "He does look like you. And if he continues as he started, he will be as tall and robust as you are, as well."

"That is why I was so tired," said Judith in a pleased tone of voice. "I was carrying all that weight around with me."

"I must take him and wrap him properly," said the midwife, disapprovingly. She took the baby from Isaac and wrapped him neatly and tightly in clean linen cloths. Then she bent over and placed him gently back in Judith's arms.

"He is big, just like his Papa," said Judith again, and laughed. Her eyes closed and she drifted off to sleep.

"She is very tired," said the midwife. "A baby that size makes for a long and difficult birth. But all is well, I think, with both of them."

"You were that size at birth, Master Isaac," said Naomi suddenly. "But your poor mother had not Mistress Judith's strength and courage. I was just a child, then, but you were the first baby I had seen born, and I never forgot it."

⊷≡⊶ ⊷≡⊶

THE day following the birth of the baby, the household was in a state of turmoil—rather like a leaderless army, whose general has been rendered helpless by wounds of battle. Judith slept, waking occasionally to tend to the child and to ask whether all was well with the rest of the house. When she was assured that it was, she drifted off to sleep again. By the next day, she started to gather strength; soon after, she picked up the reins of control once more.

"And what are we going to have for the vigil?" Judith asked Raquel. "Surely to welcome another son, particularly one so strong and so like his Papa, something special must be prepared. Where is Naomi?"

And thus, the evening before the circumcision and naming of the child, the house was alive with candles and torchlight for the vigil, and the tables were overloaded with plates of delicacies.

The baby, already noticeably grown in the ten days he had been on earth, and clad in fine and beautifully worked white linen, was brought in to cries of admiration and felicitation from friends and neighbors—most of them genuine. Perhaps a few of the onlookers felt that the physician had received more than his share of prosperity and good fortune, but this was not the time to let malice flow. It was the moment when the newborn was to be enveloped in the collective wish of all for his good luck and for his protection from the malicious influences—including the fearsome evil eye—upon him.

A silver bowl filled with water was set on a table and tiny grains of gold and seed pearls were sprinkled in it; then with great care and many prayers and good wishes he was washed in the water. For his birth—and that of every healthy baby in the community—was a moment of true rejoicing. Everyone in the room except for the young children could remember the famine years and the plague years when there were ten or twenty or even thirty deaths for every birth. And even in the last year or two, it seemed there had been too many babies who slipped, wailing feebly, into life and then gave up the struggle only a few days or weeks after they were born.

"I wonder what they will call him?" whispered a young wife.

"Quiet," said her mother. "We will find out tomorrow. It is not to be spoken of today."

"I was just thinking that names were odd things," she said sulkily. "Some people's names seem to bring them nothing but bad luck. Just look at—Who's that?" she said suddenly.

"Who?" asked her mother, whipping around. "I've never seen him before," she said, staring in amazement. "Mistress Judith was not expecting any distant kinsfolk."

Standing in the doorway was a young man of about twenty years of age. He had a pale, impassive face, almost mournful in expression, more suitable to a death than a birth, and luxuriant dark brown hair that contrasted oddly with his fair skin and light brown eyes. He looked back and forth across the room, as if seeking someone he knew, and then smiled tentatively. With that smile, his eyes took on life, and his face character, revealing strong cheekbones and a sturdy beardless chin.

The silence that ensued was broken by the forceful complaint of Judith's hungry baby.

"I beg your forgiveness," the young man said. "I have intruded on a solemn occasion. I was seeking Mordecai the bootmaker, and someone told me that I would find him here. I didn't realize . . ." His voice trailed off as if in an agony of embarrassment.

"I am Mordecai," said a voice from behind him. "Why you seek me here, at such an occasion?"

"I have just arrived at the city," he said, as if that solved the puzzle. "I am the son of Faneta, your cousin from Seville."

There was not a sound in the room. Even Judith's baby stopped in mid-cry, as if he too were struck dumb with astonishment.

"Faneta's son?" asked Mordecai. "May I ask what you are called?"

"Lucà," he said. "My name is Lucà."

"You say you are the son of my cousin Faneta?" said Mordecai, looking carefully at him. The crowd stood silent, watching.

"I am," said Lucà. "May I ask what occasion I have broken in on so rudely without an invitation?"

"It is the vigil of a neighbor's young son," said Mordecai.

"That fine young baby over there? How old is he?" said Lucà. "And what is his name?"

A puzzled hush fell on the group standing near the stranger. "You say you are Faneta's child?" said Mordecai. "He is the age all boys are the day before they receive their names. And you do not know that? How were you brought up?"

Lucà shook his head and spread open his arms helplessly. "There is no point in my lying to you, cousin Mordecai, for I reveal it every time I open my mouth. My mother and father, under great pressure, became Christians shortly after I was born. I have been brought up as a Christian."

"Perhaps that explains his name, Master Mordecai," said Isaac. "What was your name before your parents converted?"

"I am not sure," said the young man awkwardly. "In truth,

sir, I do not know. If I was ever told it, I do not remember."

"Then tell me," said Mordecai. "Why do you seek me out? What do you want from me? Money? A position?"

"Nothing at all, Master Mordecai," said Lucà, his cheeks flushing with embarrassment. "I have a profession—I am a healer, well versed in the arts," he added quickly. "Although," he added, "not as well versed as I would like to be. I had heard that there was a great physician in this city, one Master Isaac, and I was hoping to learn from him, if that is possible. I thought that you might know him, Master Mordecai, and could present me to him, if you were so kind. That is all."

At that, Mordecai began to laugh. "Well, young Lucà, I expect that Master Isaac can make up his own mind if he wishes to meet you. For it is to his house you have come in such a startling fashion."

"Young Master Lucà is welcome to join us," said Isaac. "Other matters can be discussed at a more suitable time, I think."

"How did you find your way here?" asked Ephraim the glover.

"I inquired after Master Mordecai at the city gate," said Lucà, "and then at the gate to the *call*, and was told to come here, which I did directly—with, as you can see, the mud of travel still on me."

"Do you understand what position you are in, as a *converso*, or the child of *conversos*, seeking out Jewish relatives here?" said Mordecai. "We are relatively well protected, I admit, in this city, but if there are complaints and the populace become stirred up, even the Bishop or the King cannot always save us. And you, yourself, could be in even graver danger."

"I am sorry, more than I can say, for putting my Girona relations into an awkward position," he said. "But I greatly desired to meet you, at least once." The young man bowed to each of the men in turn. "Forgive me, please. I will be on my way at once. If anyone inquires about my visit to the *call*, I shall say it was on a matter of business, now resolved."

"On such an evening as this, when our neighbors come to share our joy," said Judith clearly and unexpectedly, "I cannot allow you to leave without a cup of wine and a bite of supper."

"Thank you, mistress," said the young man.

Jacinta filled a plate and poured a cup of wine for Lucà.

"Thank you, child," he said, smiling at her.

Jacinta observed him shrewdly through lowered eyelids, curtsied, and moved on about the room on her duties.

Monday, March 23, 1355

As important as the birth of a child was to Isaac's household, the rest of the community soon turned its attention to more pressing matters. The beginning of spring was not an unmixed blessing in the *call*; of all the events brought by the season of growth and renewal, the one that caused some of the most intensive preparation was, perhaps oddly, a Christian holiday. Easter was approaching, and the entire community had to band together to protect itself.

"Are the arrangements for Holy Week proceeding satisfactorily?" asked the Bishop that afternoon, when Isaac had finished manipulating and massaging his troublesome knee with soothing unguents. "With the city," he added delicately. Arrangements between the city and the *call* sometimes did not proceed as smoothly as those between the diocese and the *call*, but it was from the city, by established practice, that the Jewish community hired the guards to prevent rioting outside its perimeter.

"I believe there were meetings yesterday and today, Your Excellency," said the physician. "I will find out tonight what the arrangement with the city is."

"I am sure that my knee will need further treatment tomorrow," said Berenguer. "If you could return before vespers, I would be most interested in hearing a report from those meetings."

"Then I shall return tomorrow, Your Excellency," said Isaac, rising to his feet.

"Could you spare me a few more moments, Master Isaac?" asked Berenguer.

"Certainly, Your Excellency. Are you troubled again by the beginning of gout?"

"No, Master Isaac. I have no trace of the gout or, at the moment, any other ailment," said the Bishop. "I wished to ask you a few questions about someone. You might be able to answer them."

"If I can, Your Excellency, I shall certainly hasten to do so."

"What do you know about this young man who has set himself up as an apothecary?"

"Lucà? I believe, to be precise, that he calls himself an herbalist. Sometimes he refers to himself as a healer. I have never heard that he calls himself either an apothecary or a physician."

"That is interesting," said the Bishop. "He is a careful young man, then."

"I doubt that he possesses a licence to practice medicine or set up shop as an apothecary—or certainly not one that would be valid in this city, Your Excellency."

"That is what I have been asked about. Or at least, that is one thing that I have been asked about. What do you know of him?"

"He lodges with Romeu the joiner," said the physician.

"That is something everyone seems to know. I'm afraid this has not helped me, Isaac," said the Bishop.

"I am very sorry, Your Excellency. I know little about the young man."

"Well—I know something about him. He is a young man who likes to talk, my friend, and since he arrived, he has claimed, or indicated, perhaps, that he is from Genoa, or perhaps from Alghero, or from Mallorca."

"He told us that he was born in Seville, Your Excellency. His voice told me that he came from Mallorca. About Alghero and Genoa, I am afraid I know nothing concerning him. Does he have permission to settle here and treat people?"

"He has something," said the Bishop. "It is a worn and tattered piece of parchment, signed by the secretary to His Majesty's procurator, Don Vidal de Blanes. When he was asked about its condition, he claimed that it was caused by an accident in which he fell into the sea."

"Into the sea?"

"The trouble is, Isaac, that he seems to tell a different tale to everyone he meets. If he would talk less, he would do better here."

"If I hear of anything that could be of interest to you, Your Excellency, I will let you know at once."

"ISAAC, my friend," said Mordecai. "I trust you are not here because you have been summoned. I am under the impression that I feel quite well."

"Certainly not, Master Mordecai," said the physician. "You sound as if you are in excellent health. It is I who come here to make a request of you."

"Surely you are not in need, Master Isaac," said Mordecai. "But if you are, my coffers are open to you, without question."

"Not at all. In spite of what you might have heard," said Isaac, laughing, "prosperity has not fled from our door, for which the Lord must be thanked."

"The Lord and your exceptional skills and hard work, Isaac. But if it is not money you need, then whatever can I do for you?"

"I am curious, for some serious reasons, to know what you can tell me about this young man who claims to be your cousin's child."

"Young Master Lucà?"

"That same young man."

"I wish I could tell you a great deal more about him. I have spoken to him a few times, trying to discover what I can. When pressed about his background, he stammers and stumbles and contradicts himself, which is not very encouraging. But if you will give me a moment to gather my thoughts," he added, "I will tell you what I know."

"Of course," said Isaac. "Take all the time you can spare me."

Mordecai opened a leather-bound box on his desk and extracted a piece of paper. "I have notes here, that I have made after each conversation," he said. "First of all, he claims to have been born in Seville, to a mother from this city and a father from Seville. That would be correct if he were Faneta's son. What puzzles me is that he speaks little of the tongue of Seville, but he speaks our tongue like a native. Not of here, Isaac, but of the islands. This, he says, is because he was raised by his grandmother, who is from Mallorca."

"It is interesting," said Isaac.

"His grandmother apprenticed him to an herbalist, he says.

His master took him to Genoa and Alghero where he learned much more. When the herbalist died, he returned to Mallorca and his grandmother suggested that he come here to take up his profession."

"Your cousin Faneta's mother came from Mallorca, did she not?"

"Perla? Yes, she did." Mordecai paused, as if not sure what to say. "Uncle Ezra died shortly after Faneta was sent away to Seville to be married, and as soon as my uncle was buried—within a few days—Perla returned to Mallorca."

"Why the haste?" asked Isaac. "It seems . . ." He allowed his voice to trail away. "She could not have had time for his affairs to be settled."

"I undertook all of that and helped her with her immediate needs," said Mordecai.

"Of course, my friend," said Isaac. "You have always been the kindest of men."

"I wish I could believe that kindness had been my motive," said Mordecai. "But the truth is that I would have done anything for her, I assure you. When Uncle Ezra took her as his third wife, he was a man of forty and she was seventeen. A lively, joyous creature, Isaac. I was a boy of eleven, and I had never seen such a beautiful woman in all my life. I fell in love with her, and suffered in silence, of course—mostly for fear of ridicule."

"I remember her, Mordecai. She was a very handsome woman."

"When you arrived here, Isaac, Uncle Ezra had driven all the joy and life out of her. She looked like some wild animal trapped in a cage. Her eyes were full of despair and they haunted me."

"Ezra ben Rubèn was an upright, honest man, as I remember," said Isaac.

"Oh, he was, Isaac. He was also a cold, unpleasant one, quite unlike my father, his brother. Her only joy in life was her daughter. But when Faneta was fifteen, he married the poor child off to a man twenty-five years older than she was, who lived in the most distant place he could find."

"Deliberately?"

"I thought so at the time, Isaac, for he could easily have found an excellent match for her here. She was a sweet, pretty girl with a handsome dowry. Many families had their eye on her as a wife for a favorite son. He claimed that her husband was the wealthiest man he had ever known. Perhaps that had been true once, and that was his motive. Certainly he was the son of a man with whom Ezra had done a great deal of business years before." Suddenly Mordecai clapped his hands. "But Isaac, I have offered you nothing, and here I find myself in a reminiscent mood." When the maid came into the room, he gave orders for some refreshment.

"I find your reminiscences most enlightening," said Isaac.

"We had remained friends," said Mordecai. "Then, when Uncle Ezra died, and she was left a widow, she told me that she was going away. I was almost mad with despair. My poor wife was still alive, then, a most estimable woman of whom I was very fond. No man could have asked for a better wife. But Perla told me that she did not think she could bear to stay in a city where she had been so unhappy. With all her heart she wanted to return to Mallorca, where, she said, there was light and joy and friendship. Then a year after Perla left, my wife died, and in mourning her I also regretted, to my great shame, that she had not died before Ezra. I have never told anyone anything of that, Isaac," he said sadly.

"I would not speak a word of your affection for her, nor of her feelings toward her husband, Mordecai."

"You are very guarded in that declaration, Isaac," said Mordecai, laughing. "But you are right. Nothing else was secret at the time."

"What puzzles me is that she would have recommended to her grandson that he come to a city she detested."

"There is a reason for that," said Mordecai, "which makes very good sense. But what I cannot believe is that any young man raised by Perla, *converso* or not, would know so little about his religion. Yet this Lucà has only a passing acquaintance with our faith, Isaac. He was not born in it, nor raised by members of the community."

"Could that be because they were trying to protect him?" said Isaac.

"I considered that, but I still think he would know more. It is a question of great importance to me, Isaac, the question of whether that young man is my cousin Faneta's son."

"Why is that?"

"I am entrusted with a certain sum of money that was left by my uncle to his grandson, Rubèn. If this young man, Lucà, is that same grandson, he should—he must—have that money. Otherwise, it should go to the real grandson. Some time ago, just after the arrival of the first Rubèn, I sent a letter to a rabbi of my acquaintance in Seville, asking him to institute inquiries, for the time is coming when the money is to be handed over."

"Perhaps it would be more useful to send someone to Mallorca to discover the truth," said Isaac.

"It might be," said Mordecai. "I may have to do that. But I would prefer to wait until I receive a reply from Seville. If I do send someone, he would need to be sensible, reliable, and discreet, who can talk easily with strangers. Perhaps if such a person were going to Mallorca, I could entrust him with it. But for now, I shall await a reply from Seville."

"THE city is refusing to listen to our arguments," said Bonastruch Bonafet to the assembled council and interested members of the community. "And so we must hire five more guards this year at the new rate, because last year there was trouble."

"Did you tell them that the trouble occurred because their guards were drunk and fast asleep on the stones outside our gates?" said Vidal Bellshom.

"I mentioned that," said Bonastruch dryly. "They were not impressed. This is a bad year for complaining. His Majesty is still in Sardinia, the procurator has said that it is a local matter, and the city is short of money because of extra levies for the war."

"We too have contributed much to the war," said Mahir Ravaya.

"Indeed, we have," said Bonastruch. "But most of us have had a good year, and partly because the war has brought us increased trade. I suggest that we consider this to be an extra tax and put it to one side as unimportant."

There was a confused murmur of assent and dissent that Bonastruch wisely interpreted as agreement.

"I should think that the most important question is the safety of the *call*," said Astruch Caravida.

"It is. How long do we remain closed, and how closed is closed?"

"Last year, I think," said a dry voice from the darkest corner of the room, "we were overoptimistic. It will not hurt us to stay within our walls from sundown on the Wednesday before this so-called holy time until sunrise on the Monday after it. That is eleven days and twelve nights."

There was a pause as everyone considered this. The voice of the learned Shaltiel carried great weight.

"And what of emergencies?" asked Vidal Bellshom at last.

"I cannot think what emergencies could call us out into that world, but should there be one, we can quickly meet and decide what should be done on its merits."

"If we are to do this," said another, "it must be agreed upon now, I think, because many people will want to make preparations. Those who have workshops will need sufficient materials so that they are not idle when they do not wish to be."

"I believe many of us have already prepared ourselves to some extent," said an armorer. "I told my clients some weeks ago that they must order what they needed for the spring and summer early. And they did, so that I have materials already to hand."

"I can foresee problems with the bakers, the butcher, and the fishmonger," said Vidal. "It is fine to lay in a stock of metal, or cloth, or leather. But you cannot lay in a stock of meat and expect it not to spoil."

"We know the days and the times of day when trouble is likely to start," said Bonastruch, whose skills in preventing strife were formidable. "If the town is quiet. I do not see why we cannot open up in the morning for a few hours when there are no troublemakers about, and before people start drinking."

Several people began to comment at the same time on the merits of the suggestion. In another corner of the room, two men who were sitting together began to chat as well. "You are very quiet, Master Isaac," murmured Mordecai in his ear.

"That is because almost every year the same points are raised and they are modified in the same way each year. It is very necessary to have this meeting," said Isaac, "but I do not feel I have much to say on the subject. What is most important is how firmly we lock up when we do lock up, and how vigilant we are when the gates are open."

Bonastruch Bonafet rose to his feet. "Neighbors, please," he said. "If everyone speaks, no one can listen."

"What do we mean by locking up?" asked Mahir.

"When we lock up, we do just that," said Bonastruch. "Every gate, every door in every house that gives out to the rest of the city must be locked and barred, every window shuttered and barred. Agreed?"

There was a murmur of agreement.

"How do we know everyone will do it?" asked Mahir. "Three years ago, when the baker . . ."

"Every house on the perimeter will have to be inspected," said Bonastruch. "Every day, if need be."

EIGHT

Metge escient no té lo cas per joc

A wise physician does not take the case lightly

LUCÀ appeared to be as good as his word. He stayed more or less away from the Jewish community, visiting the *call* only for the reasons that any other Christian in the city would—to look at a pair of gloves at Ephraim's, to buy a loaf of Mossé's bread, to inquire about the cost of having new boots fitted—except that it was noticed that he paid the occasional brief visit to Mordecai. Otherwise it was clear that he had settled comfortably into the Christian community.

But if Lucà was studiously ignoring the Jewish community from which—according to him—he had sprung, the community was studying him carefully as an interesting source of gossip. "I hear that the young man who burst in upon little Beniamin's vigil—for thus was Isaac and Judith's youngest son named—has found himself lodging with Romeu the joiner," said Dolsa, who had come over to visit Judith, and see baby Beniamin, now three weeks old and dozing peacefully. Thoughtfully, she had brought her nephew, Daniel, with her. In the hectic days since the birth of young Beniamin, Raquel and Daniel had had few moments in which to speak, or even to exchange smiles with each other.

"It is better than staying at Rodrigue's tavern with all the rabble that haunt the place," said Judith. "Do you know how

Mistress Regina is faring?" she asked. "I had heard yesterday that she was no better."

"Romeu is making a new counter for the shop," said Dolsa, "and so we see much of him. Our old counter is so warped and crooked that if Ephraim sets out a glove and places beads or jewels on it so a customer may see the effect of this or that decoration, the beads all roll away, sometimes onto the floor."

"Romeu's work would not be like that," said Judith.

"No, indeed," said Dolsa. "Romeu is an excellent workman. And he likes to be certain that he knows what we want. Every time he brings in new wood to his workroom, he and Ephraim have long talks over it. The last time that happened I went along and took a moment to visit poor Regina. I was shocked to see her."

"She is no better?" asked Judith. "I had hoped she was improving, since Romeu has not called for Isaac in months—since long before the baby was born."

"She is much worse. She keeps to the house all of the time now, refusing or unable to go out. I brought her a very delicate dish of sweetened egg, with lemon and spices, thinking it might tempt her to eat just a little, but she said to me that she cannot eat. The sight and smell of food make her sick, she said, although she tries to eat a little for her father's sake."

"What does she do?" asked Judith.

"She keeps the house as best she can. She told me that she keeps at her work, but finds it difficult. She mends Romeu's clothes and is trying to make him a new shirt, but she cannot sleep when she should, and whenever she has to sit and concentrate on something, she falls asleep—or starts to weep again."

"Something should be done for her," said Judith.

"Romeu told me he has given up. She tells him it is useless to waste his money on a physician for she is not sick, just unhappy. But Judith, if you could see her! She is as thin as a willow branch, and as pale as can be. She cannot live without eating, and I am sure she does not eat enough to keep a fly alive."

"Poor thing," said Judith. "She was such a pretty, pleasant girl that I was sure another young man would come along for her. But if she loses her looks and her pleasant ways, how can that happen? It is not as if she were rich."

"Her father is prosperous," said Dolsa. "But I don't suppose that he is rich. She should not have had any difficulty finding a husband, not a good, hardworking, clever girl like her, with a sufficient dowry. But you would think that she was doing this deliberately." Dolsa shook her head in disbelief. "I do not understand it," she added, her kind eyes filling with tears. "When the world has so much suffering in it, why does she not make every effort to forget her unhappiness?"

"Perhaps she has tried and cannot," said Judith briskly. "Remember that her mother also died recently. She was not a woman to be easily forgotten. But how does young Lucà who is staying with them earn his bread?" asked Judith. "Or is he living from Romeu's generosity?"

"He claims to be a healer and a dealer in herbs," said Dolsa carefully, without a glance at her neighbor. "I believe he earns a little money by selling herbs and mixtures to people who believe that his concoctions will help them."

WHILE Dolsa amused Judith with the latest gossip about him, Lucà sat in his small room under the eaves in the neat little house of Romeu the joiner, and examined a collection of dried herbs set out on the table in front of him. He, too, was thinking of the small amount of money his herbal mixtures were bringing him. Were it not that Romeu was a generous landlord, feeding the young man and housing him for half of what such lodging would cost elsewhere in the city, he would be forced to move on and seek a living elsewhere. He sighed and began to choose the elements of a simple preparation to soothe the throat of one of his few patients.

"I do not understand why you don't cure that daughter of Romeu's," said the old lady. "If you can cure my throat," she said, "and the pains in my belly a little, you ought to be able to do something for a healthy young thing like her. You should have seen how pretty she was before all this."

"Before all what, Mistress?" he asked casually. "You forget

that I have not been in the city long. I don't know people here the way you do."

"Who do I know?" she said contemptuously. "Nobody at all."

"Most of the city, mistress," said Lucà. "There is no one I meet who does not speak of you in terms of highest praise."

"That is kind of you, young man," said the old lady, her eyes sparkling, "but I know what they say of me. I can tell you, though, that before Regina's young man went off to the army to fight in Sardinia for the King—now he's away in some godless place at the other end of the world, not meaning to come back . . ." She coughed and then swallowed with some difficulty. "I still have some pain . . ."

"Here, Mistress. Take another half-cupful of this mixture," he said, handing her a cup of sweet wine, honey, and herbs.

She drank it, smiled, and returned to her tale. "She has not always been pale and thin, weeping continually. Everyone knows that without a miracle, she will die. I pray for her miracle, but I have been a wicked woman in my day," she said, laughing, "and I don't suppose the good Lord listens much to my prayers."

"A miracle," murmured Lucà. "Well, Mistress," he said cheerfully, "it does me good to listen to you, and hear how much better you sound than you did yesterday. If you have a jug I may use, I will mix up more of this new compound. Don't touch it yet, but when the bells sound again, stir it up well with a spoon, and take a half-cupful. From then on, take more every time the bells sound as long as you need it. No more than half a cupful, now," he said, shaking a finger at her and smiling. "Too much is bad for you. I will come back tomorrow to see how you do."

◈═══ ═══◈

Lucà walked slowly, very slowly, back to the neat stone house in the suburb of Sant Felíu where Romeu had his work-room and house. He was considering the state of his boots and of his tunic, and then the thinness of his purse, even though he paid Romeu only pennies a week for a clean room and bed, with shelves for his herbs, and three good meals a day.

People liked him. He knew that. Almost everyone liked him, except perhaps for some in the Jewish community who

were suspicious of him after he had blundered in two weeks ago
to Master Isaac's house. It had seemed such a perfect opportunity, he thought ruefully. Going there to seek his cousin at the
house of the physician, the two men he had wanted to meet.
But it hadn't worked out, and except for the old lady, and three
or four others who had called him in out of curiosity, no one
seemed interested in his cures. A miracle, that's what he
needed. Just what the old lady said. A miracle. To cure the
landlord's daughter, he mused. Romeu's pale, sad daughter.
That would make the town notice him.

THE end of that week was Palm Sunday. A cool wind from the
hills ruffled curls, snatched at veils, and tossed the hems of
gowns, but the sun shone brightly and the birds poured their
hearts out with song. Lucà didn't wake that morning until the
bells of the great church of Sant Feliu joined with the cathedral
bells to call the faithful to mass. He jumped out of bed,
washed, and dressed in a moment. As he opened the door to his
room, he heard his landlord's voice, vehement but not loud,
coming up the staircase to his room under the eaves.

"Regina, you must get up. It is Sunday, the Sunday before
Easter. I would like you to come to church with me," said
Romeu.

"I cannot, Papa," said the voice he had scarcely heard speak
before. "I cannot go out in front of all those people and have
their pitying glances on me. I am too tired, and too miserable.
How can I go to church if I cannot stop weeping?"

For the first time, Lucà actually began to consider what
might be wrong with the Romeu's daughter. No one had spoken of her to him, except the old lady. Romeu seemed to think
that he should know; everyone else just sighed, or shook their
heads, or said "Poor Regina!" as if what was wrong with her
were clear.

She came down for meals, and ate almost nothing. She was
thin. She didn't talk. She behaved as if he didn't exist.

Lucà went off to church on his own, and puzzled over the
Regina question.

Monday, March 30

"WHERE have you been, Papa?" asked Raquel, running lightly down the steps into the courtyard as Isaac came in the gate. "Mama was asking for you."

"Is there something wrong?" asked Isaac.

"I don't think so," said Raquel. She paused. The bells for sext began to ring out all over the city, temporarily drowning out conversation. From the kitchen the smell of braising meat started to drift down into the courtyard as Naomi and Jacinta set to work on dinner. "She seems to worry more about everything right now."

"She always does after a baby," said the physician. "It is part of her nature. She likes to know that everyone is where he's supposed to be. But let us sit down and have something cool to drink. The March sun can sometimes be almost as warm as June when there is little wind."

"There is a jug of bitter orange and honey drink on the table. Naomi decided that you would be hot and thirsty when you returned. Have you walked far?"

"Not far at all. I have been to visit Master Mordecai. We were chatting about the herbalist for a while," he said. "He seems to be the favorite topic for all of the gossips of the town right now."

"I saw him this morning," said Yusuf, who was sitting in a sunny corner, bending over a small book bound in stiff leather. "While I was gathering herbs. He seemed to be following me around, picking the same things I was, as if he wanted to find out what we used. He talks a lot," said Yusuf.

"Whatever about?" asked Raquel.

"Anything," said Yusuf. "He was telling about the herbs that grow around Genoa and what they're used for, and how dangerous some of them can be. And then he asked me if we used any of them, but I didn't recognize them by the names he used, and when he looked around for them he couldn't see any."

"Each plant goes under many names," observed Isaac. "That is why it is important to know them well, and study books that depict them accurately, because otherwise you can make very grave mistakes."

"He offered to trade recipes with me for various complaints," said Yusuf casually. "He said it would be of great benefit to both of us."

"And did you?" asked Isaac.

"Certainly not," said Yusuf. "I think he was trying to find out all your cures, lord, so that he could steal them and try to take away all your patients."

"There is more to treating people than being able to pick the right herbs, Yusuf. You know that. The next time he suggests some such thing, do not refuse to help him, Yusuf."

"But why should I give him your secrets?"

"Do not think of it that way. I urge you to heap assistance on his shoulders. If he is an honest man, it will help him to help others; if he is driven by evil desires, it might act like a poultice, bringing the evil to a head and allowing it to be drained and cleaned out."

"Are you sure of this, lord?" said Yusuf. "People tell me that he is already visiting some of your patients."

"And do you worry that I am not busy enough?" asked Isaac. "It seems to me that we have more work than we can do."

"True, lord," said Yusuf, somewhat chastened but stubbornly intending to make his point. "He offered to sell you—you, lord—some of his supply of a special medicinal tonic. He said that it tastes of bitter herbs and—in the time it takes water to boil on a hot fire—anyone who drinks it feels better, he says. It doesn't matter what his problem might be."

"You have just given me a useful idea, Yusuf," said Isaac. "Our esteemed neighbor, Mordecai, has been feeling weary and in a curious way, not well. I think I shall ask him to send for his kinsman, young Master Lucà, in order to request some of this miraculous compound. Perhaps it will make him feel better."

"Master Mordecai, Papa? I saw him yesterday, walking up the hill to the gate like a young deer. How can he be ill?"

"Believe me, my dear, if I say he is ill, he is. Now I must go and speak to him. I am very glad you mentioned this to me, Yusuf. Raquel, please tell your mother I will be gone from the house for no more than a few moments. If nothing else, the smell of our dinner cooking will draw me back long before it is ready."

"FEIGN illness? My good friend, Isaac, anything else, but not that. It is impossible."

"I recollect someone offering to do anything . . . without question," said Isaac.

"That was money, Isaac, or any kind of material comfort I could offer you, but to take myself off to my bed and turn away all my clients—I am much too busy right now. You cannot believe how busy I am. For twelve days starting on Thursday no one will be able to do business with us here in the *call* and at the moment there are at least two good men out there, long-standing clients, who could be ruined if I do not take care of their requirements now. They are depending on my aid to pay for goods that are being brought into the city next week: My reputation would never recover."

"It does not have to be done right now," said Isaac. "I doubt that any real harm will come to anyone at all, and certainly not in the next week or two. But if you could do that for me at some time when you can afford to appear to be ill for two or three days, it would be interesting and useful. There is no need for you to take to your bed. Keep on quietly working in your study, but for those days refuse to see visitors."

"Well," said Mordecai. "I shall consider how this might be done. After all, you have promised to find me someone discreet and reliable to travel to Mallorca and visit Faneta and her mother."

"I have promised, Master Mordecai?"

"Of course. It was your idea, was it not?"

"I admit to the idea," said Isaac.

"And now I think is a good time to carry it out," said Mordecai.

"And why is that?"

"Because I received a reply to my letter to Seville," he said. "Much of it is unimportant to anyone but me, but I shall read you what he says concerning my kinfolk there."

"I would be most interested," said Isaac.

"He says, 'Mistress Faneta and young Rubèn left Seville some three years ago for Mallorca shortly after the death of her husband. The boy was then almost twelve years old. They were to live with Perla, Faneta's mother, but I have not had word of them since. I can see no reason why a young man claiming to be. Faneta's son should speak like a Mallorquin. The boy spoke like everyone else in the *aljama* in Seville, but spoke to his mother in her native tongue, although she often lamented that he spoke it badly. Rubèn is a nice lad, but not gifted in tongues, as I know to my cost. It was my painful task for a while to try to teach him some Hebrew, and a great trial it was of my patience.' That is all that he knows about the boy or his mother, Isaac, and so I would imagine that to find further information, someone must seek it in Mallorca."

"And let us hope that when I do find someone, he discovers the truth that lies behind these jugglers' games."

"Jugglers' games, Isaac?"

"Can you have forgotten that this is the second time that a cousin who says he is Faneta's eldest son has appeared on your doorstep, Mordecai? Tell me, does either one of these cousins look like Faneta or Perla or your uncle or any other member of your family?"

"I searched both of their faces, Isaac, and found not a single feature that reminded me of any of those you just spoke of. If declaring that I am ill and hiding myself away will help to unmask an impostor, then I will do what you ask, but in a week or two."

"Thank you, my friend."

"But first tell me, Isaac, what do you—as a physician— think of our new herbalist?"

"Me? I have no opinions," said Isaac. "Except that he seems to be the perfect physician."

"Perfect?"

"Indeed. He panders to all tastes. To Jews, he is a Jew, forced to hide his religion; to Christians, he is a Christian, forced to consort with Jews. To mothers, he simpers like the devoted son they never had, and to daughters—well, I gather that when he breathes deep sighs he even cures their fevers."

"You don't like him, Master Isaac?"

"I like him, my friend. I think he is immensely likeable. For the moment, I do not trust him. And I am not sure that he trusts himself."

Tuesday, March 31

THIS morning Lucà was up with the birds once more and out on the hilly meadows to the southeast of the city with a broad basket over his arm. Except for a slender figure some distance away, he seemed to be alone. When the figure approached, he waved.

"You're out here early," called the youth cheerfully.

"Hola, Yusuf," said Lucà. "I am still looking for that same flower. I was hoping that there might be some early ones on these slopes."

"You won't find any around here for a month or more, even if the weather is very warm," said Yusuf. "But since you needed it, I checked our herb supplies, and we still have much left from last year. Or does it have to be fresh?"

"No, not at all," said Lucà.

"Then I brought some with me, in case you needed it," said Yusuf. "You're welcome to it."

"But what if your master notices that it is gone?" asked Lucà.

"He told me to let you have some if you needed it," said Yusuf. "We have enough. I hope you have a pleasant day," he added. "I must go now. I have a class at the cathedral."

And with that mystifying remark, Yusuf bowed slightly and raced down the hill.

⊹══ ══⊹

"I have met the new healer again, lord," said Yusuf, when they had gathered for dinner. "Lucà. He is gathering herbs to make a mixture against melancholy."

"That's the young man who came here, is it not, Isaac?" asked Judith.

"It is, my dear. And how do you know he is treating melancholy?" asked Isaac.

"Because he was searching for the flowers of that plant that witches make spells with. The one with the bright yellow little flowers, that grows sometimes as high as my knee, that I call witches' flower. That was one of the plants he was looking for when I last saw him. He said he needed it for a patient with burns."

"It will soothe burns," said Isaac. "But why do you think that he wanted it for melancholy?"

"I chanced to see in his basket, which he had heaped with betony and a great deal of rosemary, nothing more. They are not of much use for burns, are they, lord?"

"Perhaps not," said Isaac.

"And since I remembered what you had told me to do, I had brought a little packet of dried witches' flower with me, because he is often out in the morning these days. I hope you do not mind, lord," he added. "We have a great deal, and will be replacing it when the plants bloom again," he added hastily.

"You did right, Yusuf," said Isaac.

"Well, as soon as I gave it to him, I said I had to leave, but when I looked back, he was moving as hastily as he could in the direction of Romeu's house."

"Perhaps he seeks to cure his landlord's daughter," said Isaac.

"Where you have failed, Papa?" asked Raquel.

"How did you describe him to me, Raquel?" said her father. "A young man, with beautiful brown hair, soft brown eyes, and a strongly marked, handsome face?"

"How do you remember all my silly words?" said Raquel. "But he is a handsome young man."

"It may be that your mother's prescription for Regina will be better than mine, and if Lucà can charm her into eating and soothe her melancholy with his soft eyes, perhaps she will be cured. No doubt a few soothing herbs will help. I wish him good luck."

LUCÀ spent the rest of the morning making infusions of each of the three herbs. When they seemed to have reached the proper strength, he tasted each one, and then mixed them, wishing most heartily that he had someone to tell him how much of each to put in his mixture. The result was strong-tasting and bitter. He added a little honey and a small amount of wine. They gave it an odd, but not unpleasant flavor. After considering the situation for a moment, he drank a sizable dose. For his heart sank at the thought that he might increase her suffering by giving her a drink that turned her stomach or did her harm.

That evening, after Regina had excused herself and gone off to her small bedchamber, Lucà turned to his landlord. "Romeu, sir," he said, "I cannot help but notice that your daughter, Regina, seems to be unhappy to the point of illness. Would you permit me to try to help her?"

"Help her?" said Romeu. "How? Are you to go to Athens and convince her young man that he would rather return here and work as a laborer than fight and become rich? Good luck to you if you try."

"I could not do that," said Lucà. "I am an herbalist, not a worker of miracles. But my master taught me how to make a mixture that eases the spirits, takes away the headache, and brings sleep and appetite back. I have gone out to the hills and meadows and found the ingredients, brewed them, and mixed them. I have tasted them all at every stage, and they have brought me no harm."

"Have they helped you?"

"My head does not ache, I already sleep well, eat well, and feel cheerful most of every day, so that I'm not sure that they would change anything for me. But late this morning I took a large dose, and remain unharmed."

"If she wishes to take this mixture, then you have my permission to give it to her," said Romeu. "But first you must tell her what you are doing. I do not want my daughter deceived, even for her own good. She has had enough of man's deception."

"May I try it now?" he asked.

For his answer, Romeu stood up and walked over to the stairs that led up to the chamber above. "Regina!" he called. "Would you be kind enough to come down?"

<hr />

SOME five minutes later, looking somewhat flustered, Regina came down the stairs, tying the laces at her bodice and straightening her shawl. Her eyes were red with weeping.

"My dearest child," said Romeu, "Lucà would like to give you something to ease your pain and sorrow a little."

"And how can he do that?" she said in a dull voice. "No one can. Papa, I am sick of being dragged in front of physicians and healers and all manner of men who do not understand why I suffer. Please let me be."

"Please, Mistress Regina," said Lucà, "I have cause to feel much gratitude to your father, and it pains me to see how he suffers because of your grief. If I could ease that grief just a little, then it would lessen his suffering as well."

"How can you?" she said with a sudden flash of anger. "Do you think I suffer from a bee sting, on which you can place crushed leaves and draw out the poison and the pain? My poison and pain are here, deep in my very being, where no one can touch them."

"Let me try," he said. "Give me just three days, at least, and then if you wish, I will never speak of it again."

"You might allow him to try, Regina," said her father gently.

"If you wish it, Papa," she said, returning to her state of dull apathy.

Lucà placed his basket on the table and took out a flask sealed with cork. He shook it to mix it thoroughly, uncorked it, and filled a wooden cup with the mixture to the brim. "This is what I have mixed for you," he said, showing it to her. He raised the cup and drank half of it. "There," he said. "You see that I am not afraid to taste my own medicines. Will you do me the honor to drink the rest?"

"If you then will allow me to return to my chamber, I will drink it." She drank the mixture, curtsied to both, and went back up the stairs.

"Do you think she will continue to take it for three days?" asked Lucà.

"She has agreed to it," said Romeu. "She will not go back on her word."

"Then we should see at least a little improvement," he said.

"I certainly hope so," said Romeu. "Because if I see her getting worse in any way, you will be very sorry you decided to lodge here with me."

NINE

Fortuna és sobtós canviador

Fortune is a sudden changer

WHEN Regina came downstairs the next morning, she was moving slowly and yawning. Romeu had already set out the morning meal of a loaf, a cured sausage, and a large piece of cheese.

"You look tired, my dear," said her father. "Did you not sleep?"

"I did sleep, Papa. More than I usually do. So much that I woke up only a minute ago, and still feel very sleepy."

"I am glad you slept, my dear. Now try to eat something."

"Yes, Papa," she said. But although she helped herself to a small piece of the loaf and a little cheese, she only nibbled at it, leaving most of it on the plate.

The morning after that, Regina came down the stairs a little more briskly and set herself to putting breakfast things on the table. Romeu glanced at her and refrained from comment, except to bid her a pleasant "Good morning."

Lucà came in shortly after, and after greeting father and daughter, helped himself liberally to the food. As he ate, he exchanged remarks on the weather, and his patients, and Romeu's latest projects, with its difficulties, but like Romeu, was careful not to observe whether Regina was eating or not.

After Romeu went down to his workshop, which took up almost all of the ground floor of the house where they lived, Lucà lingered at the table. "Your father manages very well," he said. "Cooking and helping around the house. But I am surprised he has not sought himself another wife."

"My mother died less than a year ago," said Regina, her eyes filling with tears. "My father took that blow very hard. I doubt if he has yet recovered."

"She must have been a good woman," said Lucà.

"She was more than that," said Regina. "She was very good and honest, but she was also lively and cheerful. The house was always full of songs and laughter. Whenever I was ill or the weather was horrible, she would sit with her work and tell me tales better than those of the famous poets. I miss her so," said Regina, now choked with tears. "If she had lived, she would have known what Marc would do to me, because she saw everything, and knew so much about people. She would have told me—she tried to warn me a little before she died—and she would have known how to help me." Regina dropped her head down on the table and sobbed, brokenhearted.

Lucà came around the table and sat on the bench beside her. He put an arm over her heaving shoulders and grasped her hand in his, making soft, soothing noises as one makes to an unhappy child. Gradually her sobs eased and she became calm. She searched for a cloth to mop up her tears, and he handed her his kerchief. "Take this," he said, and went over to the jug on the sideboard and poured her a little wine, which he mixed with water. He brought it over along with some dried apricots and nuts on a plate and set them by her elbow.

Regina drank a little of the watered wine and set down the cup. "It was just after Mama died that Marc said he was going to fight in Sardinia with my lord Francesch de Cervian. I begged him not to go, and he said he was tired of being poor, and that until I recovered from Mama's death we shouldn't marry, because I wasn't fit to live with. He said he was sick of misery and sorrow. He'd rather fight and die than work constantly and be poor and miserable."

"And you had no one to go to?"

"No one," said Regina. "Papa was so unhappy that I didn't

want to pour my miseries onto his own. And then when we heard from my lord Francesch what Marc had done, my father was so angry at him that I couldn't even mention his name because then he would roar about how worthless and deceitful he was, how he hoped he would die ignominiously in some brawl over there, and that didn't help me at all." Her tears had dried for now, and she stared out the window at the clear sky, as if seeing her life history, brief as it was, written up in the heavens. Without even a glance at the plate, she picked up a nut and ate it, and then drank a little more.

⊹⊱ ⊰⊹

LATE the next morning, Good Friday, Lucà found her in the courtyard, in the bright sun, bending over the herb garden. "These poor things," she said. "I have neglected them so. I have just been pulling out the weeds and tidying them up. They look better, I think."

"Herbs appreciate attention," he said. "But you should not overtire yourself. Let us sit in the shade with something cool to drink."

"I will fetch it," said Regina. "Since I was tidying up the herbs I made some mint and lemon drink for Papa when he comes back from church." She returned with a jug filled to the brim and two cups and then went back for a small bowl heaped up with fruit and nuts. "You have told me nothing about yourself," said Regina. "I don't even know where you come from. Someone said from Seville, but you don't sound like it in your speech."

"That is because I didn't grow up in Seville," said Lucà. "I remember very little about it. But I will tell you my story later. What is important now is how you are feeling."

"The worst of my pain—"

"What kind of pain is it?" he asked, looking at her intensely. "Can you tell me?"

"Here," she said, touching herself just above the waist. "And here," she added, touching her breast. "For months I felt as if they were piling great rocks on me here and here, so I could scarcely move and neither breathe nor swallow. That has eased, and now I feel—nothing. Numb, unless someone reminds me of my misery, and then I cannot keep from weeping." She looked at him, her eyes bright with tears for a moment. "But it is better than the pain. And being in the garden helped me." She picked up a dried apricot and began to nibble on it. "You know about herbs. Do you think the mint will grow back? It was so choked with weeds that it was almost dead. I used almost all of it for this pitcherful."

"Oh yes," he said. "Mint is very strong. When you take away what is choking it, it recovers very quickly, you'll see. The way strong people who are weighed down with care do when someone helps them a little to clear away some of the cares. People and herbs," he said smiling. "They both need a little help now and then."

"You, sir, are preaching at me," said Regina, and for the first time in nearly a year, she smiled.

THE next day started with heavy rain, which gave way to gusty winds and then to bright sunshine mixed with bands of fast-moving clouds. Romeu rose early and worked until dinnertime without a pause. "There," he said, "I have finished the big piece for Master Ephraim, except for smoothing it down one last time and polishing it. That can wait until Monday. From now until then we will rest. I have a fine piece of mutton to braise for us to feast upon tomorrow."

After a simple dinner and a rest, Regina put on her second best gown and came into the kitchen where her father and Lucà were sitting, deep in conversation. She looked at both of them, one after the other.

"I noticed that the sun is out. The wind seems to have dried the paths. I thought it might be pleasant to go out for an evening stroll," she said. "Perhaps along the river a little way."

"What an excellent idea, Regina," said her father. "I hadn't noticed how pleasant it had become. Let us all go out for a walk."

And moving slowly, because Regina tired easily, they strolled down to the river. "There are so many people out," she whispered.

"That is because the weather has been cloudy or rainy until this afternoon," said her father.

"Who is that man, Papa?" she asked, nodding at a group crossing the bridge. "He must be a newcomer."

"Which man?" asked her father.

"The one with the light hair and the dark beard," she said, pointing. "I saw him walking up the street toward the gate yesterday when I was airing the beds."

"I don't see him. Do you, Master Lucà?"

Lucà stared at the people on the bridge. "No," he said. "For a moment I thought it was an old friend, but he doesn't look at all like him. I'm afraid I still don't know who are newcomers and who were born and bred in the town," he added apologetically.

"I must get out more," said Regina demurely. "Before I become as ignorant as Master Lucà."

Her father glanced over at her and for a moment could have sworn that she had winked at him. "I think we should go back," he said. "Before you tire yourself too much with unaccustomed exercise."

It was then that the first of the talk began. The neighbors had been expecting their next news of Regina to be that she was about to be buried. And there she was, thin, not the lively creature she always used to be, but outside, and on her feet, with a tiny bit of color in her cheeks from the fresh air and the wind and the sun.

The next morning, she rose and put on her best gown. She arranged her hair and veil with great care. "This hardly fits me," she said, coming into the kitchen where her father was sitting. "Look at it, Papa. It hangs upon me like a sack."

"Either you must take your needle to it or add a little flesh to your bones," said her father, laughing. "But I think it looks right pretty on you. Are you coming with us to mass? It is Easter."

"I know it's Easter, Papa," she said. "And of course I'm coming with you." Today, her step was a little quicker, and she was not quite so pale, details that were noticed by all those they met on the way.

"It's a miracle," said one housewife to another. "I've heard that he's been treating her with a special concoction of his own, and in one week has brought her back from the grave."

"I wonder if he can do that to my wife," said a tradesman. "She's as silent and miserable a creature as any woman on earth. It would be nice to see her with a little life in her."

"Then stop yelling at her and hitting her every time you're

out of temper," said his neighbor. "It'll work better than Master Lucà's herbs and be a lot cheaper, too."

"I don't yell at her," said the tradesman. "And I hardly ever hit her."

"She's happy enough when you're not there," said his neighbor's wife. "It's only when you come home she's too frightened to speak. And Regina's return from the grave might have more to do with having a cheerful—not to say, handsome, too—young man around the house than any potions he can mix. The poor thing was very lonely," she added. "Romeu had best keep an eye on her."

But almost everyone else in town decided that the young herbalist could work miracles, and suddenly he had more patients than he knew how to deal with.

Easter Monday, April 6

THE *call* had been closed for five days. Although life carried on busily enough inside the walls, these days had felt like an endless Sabbath to Raquel, without the calm and peace the Sabbath brought. She had been restless all day, going out with her father to see two patients, staying with her mother to give help that never seemed to be needed, wondering if she should simply throw on her shawl and wander over to visit Daniel—or Daniel's Aunt Dolsa, who would make sure that Daniel was there. Without a word to anyone, then, since no one seemed to be interested in where she was, Raquel slipped out to the glovemaker's house. Mistress Dolsa greeted her with all her usual warm affection, excused herself, and returned quickly with Daniel. With many apologies, she left them to entertain each other, as she put it, while she went to find out why refreshments had not arrived yet.

"Daniel," said Raquel, "I have been so miserable without you."

He pulled her into his arms and held her tightly. "Then why, my darling," he said, releasing her a little, "can we not get married?"

"I told you, Daniel. I don't know any more. When I ask Mama, she says how can you bother me with this until Beniamin is a little older and I have recovered from his birth. When I ask Papa if he knows the reason for the delay, he smiles in that odd way he has and says that we will be married soon, very soon. But when you're older, soon seems to come later and later."

"They cannot make us wait longer than after Passover. I shall speak to my uncle and see if he can move your parents. For indeed, everyone says that there is nothing to keep us apart."

In the moments that followed, they were both too preoccupied to hear the voices and footsteps inside Ephraim's house. It was not until Raquel heard the familiar tap of her father's staff on the tiled floor at the entrance to the courtyard that she pushed Daniel away and listened.

"Raquel?" said her father. "Is that you? Are you here?"

"Oh, Papa, are you following me about now?" she said, half in jest and half in exasperation.

"Not at all," said Isaac. "I had no idea you were visiting Mistress Dolsa. I came seeking Daniel and was told that he was here in the courtyard."

"And is there something that can I do for you, Master Isaac?" asked Daniel, in his courtesy forgetting—as he always did—what strange events those words could herald.

"There is, Daniel," said the physician casually. "I would very much like you to travel to Mallorca, to the City, on an important errand for me. It would not take you long, unless the winds are extremely contrary," he said.

"To Mallorca!" said Raquel. "Papa, what are you saying?"

"How long?" said Daniel suspiciously.

"Daniel," said Raquel. "Don't you dare!"

"Three or four days out," said Isaac, "and three or fours days back, if the winds are relatively favorable and nothing goes wrong. Then you would need to spend perhaps three days there as well as travel from here to Barcelona and back."

"And if the winds are contrary?"

"You might have to wait for a week or ten days for a wind, perhaps, but probably not both ways. If you left tomorrow—and I can assure you that there is an excellent ship sailing Thursday—you would be back in time to spend Passover with us, and while you were gone, Raquel could make final preparations for her wedding. Passover ends on Monday; the following

Sunday would be a happy time for a wedding, I think. But you may pick any day of that week, or later if you prefer."

"But why do you want me to go to Mallorca tomorrow?" asked Daniel.

"To visit a lady by the name of Perla who lives in the city, and to ask her a few questions. If you agree to do this, then I will tell you what you must ask her. She is a very pleasant woman, Daniel, and she is old enough to be your grandmother, Raquel. Talk it over. I shall return to Ephraim," said Isaac. "He is quite willing for you to go, Daniel, especially if you have a moment to look over some goods for him while you are there."

"And then we may marry at last?" said Raquel.

"By then your mother's days will be finished, and she will be back to her usual self, as well. There will be nothing to keep you apart." He rose and turned toward the house. "I look forward to your response."

"But to leave tomorrow," said Daniel. "I have no travel permission, no plans . . ."

"Master Mordecai has arranged all that," said Isaac. "You will find there is nothing for you to do but put some linen in a bundle and ride out on one of his excellent mules."

"Master Mordecai? I can feel the hand of fate on my shoulder," said Daniel. "Never, since Jacob labored for his Raquel, has any man been forced to do more to gain himself the wife he desired—desired more than anything on earth. Shall I go, and we will see if this time they mean to keep their word?"

"If Papa says that we are to marry on Sunday, not much more than four weeks from now, he means it," said Raquel. "He does not change his mind lightly. And he will have talked about it already to your uncle."

"Then I will go. Rise early tomorrow, my dearest," murmured Daniel. "I will come by your gate before I leave. Now I must speak to Uncle Ephraim and find out what is happening." After a quick glance around the courtyard, he kissed her, holding her fiercely to him, turned and ran toward the house.

"Daniel—are you on your way back to work?" asked Dolsa. "I had just brought a little something for us to nibble on."

"I cannot stay longer, I'm afraid," he said. "But I'm sure that Raquel will."

"Excellent," said Dolsa. "Then we will have a chance to talk about the wedding."

———— ◦———◦ ————

RAQUEL slept badly all that night. Between hopes and fears—not the least of which was oversleeping and missing Daniel in the morning—she could not do more than doze fitfully. She got up from her bed at the sound of the first birds and the raucous cries of roosters that echoed back and forth between the hills. She washed and dressed herself in the faint light of dawn and slipped quietly downstairs into the courtyard.

Almost before there was light enough to see from the stairs to the gate, she heard footsteps and ran over. She battled for a few moments with the gate until at last it gave way, and she slipped out into the relative darkness of the street. "I have no time," said Daniel. "I am going with a friend of Mordecai's and he waits at the gate with the mule."

Raquel threw her arms around him and held him tightly in an embrace and then drew back. "This is for you, my beloved," she said. "It is my very best curl, to remember me by." She handed him a gold case on a thin chain.

He opened it and found a thick curl of Raquel's hair. He closed the case again and put chain around his neck. "It sits on my heart," he said. "I will be back soon." He kissed her once more and ran off.

It was not much later when Yusuf wandered into the courtyard, eating a piece of bread with a chunk of cheese sitting on it. "You're awake early," he said.

"Where are you going?" she asked.

"To gather herbs. The gate is to be open for a little while this morning, and I shall profit from it. I really am going to gather herbs," he added crossly. "And do a few other things. But there are herbs we need. You look tired, Raquel. If I were you, I would go back to bed."

With a profound conviction that Yusuf knew exactly why she was up early, she glared at his retreating back, locked the gate again, and headed for the kitchen to see what she could find.

Arming herself with a breakfast of fruit, bread, and cheese,

Raquel slipped silently up the twisting staircases that led all
the way to the attics and the roof. She moved on tiptoes between the racks used for drying food, pushed open the shutters,
and went out a small window. From here she could see the city
gates and a small procession with Daniel in it riding out in the
silvery light before dawn. Long after he had disappeared from
sight, she sat there, thinking, until her eye was caught by more
movement—not on the road, but on the hillside beside it.

There were two figures on the slope, both bent over, gathering herbs. One, without a doubt, was Yusuf. That slight dark-
haired figure and those lithe movements could only be his. So
he really was gathering herbs. Then over by the trees, she saw a
bay mare, grazing peacefully. Yusuf's, she thought. He was
making the most of these moments of freedom of movement.
The second figure was behind Yusuf, and even as he bent down,
apparently also to gather herbs or perhaps to pick mushrooms,
he was moving fairly quickly in the direction of the boy.

When he drew close enough to attract Yusuf's attention, he
stood up. He was tall and broad-shouldered in comparison
with Yusuf, thought Raquel. Not another apprentice lad, sent
out at dawn by his master. In fact, he was probably Lucà.
Hadn't Yusuf complained that he followed him around? After a
few moments of what seemed to be conversation, Yusuf bent
over to his basket and handed something over to the other.

Raquel grinned. She would have some interesting moments
finding out just what had gone on in that meadow. As she considered her attack, her eye was caught by something else. A figure was standing in the trees, watching Yusuf and Lucà. As they
moved across the slope, he bent over to pick up a bundle and
moved sideways to keep them in his line of sight, stepping out
from the shelter of the trees. At that moment, the first red rays
of morning sun broke obliquely over the hilltop and turned the
newcomer's head of light-colored hair into a halo of fire.

The newcomer sat down on the grass, his bundle beside him
and his arms around his knees, settling himself to observe the
two gatherers of herbs with the liveliest of interest. Raquel
shook her head and moved back out of the attics, puzzled by
what she had seen.

Tuesday, April 7, 1355

DANIEL, carrying a half-loaf of bread stuffed with a generous portion of cheese that was to serve for his breakfast,
mounted the amiable mule supplied by Master Mordecai and
urged her onto the highroad. The waning moon floated palely
in the southwest, still providing more light than the emergent
dawn. "Why do we set out so early?" he asked Salomó Vidal. "I
thought that the ship did not leave port until tomorrow morning. Surely we cannot be that far from Barcelona now."

Salomó was the merchant who had agreed that Daniel could
travel with him and his two burly servants, as long as Daniel
did not hold them up or inconvenience him in any way. He put
spurs to his mule and gestured to Daniel to keep up. "I know
this ship's master," he said. "Cargo to be shipped has to be in
place by this morning. He'll start the heavy pieces now, and if
there's a favorable wind, he'll sail as soon as it's all on board. If
we're there, he'll take us. If we aren't, he won't hesitate to leave
us behind. So hurry up, lad."

"But there's no wind at all," protested Daniel.

"There will be," said Salomó. "So don't forget it and go back
to sleep. If it's blowing from the north, he'll be spreading his
sails well before dinnertime. I won't be pleased to miss him."

"I'll be happy to be there and back as soon as possible," said
Daniel.

"Good," said the merchant. "But I warn you not to count on
anything. You never know with the spring winds."

"Are the winds more reliable the rest of the year?" asked
Daniel in all innocence.

The merchant began to laugh, a deep hearty laugh that woke
the neighborhood dogs and evoked a cockcrow from somewhere
nearby. "You have me there, lad," he said. "You're quite right.
You never know what you're going to face."

⚓ ⚓

THEY arrived in Barcelona the next morning at about a half
hour past terce. The housewives and servants were out, squab-
bling over poultry, and fish, and meat, and fruit. By the time

the sun was high, the market stalls would be empty, leaving nothing but picked-over scraps for the lazy or disorganized. They stabled their mules outside the city walls, the two servants hoisted the pack mule's cargo on their own shoulders, and they all walked down to the strand where ships' boats were scurrying back and forth, loading the vessels that rode at anchor a safe distance out from shore.

"There he is," said Salomó. "That villainous-looking pirate over there."

"I trust he is not as villainous as he looks," said Daniel uneasily.

"He is," said the merchant. "But once he takes our money, his villainy is on our side. That's why I like to ship with him. I always know where I stand."

"But there are honest masters out here," said Daniel. "I have sailed now with two of them."

"Indeed there are," said Salomó. "And if you have a big cargo, and have chartered the boat to ship it, you should engage one of them. But if you only have a small shipment, like me, those ships will charge you as if you were carrying all the spices of the East on board, and a few lions and tigers to boot. Giovanni, here, will fit us in and treat us well, and not charge too much, as long as we don't hold him up, or try to tell him what to do."

"Giovanni?" asked Daniel.

"Don't ask me—or him—where he comes from," said Salomó. "I think by now he's not sure himself."

⟡ ══ ══ ⟡

AND, indeed, not long after the four men arrived where the boats were loading, Giovanni himself came over and greeted them. *"Hola,"* he said. "We leave soon. Next boat. Which is your cargo, Salomó?"

"It's being loaded into that boat right now."

Giovanni went over to the crew of the boat and screamed something incomprehensible at them.

"What tongue does he speak?" asked Daniel.

Salomó shrugged. "What does he speak well? None, I suspect. Badly? All you have ever heard of. He just told them that my cargo comes off first, that I am sure of, but what else he said, I could not tell you, and I speak many tongues."

They scrambled, with three other passengers, onto the next boat and were rowed quickly out to the ship, the *Santa Felicitat*, a broad-beamed, high-prowed, two-masted vessel that rocked in the wind that was blowing down from the northwest. The four of them were pushed, rather than ushered, into a tiny cabin, part of the sleeping quarters built onto the stern. It had two narrow wooden bunks and hooks for two hammocks. "I think," said Salomó, sitting down on a bunk, "that we are about to sail. They want us out of the way."

With loud and indecipherable cries from the crew, and creaking, groaning, and rattling from wood, metal, and rope, the sails were hoisted. The creaking of the hull took on a rhythm that Daniel recognized at once, heightened by the slap of water against wood. They were under way, blessed with a wind, which he hoped was heading them south to the port of Mallorca. He leaned back against the side of the ship and began to calculate happily how soon he would be back home. Then he found that he was at home, sitting in the courtyard in the blazing sun, with something pressing against the head. Painfully, he opened his eyes, and with a deep sigh, remembered where he was.

PART IV

MALLORCA

✣

TEN

car vostre cos és de verí replet

for your body is of poison full

THE wind carried them slowly out from port, with much shouting and activity from the crew. "What's happening?" asked Daniel. "Why is everyone so upset?"

"They aren't upset," said Salomó. "Irritated, perhaps. If we were heading for Genoa, no one could ask for a better wind. It's not perfect for the islands, though."

"And they don't wish to go to Genoa," remarked Daniel.

"They most particularly do not wish to go to Genoa, where many of them could well be hanged for various acts that the Genoese might call piracy. But they're a clever crew on this old tub of a ship, and they can do a lot even if the winds are not perfectly in their favor."

As if his words had been a challenge, the canvas above began to rattle; the pennants flapped aimlessly once or twice and drooped. The wind had died.

"Now what?" said Daniel.

"Now nothing," said Salomó. "Unless you want to take one of the boats and tow us," he added with hearty burst of laughter. "But don't worry. This time of year we're bound to find a wind at some point."

The ship rocked gently on the quiet sea throughout the

longest afternoon of Daniel's life. Activity on board slowed and then finally stopped. The only crew members left working were the lookout in his station, the man standing uselessly at the wheel, and the first officer, who lounged about on deck, keeping a languid eye on the crew.

The crew had finished their suppers when suddenly a sharp gust of wind snapped the drooping pennants on the mast and then steadied. A shout went up. The idle crew started to move to the ropes and up the rigging. Within moments, it seemed, the sails were raised and filled with wind; the heavy-bottomed, broad-beamed, lumbering cargo ship that Daniel had been cursing for the last eight hours or so turned into a seabird, flying over the water. Then on Friday morning, on the third day after they had set sail from Barcelona harbor, a rocky shape loomed up to port on the horizon. "What's that?" he asked.

"The islands," said the sailor sitting with his back propped against the side, mending a piece of sail. "It's where we're going."

"When will we get there?"

"This afternoon," he said.

"They told me it would take longer," said Daniel. "Possibly much longer."

"It might," said the sailor. "If we lose the wind. It often happens."

But by the time the city was stirring itself for the afternoon's work, Salomó and Daniel were making their way up from the harbor into the city. "There is the street that will take you to the gate to the *call*," said Salomó, pointing. "You can inquire for the person you seek once you are inside. I would accompany you farther, but unfortunately I have urgent business to take care of elsewhere. Remember that the ship returns to Barcelona on Friday, early, all being well. If you are there, the master will take you."

And after bidding farewell to his guide, with great curiosity he entered the *call* of the city of Mallorca, looking for the house of a certain Master Maimó.

Under the bright sun, the *call* was a vibrant mass of color and noise. The square at the gate was filled with vendors, shoppers, passersby, and squirming children held in check with difficulty by their harassed mothers. Those who noticed him regarded him with some curiosity; the rest paid little attention. Seeking the cool and shade, he veered left into a good, broad street, wide enough to bring an oxcart up, lined with tall, narrow dwellings, many of them housing busy shops and workrooms.

Mordecai had said that Master Maimó's house was within sight of the palace, and larger than most. Daniel passed a school big enough to indicate a sufficient number of children, and then a synagogue, of a size to hold a considerable congregation, but he could find no trace of either the palace or a house resembling the one he sought. At last, he stopped in front of a bootmaker's shop and workroom, where a weather-beaten man of perhaps fifty was seated outside on a bench, working on a sandal of more than common size. "You have a good-sized customer for that pair," said Daniel cheerfully. "If his purse is as large as the rest of him, I'd like to have the making of his gloves."

"You're a glover, then, young man?" asked the cobbler, in the soft voice of the islands.

"I am. Daniel is my name."

"We have plenty of glovers here," he said.

"I would find meeting them interesting and profitable, I'm sure," said Daniel. "But I am not here in the city seeking work. I leave again next Friday. Perhaps you could tell me where I might find their shops, should I have a moment to visit them?" he asked.

"Over there," said the cobbler and turned back to his sandal.

"Can you direct me to the house of Master Maimó as well?" asked Daniel. "I am charged with a letter to deliver to him."

"You won't find him in here," said the cobbler, and spat out a thread that he was holding in his mouth. "Not grand enough in here for that family. If you hold to the way you're heading up toward the palace, you'll find it," he added grudgingly, nodding in the appropriate direction and choosing another thread.

"Thank you for your courtesy," said Daniel.

But the cobbler kept his eyes on his work and his tongue silent. The conversation was finished.

He found the gate without much difficulty. On the other side was a broad square with several streets leading out of it, any one of which might lead him to his destination. His eye fell on a ragged, sharp-eyed boy of about eight or nine years, who was importuning passersby for coins. He pulled a half-penny out of his purse and held it in front of the lad, far enough away so that it could not be snatched out of his hand. "Do you know the house of Master Maimó?" he asked.

"The rich Jew?" asked the boy.

Daniel nodded, since it had by then occurred to him that Master Mordecai's friend was, in all likelihood, rich.

"Of course," said the boy. "Everyone knows that."

"Everyone but me," said Daniel. "Take me to the house, and if it turns out to be the right one, this is yours."

At that, the boy headed off at an impressive speed across the square, so quickly that Daniel lost sight of him for a moment. He caught a glimpse of him darting between two substantial matrons and started off after him.

"It's up here," the boy called, having paused a moment to make sure he hadn't lost his client. "Just beyond the old gate," he added as Daniel caught up, pointing to the remains of another structure. "That gate," he said. "Do you want me to knock?"

"No," said Daniel. "I'll do it. I want you to wait long enough for me to find out if this is the right house."

The tall, heavy wooden gate concealed much of the house, but what Daniel could see looking upward was imposing both in size and ornamentation. Two sets of large windows gave onto the street along with several smaller ones, all built with intricately patterned stone surrounding each one. He rang the bell and at the same time peered with great curiosity through a crack between the gate and the wall. He could see part of a stair-case and of a tree in the courtyard, but the sound of someone muttering as doors opened and footsteps clattered on the stone stairway leading down to the gate made him straighten up abruptly. He stepped back just in time as the gate swung open.

"I seek Master Maimó," said Daniel.

"Master isn't in," said the surly servant, who glared at him from the courtyard, his hand on the gate still, clearly about to slam it shut in his face.

"Please give this to him," said Daniel, handing a firmly sealed letter through the small space available. "He is expecting me, I believe."

"I'll find out," said the servant. "You can wait out there."

"I told you it was the right house," said the boy, in aggrieved tones.

"Thank you for your help," said Daniel. "What's your name, should I need help finding other places?"

"Miquel," said the boy.

Daniel handed him the coin and added another to it.

The lad started to run off, paused, and called over his shoulder, "You can always find me in the square," he said. "That's where I do all my work."

Daniel turned to watch him go and then stood with his back to the closed gate, looking up and down the street. It was then that he finally saw it. Without noticing, he had climbed almost halfway up a hill that was crowned with a palace built out of the magical tales of his childhood—a palace of high towers and soaring arches. Behind its walls, he thought, must lie gardens with beautiful fountains and trees that bore every kind of fruit he had ever heard of. And now, while he stood there, hot sunshine and light flooded the relatively quiet street—light that danced off decorative marble and tile work on the houses up and down the street until his eyes were dazzled.

"It is beautiful, is it not?" asked a pleasant voice behind him. "That is our royal palace, the Almudaina. And you must be Master Daniel," he added. "I am Maimó. Come in, please."

Daniel turned and was struck momentarily speechless at the sight in front of him. The master of the house had opened the gate wide and the young man now stood on the edge of a courtyard that seemed itself to be fitting for a royal palace. Richly colored tiles in intricate patterns covered the ground; the staircase to the living quarters of the family was the broadest he had seen in a private house. All around him the walls were patterned with more beautifully crafted tiles. The western sun poured in, its heat and intensity tempered by the green of a pair of trees and an abundance of flowering shrubs. In contrast, the dark-brown silk of Master Maimó's tunic looked like simplicity itself against its rich background.

"I regret that we kept you waiting out in the street," Maimó continued. "I must beg you to forgive my faithful watchdog at the gate. Our city may look like Paradise, but it harbors some strange and hostile beings at times. And at this time of year we are forced to be particularly careful. From now on, he will treat you with absolute courtesy, unless he should see you charge at me with a sword in your hand." He laughed, and Daniel joined in, somewhat uneasily.

"WHAT brings you to our lovely city?" asked Maimó, once they were seated at a table in the courtyard with cool drinks and tiny savory titbits to revive them until supper. "Not gloves, I imagine," he said, "although we have some very interesting leathers here. In fact, when the wind blows from the right quarter, you will be aware of just how much leather we have. The tanners pursue their occupation right over there," he added, with a wave of his hand in a vaguely southeasterly direction.

"That must be—"

"It is nothing," said Maimó. "Every city has its winds and its odors. What might interest you more, of course, are the ships from all over that stop here to trade. At the moment our mercantile exchange is spread inconveniently over several buildings, but we have high hopes of building a new and spacious *llonja*. His Majesty has agreed in principle to the project, which would be most beneficial to trade. It is one more advantage to the recent change in rulers," he said, referring delicately to the conquest of the island a decade before. Maimó paused to nibble on an olive, and Daniel hastened to take advantage of the break.

"Certainly I am interested in seeing what is available, and my uncle has commissioned me to buy what I can that would be useful for us to have. But my mission here in Mallorca has nothing to do with that. I am seeking a woman who lived in Girona for a while. After her husband died, she returned to the city, finding it a—" Daniel paused to search for a word. "—a happier place to live, surrounded by old friends and old customs."

"An answer of great diplomacy," said Maimó, smiling. "And who is this widow?"

"Perla, wife of Ezra ben Rubèn of Girona," said Daniel.

"The beautiful Perla," said Maimó softly, and nodded. "Many hearts were broken when she was stolen away from us. I know her well; she is a very shrewd and yet amiable woman. I shall take you to visit her, if you wish. Would tomorrow be satisfactory? I am sure you must be too tired from your journey to venture out at the moment."

"I am indeed," said Daniel. "Although our voyage was rapid, I feel as if I have spent an immoderate amount of time on that ship. At the beginning, for the better part of a day, we appeared to be moving gently backward to the port we'd left."

Once again his host laughed. "A common experience," he said, "Our own sailors are crafty about when they set sail, but the fickleness of the winds deceives even them from time to time."

EARLY in the morning of the same day, when almost all of Girona was slumbering, Isaac was awakened by a frantic ringing of the bell at his gate. He rose from the couch in his study, threw his cloak over his nightshirt, and reached the gate sometime before the door to the porter's small chamber opened. Ibrahim came out after him, cursing quietly under his breath all patients and their families. "Who calls at this hour?" asked Isaac.

"Master Isaac," said a boyish voice. "You must come at once to our house. The master is ill, and it has taken me so long to get permission to enter the *call* that I fear he may be dead before we arrive. I had to go the palace and get the guard to say that I could enter before they allowed me in. It took so long that—"

"Who is your master?" asked Isaac quickly, before the boy could waste any more time.

"Master Narcís," said the boy. "He is in such pain, writhing on the bed and calling out—it is beyond bearing."

"One moment while I don my tunic and fetch my basket."

"What is it, Papa?" Raquel's soft voice floated down to him from the stair that led down to the courtyard.

"It is Master Narcís," said Isaac, turning back toward his study to put on his tunic. "Are you dressed?"

"I am, Papa. I dressed as soon as I heard the noise at the gate."

"Then throw on a cloak and take the basket. Come, lad. We will see your master. Ibrahim, close the gate behind us."

THE door to Master Narcís's house opened as soon as the three approached it. "Come in, master," said a voice. "Quickly. He is ever so bad."

"Is that Anna?" asked Isaac.

"It is, sir," said the maid. "He is in his chamber, up here. Bring more candles, lad," she snapped to the boy. "Don't just stand there."

The boy arrived with the candles in a large candelabra and set it up on a tall dresser to cast light over the bed as Raquel set out the contents of the basket on a nearby table.

Isaac approached the bed, listened for a moment, and reached out to find the patient's chest with his hand. He felt it and then bent over and laid his ear against it.

"He is very pale, Papa," said Raquel, stepping forward. "His jaw is so clenched I do not believe he could speak if he wished, and all his muscles stand out as though they are carrying a great weight."

"His *jaw*?" said Isaac, momentarily startled. "Then we must ease the pain, first of all. Two drops, Raquel."

Smoothly and rapidly she placed sugar, water, a little wine, and two drops of a thick, bitter concoction in a cup and stirred it vigorously. "I am ready, Papa, if you would stand slightly to one side," she asked. She raised up the patient's stiffened shoulders and head and forced the liquid, little by little, into his mouth through his clenched teeth. When he had taken all of it, she lowered him down again.

Isaac ran his hands over the man's belly and then his thighs and calves. He shook his head. "Fetch something to warm his feet," he said.

The boy raced out of the room.

"Is there water for his face?"

"There is, Papa."

"How does he look now?—quickly, Raquel."

"His jaw is beginning to relax," she said, "and I think his muscles are loosening a little."

"Mix some more, but do not give it yet," he said. "Is Anna here?" he asked, as he massaged the tight belly muscles.

"I am, master," she said quickly.

"What did he eat last? Or drink, or take in his mouth in any manner?" he added impatiently. "And where is that boy?"

"I am here, sir. I have stones wrapped in linen. They are still warm from the fire for supper."

"Put them to his feet," said Isaac.

"He had only soup and bread for his supper," said Anna.

"And did you have the same?" asked Isaac.

"Yes, sir, exactly."

"And before that?"

"He had a good dinner, Master Isaac. In the morning, Cook was out before I came downstairs and found a beautiful fish to stuff and bake, and a haunch of kid for the spit. It was excellent, and he ate a good portion of everything. There was nothing wrong with the food," she said, with emphasis on the last word.

Isaac stiffened slightly. "How do you know?"

"We all ate the same, Master Isaac. The master couldn't see the reason in Cook doing two different dinners. She always served him the best part of the meat if she could, but often he left it for us, saying he preferred some other part. And we're all fine. It wasn't the food, nor yet the wine, for we had a cup each, all from the same jug."

"Then tell me—since you seem to know—what he took that did this to him," said the physician firmly.

"Oh, sir, it was that medicine he drank last night."

"What medicine, woman?" said Isaac. "Something that I left for him?"

"Oh, no, sir, nothing of yours. It was from that herbalist. And it is all my fault that it happened."

"Papa," said Raquel, "he is trying to say something."

The man on the bed tossed his head. "So cold," he muttered. "Master Isaac. Is that you? I am thirsty, Master Isaac," he said. "Terrible thirst."

Raquel propped him up and gave him a little water, and then some more.

"We should have called you, but it was locked up, all locked up," he said, grasping the physician's hand tightly. "It was that mixture. The terrible mixture."

"Has he been sick?"

"No, sir. He hasn't. It's as if he can't bring anything up even if he wanted to."

"How many hours have passed since he took it?"

"Some three or four," said Anna, hopelessly.

"We must clean out his stomach if we can, Raquel. Can you help us, Anna?" he asked. "And tell us the rest of what happened."

And while Raquel mixed an emetic and they forced it down his throat, and coped with the spasms it created as the patient brought up what little was left in his stomach, Anna explained.

"It all started last week," she said. "On Friday—Good Friday. The night before it happened—Thursday—he had a good supper and seemed to be cheerful. Some friends visited him after, and when I came in with the wine and a few little things to eat, he seemed just as usual, if not more cheerful than usual. He was telling them that he felt better and that he had been able to do many things that day he hadn't been able to do before."

"Just a minute. I don't think we can get anything more out of his stomach, Raquel. Give him a fourth part of the fresh mixture and do not let him sleep. Do whatever you can to keep him awake." He cocked his head in the maid's direction again. "What things, Anna? Was he able to do?"

"I don't know, Master Isaac, because I had to go back to the kitchen just them."

"And the next morning?"

"He had a good appetite—he wasn't fasting or anything like that, for the priest told him that until he was stronger, he shouldn't—but he told me that he felt all stiff. He said it was his fault, for doing too much the day before because he felt so well. Then, when I was straightening the beds, he rang for me so loud I came running. He was in his study, bent over his desk, and said he couldn't move for the cramps in his back and legs. I got the boy and the cook and we helped him as gently as we could onto the couch there, and tried to send for you, sir, but the boy wasn't allowed past the gate, even though he said how sick the master was. And so we sent for someone else, who came and gave him a potion, but it didn't help. Then on Sunday I heard about the herbalist—and I wish, Easter Sunday or not, I'd never gone to mass but stayed home to look after him, for then he wouldn't be like this."

"We don't know that, Anna," said Isaac. "And even if it were true, it is not your fault. How was your master after he had taken this potion the herbalist gave him?"

"It took away the pain and the cramping," said the maid, "and as soon as that happened, my master was in great good humor, although still weary and stiff from those three days."

"Did the herbalist come back?"

"Every day, Master Isaac. He loved to sit and chat—he can talk for hours—and the master found him amusing. He was around for ever so long until yesterday, when he didn't come at all. A boy came in the evening, asking if Master Narcís continued to improve. I told the boy that Master Narcís had had a bad night and that he should tell the herbalist, and he said he would, but that he had a new mixture the herbalist said he should take when he needed it. The master took some late last night and said that it might be new, but it certainly tasted worse than the old one, and went to bed."

"Thank you, Anna," said Isaac, who had not taken his hands off his patient's body during this recital. "His muscles are cramping again," he said quietly.

"Shall I give him some more, Papa?"

"Not yet." Isaac turned away and walked toward the door of the room, followed by his daughter. He reached out and felt the door frame, then caught hold of the handle. "Come out here for a moment," he said.

"What is it, Papa?" asked Raquel as soon as they were in the hallway.

"I do not want him to hear me. Do you recognize what is happening, my dear?"

"It looks very like your description of the death of the man at Cruïlles, Papa. I did not see it, for I was sleeping. You should have sent someone to wake me. Then I could have been more help now," she added bitterly. "It was not until you asked Anna what he had eaten that I realized he had been poisoned."

"If we do not give him anything more to relieve the pain, I fear—I am almost sure—that he will die in terrible agony from the spasms that are already building in his body."

"And if we do?"

"In sufficient quantity it will stop the spasms, and he might live, except that he will almost surely die of too much of that same drug. His only hope, and that is a slight one, is that he is a strong man. But such agony as this saps the will. We can do nothing if he loses hope and prays for death. He is near to that state."

"What should we do?"

"I do not know, my child. I have looked after him so long, and he has overcome so much. I cannot deliberately bring about his death."

"Can we not give him tiny amounts, a drop of the dilute mixture at a time to control the spasms somewhat? But not so much that it stills his breath altogether. Then whatever happens, we have done something for him, but not harmed him."

"I fear that you argue like a philosopher, Raquel. But it is the only course to follow. We will do that. Be very careful, my dear."

+≡— —≡+

THE dawn was showing through the cracks in the shutters before Isaac, feeling his patient's jaw clenching tightly again, and his muscles hardening with pain, turned to his daughter. "Anna, go and send for a priest."

"Oh, no, sir," said the maid.

"Quickly," said the physician. "Raquel, give him the rest of that cup, my dear. He is in great pain."

"Are you sure, Papa?"

"I know," he said.

+≡— —≡+

ISAAC had not yet been to bed when he was ushered into the Bishop's study. He had been interrupted in the middle of a breakfast that he could not eat, by a trio of episcopal guards and a nervous messenger, who had rushed him from his table, through the *call*, past the still-protesting gatekeeper, and over to the episcopal palace. "I was told that this was a grave emergency, Your Excellency. Are you ill?"

"I am not ill, Master Isaac. But in a sense, it is a grave emergency. There is something very important that I would like to consult you about."

"You are sure you are not ill, Your Excellency?" asked the physician. "I was given to understand that you were."

"Not at all, Master Isaac. I feel in excellent health. This concerns this morning's other most unhappy business—a death. The captain of the guard and Father Bernat are hard at work at the moment to find out as much as they can. They will be back soon to report."

"You have sent them out already, Your Excellency?" asked Isaac in surprise. "I would have come over to the palace as soon as it was seemly to interrupt you, but clearly the news was ahead of me."

"Indeed," said Berenguer. "The problem of Master Lucà has now become acute. One of his patients has died, Master Isaac. This morning, just before sunrise."

"As did one of mine, Your Excellency. But surely, Your Excellency," said Isaac with great care, for he could feel the confusion rising, "if officers were sent out to make inquiries every time a sick man died, we physicians would soon be in difficult straits. For commonly when someone is dying, a physician—or a healer, or herbalist, or whatever he calls himself now—will be summoned. This does not mean that he has caused the death."

"I agree," said the Bishop. "First the physician, and then the priest. And I would have taken no note of it, except for a long conversation that I had with Master Jaume Xavier."

"The notary?" asked Isaac. "He must have been waiting at the deathbed. I take it that this was another wealthy man who has died."

"I had this conversation with Master Jaume some two or three weeks ago. The notary mentioned that he had a client—a widow, one Mistress Magdalena—who had money and property to bequeath by testament. Very properly, she left most of it to a grandson, her only living relative, but she also left smaller amounts to her faithful servants, along with fifty *sous* to young Master Lucà, for his useful remedies and his pleasant manner in treating a difficult old woman. Those were her own words, the notary assured me. Shortly after making this will, she died."

"Was there anything strange in the manner of her death?"

"Not at all. She had been failing for some time, and it was not unexpected. Her previous physician, who was treating her for the flux and for a painful complaint of the stomach, said that he was surprised she had lasted this long. And the sum, although no doubt welcome to a young man starting out, was not a great one."

"But he came to you about it anyway?"

"No. He had mentioned it while speaking of another matter. But he did remind me of it a few days ago, when he came to me about a client who called him in, saying that he wished to alter his will."

"Yes?"

"This client had lost most of his family during these last ten difficult years—between plague and famine and wars only one that he knew of had survived. During that time, he had amassed a considerable fortune."

"And now?"

"For reasons which he explained to the satisfaction of Master Jaume, he divided his fortune evenly between the diocese of Girona and Master Lucà. That will was completed, signed, and witnessed two days ago. Master Jaume's client died early in this morning."

"What complaint did he suffer from?" asked Isaac.

"I was going to ask you that, Master Isaac, for you were his physician, I believe."

"Then you must tell me who is it who has died, Your Excellency," asked Isaac wearily.

"Did I not?" asked Berenguer. "It is Master Narcís Bellfont. What can you tell me about him?"

"Then we were speaking of the same man." The physician paused. "I was in attendance on him last night when he died. It was a wrenching experience. He was a young, strong man and should not have died so soon, Your Excellency."

"Then why all this running to physicians?"

"Your Excellency doubtless remembers his accident."

"I do. Last summer, when he was thrown from his horse and broke a leg. But I thought he had recovered remarkably well from it."

"I can assure Your Excellency that although he made an excellent recovery, considering his injuries, he was still in pain," said Isaac slowly. "He had also done serious harm to his back."

"He was not a man to complain," said Berenguer.

"He had great fortitude," said Isaac. "A good bonesetter looked after the broken leg, and it healed well enough, with no trace of putrefaction or other danger, but such things are almost never as good after the injury as they were before it. He was left with a limp from the broken leg and in almost constant pain both there and in his back."

"Could anything be done for him?"

"I thought so, Your Excellency. It has been my observation that impatient people who are injured and refuse to obey their physicians in the matter of rest and care in using the affected parts suffer more at the beginning but are better off in the end. Those who patiently lie about waiting to get well sometimes never do recover the full use of their limbs."

"That is quite true," said the Bishop. "I can think of several cases. Some soldiers in particular, who cannot tolerate inactivity."

"For that reason, Your Excellency, when the leg had knitted, I encouraged him to take all the exercise he could bear, starting with small amounts. He did that, I believe, although it caused him pain. He was improving, but then I fell ill, and after that I saw him only a few times. The last time I saw him, it seemed to me that he was still progressing well. That was two weeks ago."

"So you do not think that his condition could have caused his death?

"Not that one," said Isaac. "Nor any other ordinary ill that the flesh is subject to. During that long night, I had the opportunity to talk at length with those who attended him. I am certain that he was poisoned, and I would risk my life and good name against the servants in the house having had anything to do with it."

"You believe that Master Lucà's medication for his pain poisoned him?"

"I do not know who mixed the drug he took, Your Excellency. But I am reasonably sure it was the cause of his death. It was not a case of too strong a dose of a powerful medication, which can kill a man. Patients who die from that come to a

very different end, Your Excellency. This drug had been concocted to kill the person who drank it."

"You may not know how active our new herbalist has been
in the past few days. The *call* has been too heavily guarded, I
would think, for news and gossip to move back and forth."

"Quite the contrary, Your Excellency. Yusuf, for whom
walls are highroads and locked gates are passageways, seems
to have been slipping back and forth between city and *call* as
he pleases. He brings me a constant stream of reports, news
and gossip—all of interest to him, of course."

"What has he heard?"

"The common gossip is that young Master Lucà is pursuing
Romeu's daughter."

"He cannot be unduly greedy, then," said Berenguer. "There
are wealthier unmarried women in the city."

"It seems that he was living on Romeu's charity until the
word got about that he had cured Regina, Romeu's daughter,
from her deadly complaint."

"Which was?"

"Her melancholy, Your Excellency."

"She had much to be melancholy about, poor child," said
the Bishop. "But I would have thought that time had cured it."

"Time no doubt helped," said Isaac. "As did a gentle remedy
he concocted, Your Excellency. But when I was trying to help
her, I noticed, sadly enough, that she had few friends, now that
she had lost her excellent mother and her sweetheart. She
needed at least some moments of distraction while her sorrow-
ful heart healed itself. Instead she kept herself closer and closer
to her own hearth."

"You are saying that too much time alone made her melancholy worse?"

"I think it is possible, Your Excellency. And all the women
say that young Lucà is not only handsome, but that he also has
a most pleasant, attentive manner. If most of his attention has
been directed to her, I suspect she has found it helpful."

"That is all very well if he is sincere in his attentions," said
Berenguer. "She does not need to have her heart broken once
more. It is not his amorous adventures that interest me, however. What do you know of his remedies?"

"Yusuf told me what is in the remedy he gave to Romeu's daughter, Your Excellency. I do not think it would harm her, or any other person. But there is one that he sells at a high price to any who can pay for it. I suspect from what I have heard about it that it is dangerously strong—something I would only give to a patient who was in such pain as not to be endured—but that he mixes it with milder herbs, wine, and honey."

"What is wrong with it?"

"Nothing, Your Excellency, except when it is taken in large doses or at frequent intervals."

"And then?"

"And then, it kills you, Your Excellency. But as soon as the *call* is once more open to the world, I shall investigate that miracle medication that Master Lucà concocts."

"How?"

"I have devised a way, Your Excellency, with the assistance of a discontented patient."

Bernat knocked rapidly at the door to the study and came in. "I have brought the captain, Your Excellency."

"What have you discovered, Captain?" asked the Bishop.

"His servants tell me that Master Narcís fell ill on Good Friday," said the captain. "A most unfortunate time, because when he sent for Master Isaac, he was not able to contact him."

"Most unfortunate," murmured Berenguer.

"Then on Easter Sunday, the maid went to mass and heard all about Mistress Regina and Lucà's potion, which, everyone said, had brought her back from death. She told her master, and he summoned the herbalist. Master Lucà gave him a mixture that helped him. By Monday he was walking around, and on Wednesday he sent for the notary. But yesterday, the herbalist sent Master Narcís a flask of new medicine."

"And he drank that?"

"Yes, Your Excellency. Last night."

"Thank you. And Captain, before you go, perhaps you can tell me if anything more is known of this thief outside the walls. I have a delegation of farmers out there waiting to see me—no doubt full of bitter complaints."

"Then if there is nothing more for me for the moment," said Isaac, "I will take my leave of you, Your Excellency. I must return to the *call* before I find myself locked out until Monday in the morning."

"You can tell me nothing more about his death?"

"Just that the only substance he ate or drank yesterday that others did not, Your Excellency, was the potion brought by a messenger to his door."

"Sent by Lucà."

"So the maid says that the messenger said, Your Excellency."

"We must find the messenger," said Berenguer.

ELEVEN

e no imagín que jo'l vulla decebre

and don't imagine that I would deceive him

AFTER a sumptuous supper, Daniel had been ushered to a room with a window that overlooked the western end of the harbor. After living on shipboard for three days, both the chamber and the bed seemed to him to be large enough for six; he climbed gratefully into the clean linen sheets and fell into an exhausted sleep. The sound of bells dragged him awake, with no idea of how long he had been sleeping. Wind rattled the shutters in his chamber, and when he opened them and looked out, his view was obscured by rain pelting down. Gone were the heat and the sunshine of the day before. Shivering, he washed and dressed and headed out of the chamber in search of breakfast.

Maimó came bustling in as soon as Daniel had filled his plate. "Good morning, my friend," he said heartily. "I see you are not an early riser."

Before Daniel could refute this calumny, Maimó answered it himself.

"But no doubt you are weary from travel," he said. "Once you have breakfasted, I suggest that we seek out Mistress Perla before the morning grows much older. She, like me, rises with the dawn most of the time. But since it is the Sabbath, a time for pleasant visiting, I suggest that our visit should be a short one. I shall introduce you, and then we will carry on to the synagogue. Mistress Perla's house is on our way, more or less."

And from this Daniel understood that he was not to ask Mistress Perla any questions. He nodded in agreement.

The rain had stopped by the time they were ready to leave. When they reached the square, the sun had broken through the clouds and was beginning to dry the cobbles. Once inside the *call*, Maimó veered to the left, instead of taking the street that Daniel had come up. "Perla lives down here," he said, walking rapidly ahead. "This is a pleasant street, and quieter than the other side of the *call*."

They stopped at a house that looked much like all the others on either side of it. The front door was open, and through it Daniel could see a dark hallway and the bright sunlight of a pleasant-looking courtyard. *"Hola!"* called Maimó. "Mistress Perla. Are you there?"

"And where else would I be at such a very early hour?" asked a voice filled with such amusement that it robbed the words of all offense.

"Surely for such old friends no hour is too early," said Maimó, walking directly into the hall toward the open door at the end. Daniel looked at his boots, which seemed a little damp, and then followed.

Maimó had stepped down into a courtyard at the end of the hall and turned to draw Daniel with him. "I have brought a young friend who greatly desired to meet you, Mistress Perla," he said. "Daniel ben Mossé."

"Maimó, how could you let me gossip on and not tell me that we have a guest—I mean a real guest, not an old friend who is accustomed to stumble in at any hour. Welcome, Master Daniel." She smiled at Daniel as if his arrival were all that she needed to bring joy into her day.

"Mistress Perla, I am delighted to meet you," said Daniel, bowing. He straightened up and looked at her in amazement. He had been expecting an old woman, not this lively, youthful-looking creature with a face that could still turn men's heads. "I bring you greetings from an old friend in Girona."

"And who would that be?" she asked, the smile fading from her lips.

"Master Mordecai," he said. "Mordecai ben Aaron, who begs to be remembered to you."

She smiled again. "That is very kind of him," she said. "I remember him with fondness. Will you stay a moment?" she asked.

"We cannot," said Maimó "but I know that Master Daniel would like to see you when he has time to speak at more leisure, if that is possible."

"Of course," said Perla. "I would be delighted."

"I believe he has much to talk over with you concerning Girona and your family," he added, with an emphasis that Daniel found rather ominous.

"Does he?" said Perla. "I must hope that my memory serves me well, then."

⋙ ⋘

IT was Saturday morning before the Bishop of Girona was able to turn his attention to the question of young Lucà and the death of Master Narcís once more. The delay had not improved his temper. "Bernat," he said, "I want to see this herbalist and find out what he is doing. Have him fetched here."

"Now, Your Excellency?" asked Bernat.

"Yes, at once."

And before Berenguer could check over and read another document, a breathless young man had been shown into the room. "Your Excellency," he said, bowing deeply.

"You are Lucà, the herbalist," said the Bishop.

"I am, Your Excellency." He glanced around him for a chair, saw none within reach, and remained where he was, moving slightly from foot to foot.

"The person who treated the worthy Narcís Bellfont."

"Yes, Your Excellency," he said slowly.

"I have a question or two that I would like to ask you," said Berenguer, "concerning good Narcís's death."

"I am at Your Excellency's disposition," said Lucà, now standing completely still.

"Good. First of all, what was he suffering from?"

Lucà relaxed visibly as soon as he heard the question. "Most painful cramps in the legs and back, Your Excellency," he said confidently.

"And what did you give him? For the cramps?"

"A mixture, Your Excellency. It contained a very small amount of an ingredient that causes the muscles to relax and slow their movements. Just a drop or two to a whole flask of the mixture."

"And what else?"

"Willow bark and juice of poppy for the pain, and again, to ease the muscles, and honey and wine, because otherwise it would be too bitter for most to drink. It is perfectly safe, Your Excellency, except in excessive amounts, and I warned Master Narcís most particularly not to exceed those amounts."

"I see," said Berenguer. "And what was in the second medication?"

"The second?" he asked, looking baffled. "What second medication, Your Excellency? I only gave him one, the one for pain."

"Are you sure?" asked the Bishop. "I have heard otherwise."

"Perfectly sure, Your Excellency. I gave him a flask of it when I first saw him," he said, his voice rising. "Easter Sunday, that was. Half a cup, twice a day, enough for three days. Then I gave him another flask on Wednesday."

"And you visited him every day?" asked Berenguer.

"Until Thursday, Your Excellency. By then," he said, looking pleased, "I had so many calls to make that I had no time to visit Master Narcís. I told him that on Wednesday, saying I would see him Friday, but that if he needed me before, he should send for me, and I would come, work or no work."

"If you had told him that, why did you send a messenger on Thursday morning?"

"A messenger?" said Lucà. "Your Excellency, I sent no messenger on Thursday or any other day, to Master Narcís or anyone else." He moved his feet uneasily again and looked Berenguer in the eyes and then dropped his glance down, as if ashamed. "I don't trust boys, Your Excellency. I know what a thoughtless, irresponsible creature I was, and it pains me to pay good money to a lad who probably won't even try to deliver my message."

"You sent no messengers to Master Narcís's house?" asked the Bishop. "How did you send the second medication?"

"The second flask? I brought it with me on Wednesday, having seen on Tuesday that Master Narcís would likely need it."

"And the other medication?"

"There was no other medication," said Lucà. Sweat stood out on his brow, and his voice rose in panic. "What I gave Master Narcís was perfectly harmless. The worst it could do was to cause a man to sleep who had wished to remain awake. Master Narcís was kind to me, Your Excellency," he added. "I would not have done anything to harm him, I swear it."

"In what way kind?" asked Berenguer coldly.

"He welcomed me into his house like an equal," said the herbalist, his eyes brightening with tears. "And he praised my treatments to his friends, so that I have many more clients now for my mixtures. Why would I want to harm him?"

"That is an excellent question, young Master Lucà," said Berenguer. "An excellent question."

Monday, April 13, 1355

THE first thing that Master Isaac did on the Monday morning that the *call* was once again open to free movement between the Christian and Jewish communities was to visit his patient and patron, the Bishop of Girona.

"I will not take up your time, Your Excellency," he said, "but I wished to reassure myself that you were in good health and comfortable."

"If I had fallen ill, Isaac, you know I would have summoned you," said Berenguer.

"Indeed. But Your Excellency is not one to complain of minor ills—or even major ones, at times," said his physician. "Is there any further word on the death of Narcís Bellfont?"

"Only that popular feeling is now mixed between those who think the herbalist a magician, and those who suspect him of assassination. I ordered the notary to keep silence about the will, but I fear the knowledge is trickling out."

"Has Your Excellency examined him?"

"I have. He denies the existence of poison. He denies having any desire at all to harm poor Narcís."

"When his medication evidently caused the harm?" asked Isaac.

"He denies the existence of the second vial," said Bernat suddenly. "He claims he only sent one, and that three days before Master Narcís died. None on the evening before his death."

"It did arrive by messenger," said the Bishop. "A messenger whom we have not been able to find, and the carpenter says that no messenger came to their house for a packet, nor did young Lucà go out that night. That is the only thing that keeps us from seizing him."

"It could have been organized beforehand," said Bernat.

"I have arranged a little performance to discover what is in that medication," said Isaac. "Until then, is it possible to delay the arrest of young Lucà even longer? I need him able to visit patients."

"For how long will this be?" asked Berenguer.

"Less than a week, Your Excellency, I assure you."

⊰⊱ ⊰⊱

ISAAC went directly from the episcopal palace to the splendidly furnished house of Master Mordecai.

"I do not wish to press you on this matter, Master Mordecai," said Isaac. "But one of young Lucà's patients has died after taking a special medication for his pain."

"I heard of that this morning, Isaac my friend. As a solution to one's problems it is effective, but it has decided disadvantages," he added wryly. "Not what I would choose, if I were offered a choice, that is."

"Did you also hear that he is to benefit from Master Narcís's death?"

"I did. Under terms of strictest confidence, as well. And did you intend me to take this same medication that young Lucà gave Master Narcís?"

"Certainly not. I intend you to ask for it, since you have heard how well it works. If he is still willing to give it to you,

I will need all of it in order to puzzle out what may be in it. Do you think you can help me in this way?"

"Since the young man has loudly proclaimed in some sections of the town that I am his kinsman, I feel that I must help you, if only to maintain the honor of our family. I have already discreetly contacted some of my clients, saying that I am available now, but that I might have to travel at the beginning of next week. Friday at dinnertime would be a most convenient time for me to fall ill. Does that suit your plans?"

There was a significant pause. "I can see that Friday afternoon would be a convenient hour for you to fall ill, Master Mordecai," said Isaac. "But events are crowding in on us rather rapidly."

"I can see that," said Mordecai. "Let me consider all this more carefully. I will speak to you soon about what is in my mind."

⊹═══ ═══⊹

ISAAC and Yusuf returned home as a cool April evening was beginning to close in. At the sound of his master's footsteps on the courtyard, Ibrahim set his broom down behind the fountain and walked over. "There is someone waiting for you in the sitting room, Master Isaac. He has been there for an hour or more."

"Who is it, Ibrahim?"

"I do not know, Master Isaac. He did not say, and the mistress was asleep and Mistress Raquel was at work in her room and so I didn't want to disturb them."

"Thank you, Ibrahim. Ask at the kitchen if they have brought him anything."

"Yes, master," he muttered, and headed over in that direction, slowly.

"You had best come with me, Yusuf," said Isaac. "He could well be a sick man, and I might need your assistance."

⊹═══ ═══⊹

WHEN Isaac came into the common sitting room, it had an air of lifelessness. The twins and Judith were clearly not there, for even when they were silently absorbed in something, they always made slight rustling noises, soothing and comforting on a busy day. Instead of hearing their noise, he smelled a sharp, odd odor—not of a man, but of drying herbs in an attic or a stillroom.

Then he heard the chair by the fire creak and his visitor moving briskly to his feet. Not ill, thought Isaac. Nor injured.

"Excuse me, Master Isaac, for imposing on you in this way," said a light, pleasant, youthful voice—a voice with the soft sound of the Mallorcan islands.

"Not at all, Master Lucà," he said. "It is Master Lucà, is it not?"

"It is," he said. "But I am astonished that you knew that, sir, because—"

"Your manner of speech is distinctive and easily remembered," said Isaac. "What brings you to my door? And have you been offered refreshment?"

As he spoke, young Jacinta came into the room and without a glance in Lucà's direction, set a tray down on a table by the wall. She poured mint and lemon drink into three cups and gave one to her master, one to Lucà, and one to Yusuf, who remained standing by the door. Leaving a bowl of olives and a bowl of nuts on the small table in the middle of the room, she looked once at Lucà and left.

"I have come because I am in a rather difficult position," he said. "My cousin, Mordecai, summoned me to his aid this afternoon, just after dinnertime, saying that he was suffering from a raw throat and terrible pains in his joints, particularly in his arms and legs. I know that you treat him, and although I gave him something that I know will ease all those symptoms, I still thought that I should let you know."

"I thank you for your discretion and thoughtfulness," said Isaac, "but if Master Mordecai wishes to have his kinsman treat him, he is free to do so. I assure you you have nothing to worry about on *that* score."

Master Lucà's chair squeaked again, but he made no reply.

"Was there anything else that you wished to talk to me about?" asked Isaac.

"No, not at all," said Lucà, and Isaac heard him rising to his feet. "I thank you for your time, Master Isaac."

"Perhaps Yusuf would be so kind as to show you out," said the physician.

"Certainly," said Yusuf, sounding startled, but he set down his cup and led the way out the door.

"Is he gone?" asked Isaac, when Yusuf returned to the room.

"Yes, lord," said Yusuf. "You certainly frightened him."

"I did?" said Isaac. "When?"

"When you said that he nothing to worry about on *that* score, he jumped as if he had been bitten by a snake."

"I heard the chair squeak," said Isaac, "and wondered about his conscience. Yusuf, would you run over to Master Mordecai's and get that potion before someone decides to drink it? I must consider what it all means."

It was not until Monday that Master Maimó had been free to take Daniel with him to the house of Mistress Perla again. The door was again open and a young girl was vigorously sweeping every speck of dirt from the dark hallway in front of them straight into their faces. She glanced up, saw what she was doing, and stopped in confusion. "Pardon me, Master Maimó," she said. "I never meant . . ."

"I am sure you didn't, child," he said. "Is your mistress at home?"

"I'll tell her you're here," said the maid, and ran off, carrying her broom with her.

"If you insist on coming on a day like this, Maimó," said a voice from inside, "unless you are willing to assist us, you'll have to sit very quietly in the courtyard, and watch."

"What kind of day, Mistress Perla?" asked Maimó, taking this as an invitation to enter, with Daniel again behind him.

"Have you no nose? Can you not smell clothes boiling, and soap, and the boiled dinner from yesterday back on the fire? This week we wash. Take care, or I'll set you to lay the wet linen out to dry," she said and stopped abruptly. "I see you have brought Master Daniel with you. How delightful. Today you can see how we do the wash here on the islands," she said, and laughed.

"As you well know, I have no aptitude in domestic matters," said Maimó, "and since I have business to transact down at the exchange, perhaps I can leave Master Daniel with you for a short while. I believe he would appreciate a chance to talk to you, Mistress Perla, if you can spare him a moment this morning. I beg you to join me there, Daniel. Just ask anyone where you are to go. I will be looking at silks."

⸻ ⸻

"NOW," said Perla, "what is so important that it cannot wait until this evening, and that causes Master Maimó to abandon a guest like this?" They were seated at a table under a fruit tree with refreshments brought in by the dusty and flustered maid-servant.

"I come at Master Mordecai's behest," said Daniel. "I am only a messenger, and I am not certain that I understand everything that I am to ask you. I beg your forgiveness before I begin if my questions are offensive or painful."

"This sounds serious," said Perla. "And whatever it is concerns me?"

"It concerns your grandson Rubèn," said Daniel. "Master Mordecai would like to know everything that you can tell him about your grandson from the time he left Seville with his mother."

"Poor little Rubèn?" she said, and her eyes filled with tears. "I am sorry," she said. "But I do miss them." She mopped at her eyes with her kerchief. "There," she said. "I am better now. Mordecai wants to know everything? What a very strange question. I cannot see that it will do him any good, but I will try to answer."

"From the time he arrived in Mallorca."

"I will do my best," said Perla. "They came here three years ago. Rubèn was just twelve. He was a nice boy, affectionate and quiet, but I think he was lonely here. He still went to school, you see, but he was not a great scholar, and most of the other boys were younger than he was."

"That must have been difficult for him," said Daniel.

"Perhaps," said Perla. "He was happy enough at home, but we had a little trouble with him from time to time. I would go by the school to fetch him for his dinner and discover that he had been playing truant. Faneta blamed the move, and me, and herself. Anything but him. She said he was never like that in Seville."

"Perhaps he was just growing older," said Daniel.

"That was what I said. I said that it was time he gave up his studies, which he hated, and did something useful. And so Master Maimó arranged for him to enter a warehouse in the cloth trade, and he was quite excited about that."

"And your daughter? How did she feel?"

"Faneta had always put the problems down to being taken away from home at too early an age, although I pointed out that most boys are much younger when they leave home to apprentice. But she said this was going to another kingdom, just as she had been forced to do, and she tormented herself over it. Still, anyone could see that she could not have stayed in Seville."

"Why not?"

"Her father-in-law told her that he was going to rent her house out from under her even before her year of widowhood was up. He said that it was permitted since he was offering to shelter her himself in his house."

"That would not be permitted here," said Daniel. "As far as I know."

"I had never heard of such a thing," said Perla. "She couldn't bear the man, and as quickly as she could, arranged to come here and live with me."

"She must have been very distressed," said Daniel.

"You mean that her husband died?" said Perla, with a faint smile. "Not at all. She loathed him. If her father—my husband—had sought throughout all the kingdoms of the world, he couldn't have found her a worse husband than his friend's son. Not only was he too old for her, but he was cruel and impoverished." She paused, looking up at the sky filled with delicate bubbles of white cloud racing above. "It is possible, of course, that Rubèn missed his father, although I saw no sign of it."

"But instead of going into the cloth warehouse," said

Daniel, "why did you and his mother decide that he should go to Girona?"

"To Girona? Are you mad?" said Perla. "How could he go to Girona? He's dead, and his mother too."

"Rubèn is dead?" said Daniel, too astonished to be tactful. "How can that be?"

"They are both dead," said Perla. "My Faneta and her son. Died within a week of each other from the same ailment. How could you not know? We sent word to Mordecai."

"We didn't know. No one in the community heard a word of their deaths that I know of," said Daniel, stumbling over his words in his embarrassment at having raised such a painful subject. "No one. Mistress Perla, I am sorry to hear it, and even sorrier that I must ask you to talk about it. When did it happen? What caused their death?"

"The physician talked of a sudden inflammation of the gut, caused by some infectious agent. He said he had seen such things before and that they commonly attacked the young and strong. It happened just before the High Holidays," said Perla.

"Before? Are you sure of the time?"

"One does not forget such an event so quickly, Master Daniel," said Perla.

"Of course not, Mistress Perla. I apologize. It is just that the time is important. Could you tell me what Rubèn looked like? I beg you. It too is important."

"What he looked like?" Perla caught her hands together in her lap and stared at them, as if conjuring up his image. "He was a pretty lad. Slight and boyish still," said his grandmother. "But tall. He had his mother's eyes—somewhat green of hue— and a face rather like mine in shape. But he was not as pale of skin as his mother, nor was his hair as light as hers. In truth, he was quite dark in hair and complexion. In that, Faneta told me, he resembled his father. I cannot think of much else to say of him. He had no oddities of appearance that would make him stand out. Why do you ask?"

"Mistress Perla, just after the High Holidays Rubèn came to Girona," said Daniel. "Or someone who said he was Rubèn."

Perla shook her head firmly. "No. Clearly he was not my

Faneta's Rubèn," said Perla. "It is not so strange a name for a boy to have. There are other Rubèns here in the city of Mallorca. Was it for this that Master Mordecai sent you all this way? To ask me what my grandson looked like?"

"This Rubèn in Girona presented himself to Master Mordecai as Rubèn, son of Faneta, the cousin of Master Mordecai. As if he were part of the household."

"What does he look like?" she whispered. An expression of horror crossed her face, and she raised her hands as if to fend off an enemy.

"Small of stature, with fair skin and fair hair," said Daniel. "In color, rather—"

"Thank the Lord," said Perla, dropping her hands in her lap.

"Why do you say that?" asked Daniel.

"Because I myself saw my grandson wrapped in his shroud. I wept over his poor body before it was taken away to be laid in the ground, properly. I would not like to awake in the night and fear that his spirit is abroad, as the witch women would have it," said Perla. "If this Rubèn is as you say, he is no kin of mine, nor of Mordecai's."

"He is as I say. I rode with him from Girona to Sant Feliu de Guíxols."

"What manner of speech has he?"

"That of all the folk that I have heard in this city, mistress."

A crash of something large being dropped somewhere behind them caused Perla to look over at the house and then shake her head. "Some wicked imp of a boy stole Rubèn's name and went to Girona for the money," whispered Perla. "Tell Mordecai not to give him any. Tell him—no," she said, shaking her head. "Just tell him that."

"Money is not the problem at the moment, mistress."

"What is, then?"

"That particular Rubèn ran off while we were in Sant Feliu—I think because he feared that he would be discovered to be an imposter."

"Then there is no problem."

"But there is," said Daniel. "Another young man has appeared, saying that he, too, is Faneta's son, only that Faneta, in fear of her life, converted and raised him as a Christian."

"My Faneta?" said Perla, in tones of contempt. "She would never have converted. Her husband couldn't frighten her into submission with beatings, nor her father-in-law with threats and money. Why should she bow to a mob? After the life of misery she led once she had left home to be married, she said to me when she came here that death had no terrors for her. But she didn't convert, I assure you. Nor did she bring Rubèn up as a *converso*."

"You do not know who these impostors might be?" asked Daniel. "Either one of them?"

"Excuse me, mistress," said a voice from behind Daniel. He turned and saw a woman, thin, her work-reddened hands on her hips and her hair tied up in a kerchief, standing in a doorway on the ground floor. Beside her, dragging a basket filled with wet linen, was a boy of about eight or nine years of age.

"Yes, Sara?"

"May I lay out the linen in the courtyard?"

Perla cast an oblique glance at her guest, who began to rise. "Yes, do," said Perla. "Is there anything else, Master Daniel? I will be glad to answer other questions, but right now . . ." She indicated the modified chaos that seemed to be going on in her house.

"I will be here in the city of Mallorca until Friday morning," said Daniel. "I will think over what I have learned, and if I need to do so, may I return?"

"Of course," said Perla. "I would be delighted to see you. The afternoon would be a quieter time, I think, if that is possible."

"I will return tomorrow or the next day, in the afternoon. Thank you, Mistress Perla. You have been very kind."

As soon as the door to the house closed behind him, Daniel remembered that Perla had not answered his last question. Turning, he raised his hand to knock at the door and paused. He had already seriously disrupted the routine of Mistress Perla's house, and he was expected at the warehouse to meet his host. Surely he could wait until tomorrow for the answer to his question. He let his hand drop and hurried down the street in search of the warehouse, or someone who could tell him where it was.

Somewhere behind him, a heavy door opened and closed again. He glanced back and caught a glimpse of a small boy darting off in the opposite direction, raising a hand in glee, Daniel decided nostalgically, at running free in the sun and wind.

TWELVE

caent en man d'enemics tan mortals

falling in the hands of enemies so deadly

WITHOUT thinking, Daniel had turned to the right, away from Master Maimó's house. He had passed a dozen houses at least, when it occurred to him that he should be looking for the gate he had first used to enter the *call*. After all, he had been coming from the waterfront, and that was where one would expect import and export facilities to be. Feeling rather foolish, he turned back toward Mistress Perla's house to ask directions.

This time, the laundress was in the open door continuing the sweeping that Daniel's arrival had interrupted. As soon as she saw him, she paused, leaning the broom against the door frame. "Did you wish to see the mistress?" asked the woman, coming uncomfortably close and looking at him as if she were intent on reading the darkest secrets of his soul. Her eyes were a darkly brilliant blue and stood out against her weathered and sun-darkened face like a wax candle on a moonless night.

Daniel dragged back his wandering thoughts and smiled. "I doubt that I need to see Mistress Perla," he conceded. "I am looking for Master Maimó. He assured me that he would be looking at silks at a cloth warehouse. Could you tell me where that might be?"

She frowned. "You'd have to cross the bridge to get there,"

she said. "That warehouse is in the lower city, and right now we're in the upper city. I have business there myself that I should settle before dinner. If you will permit me, sir, I will take you across the river and point you in the right direction for the warehouse. The mistress is very busy right now," she added, and disappeared quickly into the house.

In a moment or two Sara returned, having left apron and broom behind. Without a further word, she set out at a lively pace in the direction of Maimó's house. At the square, however, she turned left down another street, veered to the right and began climbing briskly up past the cathedral and the palace.

The streets and squares were filled with children running, women hurrying, and men strolling as they talked about business; the shops and market stalls were crowded with people anxious to buy. Everywhere Daniel heard the chink of coins changing hands and the cries of the vendors hawking their wares. Sara had plunged into the middle of the crowd, giving Daniel little time to notice the impressive beauties of the palace and cathedral in his attempts not to lose sight of her. Suddenly she paused and looked back to make sure he was still in sight. Beckoning him to hurry, she plunged down a hill and crossed the bridge at its foot.

The bridge spanned a deep riverbed containing a sizable stream. Its tumultuous speed and the muddiness of its water testified eloquently to the sharp and sudden rains of the night and morning. When Daniel caught up with the laundress on the other side, she was standing at the convergence of several narrow streets, deep in conversation with a large man clad in a short tunic of coarse cloth such as a porter might wear. He stepped back when Daniel approached.

"I must leave you here, Master Daniel," said Sara. "I have business to attend to elsewhere. But Esteve will show you the way. You cannot miss it. Walk down that street," she said, pointing down a dark and narrow street—too narrow for the two men to walk comfortably shoulder to shoulder.

As Daniel reached into his purse to reward her for her assistance, Sara turned away. He stepped cautiously into the darkness. "Is it far?" he asked, looking back, and discovered that, for the moment, he seemed to be alone.

The alley sloped sharply down. Daniel, his eyes still not

adapted to the abrupt change out of brilliant sunshine, peered blindly into it, unable to distinguish where it went. Farther inside this warren, even when his eyes had become accustomed to their surroundings, the light was perilously dim, blocked by a number of tall, narrow buildings that had been joined together by arches over the street. He looked up uncomfortably at them, wondering whether the motive for the arches had been to squeak living space for another room or two out of each house, or if they had been added in hopes of keeping the two sides of the street from falling together. The buildings that were not physically joined leaned ominously close to each other, cutting out any possibility of sunshine ever reaching street level.

Steps had been cut into the steepest part of the slope, and Daniel picked his way carefully down them. They were wet and muddy from the morning's rain, and slippery with rubbish of all kinds. At the foot of the steps, Daniel stopped. The street flattened out into a slightly broader space—almost a square— before making a sharp turn to the left. He was facing the front of a tall, thin house, its battered door slightly ajar.

The street continued on to his left for a short distance; ahead he could see sunlight on the cobbles of a broader avenue, and he moved toward it with a sense of great relief.

The light ahead of him was blocked by two more massive figures. "Pardon me, sirs," said Daniel. "But—"

The two men in front of him made a lunge in his direction. He stepped back, stumbled, reached out a hand to recover himself, and found himself falling into the partially opened doorway at the bottom of the street. Then a pall of black fell between him and the world around him. Someone had thrust a heavy piece of itchy, dirty cloth over his head, someone else had seized his arms tightly, and he was furious. Daniel kicked out, made contact with some kind of flesh and kicked again. At the same time he struggled furiously against the hands holding his arms.

"Get him out of here," said another voice. "Before someone else turns up."

They were dragging him backward, he thought, back toward the filthy stone steps. They paid no attention to his struggles to free himself, and his yells for help were muffled by the cloth surrounding his face. He fell on a hard surface, jolting his elbow and shoulder, and something—a boot, he thought vaguely—hit him just below the rib cage. He could scarcely breathe with his face covered, and now he was enveloped in a wave of nausea. He couldn't tell if he were in the house or on the street, had no idea where he was being taken, no idea what direction it was in, no notion what they had in mind for him. All he could feel was a massive regret that he had allowed himself to be sent away from Girona, from Raquel, to lose all he desired just when it seemed within his grasp. His strength drained from him as the regret overwhelmed him, and he gave up the struggle.

"He's fainted," said a voice.

"This is where we leave him, anyway," said another. "I'm going, before the whole world turns up."

DANIEL had no idea how much time passed—if any—before he began to assess his position. He was lying on his side on a cold and bumpy surface. His shoulder ached, but not unbearably; his side hurt where the boot had landed; his nose and mouth were filled most unpleasantly with dust. His arms were tied behind him at the wrists, but his legs were free. Slightly heartened that he did not seem to have further injuries, he tried to roll over and sit up and found out that it was possible, even with the awkwardness of his position.

He considered the possibility of standing up and decided against it. He had no idea how high the ceiling of this space might be and had no way to judge it without actually scrambling upward and cracking his head against something. Reduced to the movements possible while seated without use of his hands, he moved backwards in a series of bumps until he reached a wall. It seemed to be roughly plastered and felt as cool and damp as the floor. He suspected that he was in a cellar and was glad he hadn't risked getting to his feet. He wriggled sideways to his left and very shortly hit another wall. Leaving that for later exploration, he started moving to his right across the first wall he had backed into. In a startlingly short distance he hit another wall with his already bruised elbow. He emitted a muffled curse and stopped moving. What kind of place was he in? Some sort of minute cell? An empty storage bin?

He wriggled into the corner to allow his fingers to explore this surface. It was stone, unlike the original wall. Solid stone, he thought. He moved along it in a crabwise manner and it disappeared. Beside it, there was nothing. Space.

He shivered. What was he beside? A pit designed for him to fall into should he be foolish enough to try to change his position? He touched the surface behind him. The stone wall came to a corner and turned away from his exploring fingers. He leaned over sideways and felt the stone flooring. As far as he could tell, the floor continued peacefully along, even though the wall did not. Very gradually, he edged his way far enough over to feel where the wall was. It carried on, but curiously enough, instead of being cold and damp to the touch, now it was dry and faintly warm. Then his fingers encountered a rough, thick piece of metal; sticking out at an angle from the stone wall. Under it was a smoother piece of metal, somewhat rounded. When he touched it, it rocked back and forth with a sloshing sound, for all the world like a kettle.

A hearth, with a kettle. He was in a kitchen.

Surely a kitchen would have something to cut a rope with, he thought. But even if it did, where would it be?

As he considered this, he heard a soft movement somewhere close by and froze. "Who are you?" asked a high-pitched little voice. "Why do you have that thing on your head?"

"Someone put it on me as a joke," said Daniel, as calmly as he could. "Can you take it off?"

There was no reply, just a faint rustle of movement. Then he felt a tug on the cloth. Next his would-be rescuer grabbed the two sides of the covering and tried to push them upward, scraping its tiny fingernails on his skin. He could feel some movement upward. "Can you grab the top very hard and pull up?"

The hood got caught painfully in his hair; it snagged on his chin and his nose, releasing untold quantities of dust and dirt; at last it popped free of his head. His rescuer giggled. "You're all dirty," she said.

"It was a dirty sack," said Daniel. "But I'm very glad to get it off." He sneezed three times, and his rescuer giggled again. He blinked to get the dirt off his eyes and looked to see who had saved him from the sack's choking confines. She was a little girl, no more than four years old, who was regarding him seriously. They were standing in what was likely the main room of her family's share of the house. In addition to the hearth, it had a bed, a table with a chair, and a dresser. On the dresser were a number of various implements.

"Why are you sitting like that?" she asked.

"Because my hands are tied behind my back. Can you—what is your name?"

" 'Guda," she said.

"Benvolguda?" he asked.

She nodded.

"That's a very pretty name. Well, Benvolguda, I don't suppose you can untie a knot." She didn't answer, merely stared at him with huge, brown, interested eyes. "But if you could get me a knife, I could cut myself free, and then the joke would be on them."

"It wasn't a joke," said Benvolguda.

" 'Guda, 'Guda, where are you?" said a sharp, woman's voice. "Are you in the kitchen? I told you to stay out of the kitchen."

"No, Mama, I'm going outside."

"Stay out of trouble," said the voice.

The little girl went across the kitchen, pulled something off the dresser, and dragged it back behind her. "It was Mama's friend. He told her to look after you, but she wasn't, so I am."

"Thank you," said Daniel. "What do you have there?"

"Knife," she said, dragging a knife almost as tall as she was from behind her.

"Can you set it on the floor just beside me?" asked Daniel.

With some trouble, she pushed and pulled it into the correct position and backed away. Daniel maneuvered it so that the sharp edge was upright, held it there between two fingers with his left hand, while he drew the rope over its surface with his right wrist.

"Mama's coming to see where I am," remarked Benvolguda.

"If you come out in the courtyard I'll show you the secret way out. It goes down to the sea. But hurry."

"Just a minute," said Daniel as the ropes fell away from his wrist. He gathered them up, along with the hood and stuffed them into his tunic. He picked up the knife and put it back on the dresser. Dipping into his purse, which he still had, to his great surprise, he took out a penny and gave it to the child. "Hide that somewhere safe," he said. "Now—where is the secret way?"

As he darted under a broken piece of wall into a patch of empty ground, he heard a woman shriek. "How could I know where he is? I never set eyes on him."

"What about the kid?" said a male voice.

"Don't be stupid," said another. "What's she going to do?"

"She has eyes," said the woman. " 'Guda? Did you see a man go through here?"

"Yesterday," said his rescuer. "Papa went through here yesterday."

◆══ ══◆

"WHAT has happened to you?" asked Maimó, shocked for the moment out of his customary courtesy. "You are covered in soot."

"I'm afraid I had a memorable morning after leaving you, Master Maimó."

"I had intended to introduce you to some useful acquaintance this morning, but I think instead I shall take you back to wash and change. Then you may tell me your story in calmer surroundings."

An hour later, comfortably in time for a glass of wine before dinner, Daniel, scrubbed free of soot and in impeccable linen, finished off his tale of his morning's adventure.

"Who were these men?" asked Maimó. "Do you have any idea?"

"They were just black shapes against the bright light," said Daniel. "I have no idea who they could have been. The woman lived in that house at the bend in the street. But I am not harmed, and they stole nothing from me."

"Excuse me for a moment," said Maimó, rising. "I have orders to give regarding dinner." He bowed courteously before and walked quickly into the back of the house.

It was a relief to have a moment to reflect on the morning's happenings without having to deal with his host's concern or curiosity. Oddly, though, Daniel thought, Maimó appeared distressed over his mishap, but not alarmed or even surprised. Perhaps attacks of this kind were commonplace on the island.

"And you were rescued by a four-year-old child," said Maimó, appearing in the courtyard again, and laughing. "Well, I am glad of that, and I am very glad that you seem to have come through your ordeal safely. But you must have a few bruises."

"Here and there," said Daniel. "One on my shoulder, which scarcely bothers me at all, and another on my knee. Otherwise I was not harmed. What puzzles me, Master Maimó, is why it happened. What reason could those two men have to wish me harm?"

"They could have been acting for someone else," said Maimó. "No—that is absurd. You are not known here. It was a theft that went wrong, nothing more than that."

"My purse was not carefully hidden," said Daniel. "But no one seemed to have the slightest interest in it."

"Doubtless they thought you were someone else. And after hearing your tale, I do not think we need to take it all that seriously. But it will be looked into. Now—I hope that this affair has not taken away your appetite. My cook observed you carefully as a young man who appreciated excellence at the table, and poured her heart into this dinner. Today you shall meet my secretary, my son, my daughter, and my son-in-law over some of the best delights that this island can furnish a man."

THE dinner was sumptuous, leisurely, and pleasant, with dishes to please every taste, from tiny fish to lamb on the spit. "I am overwhelmed by your hospitality, sir," said Daniel, once the cloth had been taken away and they were left to chat over bowls of fruit and small sweet delicacies. "I believe I have never eaten better in my life, nor with such pleasant company."

"I assure you, Master Daniel," said Maimó's son, a young man of Daniel's age, or slightly older, "that we do not eat like this every day. Our cook likes an appreciative audience, and I fear that we are so accustomed to her excellences that we skimp on our praises. We have reason to be grateful that you are here."

"We have much reason to be grateful," said Maimó. "I don't know if you are aware of the difficulties the community suffered in the time of the old kings."

"I had heard only that things are better now," said Daniel.

"Well—between taxes, and heavy penalties for infractions of this or that regulation, and restrictions on movement and professions, we were stretched to the limits of our ability to survive," said Maimó.

"To taste lamb more than once a year was rare," said his son with feeling. "I remember that well."

"Even you, Master Maimó?" asked Daniel.

"Everyone suffered. But now, the entire city prospers, and we prosper along with it. I only hope that it may last."

"Do you see signs of it ending?" asked Daniel.

"I always see signs," said Maimó. "For that reason I was concerned about the incident this morning. But it did not seem to me to be an attack because of your faith."

"No," said Daniel. "I had the feeling they would have attacked me no matter who I was or what my religion. It was odd. Almost a crime without malice."

"It was odd, indeed," said Maimó. "The next time you go down to look at the warehouses, my son or I will accompany you. There are safer ways than the one that Sara pointed out to you."

THIRTEEN

que per traidor on fos tot malifet

than by a traitor where all is badly done

BETWEEN the strange surroundings and his bruises, Daniel
had slept uneasily that night and awakened early to a bright
and clear morning. The house was silent; outside his window
the noise of the city had been reduced to single sounds—a door
shutting, the warning bark of a dog, the whimper of a fretful
baby. Having broken one law of hospitality the previous morning by rising late for breakfast, he stayed in his bed to avoid the
opposite, more heinous infraction of coming down in the
morning before the housemaids.

For the moment he had leisure to think without interrup-
tion. He brought the little gold case with its lock of hair to his
lips. His nostrils caught the scent of the delicate jasmine oil
that Raquel smoothed on her hair and was pierced with sharp
longing for this endless month to be over. Today was Tuesday.
On Friday morning, if the winds were favorable, he would sail
for home.

Pushing those thoughts aside with difficulty, he considered
the information he had gathered from Perla. Aside from the
crucial point that her description of her grandson eliminated
both Rubèn and Lucà, she seemed to know remarkably little
about the boy. Or she had not told him what she knew. He or-

ganized a list of questions in his head and worried over them like a dog worrying a bone. It was true, as Master Isaac had once remarked, that proper questions were much more important than proper answers, even if you weren't speaking of medicine. He would do what he could today. No one would expect more. Otherwise he intended to pass the rest of the time furthering his own and his uncle's affairs by visiting the exchanges and some of the glovers' shops.

AT the end of dinner, when the board was cleared and the others had excused themselves, Maimó reached over and filled Daniel's goblet with wine. "Stay here a moment, Daniel," said his host. "I must admit to you that while you were deep in conversation with my good friend, Benvenist, over questions relating to the glovers' trade, I slipped over to Mistress Perla's house."

"I hope she is well," said Daniel cautiously, not quite sure where this conversation was heading.

"I presume so," said Maimó. "I would not want you to think that I did not take yesterday's difficulty you had seriously. I did, and still do. If there appears to be some remedy that can be obtained for it, I will do what I can to pursue it."

"Surely you do not think Mistress Perla can have anything to do with what happened," said Daniel.

"Mistress Perla?" said Maimó. "Certainly not. It would not help anyone in whom she has an interest to have you harmed in any way. I assure you that if someone presented a threat to someone she valued, that Mistress Perla would be a formidable enemy. But you do not. I am sure of that. But I did not go to see her."

"I beg your pardon?" said Daniel, puzzled.

"No—I went to discuss matters concerning the laundry that had been neglected until the sun was almost too low in the courtyard to dry it. I spoke to Sara, the laundress. She, after all, was the one who turned you over to Esteve, and although Esteve may not have had anything to do with the attack on you, he certainly made no effort to help you."

"Did you discover anything?"

"I discovered what I expected—that the connection between Sara and Esteve is certainly reprehensible, but it is not a criminal connection. Esteve, as far as I could discover, is not a thief or assassin. Sara insists that he is, by his lights, an honest man, who would not indulge in assassination merely to please his ladyfriend. He is, as you surmised, a porter, and those who have hired him have found him reliable."

"I am surprised that Mistress Perla employs her, if that is the case."

"That is another question altogether, and one that has its roots in her girlhood here in Mallorca," said Maimó. "I do not know why, precisely, but Perla sees herself as Sara's protector. When she returned, she was instrumental in obtaining a pardon for the woman so that she could return from banishment. Perhaps," he added, "laundresses are hard to find, but I think it is rather that Mistress Perla has a very kind heart and knew Sara when she was a child."

"Perhaps I should seek Esteve, and ask him what he knows of my attackers," said Daniel. "Since it seems possible that he wasn't one of them."

"I think that would be a most unwise idea," said Maimó. "One look at you and the man might panic. I would not like to see you involved in another incident. My friend Mordecai might feel that I take poor care of the guests he entrusts to me." With an amused smile, Maimó rose and excused himself.

THE city of Girona was just beginning to come alive again for the afternoon when a timid ring of the bell at the gate brought Raquel down to the courtyard. As she suspected, Ibrahim was nowhere in sight, and was unlikely to respond to such a delicate summons. Her little brother cried and was being hushed; the rest of the house was moving about, but slowly.

When Raquel pulled open the gate, a veiled woman, whose gown hung loosely on her, almost fell into the courtyard. "Thank you, Mistress Raquel," she whispered, throwing back her veil.

"Mistress Regina," said Raquel. "You are most welcome."

"I can only be here a few moments," said Regina. "I came to

the *call* with Papa, who had some matters to go over with Master Ephraim concerning the new counter, but I must talk to your father. I must!" she reiterated in tones of desperation.

"Mistress Regina," said Isaac from the doorway to his study. "You are indeed welcome. Raquel. Our guest needs some refreshment."

"Certainly, Papa," said Raquel, and she ran quickly up the stairs to the kitchen.

"Please sit down, mistress. Over here, by the fountain. Now, why must you talk to me?"

"Master Isaac, it is about Lucà. They are accusing him of killing Mistress Magdalena and then Master Narcís, and he cannot have done it. He cannot."

"Why do you say that?" asked Isaac. "For if what I have heard is true, his remedies are powerful, and therefore could be dangerous. You should know that, having been helped by him almost against your will, I would guess."

"No, Master Isaac, that is not the case," she said with vehemence. "I know that is what everyone thinks, but it is not true. It was my own fault that I allowed myself to become so ill, I swear it. I was so miserable and I felt so abandoned by everyone, even my poor papa, that I didn't want to get better."

"But surely your father never abandoned you, mistress."

"In his sorrow he could barely speak, Master Isaac. We could not speak of the past, and if something reminded him of it, he would become enraged over what Marc had done to me. I just wanted to stay away from everyone and be left alone." She took a deep breath to control her shaky voice and continued. "Master Lucà was very kind. He never asked me questions that I couldn't answer and never seemed to think that I should be cheerful and friendly to everyone. His remedy helped me to sleep, yes, I think. But what he did was more than that. He explained why he wanted to help me."

"Why was that?"

"It was because he so liked my papa and could not bear to watch him suffer because of me."

"Do you think he was being honest when he said that?" asked Isaac. "After all, it was to his advantage, was it not, to have you support him?"

"I don't think he was being dishonest. It was true. He really does like Papa. He spends many hours talking to him after supper, when it is too dark to work. They talk of all sorts of things, and I think Papa's sorrow is gradually easing. In my selfishness I had not seen that my unhappiness and illness were troubling him as much as my mother's death. I might as well have been killing him by digging knives into his flesh. And so I tried to get better, and once I had decided that, it was easy. I only took the drops for two days. They tasted awful. Do you understand what I am trying to tell you?"

"I understand very well," said Isaac.

"And now Lucà and Papa spend even more time together, talking and working."

"Is Lucà also a cabinetmaker?"

"I don't think so," said Regina, her voice filled with doubt. "How could he be? But many times Papa needs someone to steady a piece of wood or some such thing, and since he lost his last apprentice he has had to find a neighbor to help him. So Lucà will stop his own work and help Papa. They are friends, and Lucà is a good man—he really is. He told me that he did some very foolish things when he was a boy, not very long ago, things for which he is very ashamed, but that he has never harmed anyone."

"What do you wish me to do?"

"You understand these things," said Regina. "Could you not smell some of his mixtures and see if they are poisonous? I can tell you what goes in them. I brought vials of his two mixtures."

"Excellent," said Isaac. "There should be an empty basket on the table. Set them down in there."

Regina stepped over to the table and took two vials wrapped in pieces of cloth out of her purse.

"Can you also bring me a pinch of every different herb he has—the ones he compounds these from?"

"Tomorrow morning," said Regina. "When I go shopping. You will do it, then? And you will speak to the Bishop?"

"I will do what I can, Mistress Regina," said Isaac. "Now, will you do something for me?"

"If I can, Master Isaac," said the young woman.

"Can you remember back to the evening before Master Narcís died?"

"Yes," she said. "I remember that . . ." Her voice died away.

"Were you at home?"

"We were all at home," said Regina. "I had cooked a special supper of eggs and mushrooms, with onions and herbs. It was very good and—" She paused. "—and everyone liked it. Before supper, Lucà was in the workshop with Papa, and when I had everything ready to cook, I went down and watched them. Papa was showing him the special way he has of smoothing fine wood until it shines, and it took a long time. When they were finished, I cooked the eggs—it only took a moment—and we ate and sat around the table all evening, talking." Her voice broke at that, and Isaac intervened.

"Thank you," he said, "that was very helpful." But if Raquel had stayed in the courtyard, she would have known that her father was puzzled.

⊹══ ══⊹

HAVING spent the intervening time at the mercantile exchanges and various glovers' establishments, it was late Wednesday afternoon before Daniel finally reached Perla's house once more. The sun was low in the heavens, and her establishment had an air of ordered comfort.

"You have escaped the rest of the laundry," said Perla, her voice almost gurgling in unexpressed laughter. "I am sorry that I couldn't entertain you more completely yesterday, but my cook and the maids become completely distracted when the laundress arrives. It is a hopeless situation."

"I met up with your laundress yesterday after I left your house," said Daniel, unsure how much she knew of the incident. If she had been told what had happened, it would seem odd not to mention it. "She was kind enough to direct me on my way to the exchanges," he added, leaving her to define how much he revealed.

"Is that what happened to her?" asked Perla. "She disappeared just like that, leaving armloads of wet linen about, and then appeared again an hour or two later. Everyone was out spreading sheets and towels in a panic. It caused quite an upset in the house."

"She said she had some business to attend to across the river," said Daniel.

"Ah, well," said Perla. "No doubt she did. Sara is a strange one. She has not led an exemplary life, I'm afraid, but she is strong and hardworking when she appears, and so I continue to employ her. Her life has not been easy."

"Really?" said Daniel.

"She was widowed very young," said Perla, as if that explained everything. "She left the island and came back just after I did. I do what I can for her."

The shadows were growing very long, and Daniel remembered that he had questions that ought to be answered before he reported back to Mordecai. Casting aside subtlety, he plunged into the heart of his list. "Mistress Perla, who knew Rubèn well enough to try to borrow his identity? I mean, if you go off to a man's kin, claiming to be him, there are many things you have to know."

"What boy? Truly, I do not know," said Perla. "Rubèn didn't have many friends here—and no close friends that we knew of. Those boys he knew were at the school."

"What did he do when he wasn't at school? When you thought he was?"

"I asked him that, Master Daniel. And he shook his head, but he finally told me that mostly he went out and sat by the sea, dreaming of sailing far away somewhere, somewhere different from Seville and from the City here. I said to Faneta that, young as he was, he wouldn't be happy until he had a wife who loved him. Some men cannot do without a wife for company. I cannot really tell you any more about him," she added. "He was a quiet boy, who felt things deeply, I believe, but hated to speak of them."

Suddenly very sick of intruding on a grandmother's grief, Daniel rose. "Thank you for your patience and generosity in answering all my questions," said Daniel.

"Please carry my most affectionate good wishes to dear Mordecai," said Perla. "Happy as I am here, I remember him always with great fondness."

"I will, mistress," said Daniel.

＊≻ー ≻ー＊

ON the Monday afternoon that Isaac had requested the move, Mordecai had retreated to his bedchamber and its attached sitting room, having given a few hours of concentrated thought to the problems likely to arise from his enforced absence from business. He quietly transferred some important materials into the sitting room, took his housekeeper into his confidence, at least partially, and left gossip and rumor to do the rest.

On Tuesday, the housekeeper, distraught at the domestic difficulties that had already arisen, and convinced that, no matter what he might say, her master must be ill to behave so strangely, sent for Master Isaac to hasten to his aid. "I did not know what to do," she confessed. "Especially since Mistress Blanca and Mistress Dalia are both in Barcelona right now, and Mistress Dalia won't be back for another week. He said I was to send for that other person, but I don't trust him . . ."

Master Isaac told her to do exactly what she had been instructed to do, murmured reassuringly, stayed with his patient for a while, left various medications, and went away again.

No one was permitted in the master's room, or even in the part of the house that contained his room, except for the physician and the housekeeper. Word spread like lightning through the house, then the call, and then the city that he was ill, very ill, possibly close to death.

It soon became widely known that Master Mordecai had failed to improve in spite of the best that the physician could do. After another day of wringing her hands in despair, the housekeeper yielded to her master's commands, as well as to the advice of friends and neighbors, and sent for young Master Lucà.

＊≻ー ≻ー＊

THE next morning, as soon as the hour seemed reasonable, Daniel headed off once more to the *call*, seeking the young man who would have had the most to do with tutoring Rubèn.

"Oh, yes, he was a problem to us," said the tutor. "He was

not difficult or rude, but he was . . ." The young tutor paused, as if seeking some manner of expressing himself.

"Perhaps he was not interested," said Daniel. "I have known many boys like that."

"Either that," said the tutor, "or he was simply not a quick wit. Whatever it was, the other, younger boys learned things much faster than he did. In truth, he was too old to be at school. He was a full year older than any of the other boys, and three or four years older than most. And at thirteen and fourteen, each year makes a great difference, you know."

Daniel agreed that it did and wondered that any lad could bear with patience being in a schoolroom at fourteen, surrounded by nine- and ten-year-olds.

"Then he began to slip away. One day he might not turn up and the next, perhaps, he would leave early. All the tricks that schoolboys have."

"Where did he go?"

"I don't know, although someone told me that he was seen over in the Lower City, near the outer walls, and someone else told me that he was often down beyond the tanneries—not a very respectable area," he added primly. "Many whores and thieves and other such common folk congregate there. But I never saw him in either place with my own eyes."

Daniel thanked him profusely and offered him a donation—leaving it unclear whether he was to consider it personal or for the benefit of the school. The tutor accepted it cheerfully, and to judge from the condition of his tunic, it seemed to Daniel that it would be better going to the young man himself.

Daniel walked slowly back up toward the gate to the *call*, considering what to do next. He could ask Master Maimó for advice, but he had a feeling that it would be indelicate to pour out the whole situation to someone who knew both Perla and Mordecai quite well. If Mordecai had wanted Master Maimó to know all about this, he could just as easily have written to him. And that word *discreet* popped up again in his head. That was what he was supposed to be. Discreet.

Then as he crossed the square, a hand plucked on his sleeve. "Can I take you anywhere today?" asked a hopeful voice.

"*Hola*, Miquel," said Daniel. "Perhaps you can. Come over here and sit down."

They settled down on a shady piece of ground under a tree where they could speak in relative peace.

"Tell me, Miquel," said Daniel. "Did you ever know a boy named Rubèn? He lived in the *call*, but I think he spent a lot of time away from it—either with friends or alone."

"How old?" asked Miquel.

"He'd be fifteen now."

Miquel measured that against his own age, as much as he knew it. "What did he look like?"

"Thin, tall, black hair, skin the color of that man," said Daniel, pointing discreetly at someone who seemed to be of the complexion described by Perla. "And green eyes."

"Like a tree?" he asked, with considerable interest.

"No, sort of grayish-brownish-greenish color."

"Oh, that. I knew him, sort of," said Miquel. "But I never knew his name. I didn't know any of their names. He talked funny. Like you, only more. Then someone said he died."

"He did, at the end of last summer. But I think we're talking about the same person. Can you tell me anything about his friends?"

"Well—they were old, much older than me, master. They never talked to me. He did, but they thought they were too important."

"Did one of them live near the tanneries?"

"Sure. His mother's a whore, that's why he lives there."

"And the other over by the outer wall?"

"Maybe," said Miquel. "I followed them once, so I know what street they went to, but I don't know which house."

"Will you take me there?" asked Daniel.

"Which place?" asked Miquel.

"Both of them," said Daniel.

"It'll cost you a penny to go to both," said the boy, looking assessingly at Daniel.

"You'll get more than that if we can find what we're looking for," said Daniel.

Miquel jumped to his feet and turned to his employer. "Where do you want to start?"

After some disagreement over which route would be more efficient, they compromised by starting at a stall selling substantial portions of grilled meat. Daniel then bought a couple of bread rolls, stuffed the meat into them and gave one, wrapped in a vine leaf, to Miquel. He had decided that he'd get more from the boy if he fed him first. From there they headed over to the bridge into the Lower City and the place by the outer walls.

Miquel trotted confidently along in front of Daniel, pointing out places that he deemed to be of interest as they passed by them. "Two sailors were killed here," he said, "and just down there the whole street was under water when the river flooded, and I saw a dog and a man that were drowned." The patter continued throughout the journey, at times gruesome, at times amusing, and at times only of interest to a boy.

"This is where they went," said Miquel, pointing to a narrow street that appeared to be better swept and not as dark as the one Daniel had come across earlier. "Do you want me to ask?" he said, as if he doubted Daniel's ability to ask anything about anyone and be understood.

"I'll start," said Daniel, "and if I have problems, you can help." There was a woman sweeping the street in front of a shop, and she seemed like the obvious person to begin with.

"Mistress," said Daniel politely, "I am in search of a young man. I believe he worked or lived on this street until he left the island, not very long ago."

"What's his name?" she snapped impatiently.

"I'm not sure," said Daniel.

"What did he look like?" she asked suspiciously.

"Moderate to tall in height," said Daniel, "with brown hair, lighter than mine, light brown eyes, and a fair complexion. He is broad in the shoulders and has a pleasing smile and manner."

"That's him," said Miquel admiringly.

"And that's your friend that you're looking for, is it? Well, let me tell you that I'm looking for him too, and if I ever find him and that thief of a master of his, I'll set the officers on them both. Sick he said he was—well, he didn't look sick to me. Half a year's rent he owed me when I last saw him, and that was before Michaelmas, and I still haven't rented the premises—"

"You haven't seen the young man since Michaelmas?"

"Him? I haven't seen him in a year or more. At the first sign of trouble he disappeared, didn't he? You can't trust young men these days," she added, with a shake of her head. "Never could, either, or I wouldn't be in this fix. His master said he'd be back and then they could work regular-like and pay the rent, but he never did, did he? And the old man left, too, and I didn't know they weren't coming back, and then all the people who wanted it had found other places." She raised her broom in fury and shook it at Daniel. "You tell them that."

"What did his master do? In the shop?" asked Daniel, wondering how much of her message she expected him to carry in his head.

"Made things of course," she said. "If you knew him, you must have known he was a joiner—and a good one, too. He mended my table for me and it's still good as new. He wanted me to take that instead of rent. A few trifling repairs. I won't put up with that sort of thing."

"Thank you for your trouble, mistress," said Daniel, and pressed a penny into her hand.

"You shouldn't have done that, master," said Miquel as they walked away. "Not when she was so rude to us."

"Don't worry, Miquel. It's not my money I'm spending, and she told us some useful things."

+=—— ——=+

THE shortest route to the tanneries, according to Miquel, was a rather complex one, involving zig-zagging through a succession of streets that met each other at sharp angles. After four or five turns, Daniel had no idea what direction he was moving in. He had little choice but to put his faith in the boy, who, after all, had not as yet steered him wrong. His nose soon told him that the faith was justified.

"The tanneries are over there," said Miquel, "but that's not where we're going. The boy you're interested in used to go down here sometimes, and I'd see him with one person or another. But this is where he usually went." Miquel was pointing at a ramshackle lean-to built onto a more substantial building. He knocked firmly at the door, and a woman opened it.

"What do you want?" she asked, looking at the boy. "Go away. You're too young to be hanging around here."

"We're looking for Sara," said Miquel. "It's important."

"She's gone," said the woman. "Moved away."

"Where to?" asked Miquel.

"How do I know?" said the woman. "Go home."

Daniel decided it was time for him to step into the middle of the misunderstanding. "I am the one who is looking for Sara, mistress," he said politely. "Not the lad. He was kindly showing me the way. I have business—"

"What kind of business?"

"I'm from Girona, and I'm trying to find—"

"Get out!" screamed the woman. "Get away from here! Or I'll call for friends who'll make sure you do!"

"I am not trying to cause any trouble for Mistress Sara," said Daniel, stepping toward her.

"Help!" she shrieked. Doors banged open, and soon the empty street seemed filled with people.

A voice said in his ear, "Give me your purse, master, and I will fetch help for you."

Without thinking, Daniel grabbed it out of the sash of his tunic and slipped it to Miquel, who disappeared into the crowd like a ferret down a rat's hole.

<hr />

HIS feet slipped from under him, and Daniel landed on the wet ground. He raised his arms around his head, trying to protect himself from the throng of angry feet surrounding him. Suddenly the noise around him increased considerably. The blows stopped. He had been driven close to the wall of Mistress Sara's former house and now used the surface behind him to help get himself on his feet. The crowd, of whose number he had no clear idea, had been reduced to three men with stout staves. They had, obviously, been using them to good effect.

"Master," said Miquel, "are you all right?"

"I'm muddy," said Daniel, "and I think I've collected one or two more bruises, but mostly I'm baffled. Why did they all turn on me?"

"They thought you were trying to harm her, see?" said one of the men. "And they try to help each other out. But Miquel said you weren't, and anyway . . ."

"I promised them a penny each," said Miquel, restoring his purse to him. "Is that all right?"

"Since otherwise I might have been dead or a mass of broken bones by now, it certainly is," said Daniel, giving each the promised amount and more. "And now let us go back to Master Maimó's."

+·✦═══   ═══✦·+

"AND from now until I leave the City of Mallorca," said Daniel to his host, "I swear I will not ask anyone I do not know a single question. I seem to have the gift of asking people things they do not wish to tell me."

He was cleaned up, the boy Miquel had been generously thanked, and now Daniel was sitting in the courtyard with his host, drinking a glass of wine.

"I think it would be wise if you stayed in the house until tomorrow morning," said Maimó, "when you will be escorted to the embarkation point for your ship. You have, one way or another, innocently, I'm sure, stirred up trouble amongst some group of people."

"The woman that Rubèn used to visit was called Sara," said Daniel. "Do you suppose she could be the same Sara who works for Mistress Perla?"

"It is possible," said Maimó. "It is a common name, but he would have known her—because of the laundry. We do keep stumbling into that laundry of Mistress Perla, do we not? Have a little more wine, Master Daniel."

"I believe you are trying to render me incapable of going out," said Daniel.

"It would doubtless be an excellent idea if I were," replied his host smoothly.

+·✦═══   ═══✦·+

THE next morning, Daniel awoke to the knock on his door and the voice of his host. "Master Daniel," said Maimó. "The wind sets fair for Barcelona, and your breakfast awaits you. I beg you to hasten a little."

He climbed out of bed in the pearl-gray dawn, washed, dressed, and fastened up his bundle. Waiting for him in the dining room was an abundant breakfast of steaming rice with fish and vegetables in broth, along with freshly baked bread and a bowl of fruit. Beside his place was a basket. "My cook packed that for you. She worries that you will starve on shipboard," said Maimó. "I suspect there is enough in it to feed you even if the ship is becalmed for weeks. Perhaps you could give away what you cannot eat yourself. And can I trouble you to carry a packet of letters to Girona for me?" he asked. "I have sealed them up as tightly as I can so that they will not be damaged during the voyage if the weather turns stormy. When you open them in Girona, each is marked with the name of the recipient."

Daniel assured his host between mouthfuls that he would conscientiously deliver all the letters, and with an exchange of compliments, gifts, and good wishes, he was whisked off by a trio of stout attendants to the waterfront.

※＝ ＝※

WHEN they arrived, one boat was waiting in shallow water. It was being filled by longshoremen, who trudged back and forth with boxes and bales of cargo. A clerkly looking man with a copy of the ship's manifest in his hand checked off each item as it was transferred. There was, as well, a small group of men standing apart from the working group, some of them deep in conversation, others staring gloomily, or sleepily, at the horizon. Daniel surmised from their dress and bearing that they too were travelers, out in the dawn to wait with varying degrees of impatience for their turn to be loaded into the boats after the cargo.

Two of the people, however, were staring intently up at something behind the shore. Daniel glanced over as well, wondering idly what could be so fascinating that early in the morning. It was not difficult to find what attracted their attention. On a turret at the corner of the city wall stood a woman, gazing like a sentinel out over the harbor. A sudden gust of wind ripped her veil away from her head and whirled her hair out like a peacock's tail. At that moment, the morning sun broke through a layer of low-lying cloud and caught the golden-red hair of the woman in its light.

"Who is that?" Daniel asked the man standing next to him.

He looked up and shook his head. "I don't know," he said. "She's too far away for me to see. I do not have the sharpest of eyes."

"I suppose she's bidding farewell to someone," said Daniel, thinking of Raquel standing at her gate as he ran down the short street on his way on this journey.

"Or waiting for someone to come sailing home," said his fellow passenger.

The woman pointed down at the waterfront, like a strange exotic queen surveying her world. At that moment, a soldier in helmet and breastplate appeared behind her. He stepped close and caught her around the waist. She whirled about, tapped him coquettishly on the tip of his nose, and disappeared from sight, dragging him after her.

"Shouldn't allow goings-on like that when someone's on guard duty," said a disapproving voice behind him. "In my day—"

"In your day they didn't even bother to keep a guard up there most of the time," said someone else. "And look what happened."

Daniel smiled and shook his head. His glorious vision of queens and brokenhearted lovers faded suddenly into a tale of a common soldier and his tart. The ship's boat came in to ferry them out, he picked up his bundle and his basket, and along with a handful more new arrivals, made his way over to it.

"You are Master Daniel?" asked the passenger who had been standing beside him, after they had clambered into the boat.

"I am," he said. "But how—"

"I am Jafuda. I am in the cloth trade, primarily, but I go to Barcelona to arrange for various materials to be brought over. Master Maimó asked me to keep an eye on you. He seems to feel that you are prone to trouble."

FOURTEEN

Veles e vents han mos desigs complir
faent camins dubtosos per la mar

*Sails and winds have to fulfill my desires
making doubtful roads across the sea*

ON Thursday morning, a flustered housemaid ushered Master Isaac to his friend Mordecai's bedchamber. "He asked that you be brought to him at once, sir," said the maid, breathless with haste.

"How are you, my friend?" asked Isaac as soon as the door to the bedchamber had been firmly closed behind him.

"I am already weary of all this isolation," said Mordecai. "I warn you that unless I have a miraculous recovery I shall go mad with boredom. Either that or my business ventures will become too complex to be sorted out again. But I have your mixture for you." He went over to a heavy, carved dresser and took out a vial of a darkish substance.

AS soon as he reached home, Isaac summoned Raquel and Yusuf. "I need a clean cup and a pitcher of pure water," he said.

Mystified, Raquel fetched the water from the fountain; Yusuf went into the house for the cup, annoying Naomi by insisting that it must be clean. "As if any cup that is on the shelf in my kitchen were not clean," she hissed at Jacinta, who

agreed that it was an unwarranted insult to suggest anything
else.

Isaac went into the courtyard and uncorked the vial that he
had brought from Mordecai's house. Holding it some distance
from his nose, he sniffed at it, and then held it to one side, taking deep breaths. He repeated the process, bringing it closer
and closer, sniffing it each time. "Do this exactly as I have done
it," said Isaac. "And note what you can smell. If it smells of bitter almonds, cork it at once. If it begins to choke you, do the
same. Otherwise, note carefully its characteristics."

Each did the same, corked it, and returned it to the physician. "It has an unpleasant smell, Papa, covered over with
something almost flower-like," said Raquel.

"That is because it is a mixture," said her father. "And your
nose is trying to unmix the elements within it, and tell you
what they are. Now, bring me a half cup of clear water and
place one drop of the mixture in it."

The pitcher and the cup were already on the table in the
courtyard. Raquel poured the water and carefully allowed one
drop of the mixture into it. It was somewhat viscous in consis-
tency and left a reddish-black pattern as it drifted down
through the water. "The mixture is thick, Papa," said Raquel.
"It is slowly moving through the water, but clinging to itself
in threads."

"Then fetch a clean implement and stir it," he said. "Until it
is well mixed."

Raquel nodded at Yusuf, who sped off to fetch the required
implement and returned with a spoon. Raquel stirred the liquid gently but thoroughly. "It is well mixed now, Papa," she
said.

"Where is it?" he asked.

His daughter set the cup on the table just in front of her father. "In front of you, Papa, a hands' breadth from the edge."

He reached down delicately and picked up the cup in his
left hand. He dipped his right index finger into the mixture
and rubbed his fingers together, then dampened the tip of his
tongue with it. He set it down again. "Try that," he said.

Raquel did the same, screwed her face up in distaste and
handed the cup to Yusuf.

"Oof!" said Yusuf. "That's awful."

"In what way?" asked his master.

"At first it seems very sweet, and then there is an awful taste that seems to cling."

"Bitter? Sour? Rotten? What kind of awful taste? It's important."

"I can't tell," said the boy.

"I thought it was bitter," said Raquel, "but there's more than that."

"Rinse your mouths out with clean water and then pour that mixture onto waste ground," said Isaac, going over to the fountain and taking a handful of water to rinse his mouth. Raquel took another cup, rinsed out her mouth, handed the cup to Yusuf, and then carried the mixture over to the darkest corner of the courtyard and poured it away.

"It is done, Papa."

"Now, I want two drops in clean water."

Raquel repeated the process.

Once more the physician picked up the cup and placed a minute quantity on the tip of his tongue. He handed the cup to Raquel, repeated the experiment and then gave the cup to Yusuf. She went over to the fountain at once and rinsed out her mouth. "It is sickly sweet, Papa, and after there are two different bitter tastes—first one and then the other. I cannot describe them."

"How does your tongue feel?"

"Strange," she said.

"And Yusuf. Can you describe the taste?"

"No, lord," he said. "I cannot. But I will never forget it as long as I live."

"Good, because you will live longer if you spit it from your mouth as soon as you recognize it."

"Was Lucà attempting to poison Master Mordecai?"

"No," said Isaac. "Because he was instructed to take two drops in a half-glass of wine. That strange feeling you have on your tongue would have pervaded his entire body, causing his limbs to feel heavy and relaxed and every part of him to slow mightily. This can be useful if your patient is suffering from cramping of the gut, or the limbs or some other painful condition, but it is very dangerous, for too much of the substance will cause death. Here, you should recognize, he has mixed ordinary willow bark with the juice of the poppy, dried leaves of henbane, and mandrake root. Then he adds quantities of sugar to cover the taste, as would the wine with which you are instructed to take it."

"Which is the horrible-tasting one?" asked Yusuf.

"Henbane, I expect," said the physician. "You can tell it by its somewhat rotten smell and taste."

"But, Papa, surely you too use some of these substances," said Raquel.

"I do, for pain that cannot be endured, but not mixed like that, and not for what Mordecai was supposedly suffering from. This is rather like curing a bruised finger by cutting off the arm. But I acquit him of desiring to poison my friend Mordecai."

"What will Master Mordecai do now?" asked Raquel.

"I will visit him this afternoon to give him the good news—for no man likes to think that he might be targeted for assassination—and then give him permission to recover in time for the Sabbath. He is anxious to resume his usual life. He does not enjoy isolation."

⋆⟡═ ═⟡⋆

ON Saturday morning fate dealt Mordecai a cruel blow. After being forced to pretend for five days that he was mortally ill, Mordecai awoke with a real sore throat. He rang angrily for the housekeeper, who was still in her shift; she screamed for the maid, who was down in the kitchen, getting herself something to eat; soon the entire household was gathered outside his room.

"I don't know why you can't do something simple without gathering the whole world at my door," complained Mordecai. "I need something hot for my throat, and someone to fetch the physician."

"Which one, master?" asked the housekeeper.

"Master Isaac!" he roared, and then winced as the effort made his throat all the sorer. "What other physician do I see?"

"I apologize most heartily for laughing, Master Mordecai," said Isaac. "And for having asked you to carry out this masquerade."

"Why for that?"

"Because it is clear that you do not appreciate rest and quiet. If one keeps you away from hard work, difficulties, people suffering from illness, and other problems, you promptly fall ill yourself. But I think we can ease this condition quite soon. Continue drinking warm broth and eating what you can. It is not good to allow yourself to become weakened further with poor nourishment. I shall leave you a quantity of a draught to ease your throat. Take a cupful as soon as it is prepared, and then another in a few hours—perhaps when the bells ring once more. Allow at least that much time to go by before taking another cupful. Send for me at once if you feel worse," rising to leave the room.

"Stay but a moment longer, please," said Mordecai. "I am in a quandary, Isaac, and that is why I have fallen ill. As soon as I had nothing more pressing to do, I began to fret about it, and this is what happened."

"What is your problem?" asked Isaac. "If I may be allowed to ask."

"Isaac, I do not know what to do. In spite of what I may have said to you, I think it is possible that the boy who came here, saying he was Rubèn, might have been Faneta's son. And that he is alive. The account of his death was not convincing. The body that was found could have been of any poor soul who could afford boots."

"Tell me, did you write to his mother, telling her of his death?"

"No," said Mordecai abruptly.

"Why not?"

"Because I didn't believe he was Faneta's boy, and also because I wasn't sure that he was dead. But Isaac, if Faneta's son is still alive, he must receive that money before the end of the month of *Nisan*."

"You have little more than three weeks, then," said Isaac.

"I have received a most polite inquiry from the community

in Besalu, wanting to know whether there is an heir to the money or if they can expect to receive it. And what is more difficult, I have received a letter from the boy himself. Now I cannot simply ignore the problem."

"A letter from the boy? From where?"

"From Mallorca."

"How did he explain his behavior?" asked Isaac.

"He said that he was captured by pirates in Sant Feliu de Guíxols when he went out to see what was happening. But fortunately he had a small store of gold pieces with him, sewn into his clothing, he said, and he was able to bribe them to set him down farther along the coast. From there he made his way back to Mallorca, where he spent the winter with his mother and grandmother."

"It sounds possible," said Isaac.

Mordecai shook his head. "Yes, but there is much that it does not explain. According to my agent, and to Daniel as well, he didn't venture out to look, he raced away as if he were escaping."

"They may have misinterpreted his actions," said Isaac.

"I will admit the possibility. And to support his claim, he spoke of events in the City of Mallorca and the *call* that I know happened this winter. So I would think that he had been there. Then he said that he had found work, and when he had earned enough to return here, he would do so. He hoped it would be soon."

"I would not be surprised if it were very soon," said Isaac slowly.

"Yesterday I sent for the notary," said Mordecai. "I described the problem to him and asked for his advice. I also appointed him to administer this money should something happen to me in the next short while. It is wonderful how these events sharpen the mind, Isaac."

"It is unlikely that this little sore throat will be the end of you, Mordecai," said Isaac, "but I wish that you had not sent for your notary. I hope that you will take every precaution in what you eat and drink."

"I shall," said Mordecai. "But I hardly think I am in danger. I am not planning to leave all my money to Master Lucà."

And as soon as Isaac had had a word with the housekeeper about his friend's care, he returned home to his breakfast.

As often happens on days in spring, a sunny morning in Girona turned into a cloudy afternoon. By nightfall, rain had started; by suppertime, it had settled in to soak the ground and fill the streams.

The bell sounded at Master Mordecai's gate just as the rain reached its greatest ferocity. When the porter opened it, muttering curses under his breath, all he could see was a drenched hood and cloak, and streaks of wet hair clinging to a white face. "I have a packet for Master Mordecai, from Master Lucà, with apologies for not having sent it earlier." The lad smiled sweetly at him, turned on his heel and ran for a place of shelter.

"I dropped by, my friend, to find out how you were faring," said Isaac. The rain had carried on through most of the night, but now the sun was shining valiantly, and clouds of steam arose from the cobbles where the sun shone on them.

"A most curious thing has happened," said Mordecai, who was sitting up in his bed with many cushions behind him to support him comfortably.

"And what is that?" asked Isaac.

"Last night, as my secretary and my housekeeper, along with the servants, were finishing their supper without the constraints of the master's presence to annoy them, a messenger arrived with a packet from Master Lucà, containing the medication the lad seemed to believe I had requested."

"Had you?" asked Isaac. "Out of curiosity or any other motive?"

"No, Isaac, I hadn't. My throat was still a little sore, but your earlier attentions had helped, as did the incessant attentions of my housekeeper. I was quite comfortable and set the medication to one side in my chamber."

"Yes?" said Isaac. "Is that all?"

"No, that is not all. Shortly after, I fell asleep, very deeply asleep, awaking in the clamor of the bells before dawn begins to break. Things were very different in the middle of the night."

"They often are," said Isaac.

"My head ached, my limbs ached, I was hot and drenched in sweat, and my throat felt a hundred times worse. I reached for water, and then thought that I had this new medicine. It also struck me that you had pronounced Master Lucà's medications harmless, even though you had also said that you would not give them to a sick dog."

"Hardly harmless, Mordecai. Powerful, possibly dangerous, but not deliberately poisonous."

"Well, at that hour, I was mostly concerned with the not poisonous part, and so I decided to take a small amount to see if it might help me."

"And did it?"

"You will see. Lacking a pitcher of wine in the room, and not wishing to wake up the household, I determined to take it in some water, as you had described your experiments with the original quantity. I drew close to the candle, filled a cup half full with water, and very carefully put into it the two drops that I had been instructed to use. I took a small sip of the liquid, and motivated by some natural caution, or perhaps by your earlier suspicions, I did not swallow it immediately, but held it in my mouth. It was a terrible sensation, Isaac, my friend, and it remains with me still to some extent. I spat the liquid out into my hand and washed it away."

"What was the sensation?"

"It burned or tingled in my mouth in a way that I cannot quite describe, but then I could feel a terrible numbness—that was when I spat it out and rinsed my mouth clean with fresh water."

"And how do you feel now?"

"My sore throat is no more, but I have a odd feel and taste in my mouth, and a deep sense of relief and thanksgiving that I did not drink that medication. The shock of almost drinking it seems to have cured me, the way a man who has taken too much wine will be cured if he falls into a pool of cold water, as long as he escapes before he is drowned."

"I suggest that you spend the day eating lightly, drinking

cool liquids, and sleeping whenever your body wishes it. Try not to agitate yourself in any way. It is a pleasant day; you might wish to sit comfortably in your courtyard under a tree, but do not allow yourself to become chilled. If you feel any change in your condition, then please, send for me. I would miss you if you carelessly allowed yourself to be poisoned."

"You think there was poison in that vial?"

"I know there was," said Isaac. "What I do not know is whether it arrived there through malice or through young Master Lucà's ignorance of his trade. Will you allow me to take away the vial in question? I would like to examine the contents more closely."

"With all the best will in the world, Isaac. I do not want such things in my house."

ISAAC brought the vial home and, fetching a small, lockable chest from his study, set the poisoned concoction in it and placed the chest on the table.

"Why have you brought Master Lucà's medication out again?" asked Raquel. "Are you not satisfied with your results?"

"This is not the same vial," said her father. "But we need to examine it all the same. I will need two large cups, a pitcher of water, a lantern with a candle in it, a scrap of paper or cloth, and a spoon for stirring. Bring it all out here."

"Would it not be easier to work in your study, Papa? It is breezy out here, and—"

"That is why we are here. I prefer to have a nice, clean wind blowing past us. Can you summon Yusuf from his studies, as well? We can do with another nose, I think."

Once Yusuf was summoned, and the objects all assembled, the three gathered around the board set up in the courtyard.

"It is all ready, Papa," said Raquel. "I brought a scrap of linen."

"Excellent. Now I wish to feel the size of the cup," said Isaac.

"Yes, Papa," said Raquel, moving it over until it was in front of him.

"Thank you." He picked it up, surrounded the circumfer-

ence with his fingers, and then set it down, measuring the
depth against his hand. "That will do," he said. "Now fill the
cup with water, Raquel, if you please."

She poured water in it until it was almost at the top. "It is
full, Papa," she murmured.

Isaac checked the level of the water with his fingertip. "Excellent. Now uncork the vial and sniff it as you did the other
day. Then give it to Yusuf to do the same."

"It doesn't smell the same, Papa," said Raquel, passing it
over to the lad.

"Except for that almost rotten smell," said Yusuf, placing
the vial in Isaac's fingers.

"Indeed, I think you are right. Raquel? Is he right?"

"I'm not sure, Papa."

"Then put one scant drop in the water and stir it. When
you've finished, smell the vial once again, but don't get too
close to it."

"I can see what he means," said Raquel. "That rotten cabbage smell, or something like that."

"Fill the other cup with clean water and put it within my
reach," said her father. Then he moistened his fingertip with
the liquid and touched it to his tongue. Very rapidly, he
swilled out his mouth with the clear water and spat it out.

"Should we try that?" asked Raquel.

"Hold the cup of water in your hand so that you can get it
quickly to your mouth," said her father. "And for all our sakes,
do not put too much on your tongue."

In silence, Raquel did what she had seen her father do. "I am
not sure that Yusuf should try this, Papa," she said in an odd
voice and coughed. "He is slight and younger than I am, and
may be worse affected."

"You feel the effects, my dear? Remember them, and that
smell. Yusuf may try it too, but remember how quickly the
mouth must be cleansed of the drugs."

"That was horrible, lord," said Yusuf in an awe-struck voice.
"My mouth feels as if it belongs to someone else."

"I would like to find out what happens if we heat up a drop
on the cloth," said Isaac. "Put one drop on the piece of linen,"

he added, "and set it on top of the lantern. Stay away from it, but observe it."

"It's turning dark, Papa, and the smell is stronger than it was in the vial. Especially the rotten cabbage smell."

"I can smell it from here," said Isaac, mildly. "Now—those are three ways of unlocking the secrets of a mixture. The dried henbane, which has the odd and unpleasant smell, gets worse with heat. Those who have exceptionally keen noses, like Yusuf, can smell it at this stage, and do not have to taste it. Tasting is always dangerous. Here, for example, I believe he has added the dried root of the plant the Greeks called 'the plant of death.' A portion of a drop of the essence of it will kill some men.

"Then why do you do it?"

"Because if you are unsure of what is in a compound, it can tell more secrets than any other test."

"What are you going to do now?" asked Raquel. "Clearly Master Lucà sent Master Mordecai a vial of poison."

"No, Raquel. A messenger brought Master Mordecai a vial of poison, saying it was from Master Lucà. We cannot be sure who mixed it and who ordered that it be sent. But I shall place the problem before the Bishop, along with other matters, since it seems at least possible that a Christian has committed a crime against a Jew, and that His Excellency is the proper person to pursue the matter."

THE bells had not yet rung for terce on Monday morning, when Isaac and Yusuf made their way to the Bishop's palace. "Welcome, Master Isaac and friend Yusuf," said Berenguer. "I had thought you had completely forgotten my request."

"I have been working on it as busily as I could, Your Excellency," said Isaac calmly, "and have, I believe, some important information to add to your inquiry."

"Good," said Berenguer. "Because I grow tired of being annoyed by the city authorities. They have been murmuring that they have every right to hang the man, and so it is time that I lifted my ban on seizing him. It is a question of jurisdiction, now, and one that can become quite difficult."

"Your jurisdiction over Lucà's person is very clear, Your Excellency."

"Is it indeed? I am glad to have a definitive opinion from you, Master Isaac. And under what provision of canon law," he added with heavy sarcasm in his tone, "do I derive this jurisdiction?"

Isaac continued smoothly along, ignoring the Bishop's evident ill humor. "Young Lucà, a Christian whose parish is unknown to me, is accused of having given in the guise of medicine a noxious poison to Master Mordecai ben Aaron, a Jew of the diocese. As you well know, His Majesty not being here to dispute the issue, I think that the only court that can deal with the accusation is yours, Your Excellency. Since the other matter—the death of Master Narcís, is also simply an accusation, then I believe that Your Excellency has an excellent case for jurisdiction over his person."

The Bishop paused for a moment to consider the question. "That is interesting. I might not have put it in quite those words, and I am not entirely positive that you are right, but whether you are or not, I shall exercise my right to jurisdiction. We can argue later," said Berenguer. "Now tell me, what happened to Master Mordecai? Surely he is not—"

"It is a somewhat lengthy tale, Your Excellency," said Isaac.

"You have my complete attention," said Berenguer, "but I think we need witnesses to this." He rang, and summoned both his secretary, Bernat, and Bernat's scribe to note and witness the account.

"And there you have it, Your Excellency," said Isaac when he had finished a summary of what he had discovered during the previous ten days. "I would like to add that Mistress Regina brought me vials of Master Lucà's two special preparations, as well as samples of each herb that he uses to prepare them. One vial contains a simple remedy that I frequently give to patients for mild disorders, and the stronger remedy that he sent at first to Master Mordecai contains two ingredients that in great strength are dangerous, but when used in small doses, can be most efficacious."

"Has Master Lucà explained the second vial sent to Master Mordecai? The one that is not quite so benign?" asked Berenguer.

"No one has mentioned it to him."

"How many people know of the incident on Saturday night?"

"Seven, Your Excellency. Master Mordecai, my daughter, Yusuf, and I, as well as the three in this room who have just heard of it."

"No one else? The servants, perhaps?"

"Not even they, Your Excellency. I asked him not to speak of it until I could bring it to your attention."

"That is good. And you believe the girl, Regina, to be truthful?"

"She always has been, and her account sounded very like truth to me."

"If we could find the messenger," said Bernat. "It would be of great use. Do you have any idea who it might have been?"

"A boy, Bernat," said the Bishop. "One boy amongst a horde of boys in the city and outskirts."

"I shall try to find him," said Isaac. "But first I must get a description of him from those who saw him."

＋═══ ═══＋

WHEN Daniel had awakened on Saturday morning in the cabin of the ship *Santa Felicitat*, there had been an unnatural quietness in the air that had made him uneasy. He had stood up, very carefully, picked his way softly over to the companionway, and walked onto the deck to look around. Nothing had been happening. The sails had been lowered. The crew had been sitting around, chatting quietly, or sleeping on the deck. He had walked over to the side and looked down. The ship had been moving gently up and down on an almost still sea. There had not been a breath of wind. And behind them, just on the horizon, had been a land mass that looked discouraging like the island of Mallorca.

That was the morning before. In two days they had traveled no more than ten or twenty miles farther along, having taken advantage of a few fits of favorable wind. The ship still sat as it had been, the air was still calm, the sea quiet as a sleeping baby. "How long will this go on?" asked Daniel of a passing seagull.

And to his surprise, a sailor standing nearby said, "I think it's over. I can feel a wind coming."

✦══ ══✦

ANNA, Master Narcís's maid, shook her head. "I do not know what I can possibly tell you," she said. "It was a dark night. The moon had not yet risen when the boy came to the door."

"What did he wear?"

"His clothing?" said Anna. "That was a strange thing. I wondered if he had stolen it."

"Stolen his clothing?" asked Isaac patiently.

"He had a cloak with a hood," she said. "It was a cool evening, but not cold, and it was a warm-looking cloak, thick and expensive. Not what you'd expect to find on a boy running errands like that. But because the hood was pulled down over his face, it was hard to see what he looked like."

"Was he tall?" asked Isaac.

"Tall? For a boy, yes, quite tall," said Anna.

"Could he have been a man?" asked Isaac.

"A man? Perhaps. Except that his voice didn't seem to be a man's voice. It was too light for a man, but too deep for a boy. I thought for a moment that he might be a very tall woman, but I don't think he was."

"Would you recognize his voice if you heard it again?"

"I might," she said doubtfully. "I don't think he was from the city. Perhaps he came in from the countryside. He spoke oddly—not like one from here."

✦══ ══✦

THE porter who had taken the packet for Mordecai was struck dumb at the idea of describing the person who brought it. "What did he look like? I don't know. He looked like a boy. Everyone said it was a boy. It was dark and raining, Master Isaac. And with his cloak and hood pulled around like that to keep off the rain, you couldn't tell what he looked like."

"Was he a tall person?" asked Isaac.

"Tall?" he said. "I didn't notice that he was tall. Not as tall as I am. He was just an ordinary size."

"For a boy, ordinary?" asked Isaac. "Or for a man? Or even a woman?"

"But you just said he was a boy," protested the porter. "And

I don't know. He was just a messenger. I took the package, he said he'd been paid already for delivering it, and so I closed the door. It was an unpleasant night, and very dark." He paused for a moment and then added triumphantly. "I know he was a messenger. He had one of those baskets—the tall, narrow ones you can put things in you don't want to lose. Why else would he be carrying it?"

"Thank you," said Isaac. "What sort of voice did he have?"

But this went beyond the porter's notice. "Same as anyone," he said. "He didn't say much. I couldn't tell."

THE gatekeeper to the *call* was even less forthcoming. "Saturday night," he said. "No one left the *call* on Saturday night. It was raining."

"No one at all?" asked Isaac. "You didn't open the gate once?"

"No one to speak of. I opened for a boy," he said.

"Who was he?"

"I don't know. He came in, paid his penny, and ran off. I didn't see what he looked like. It was a bad night."

"When did he leave?" asked Isaac.

"Leave?"

"Do you mean he lives here? Or did he go over the wall?"

"Of course he didn't go over the wall," grumbled the gatekeeper. "But I didn't see any stranger leave. I opened up for a small group a little later. He could have gone with them."

"Who were they?"

"Men who said they business in the town—"

"Did you know them?"

"Of course I knew them," said the gatekeeper. "Master Astruch—"

"Thank you," said Isaac and went home to fetch Yusuf.

YUSUF listened intently to what Isaac had to say. "This boy is not from the city?" he asked.

"That seems to be so. Anna thought he was a country lad."

"Then he will have been noticed," said Yusuf. "Especially if he has been earning money delivering messages. I am surprised they have not chased him away. But I will find out," he added with assurance.

"Excellent," said his master.

"And I will find out much more quickly if I have a store of small coins—farthings and halfpennies. It loosens tongues and brings people forward."

"You shall have them," said Isaac. "Now go and prepare yourself."

YUSUF was away no more than a half hour. "Have you solved our dilemma already?" asked the physician.

"No, lord. I had just started when I heard a group of men talking about Master Lucà, saying that he had already murdered three people and gained a vast fortune, and that he should be hanged and the joiner driven from his home for sheltering him. Shortly after, I heard others talk the same way."

"Come, Yusuf, we must visit the Bishop before anything happens."

FIFTEEN

e'm furtarà la mia llibertat?

and will rob me of my liberty?

"WHAT I must do, Master Isaac, is what I should have done long since. I must arrest this Lucà. It is the only way to assert jurisdictional rights over him and to ensure that he lives long enough to be tried. Fairly. Otherwise he will be mobbed, and Romeu with him. Bernat—fetch the captain."

In moments the smoothly running mechanism of the Bishop's Guard was functioning at its most efficient, and a small troop of guards had been dispatched to seize the herbalist.

"May I beg a favor of Your Excellency?" asked Isaac, once the captain had left the room.

"What sort of favor, Master Isaac?"

"Master Lucà must be seized and kept in the episcopal prison, I agree, for his own sake as well as the city's, but I beg of you, do not charge him with a crime. Not yet. He must not be tried until Daniel returns from Mallorca."

"Why is that?" asked the Bishop.

"I feel that Daniel will bring back something—"

"What?"

"I am not sure, Your Excellency, but whatever it is, I believe that it is important, and that it will relate to the guilt or innocence of young Lucà."

"And how long will it be until Daniel returns?"

"He will return before this day week, which is Passover, if he has to buy passage on the fastest galley moored off the island," said Isaac. "For he does not wish to miss the preparations for his wedding."

"A powerful motive, Master Isaac. But the course of justice cannot be delayed that long. I am obliged to try him as soon as I can bring a court together—Wednesday, I would think. That means that, in all likelihood, he will be hanged on Thursday. If Daniel returns before then, we will of course be glad to hear his testimony."

"It seems harsh that his fate should depend entirely on something as capricious as the winds from Mallorca, Your Excellency."

"I am puzzled, Master Isaac, and not pleased with this," said the Bishop angrily. "Why should you plead so eloquently on behalf of Master Lucà? I would expect you to be justifiably angry that he had attempted to poison Master Mordecai, who would be a loss to your community and to ours."

"It is only, Your Excellency, that I fear that justice may not be done if it is executed too swiftly. Also I would not like Mistress Regina, whose heart has been too often broken, to suffer once more."

＊⇒ ⇒＊

WELL before Berenguer de Cruïlles and his physician had finished their somewhat acrimonious discussion, four members of the Bishop's Guard arrived at Romeu the joiner's house. Regina saw them first, turning into their street. She had been leaning out a window, pulling in the bedclothes that had been airing in the morning sun. She forgot all about the unmade beds and flew down the stairs to the workroom. "Papa," she said. "Where is Lucà? Is he with you?"

"No, my dear," said her father. "What is the matter?"

"I must find him," she said. "He must leave, at once—go somewhere where he is not known. They are coming for him." She turned and ran up to the little room under the eaves that was bedchamber and herbarium for the young man.

"Mistress Regina," he said, turning rapidly around when she flung open his door. "What is wrong?"

"You must run. Now," she said. "Go out the back window and onto the roof. From there, go over to the neighbor's roof and down the ladder to his wall. Then follow the wall back and jump down. It will take you to the river. I know. I did it many times when I was a child."

"But why must I run?" he asked, the color draining out of his face. "What have I done? Have I offended your father?"

"Oh, Lucà! How can you ask that? Are you the only person in this city who has not heard what they are saying about you?"

"But no one believes that, Regina. You don't believe that, do you?"

"It matters little what I believe," she said. "It is what everyone else will say of you that matters." The sound of a heavy fist banging on the door resounded through the house, driving the girl to a frenzy of desperation. "They are here, Lucà. You must go. Papa cannot tell them where you are, because he does not know, and I will not tell them. Now go." She seized him by the arm and tried to push him toward the back window.

"Run?" he said blankly. "I cannot run—not again. Not any more. I have harmed no one, I swear it on my very soul, Regina. I will tell them the truth and pray that they will listen to me."

"No. I will tell them the truth after you are safely out of the city," said Romeu's daughter. "I hear them talking to Papa. They will be here soon."

She ran out to the tiny landing and closed the door firmly after her. Lucà stood for a moment listening to her quick footsteps running down the stairs, bundled up a few of his possessions, and started to move across the room.

"No," said Regina, "he is not at home. I know, because I was just looking for him. I thought he was in the courtyard, but it is empty, and so I went up to his room, but he must have slipped out earlier this morning while I was at the market. Either that, or he's in the workroom with Papa."

She stood at the foot of the stairs, daring this troop of strong, broad-shouldered men to try to move her.

"No, Mistress Regina," said the sergeant patiently. "He is not with your father. We looked there."

"Then he is out," she repeated stubbornly.

"You are mistaken, Mistress Regina," said a voice from behind her. "I was not out. Who are these gentlemen?" And Lucà appeared out of the shadows, gently moved Regina off the bottom step of the stairs, and came into the common sitting room and kitchen.

<hr/>

YUSUF returned that day after dark, cold and hungry, and as he sat at table with a plentiful hot supper in front of him, he tried to sum up the result of his searches between mouthfuls. "I am not sure that this messenger exists, lord," he said. "No one knows him in any of the places where you would expect to find someone like that—one who hopes to earn a penny or two running errands, or bearing messages. Certainly no one at all like him waits in the cathedral square, or in the market, or down by the river, or up near the bridge by Rodrigue's tavern."

"Do they know Lucà?" asked Isaac.

"Certainly," said Yusuf. "And he has never been known to hire a messenger. He always goes to his patients in person. Not only that, but a boy with a thick cloak and a hood, such as this lad is supposed to have worn, would be noticed. It is not a common garment for one like them," he added, dismissing all such boys with a wave of the hand, as though he, himself, had never been one of them.

"Therefore, whoever it is, it is not a common beggar lad," said Isaac.

"It is not even an apprentice that anyone knows of," said Yusuf. "Or someone in the lowest ranks of servants."

"Then it is likely to be a man who has deliberately assumed that disguise," said Isaac. "There are few other possibilities."

"Or a woman," said Yusuf.

"Why do you say that?" asked Isaac.

"I was talking to a lad who had been out in that rain, and

was looking for someplace where he could shelter without being harassed. He told me that he was trying to get home when he stepped under the arch of the north bridge and bumped directly into someone in a thick cloak with a hood. He said he couldn't really see it, but he could feel the cloth. This person hit him, then cursed him, and threatened him with a knife, saying he would slit his throat if he did not leave. He said he was very frightened, but that he began to wonder later if it was a woman, rather than another boy."

"Why should he think that it was a woman?" asked Isaac.

"He didn't know," said Yusuf. "It was just a feeling."

"I would very much like to speak to this lad," said Isaac. "Very much indeed."

"Most nights he sleeps in a shed on the other side of the river," said Yusuf. "But he comes into the city when the gates are open."

＊＝＝＝＝＊　＊＝＝＝＝＊

YUSUF had not quite finished his supper when the bell rang at the gate once more. "Who can that be?" asked Judith.

"We'll find out soon enough, Mama. Don't get up," said Raquel.

One set of footsteps sounded on the stairs; Ibrahim poked his head into the dining room. "Two people are waiting to see the master," he said.

"This is not a summons to someone's bedside?" asked Isaac.

"He said he wanted to see you," repeated Ibrahim. "He didn't look sick. They are waiting in the courtyard."

"Show them up here, Ibrahim," said Judith. "It is too cold a night for standing about down there. And we have much too much to do elsewhere," she added, gathering up everyone with a commanding look, "to be sitting about here gossiping. Bring your plate into the kitchen, Yusuf."

＊＝＝＝＝＊　＊＝＝＝＝＊

"MASTER Isaac," said the deep, slow voice of Romeu the joiner. "I have come here to talk to you at the insistence of my daughter, Regina, who is with me."

"I wished to add my voice to my father's," said Regina, in a low voice.

"And to make sure that I carried out my commission," said Romeu.

"And what is your commission?" asked Isaac.

"You may have heard that our lodger, young Lucà the herbalist, has been seized and is now in the Bishop's prison," said Romeu. "Although why he should be there and not in the city prison I do not understand," he added. "Since he stands accused of the murder of Master Narcís."

"I will explain that in a moment," said Isaac, "for I had something to do with it."

"That is not important, Papa," said Regina urgently. "What is important is that he is innocent."

"No," said Isaac, "I must explain. It is very important that he is in the Bishop's prison, for there I am assured that he cannot be tried before Wednesday—two more days from now. Nor could he be hanged before three days have passed. In those two days, there is a possibility of much being done."

"I do not understand what you mean," said Romeu. "I am ready to testify that on the afternoon and night that the poison was delivered, Lucà did not leave the house. He had been working with me in the workroom, and then we all had supper, and then we sat over a jug of wine and he told me tales of his life in Mallorca, and of his time in Sardinia. He could not have taken that potion to Master Narcís's house."

"But that does him no good," said Isaac. "Because no one thinks he did. The potion was delivered by someone who said he was a messenger, someone shorter and slighter than young Lucà, who is a tall, strong young man. His accusers believe that he hired that messenger to deliver it. He could have done that any time during the day."

"Then when did he concoct it?" asked Regina. "He has made four batches of medications since Easter; I know, because it is simpler for him to work in the kitchen, and I have helped him. He makes two kinds—he told me in confidence that they are the only two he knows."

"What about the mixture he gave you, mistress?" asked Isaac.

"That was based on something that he had seen his master making. He spent a long time imitating it, and drank a large dose before giving it to me, to make sure it did no harm. But each mixture has a very distinct smell, and I recognize it right away. He has done two of each, and there is some left over of each one." She said all this very clearly and deliberately, as if she were already in front of a court.

"Could he not have made a potion while you were out?" asked Isaac.

"No," said Regina firmly, "for he was in the habit of accompanying me on my errands, saying that until I was completely strong, I needed help in carrying the baskets when they were full. And if I had left him alone, and he had stirred up the kitchen fire sufficiently to brew these things, then not only would he have used wood, but also the smell would have lingered in the kitchen. I would have noticed."

"They may listen, and I am sure that they will believe you, mistress, but they may think that you deceive yourself, for he is a pleasant, handsome young man, and they will take that into account," said Isaac.

"But I know that he is innocent of these poisonings," said Regina. "I know it. I made them let me see him in prison, because I wanted to ask him what I should do, what persons could testify for him beyond us, and he just shook his head and said that he knew as he knows his own name that he did not do these things, and that God would not allow him to be punished for them unjustly. He said he had done many lesser things that he was ashamed of, but never had he killed a man, either accidentally or deliberately. Then I got angry and said that God was not going to appear before the Bishop's court and save him if he would not save himself. You must help us, Master Isaac. Please. Ask the Bishop to do something to spare him—"

"Before pleading your case before the Bishop, Regina, why do we not find the messenger?" said Romeu. "He will know who paid him to deliver the poisoned compound."

"I was planning to do that this very night," said Isaac. "Someone who saw him in all that rain is said to live on the bank of the river on the far side of the bridge. When you arrived I was only waiting for Yusuf to finish his supper before leaving to seek him out."

"I will come with you," said Romeu. "If this person lives

where you say, then he is near my house, and I can perhaps be of use. But first I must take Regina home."

"And I must fetch Yusuf, who knows who this young man is," said Isaac.

⊹⊱══ ══⊰⊹

IN the end, there were six in the group that made their way by torchlight out of the *call* toward Romeu's house. "Regina, I do not like you being alone so late. Perhaps you should stay with a neighbor," Romeu had said while the four of them were gathered by the gate. Raquel was there as well, standing near the stairs, in case something more was needed, and Ibrahim was waiting patiently to lock the gate behind them.

"Papa, it is too late to wake up the neighbors for such slight cause," said Regina. "I shall be safe at home."

"I feel uneasy, leaving my daughter alone in the house," confessed Romeu to Isaac. "It is perhaps foolish of me, but . . ."

"Then why don't I come with Mistress Regina?" said Raquel. "And perhaps we can bring Ibrahim to guard us, to keep her father from worrying."

"Or Mistress Regina can stay here," Isaac had said, "where she will be safe, I assure you. Our walls are high, our gate is stout, and my family and servants all very cautious."

"I would rather go home, Papa," said Regina, "if Mistress Raquel does not mind accompanying me."

And so it was decided, and they moved through the streets like any group of sober citizens returning from an evening with friends, chatting amicably in quiet voices so as not to disturb the neighborhood. "Why did Lucà spend so much time with you in your workshop?" asked Isaac suddenly. "Out of boredom because he lacked patients to treat?"

"I don't think so," said Romeu. "In the last two weeks he has had patients who wished him to visit every day. I know that, because they would send a maid or a boy with the message, and when I delivered it to him—for he didn't like to go to the door himself—he would say that he was too busy to come until the next day, and to me he complained that they all wanted him to stay and talk to them, and that he preferred the silence of a piece of wood and the sound of the axe, or the chisel, or the smoothing stone over it. He has a feel for wood, Master Isaac. He has been a great help to me."

The distance from Romeu's house down to the river road was not far, and soon they left the hillside and turned on level ground toward the bridge. "Is the torch still lit, Yusuf?" asked Isaac.

"Yes, it is, lord," murmured the boy. "It is a dark night, without a moon as yet."

"We must douse it," said the physician. "And make our way as best we can without it."

They moved slowly ahead until their eyes grew accustomed to the sudden darkness. When Romeu's footsteps resounded hollowly on the span of the bridge, Isaac touched him on the shoulder to warn him to keep silence. They all stopped.

The night was black, illuminated by the faint light of the stars above them; beneath them, the river ran like a ribbon of inkier black between banks whose existence could only be guessed at. A dog barked. Something moving through the grasses on the water's edge made them rustle faintly. A thud like a beast jumping and landing on its paws made Yusuf start. Then, with a splash, something fell into the water.

"What was that, lord?" asked Yusuf nervously.

"Something is abroad in the night, hunting," said Romeu softly. "I think we heard it take its prey most silently and efficiently."

"I fear we did," said Isaac. "Have you that torch still, Yusuf? And flint and steel?"

"Right here, master."

"Then light it and hurry."

Suddenly a flame leaped up and the world around them came back into existence. "Can you see anything on the bank?" asked the physician.

"We have to get closer—the shed is in the shadow of the trees." Yusuf moved ahead, bringing Isaac with him, and Romeu, looking around for whatever danger the physician seemed to apprehend, followed them.

"Here is the path down to the shed," said the boy, raising the torch. "It is rather narrow. But he should be in here, if he has not fled."

"Have you seen him flee?"

"No, lord. But—" He stopped and looked into the low, ramshackle building. "There is no one here," said Yusuf.

"Romeu, take the torch and look into the river," said Isaac.

Romeu was the first to see him. He was lying caught on a bank of gravel an arm's length away from the bank of the river, a black shape, bobbing up and down in the swirling movement of the current racing down to the sea. "Here, lad," said Romeu, turning to Yusuf. "Take the torch again and hold it high. I will fetch him out." The big man waded cautiously into the cold water; in a moment he returned carrying a young boy in his arms.

"It is the boy I spoke of, lord," said Yusuf.

"Is he dead?" asked Isaac.

"His head is bleeding, lord, a great deal. It looks as if he were badly injured and then fell into the water. How can he be alive?"

"A man does not bleed after death, Yusuf. If he is still bleeding and is not drowned . . ."

"When I got to him, his head and shoulders lay on a gravel bank, Master Isaac," said Romeu. "His face was not in the water. I can just feel his breath coming and going. But I think we should take him to our house. The night is cool."

"Excellent," said Isaac. "Let us move as quickly as we can."

⋇⟹ ⟸⋇

THE boy was laid on a blanket on the table in the kitchen. Regina supplemented the candle that already lit the room with three others. Raquel moved to the far side of the table while her father felt the bleeding head. "The skin is broken and the skull feels slightly depressed from the blow," he said. "Fortunately he was not struck on the temple, but it is difficult to judge whether he can survive. How does he look, Raquel?"

"His scalp is still bleeding," she said, "and he is very pale and sunken, Papa. He is extremely wet, poor thing, and must be cold, although I am sure he cannot feel it at the moment. He needs to be bandaged, and then may I take his wet things off him and wrap him in a blanket?"

"I have fetched the remnants of a clean linen sheet for bandages," said Regina, handing them to Raquel.

As soon as his head was bandaged, they stripped off his wet

rags. Regina dressed him in a clean shirt, soft from long wear, that had belonged to Romeu's apprentice and ought to have been returned to his family on his death.

"We cannot leave him here," said Raquel. "Is there a bed or a couch where he can stay quietly?"

"There is the maid's little room, which is behind this one," said Regina. "Or Lucà's chamber, which used to be the apprentice's. It would be the quietest."

And so the boy was taken up to Lucà's bedchamber.

"Nothing can be done for him now but watch him and pray for his recovery," said Isaac in somber tones. "Shield him from strong light and loud noises. If he is a strong lad, as I think he may be, he may live, and if he does, his evidence could be important."

The ringing of the bells of midnight stopped all conversation for the moment. Isaac stood in silence for a long moment after the last vibration left the air. "Do you still have a servant, Romeu?" he asked at last.

"Alas, I do not," said the joiner. "We had the servant girl, but she was carried off in the same fever that took my wife and my apprentice. When Regina was very ill, a neighbor came in and helped."

"For now, that is good," said the physician. "It is of the utmost importance that no one should know of the boy's existence. I am sorry to do this to you, Mistress Regina, but it must be given out that my visits here are because you have been overcome with fever and a nervous complaint at the arrest of Master Lucà. Raquel will look after the boy, if you will help her, and Yusuf will come from time to time with news and extra help if it is needed. When Romeu must leave the house, it is to be well locked up and no one—not even a dear friend or neighbor—is to be allowed in, except for those in the house right now. Regina must not go to the door; if someone other than the three of us brings you a package, mistress, no matter who it is from, do not open it unless I am there. Do you understand? If we are to save Lucà, we must do our utmost to save this boy. And I fear that he might be in graver danger from the outside world than he is from his injury."

His white-faced listeners nodded and murmured their comprehension, and the physician left, accompanied by Yusuf and Ibrahim with the torch.

"DO you expect grave danger, lord?" asked Yusuf as they walked away from Romeu's house.

"I do not expect it, Yusuf, but I fear it," said the physician. "I know she is suffering now, and that her body is still weakened from her previous ordeal, but she is brave, and I hope that her courage will carry her through."

"No, lord," said Yusuf, "I meant—"

"I know well enough what you meant, Yusuf, and instead of speculating about such ultimately useless questions, tell me what you would give to Mistress Regina to strengthen her for what is to come. What symptoms do we deal with? What are the basic remedies for each? Which ones can be administered at the same time? Come, lad. Let us see what you have learned in addition to curiosity."

And, hesitant and somewhat confused, stumbling over some of the names, Yusuf began to order his thoughts in that direction, and describe the condition. "I expect that she will be unable to sleep, and that will weaken her even more," he said. "For that I would give her . . ." He paused. "There are several remedies. I do not know which one."

"Tell me what they are and their properties—their advantages and disadvantages. In an orderly fashion. Think before you speak, Yusuf."

"We are at the gate, lord."

"Then knock, and while we wait, you can start."

As they stepped through the gate and rewarded the porter, the other late night pedestrian who had been strolling toward the city behind them apparently had a change of mind. When the postern gate closed behind the pair, he—or she—paused, turned, and walked slowly back in the direction of the bridge.

YUSUF had finally arrived at the juice of the poppy plant in his list of soporifics when they entered the gate of their own house. Ibrahim locked up, muttered something that could have been "good night," and headed toward his little chamber.

"I am afraid I had great difficulty remembering all of that," said Yusuf penitently. "I shall study harder."

"You do not need to study harder, Yusuf," said the physician. "You need to listen."

"I try, lord," said the boy. "Whenever you speak of treatments."

"You need to listen all the time, and not just to me, and you must think before you speak. Someone was abroad, behind us, as we walked from Romeu's to the gate. If I could hear his footfalls, which were delicate, he could well have heard our words. Remember how quiet the night is. He could have been an innocent traveler or not. We do not know. Now go to bed, lad. You have worked hard and must be tired. Good night."

+≈= =≈+

"WELL, Master Isaac," said the Bishop, "I have indulged your desire to speak to young Lucà, although I cannot see what possible difference it can make to the outcome of the trial. I have spoken to him myself, twice, in front of witnesses, and he has said nothing that would convince any court of his innocence. Did he tell you anything that might help him tomorrow in his defence?"

"I am bound to say, Your Excellency, that he did not, although he said nothing that might make me believe him guilty, either. He did tell me a few things that I find interesting, and that I would like to pursue."

"You are, of course, free to do so."

"The reason that I am here at this early hour disturbing Your Excellency is that I have found a possible witness—if not on Lucà's side, at least on the side of the truth."

"Then bring him forward," said the Bishop impatiently. "A witness would be a great help."

"I cannot do that, Your Excellency, because he lies, gravely injured, in a safe place. I do not even know his name."

"Explain yourself," said Berenguer. "And quickly."

"I saw him this morning, and there are clear signs that he is improving, Your Excellency," said Isaac as he finished his account of their search for the boy. "But such injuries cannot be predicted. If the poisons were not concocted by Lucà, this boy may be able to point out who the poisoner's agent is. If the wrong man is hanged, then we have someone here to whom human life means nothing. Will you but give the lad a little while to recover his wits and his memory? Perhaps until Daniel returns? For one or the other of them should be able to tell us much that we do not know."

"Are you sure you do not want me to release him as well?" asked Berenguer sourly.

"That is the last thing I would want, Your Excellency. If you were to release him, either the city would seize him or the mob would, and in either case he would have no chance at all."

"Well," said Berenguer uneasily, "I will consider this. At the moment I have done nothing toward setting up a court, in spite of Bernard's prompting, for I admit that the circumstances trouble me—even though I think it likely that the young man is guilty."

ISAAC bent over the boy and laid his head to his chest, listening intently. "Have you noticed any further changes in him?" he asked.

"No, Papa," said Raquel, "except that his color seems to be returning, although slowly."

"He is sleeping now," said Isaac, "in a more normal fashion. You must send for me the moment that he awakes. If he seems to be disturbed or excited, then you and Regina must try hard to keep him as calm and still as you can and apply cool cloths to his head. Whatever his state, get him to take water when he is awake enough to drink it."

"I have been sponging his lips with water, Papa, some of which he has swallowed," said Raquel.

"Excellent. Have you been troubled by anyone from the outside world?"

"Just the neighbors," said Regina, who had at that moment come up the stairs. "And they are only curious. I had to hide myself in the maid's little chamber when they arrived. One of them asked Papa if he had heard the noise the night before, when someone apparently fell into the river."

"And did he?" asked Isaac.

"He said he heard it, and thought it sounded like a water rat returning safely to his hole." She paused. "Master Isaac," she said, "did you see him?"

"I went to visit him," said Isaac. "He told me he was being well treated and that he felt well. Unfortunately for us and for him, he told me little else."

"Oh, no!" said Regina. "Did you say how important it was for him to talk to you?"

"I did, but he did not change his mind. Although he found it difficult to remain silent when I gave him your message," added the physician.

Raquel looked curiously at Romeu's daughter and turned back to the child on the bed.

"If only Daniel would come back," said Raquel. "I'm sure that there is so much that he could explain. I cannot understand what is taking him so long. Mállorca is not that far away, and we have heard nothing of terrible storms on the coast."

"We cannot depend on his having learned anything, my dear," said Isaac gently. "We must do what we can here."

"I want to know who hit the lad on the head and threw him in the river," said Romeu. "It was a scurvy trick. He may be a thieving little magpie who roams the street looking for pieces of bread to steal, I don't know, but whoever did that meant him to die there. For if the blow hadn't killed him, the river would have. The water coming down from the hills at this time of year is cold enough to snuff out a little heap of skin and bones like him." He drew a long breath and looked around. "Don't you think?"

"It was the person who delivered the poisoned concoctions," said Regina. "And said that they were from Lucà. Who else can it have been?"

"But who hated Master Narcís enough to poison him?" asked Raquel. "He was a pleasant, harmless man, who never hurt anyone, as far as I know."

"Who hates Master Lucà enough to kill Master Narcís in order to destroy him?" asked Isaac. Everyone turned silently in
his direction. "That may be where the answer lies."

There was a long pause. "We must ask him," said Regina.

"He will not say," said Isaac. "And I think it is because he
does not know. When I questioned him about this, he was
shocked and then sorely puzzled. He is, after all, a pleasant
young man, and not used to being hated. Perhaps the boy
knows more and will wake up in time. And I, too, would like
to know where Daniel is," added the physician, as sharply as if
Raquel's betrothed were late for an appointment. "Those bells a
few minutes ago were ringing for midday, were they not? We
have little time left."

"I hope he is on his way back from Mallorca," said Raquel
tightly. "It was your idea to send him there, Papa."

"We will not battle over who sent him, Raquel," said her father, "but despite what I say, I hope that he will bring back, either in his head or on a leaf of paper or parchment, the key to
all of this."

"And I hope he does not linger to enjoy himself once he arrives in Barcelona," said Romeu.

"I think I have taken care of that," said Isaac.

SIXTEEN

no sap los mals qui la mort li percacen

he doesn't know the ills which seek his death

ONCE the *Santa Felicitat* had picked up a steady wind that lasted for more than an hour or two, their erratic homeward journey had come quickly to an end. She arrived in the port of Barcelona under the blazing sun of noon; the sails had hardly come down before the passengers were bundled hastily into the first boat and rowed into shore. As Daniel clambered up on the stone pier, he felt a sense of enormous relief to be back on the mainland, free of the vagaries of wind and weather and with his plans under his own control, more or less. He tossed his bundle onto his shoulder and headed purposefully toward the establishment where they had left the mules on their way down.

Before he stepped onto the road, he was astonished to be stopped by a neatly dressed boy carrying a roughly folded piece of paper in his hand. "Are you Master Daniel ben Mossé?" he asked politely but firmly.

"I am. But how did you know I was here?" said Daniel.

"I've been watching for the *Santa Felicitat* since yesterday, sir. I am bid to tell you that you are to come with me to where your mule is stabled. At once."

"I had been planning to spend tonight with friends," he said. "Can't I look after this later in the day?"

"It is very important," said the boy. "Here is a letter that says why. But if you could come with me."

Daniel looked at the letter, which repeated in excruciating handwriting what the boy had said rather neatly. "What has happened?" asked Daniel, feeling somewhat alarmed, and after his Mallorcan experiences, slightly suspicious.

"Nothing, that I know of, sir," said the boy.

"You go ahead," said Daniel, "and I'll follow." And since the boy walked quickly along the most direct path to the stables, on sunny, open streets, filled with ordinary-looking people, Daniel went along after him.

"MASTER Daniel," said the jovial patron of the stables. "I am pleased to see you. The lad found you with no difficulty?" he asked.

"As soon as I stepped off the ship's boat, he was there," said Daniel. "What is this all about?"

"As to that," said the patron, "I wouldn't know. I received a package from a courier asking me to waylay you as you came from shipboard and hasten you on your way back to Girona at once. My wife has a dinner prepared for you, and some food and wine for the road. I'll put you on a fast horse, and you should be there in the evening—the moon sets around midnight, I think. You should have plenty of light. We have had a run of clear skies."

"Who sent these instructions?" asked Daniel, as he allowed himself to be pushed toward the kitchen.

"The physician, of course. Master Isaac. Do you know that once when he was a young man he came by to hire a mule, and he cured my wife of the quinsy and my best mare of the colic. They were both in foal at the time. I still have her foal, a lovely fellow he is, and that was my lad who fetched you from the harbor. We were poor in those days, and I paid him with a meal— he insisted on paying me for the hire of the mule. I owe him much. You can wash in there," he said, shoving Daniel toward a tiny room behind the kitchen with a bed and washstand in it, "while my Marta serves up your dinner."

Daniel mounted a sturdy, fast little mare, his head reeling

with instructions about her care and feeding. "Don't pay too much attention to old Roger," said a man who fell into pace beside him. "He likes to hear himself talk. Are you going north?" he asked. "Because if you are, we can ride together. I spend the night at a farm just outside Girona."

"Is that where you live?" asked Daniel, thinking that he didn't look much like a farmer.

"Me? No. Where do I live? Here, when I'm home, I suppose. I have a room at my sister's house. I'm a courier."

"I thought couriers always set out at first light," said Daniel.

"If we have any choice in the matter. It's late to be starting out, but I leave when I'm asked. And don't worry," he added with a grin, "we won't set too hard a pace. I've ridden that mare of yours when my Nineta was laid up, and I know exactly what she can do over a distance without pushing herself. It's a good idea to travel in pairs if you can."

⊶═══ ═══⊷

ISAAC left Romeu's house with no clearer an idea of where to go next than he had had when he arrived there. Logic had carried him so far, but in absence of knowledge, refused to take him further. He paused as he went by Master Pons's house, remembering that Mistress Joana was still suffering from a troublesome cough, and went in to ask after her.

"I am much better, Master Isaac," she said, "but you look troubled and that is unlike you. Is there anything we can do?"

"I am troubled, but unless you can tell me how to find someone without a name, or a face, or a voice that anyone knows or can remember—an evil person—I do not know how you can help me, Mistress Joana."

"You mean like finding the boys who were hurling stones at the birds in my courtyard and injured my kitchenmaid?" she asked. "You track them back to their lair, like a hunter. I found them and nasty little imps they were, too."

"That might work with stone-throwing boys," said Isaac, "but how can it find someone older and cleverer?"

"Not many people are that much cleverer than you are, I suspect, Master Isaac," said Mistress Joana.

"Perhaps I will try it," said Isaac.

"WHERE have you been?" asked Judith as he came up the stairs. "Someone came by and said that you had promised to visit his master, but had never come. I was worried. I thought perhaps you were ill."

"Fear not. If I had been ill," said Isaac, "someone would have come to bring you the news. People always enjoy carrying bad news. Where is Yusuf?"

"I am here, lord," said the boy. "We are about to eat dinner."

"You must eat yours as quickly as you can," said the physician, "and go to Romeu's house. Raquel might require help of one kind or another. If there is any news, bring it back here at once."

"I do not understand why Raquel must stay with Mistress Regina," said Judith. "How can she be so ill again?"

"It is necessary," said Isaac. "Now let us talk of pleasanter things," he added, as Judith put fish and bread on his plate and gave it to Jacinta to set it in front of him. "How is my son? He was sleeping again this morning, and I had no chance to greet him."

"He is wonderful," said Judith, sounding happy. "Hungry as a bear, and like a great lord, as soon as he has had his fill, he falls asleep at table."

"He cries a lot," said Miriam.

"Only when he's hungry," said Judith. "And so did you."

"I didn't know he would be so loud," Miriam added. "Are all babies that loud?"

"Your brother has a particularly strong and healthy voice," said Isaac. "In time, he will learn to moderate it when necessary."

And the physician continued in this manner throughout dinner, trying to pay close attention to his wife and the twins, eating little, and brooding over Master Lucà's behavior.

"Nathan skipped his lessons this morning," said Miriam.

"I didn't," replied her twin brother.

"Then why didn't I see you?" said Miriam. "It was during lesson time, and you weren't in your class."

"But that's not what I was doing," protested Nathan.

"What were you doing, then?" asked Miriam, with a note of triumph in her voice.

"I was . . . it doesn't matter what I was doing," said Nathan. "I wasn't staying away from my class."

"Why not tell us, Nathan?" asked Isaac. "Why do people not defend themselves when they are given the chance to do so?"

"Because you would not believe me, and Mama would think that I am telling lies," said Nathan.

"It's because his friend Mossé would get in trouble if he said what he was doing," said Miriam.

"It is because he is too stubborn," said Judith, looking at her elder son with a mixture of affection and exasperation.

"Those reasons all sound very likely," said Isaac. "Which one is it, Nathan?"

"If everyone knows why I do everything," said Nathan in a fury, "then why should I tell you?" He jumped up from the table and fled from the dining room.

Isaac left the table and went into his study. He sat in his heavy, carved chair, his hands on his knees, and tried to empty his mind of extraneous thoughts. What made people behave in a manner which seemed so extraordinary, and yet was so common to man that his son did the same at the age of eight, and no one was astonished?

What did they fear more than quick and certain punishment that was unmerited? The ridicule of disbelievers? The sting of conscience because of disloyalty? The humbling of pride required to justify oneself? Or something else? And yet no answers came. At last he stood up and went out into the courtyard. The house was somnolent; not a living thing stirred but the cat, who came over and rubbed against his legs.

"Do you know?" he asked. "You who would scorn to justify herself before any court?" But the cat's answer was an interrogative meow, and however wise it may have been, advanced his understanding not at all.

Quietly, the physician picked up his staff, crossed the courtyard and opened the gate. He made his way through the well-known streets of the *call* up to the gate and stirred up the gatekeeper, who was dozing at his post. "If anyone seeks me,

Jacob," he said, "I am visiting a prisoner at the Bishop's prison. I will be returning soon."

The gatekeeper yawned and nodded, forgetful of the fact that the physician could not see, but by that time, Isaac was walking across the square, his staff marking the time of his progress.

"Lucà," said Isaac briskly, as soon as he had obtained admission to the prisoner, "Why do you refuse to defend yourself? Are you too proud to submit to our judgment, and the judgment of the court?"

"I do not altogether understand your question, Master Isaac," said Lucà. "I am not a proud man. What have I to be proud of?"

"Everyone knows that you have a gift of pleasing others with your speech and manners," said Isaac. "That could be a source of pride."

"Only if it were true," said Lucà, "and if it were something that I had learned to do through hard work and intelligence. Some men have twisted faces and cannot smile without looking menacing. Should they pride themselves at being able to strike fear into hearts? I think not. It is an accident, not a skill."

"Then perhaps you protect someone with your silence," said Isaac. "Would your defense harm another whom you esteem?"

"Whom? Can my silence help Regina or Romeu? Who else has helped me here? Who else do I care about?"

"Perhaps someone back in Mallorca," said Isaac. "Your mother or father or other kin. Your master."

"Nothing can help them, Master Isaac," said Lucà. "Or harm them."

"Then you do not trust us to believe the truth when you speak it with your tongue," said Isaac.

"Master Isaac, if I knew wherein lay the truth, I would shout it from the rooftops. But I cannot say what I do not know, and if you do not know the truth, you cannot even lie. There, that is all there is to it. I can say no more."

⊹⊰══ ══⊱⊹

THE physician picked up his staff and left the prison, deep in thought. He had turned his mind to Lucà's answer. A man cannot lie if he does not know the truth. It was so clear and so obvious. Without the truth to guide him in his deceptions, he can only stumble about in confusion. Before his thoughts carried him any further forward, he heard the sound of feet running in his direction. "Lord," said Yusuf softly, "I think our patient is ready to talk to you, if you will come."

"Is all well?" he asked.

"The head is painful, but the behavior is what we hoped for," said Yusuf.

And having to content himself with those words, which could be interpreted in rather too many different ways, Isaac went with him to Romeu's house.

◆━━◆ ◆━━◆

"HE can remember nothing at all about yesterday evening, Papa," said Raquel. "I told him that he had hurt his head and must lie quiet."

"How long has he been awake?" asked the physician.

"Not long this time," said Raquel. "He awoke for a moment, and drank some water, and muttered something I could not catch. Then he fell asleep again. We waited for a little while to see what would happen before sending for you. Then he awoke again, very thirsty, and able to talk."

The boy lay quietly, his eyes open, watching everything in the room. Isaac sat down in the chair by the bed and listened to his breathing for a moment. "What is your name?" asked Isaac. "We cannot just call you the boy any longer, now that we have come to know you."

"Tomas," he said. "That's my name."

"Tell me how you feel, Tomas," said Isaac. "I am a physician and am here to help you get better."

"My head hurts," said Tomas.

"How many fingers do I have that you can see?" asked Isaac, tucking three fingers under his thumb and holding up his hand.

"One, of course," said the boy. "But how can you do that? You can't see, can you? I can tell. You're blind."

"That's right. I can't see," said Isaac, "but I'm clever enough to know how many fingers I'm holding up in the air. If you did the same and asked me, now, I couldn't tell you, unless you allowed me to feel your hand. Then I would know. Last night I felt your head and could tell as well as any person with sight what had happened to you. Do you know?"

"I hurt it," said the boy uncertainly.

"Do you know how?" asked Isaac.

"No. Did I fall? The lady said my clothes were wet and so they gave me a clean shirt and I'm to keep it for myself."

"Which lady?"

"The dark-haired one."

"She is my daughter, and her name is Raquel. The other lady is Romeu's daughter, and her name is Regina. This is Romeu's house. Do you not know anyone in the city?"

"I met Yusuf," he said. "I know him."

"Everyone knows Yusuf," said Raquel.

"What happened to me?"

"Someone hit you on the head, probably with a cudgel. Then he dropped you in the river."

"Papa," said Raquel. "That is too cruel."

"Why did he hit me?" asked the boy. "Do I know him?"

"I don't think you do," said Isaac. "But you saw him once, one very dark, wet night, under the bridge."

"The day I came to Girona," said the boy, sounding suddenly tired. "I was looking for my uncle. I crept under there to keep out of the rain, although it was very muddy. He hit me and cursed me, and took out a knife. Then he left and ran away."

"Ran? Like a boy?"

"Yes. He was a boy—older than I am, maybe even older than Yusuf, but not a man."

"But you couldn't see where he went."

"But I could," he said sleepily. "In the lightning. He was running up the road to Figueres. I thought it was funny because I'd just come down the road from Figueres, and I knew there wasn't nothing there . . ."

"He's asleep, Papa."

"Poor lad, he worked very hard for us. He's a courageous soul."

"Will he get better?"

"I don't know, but the chances are good. Did you notice his eyes? Were they strange?"

"One pupil is slightly larger than the other," said Raquel.

"Make sure that he is not disturbed," said Isaac. "Is the room darkened?"

"Yes, Papa," said Raquel.

"We must look after him. Even if he can tell us nothing more than that, he deserves our help."

Isaac made his way down the steep, narrow stairs of Romeu's house, from the attic room where the boy slept, down past the two rooms on the next floor, and then the kitchen and Romeu's chamber, and finally to the ground floor, which was taken up by Romeu's spacious workroom. "Romeu," he called out softly, "are you there?" It was an unnecessary question, for he had been able to hear him working all the time that he had been descending the stairs.

"I am, Master Isaac," he said. "What can I do for you?"

"I have just come from the boy's bedside. He awoke for a short time and told us something of great interest."

"He did? When Regina came down she said that he had known nothing."

"She has not had the opportunity to talk to Mistress Pons today, as I did," said Isaac. "Mistress Pons pointed out to me that if you want to find someone whose existence you can only postulate from his deeds—you can only guess at from what he does—" added Isaac tactfully, "you must track back like a hunter after his prey until you find his lair."

"I'm no hunter," said Romeu, "but I admit in all secrecy that as a boy I snared a few rabbits, and so I understand the method. But what has this to do with our problem?"

"The lad upstairs—whose name is Tomas—saw the messenger boy running up the road to Figueres. I think that he may have a safe place to hide—or possibly, to live—at a house or farm on that road."

"He saw him after he was struck on the head?"

"No—he saw him on that rainy night when Master Mordecai was taken some new medicine that could have killed him."

"And you want me to find him?"

"Someone must."

"And if I go to find him, Master Isaac, I will be leaving the lad and my daughter alone in the house, unprotected. I cannot do it. I hesitate to go out in the blaze of noon right now."

"Yusuf and my daughter will be here," said Isaac, "but before you answer, I see that it cannot be done this way. I will solve this problem some other way."

⊰⊱ ⊱⊰

ISAAC walked to the square beside the cathedral, ignoring the main entrance to the Bishop's palace, and went around to the guards' quarters. In a few moments he was talking to Domingo, the sergeant of the guards, someone who, he felt, could be trusted to the utmost. "Sergeant Domingo," he said, leaning his staff against the wall, "I am here to talk of something that you may not know about, and to ask for your assistance, if it is possible for you to give it."

"Then why do you not sit down in comfort, Master Isaac," said the sergeant. "And take a cup of wine with me, and tell me what I do not know."

"The night that Master Narcís Bellfont died, a messenger brought a vial of pain medication, telling the housemaid that it had been sent by young Lucà. He took it, and it killed him, I believe."

"All that I know."

"I thought you would," said Isaac. "For reasons of my own, I asked Master Mordecai to feign illness and call in young Lucà. After being treated in a perfectly normal fashion, receiving two vials of relatively harmless medication—which, by the way, he didn't drink, giving them to me instead so that I could test them—he was sent, by messenger, a vial of a very efficacious poison. Had he taken it, he would have suffered many unpleasant effects— a confusion of mind, great heat and dryness of the mouth and skin, unbearable pain, convulsions, and finally death."

"Like one Joan Cristià," said the sergeant.

"Yes, very like Joan Cristià," said Isaac. "So much so, that one might almost believe that the concoction had been mixed by the same cunning hand."

"Whose hand?" asked Domingo. "Lucà's?"

"I do not believe his hand is that cunning," said Isaac. "Not with plants. But there is one person who would know the author of these poisons."

"The messenger."

"Either he is the man himself, or he knows who he is," said Isaac thoughtfully. "The difficulty is that no one has seen him clearly or heard him speak with his natural voice except for one."

"The poisoner?"

"No. A harmless lad of perhaps nine years, named Tomas, who came here from the north the day of the storm. That was the night when Mordecai received his vial of poison. The messenger was clad in a warm, woolen cloak and hood, as he had been before—a cloak and hood much too fine for such a lowly lad. During the worst of the rain, he and Tomas clashed over a bit of shelter under the north bridge on the far side of the river. Cloak and hood ran off in the direction of Figueres. I think he might live somewhere in that direction at the moment. Tomas saw him quite clearly in the light from a bolt of lightning."

"Why has he not been brought forward then?" asked Domingo.

"Because the day that we found out about his existence," said Isaac, "someone cudgeled him on the head and threw him into the river to finish him off. Fortunately, he landed with his head on a sandbar and his face out of the water."

"Where is he now?"

"At Romeu's," said Isaac. "Romeu feels responsible for Lucà. After all, he is his lodger."

"And, if he survives, could well be his son-in-law, I hear," said the sergeant. "Although there can be no lack of candidates for that position."

"But Mistress Regina does not give her heart away easily," said Isaac. "I hope she has not transferred her affections from one hopeless case to another."

"And you want me, in spite of my orders, and my responsibilities, to desert my post and go off wandering up the road to Figueres, looking for someone in a cloak and hood."

"I do. I suspect he would be someone who has not been here for much more than a month. And he may have a friend in a notary's office."

"I wouldn't do such a mad thing for many men, Master Isaac," said Domingo, "but I owe you a favor or two, it seems to me. I will take worthless Gabriel with me. With his sharp eyes he can see in the darkest nights—although tonight there is a moon. How far away do you think he might be staying?"

"An easy walk away, I would think," said Isaac. "At the most, three or four miles. He seems to come back and forth a great deal."

"Very well. A lad with a thick cloak and a friend in a notary's office. Shouldn't be too difficult," said Domingo, finishing off his wine.

⋇══ ══⋇

THEY had already visited five farmhouses on the road north and were approaching the sixth when Gabriel spoke. Up to this point, he had wisely kept silent, having learned from painful experience that it was the best way to avoid the sergeant's often blistering tongue. "It just happens, sir," he said, "that I know someone here."

"You do?" said the sergeant skeptically. "And who would that be, the lady of the establishment?"

"Oh no, sir," said the guard. "Her maid. And at this time of the evening, she'll be in the kitchen, chatting with the cook. This is when she's free. I don't think it would do us much good to speak to the lady. She is not very—" He stopped, unable to think of a tactful way of explaining what she was like.

"You mean she wouldn't say anything to someone like you or me."

"Meaning no disrespect, sir, but it's possible."

"Then let us go to the kitchen, by all means," said the sergeant.

Gabriel nudged his horse forward onto the narrow road leading to the main entrance of the substantial house. The sergeant was amused to note that the sturdy beast immediately swung over to the right, and onto a path that led around to the back. He broke into a trot and headed straight for the kitchen door.

"He's used to getting a little something here from the

cook," said Gabriel, turning pink, but whether it was from the light of the setting sun or embarrassment, Domingo could not tell.

"Gabriel!" said a pretty girl coming out of the door as the guard dismounted lightly. "And Neron. How are you," she murmured to the horse, who nuzzled her apron. She brought her hand around from behind her back and held it out. On it were two big pieces of carrot. "What brings you here this evening?" she asked. "I thought you had to be on duty?"

"I am," he said rather desperately, glancing behind him.

"Goodness," said the young woman. "I didn't see you, sir," she added, dropping a small curtsey.

"This is Sergeant Domingo," said Gabriel.

"*You're* Sergeant Domingo," she said in a surprised voice.

Domingo dismounted and came forward. "Yes, mistress, and I am human," he said, smiling, "no matter what young Gabriel has told you, not the devil incarnate. And you are Mistress—?"

"Blanca, sir, is my name," she said prettily. "Do come in. It's cool outside, and we're having a little wine and some hot soup."

<hr />

"A newcomer?" said the cook, after checking that the hot dish for the master's supper was simmering as it should by the fire. She pushed a cheese and a knife over to the two men. "How old? Because there's Mistress Alicia's brother. He came to stay with her at the beginning of the winter, but he's something of an invalid and doesn't get out much."

"Someone young and lively," said the sergeant, helping himself to cheese and more of an excellent loaf. "I would guess he is something more than a boy, and not yet a fully grown man. Younger than Gabriel here—I go by the way he was described as running. Like a boy, said the person who noticed him. Yet as tall as a moderate-sized man."

"One of those skinny, lanky creatures," said Blanca scornfully, dismissing him and giving Gabriel a meaningful look. "I haven't noticed one around here."

"But there's that new lad over at the *finca*," said the cook. "Not been there more than three or four weeks, I'd say. Now there's a pretty creature. All angelic smiles and golden curls, with a curling little dark red beard. He's a clerk to the steward. Studied with the brothers, he said, but decided it wasn't the life for him and went off on his own."

"You met him?" said the sergeant casually.

"I saw him," said the cook. "But my sister works there, and she knows him. Very talkative and pleasant, she says. And so quick and clever with his hands. He mended my sister's favorite little necklace that was broken. He comes all the way from Valencia. Can you imagine? Such a long way."

"Not if you're a soldier, mistress," said the sergeant, leaning forward and smiling confidentially at her. "We've been all over, but we always come home if we can." He patted her hand as it lay on the table across from him. "Is there no one else you can think of?" he asked casually. "Because if he's golden-haired and from Valencia, he can't possibly be our lad."

"He's no one's lad," said Blanca, "if you want my opinion. He looks more like a girl with a beard than a man. I wouldn't have him if he came with a bag of gold on his back."

The sergeant grinned at her, and then rose to his feet. He cast a look a great regret at the food still remaining on the table. "Where is this *finca*?" he added. "We can save ourselves a little work by not going there."

━━◆━━ ━━◆━━

"I'M sorry about that, sergeant," said Gabriel miserably as their horses walked down to the main road. "I thought we had something there."

"Oh, we did, lad, we did," said Domingo cheerfully. "We've found him, sure as certain. But the cook's sister sounds fond of the vicious creature, and she'll warn him if we're not careful. Who lives up there now?" he asked. "For I heard that the old family has died out and newcomers have taken it over."

"A prosperous gentleman and his wife, who is sister to Master Jaume, the notary, sir," said Gabriel. "I cannot imagine them to be involved in any evil. Everyone speaks highly of them."

"However did he come to be employed by such a household, I wonder," said the sergeant. "Perhaps through Master Jaume."

"Shall we go over to the *finca* and get him now?" asked Gabriel. They had stopped at the road, and the horses were getting restless.

"Not this evening," said the sergeant decisively. "I think we should return and report to His Excellency."

⁘⸻ ⸻⁘

THE bells for compline were ringing as Jacinta, the kitchen maid, cleared the plates from supper. For once, there had been little conversation for the bells to interrupt. When their clamor ceased, an oppressive silence fell over the dining room. The twins had gone to bed almost with the sun; Beniamin was dozing peacefully in his cradle. Raquel looked at her silent parents and made as if to rise, but changed her mind. No one else moved.

"Was that footsteps outside our gate?" asked Isaac suddenly.

"No, Papa," said Raquel. "I wonder if we should go back and see how everything is at Romeu's house."

"Yusuf will bring word if we are needed," said Isaac. "I prefer to wait here. Perhaps you could read to me, Raquel."

The baby cried out. Judith looked up from whatever waking dream she had fallen into and waited. He cried again. This time she rose and left the room.

"Certainly, Papa," said Raquel. "What would you like me to read to you?"

"In my study are copies of several different manuals on herbs," he said. "They should all be together. I have been straining my memory to place which mixtures are recommended by each of the different schools of learning. Get Ibrahim to help you carry them up here."

"If you wish," said Raquel. It seemed to her that her father knew the proportions, the properties, the dangers, and the uses of hundreds of mixtures already and had little need at the moment to find out more, but anything was better than sitting doing nothing in this tense silence.

RAQUEL had been reading for what seemed like hours, although she had only worked her way through one of the volumes, searching for and reading out the material on some ten or twelve plants. Naomi had come into the room to point out that the mistress had fallen asleep with the baby and what should she do? "Send everyone to bed, Naomi," said Raquel. "I am sitting up with Papa and will take care of anything that arises. You go to bed as well."

She continued reading, wondering when her voice was going to turn too hoarse to carry on. Suddenly her father raised his hand. "Sh," he murmured and turned his head toward the door. "Is that someone walking up to our gate?"

"I don't think so, Papa," said Raquel. "Do you want me to go on?"

"Very well," he said. "Read me what—"

"Papa, now I hear footsteps coming near."

"Excellent," said her father. "It may be the good Sergeant Domingo, whom I sent on a mission on our behalf. Let us go down and find out."

THE bell sounded as Raquel reached the foot of the stairs just behind her father. "I will see who it is," she murmured, then stepped around him and went over to undo the lock and lift to the gate. "Daniel!" she cried out, as she pulled the heavy gate open.

"I am so happy to see you," murmured Daniel as he stepped inside and caught her in a fast embrace. "But I understand that there is some powerful reason that I was to get home as early as possible. What is wrong?"

"Now that you are here, nothing is wrong," said Raquel.

"That is not quite true, my dear," said her father. "I too am delighted at your return, but there are indeed reasons, powerful reasons, why your presence back here was needed as soon as possible."

"Am I too late, then?" he asked. "I rode on as quickly as I could."

"Who did you travel with?" asked Raquel.

"At first, with a courier, carrying letters to Perpignan," said Daniel. "He stopped at a farm with stables just outside the city where he often spends the night. I left the horse with them and walked on alone. It seemed easier than waking up everyone."

"I am glad you did," said Isaac. "You timed your arrival to perfection. Have you been home and been given an opportunity to wash and change clothing?"

"I have not, Master Isaac, and although I would appreciate being able to wash off the dust of travel, I can wait to change until I have heard what you have to say."

"Excellent. You will find water and everything else you need in my study. Raquel, would you get a candle for Daniel? We will be waiting in the sitting room."

When Daniel came in, there was an empty chair by the fire, with a table set beside it. On it Raquel had set out the remains of their supper: a bowl of hearty mutton soup that smelled of herbs and spices; an array of cold meats; bread and olives. "This is splendid," he said. "I hadn't realized how hungry I was until this moment. Now, sir," he said, turning to Isaac, "I had already conjectured while riding back here that you had some reason for needing to know as soon as possible what I discovered. And although I have it in written form somewhere in my bundle, most of it is sitting securely in my head."

"I do indeed most urgently need that information," said Isaac. "Continue your supper, please, for you must be hungry, but between bites, tell me what you discovered about Mordecai's cousin's child."

"The most important thing I discovered is that Faneta's son is dead," said Daniel directly. "As is Faneta herself. They died just before the High Holidays, this last autumn. Neither imposter can possibly be the boy Rubèn."

"Dead? You are sure?"

"Mistress Perla, who is Faneta's mother and Rubèn's grandmother, says that it is so," said Daniel. "And even if they weren't dead, neither one of the men who came here saying that he was Rubèn looked at all like him. Faneta's son was thin, tall, dark of complexion and hair, with green eyes. He did have a friend who could perhaps have been Lucà," continued Daniel.

"I found a boy in the market who had seen them together many times. The friend lived some distance away on the edge of the city, and has been gone from Mallorca for at least a year."

"Where did he go?" asked Isaac.

"He was an apprentice," said Daniel. "As soon as he finished his apprenticeship, he left the city. The landlady at his master's workshop had no idea where he went. According to her, he had told his master—who was ailing—that he would return. But he didn't. I couldn't talk to the master, because she didn't know where he was. Dead, most likely," said Daniel. "I was not able to find him."

"What was his master's trade?"

"He was a cabinetmaker," said Daniel.

"That is interesting," said Isaac. "Anything else?"

"Well—the boy had another friend who lived in a most disreputable part of town near the tanneries. I don't know what his name was, but my little informant took me there. When I told the woman who lived in the house what I wanted, I was set upon by the neighbors—I wasn't injured," he added, "but it wasn't pleasant," he said, helping himself to some cold meat and bread, and pausing while he ate it. "And that wasn't the first time I was set upon. There seemed to be someone in the City who resented my inquiries."

"It was not that there was trouble in the City?" asked Isaac. "After all, at this time of year . . ."

"There didn't seem to be," said Daniel, cheerfully helping himself to more bread and cold meat. "They seemed to be after me because I was me, not because there was feeling against the community—the first time it happened I was captured and tied up and left in someone's kitchen."

"Captured and tied up?" said Raquel, torn between laughter and fear. "I can't believe it. What happened then? How did you get away?"

"A little girl helped me," said Daniel. "Her name is Benvolguda. They hadn't tied me up very tightly, and she brought me a knife. Then she showed me a hole in the wall where I could crawl through. It wasn't very heroic, I'm afraid. I got very dirty and quite shocked Master Maimó, who is a most elegant gentleman."

"You appear to have had an eventful journey," said Isaac, in his most noncommittal manner.

"It was certainly an interesting one," said Daniel. "Someday we must go there," he added, turning and placing his hand over Raquel's for a moment. "It is a beautiful place. But aside from that, I have brought a packet of letters for Master Mordecai," he said. "I do not know whether they have anything to do with the purpose of my voyage or not, but I suppose I should go over there and deliver them now." He rose with great reluctance.

"I think that would be an excellent idea," said Isaac briskly. "Raquel, perhaps you would be kind enough to show Daniel out. I must return to my study." He led the way down the corridor and the stairs to the courtyard. "I beg you to speak softly," he added. "Your mother has fallen asleep with the baby, and I am hoping she might be allowed to sleep until morning, if your little brother permits."

Isaac embraced his daughter, murmuring something softly in her ear, and walked over to the door of his study.

Raquel took Daniel's hand and pulled him over to the bench by the fountain. "Let us sit here a moment before you must leave," she said quietly.

"What did your father say?" asked Daniel.

"He suggested that there was no hurry that he knew of to force you to leave quite so soon, and that he had many things to think out before he could retire to bed. I think he means that if we stay quietly here, he will not interrupt us."

Daniel took her hands in his and brought them to his lips. "Your hands are beautiful in the lantern light," he said, "They are so graceful and strong, and yet when they lie still, they look like warm marble. When you are listening to someone, and set down your work, your hands rest in your lap, or on the table, completely still and relaxed. Did you know that? They never move in meaningless gestures like other woman's hands, and right now they make me realize that it is much too late to disturb Master Mordecai. I shall stay here as long as I can take him his letters early in the morning."

"Do you really think this is what Papa had in mind when he

retired to his study?" asked Raquel, with a tiny well of happy laughter bubbling up in her throat.

"I am sure it is," said Daniel. "He too is made of flesh and blood."

SEVENTEEN

No cal dubtar que sens ulls pot home veure

One can't doubt that without eyes a man can see

Isaac said his evening prayers and prepared himself for the night. Instead of finding his couch, however, he wrapped a large shawl over his shoulders for warmth and sat comfortably upright in his heavy chair.

All his learning and all his instincts told him that if nothing were done to prevent it, tomorrow an innocent would be tried for murder, convicted, and turned over to the city to be hanged the next morning. Daniel's information explained some things, and was interesting in many ways, but it would not save Lucà.

His certainty that the young man was innocent, he argued to himself, must come from somewhere. And therefore somewhere, even without knowing who was the actual culprit, he must possess a fragment of knowledge, a thread of logical proof, that could convince the Bishop's court that Lucà was innocent. Or did his belief come simply from arrogance and from his pity for Romeu and Regina? Did he believe that since he had said that Lucà was innocent, that he must be right, because he was himself and therefore right? He shivered. Only a madman or a divine being could think that, and he hoped—no, he knew—he was neither.

He stared into the fathomless darkness and listened to the

voices registered in his mind. "He spent two days recreating a potion he had seen his master make." That was Regina's soft voice. "He told me all about the herbs he found around Genoa." And that was Yusuf's. "He spoke of his days in Mallorca and Sardinia." That was Romeu. Not Genoa, but Sardinia. Why would he lie about where he had been? Or had he been in both places? What had a journeyman cabinetmaker been doing collecting herbs in Genoa—or Sardinia? And with whom?

Before he could think of a reasonable cause, he heard a knock so soft on the door that it could have been a leafy branch brushing against it. "Yes?" he said quietly.

"Are you awake, lord?"

"Come in."

"Tomas is awake and feeling better," said Yusuf. "His eyes look the way they should, and there is something that he remembers."

"Then we must leave at once. But we will go through the gate this time, Yusuf."

"How do you know that I did not use the gate?"

"Because I did not hear anyone speak to you as you came in, nor did I hear you rouse Ibrahim, nor did I hear the creaking of the gate itself, which could awake the dead when you come in the proper way."

"That is why I don't, lord," he said, in a tone of injured innocence. "I do not wish to disturb those who seem to be in the courtyard, nor to awaken the house. But now I will go and open it, as quietly as I can."

"Not as quietly as you can, Yusuf, but with only sufficient noise to attract Raquel's attention." Isaac picked up his light cloak, threw it over his shoulders, and followed the boy into the courtyard.

"Papa?" said Raquel softly.

"Are you still here, my dear?" asked Isaac. "I must go over to Romeu's house. Is Daniel still with you?"

"I am, Master Isaac," he said.

"Then I have a favor to beg of you. Could you sit with Raquel until I return? If you are chilly, there is a warm cloak in my study that you may borrow. That way the gate can be barred behind us and no one will have to be disturbed when I return."

━━◆━━ ━━◆━━

THE boy was lying in bed, eyes wide open and a piece of bread in his hand. Beside him on a stool was an empty bowl with traces of soup in it. "Physician," he said, "I can remember so many things now."

"Excellent," said Isaac. "I am very pleased. And how does your head feel?"

"Sometimes it hurts still," he said, "and sometimes I can't feel it at all."

"Why don't you show me how much you can remember by telling me about yourself?" asked Isaac. "I'm interested in how you came to be here in Girona. You are from Figueres, you said?"

"Oh, no, sir," the boy said. "I just went there because they told me that my uncle, my father's brother, had gone there during the Black Death. But I couldn't find him, or anyone who had heard of him, except one man who said he had only stayed a little while and then gone to Girona. So I came here."

"Where did you come from?"

"Sant Feliu," he said. "We lived by the sea. There was one of those raids and my mother died, I think, but I was hidden and no one saw me. Some people were going to Figueres and they took me with them," he added. "But that was what I remembered, you see, sir?"

"What was that?"

"His voice," said the boy. "He sounded just like my mother when she drank too much and got mad at me. And the words he used, they were the same, just like my mother. For a moment it made me feel sad for home." His voice slowed down as sleepiness began to invade it.

"Why did his voice remind you of your mother?" asked Isaac.

"They come from the same place, didn't they?" said Tomas, yawning.

"Where was that?" asked Isaac.

"Mallorca of course," said Tomas, and fell asleep.

"So the lad has no one," said a deep voice behind Isaac.

"No, Romeu, I don't believe that he does," said Isaac. "Not any longer."

"But you knew he didn't," said Regina, from her stool at the foot of the bed. "Why else would he be sleeping in that old hut by the river?"

"He might have run away," said Romeu. "And if he had, then someone might come after him. He seems a likely lad. Sharp, you know, and clever."

"How can you tell that?" asked Regina.

"He's still alive," said Romeu dryly. "That's how I know."

"I must return home," said Isaac. "I am still hoping to hear tonight from someone who might have useful information. If Tomas awakes before I return, ask him if the boy in the cloak carried a basket. If he did, ask him what shape the basket was. Good night."

"DOES the captain know where you have been, sergeant?" asked Berenguer coldly. "And what you were doing?"

"No, Your Excellency, unfortunately the captain had business elsewhere to attend to, and I was unable to inform him," said the sergeant, his face expressionless. "I set the best of my men to replace me for the hour or two that I was away and went to see if there was any truth in the rumors I had been hearing."

"And was there?"

"We discovered something interesting, Your Excellency. A young man, perhaps seventeen years of age, has been taken on as a clerk to the steward of the large estate just to the west of the Figueres highroad, a mile or two beyond the city. He was hired on the recommendation of Master Jaume, the notary, to whom he had given a letter from someone of his acquaintance in Barcelona."

"That seems a slender line of recommendation," said the Bishop.

"It is indeed, Your Excellency. But as I am sure Your Excellency remembers, many people have difficulty finding well-trained, clever, hardworking young men to assist them these days. They are happy to take on anyone who declares himself to be competent and looks fairly honest."

"I am aware of that, sergeant."

"I spoke to the cook at the farm adjoining the *finca*," said the sergeant. "I asked her, as I had asked everyone this evening, if any newcomers had arrived in the vicinity. She spoke of a lad who said he had studied with the brothers, who was pleasant and talked a great deal, and said that he came from Valencia."

"And you have disturbed me over this?" asked the Bishop.

"No, Your Excellency. But she also said, if I remember the words aright, that he was 'a pretty creature, all angelic smiles and golden curls, and so quick and clever with his hands that he mended my sister's favorite little necklace that was broken.' That made me think of someone with the face of an angel who could steal gold *maravedís* out of a man's purse and replace them with copper pennies without anyone noticing but a sharp-eyed and suspicious innkeeper."

"The angelic-looking youth called something like Rafael," said Berenguer, with a smile—quickly suppressed—suddenly breaking out across his face. "I wonder what this one's name is."

"And who came out of nowhere with a letter from a distant acquaintance of Master Jaume, the notary. I took the liberty of speaking to him before disturbing you, Your Excellency, for if Master Jaume could give the young man a reasonable background, then I had no grounds for my suspicions."

"But he did not?"

"No. The young man came in, presented his letter, and asked if there might be a position available. Then Master Jaume's clerk reminded him that his sister had inquired if anyone were available, since their steward was overwhelmed with work and needed a hardworking junior assistant to take some of the load off his shoulders."

"The *finca* must be doing well," remarked the Bishop. "And I must remember to tell Bernat. Whenever we seek donations to feed or house the poor and sick of the diocese, the mistress raises a pitiful cry of hideous poverty."

"When I asked if the letter could possibly be fraudulent, he considered for a moment and said that he had not written to this business acquaintance at the time, but that he would at once. And would the diocese indemnify him for the cost of sending the letter by messenger?"

"It can go in the diocesan bag," said Berenguer. "We expect the Barcelona courier tomorrow."

"I will let him know, Your Excellency," said the sergeant with an impassive look on his face. He had already pointed this out to Master Jaume. "Then it seems, Master Jaume's clerk walked to the *finca* with the young man and presented him to the mistress."

"What is he calling himself?" asked Berenguer.

"Raimon, Your Excellency."

"Raimon, by all the saints in heaven!" said the Bishop. "I want to speak to that young man. Take a sufficient troop and fetch him."

<hr />

BUT when the sergeant and his six men arrived at the *finca*, their bird had flown.

"I don't know where he can be," said the mistress, looking very alarmed. "He was here for supper, I know that. I do hope he has not come to any harm. He is not one of those rough young men who are accustomed to brawling and fighting."

"Where does he sleep?" asked the sergeant.

"He has a room above the steward's office," she said, pointing across the courtyard to a small wing of the house that formed part of the wall of the courtyard itself. "It is very convenient for him."

When they went over to inspect it, they could see just how convenient it was, for the stairs within the courtyard leading down from the clerk's little chamber ended at a small gate, wide enough for one man to pass through at a time. It had been left closed, but neither barred nor locked, and the bedchamber above was deserted.

An hour-long search by lantern light of the house and the outbuildings revealed nothing at all. It was as if he had never been there.

<hr />

ISAAC rang the bell at the gate once with delicacy; after a pause he heard quick, light footsteps, and then a rather breathless struggle with the bar across the gate. "Raquel?" he said. "Where is Daniel?"

"Sh, Papa," she said, setting the bar up and pulling open the gate. "He's in your study, asleep."

"On my couch?"

"Where else? Oh, Papa, he was so exhausted from all that travel that he could not keep his head upright. I suggested that he might be more comfortable lying on your couch, and since he seemed chilly, I spread your cloak over him. In a minute he was asleep, and has been asleep ever since. I will go and wake him."

"Do not disturb him, my dear; I will sleep in my own bedchamber with your mother. And Raquel, there is something else that I would like to suggest to you. Come over here and sit by the fountain with me."

Raquel listened attentively to the soft voice, nodded a few times to herself, and turned to her father. "Certainly, Papa," she said. "It may be a little difficult, but I will look after everything. It is fortunate that Mama is so taken up with the baby."

"Do not discount your mother's shrewd eye and sharp ear, my dear," said her father, patting her on the knee.

THE servants had hardly rubbed the sleep out of their eyes when Isaac appeared the next morning at Mordecai's gate. The porter could not believe that anyone could be so unfeeling. It was impossible that someone who had been an honored guest of the house on frequent occasions would arrive at such an hour, and then expect to be taken up to the master's bedchamber. He stared at him helplessly for a considerable length of time before coming to the conclusion that he could not simply send him away. He put him in the room where clients were accustomed to wait, and went up to alert his master.

"Well, bring him up here, man," said Mordecai, who was not fond of being dragged from a sound sleep so early. "We have many things to talk about. Put him in the sitting room and have someone bring us refreshments."

"Yes, Master Mordecai," said the porter, feeling aggrieved that his master showed no signs of dismissing the physician at once.

"Isaac, come in. I gather from the reaction of our porter that the hour is early."

"I fear it is early, but I must speak to you before the business of the day begins."

"Have the bells gone for the first hour?" asked Mordecai.

"They have, Mordecai. I would not have awakened you before then unless I had no choice. But the reason I am here——"

"Yes—why are you here? Has something happened?"

"No, except that a courier arrived with a bundle of letters intended for you, and I wished to give them to you."

"That was why you awakened me? Doubtless they are matters of business, Isaac. This is very kind, but you did not need to make such an effort."

"I wasn't sure. They are from your friend Master Maimó."

"From Maimó? Does that mean that Daniel has returned from his mission? I will look at them now in that case," he added, without waiting for a reply. "It won't take long to find out whether they have to do with my inquiries."

"I shall wait with what patience I can command," said Isaac.

Mordecai broke the seal on the oiled silk of the package that Isaac had brought him and took out a bundle of five letters. He examined each one, set three to one side on the table beside him, and broke open the seal of one of the other two. "This is from Maimó himself," he said, with an air of abstraction as his eyes ran quickly over the neatly written contents. "It is largely to do with business other than that which I sent Daniel over for. Perhaps the second letter is of more interest."

As he was breaking open the seal of that one, the housekeeper entered with one of the manservants, who was laden down with an abundance of food and drink. Mordecai sat silent while a breakfast of fruit, bread, a good cheese, a rice and lentil dish with aromatic herbs, and some refreshing mint drink, was laid out on the table. He made sure that his guest had been adequately supplied and sent away the servants who had brought it all in. He waited until the heavy door to his private sitting room closed firmly. "I prefer that the contents of this letter not be a subject of conversation among my servants," he said. "It is from Perla, Ezra's widow. It was written on Thursday, the day before Daniel left to return home. Now that we are alone, I will read it to you."

My Dearest Mordecai,

This letter is being written for me by Arnau G., a letter writer in the City of Mallorca, and sets down each word as I have spoken it.

I have been thinking much in these last few days, since your friend, Daniel ben Mossé, came to visit me to ask questions on your behalf. I fear that, although I did not lie to him, I did mislead him by omitting many things that should have been said. Please forgive me. A mother always tries to protect her child; a grandmother always desires to shield her grandson's good name.

In talking about my poor Rubèn, that sweet boy, I led Daniel to believe that he had no friends, meaning to indicate that he had no friends inside the call. Most unfortunately for all of us, that was not true. He had two friends. One was a Christian, older than he was, whose company he enjoyed; the other was Josep, the son of my laundress Sara. Sara's Josep was clever, poor, and ambitious. It was clear to me that he considered us—me and my family—wealthy beyond belief, and hoped to gain considerable advantage from us.

I have known Sara for most of my life. She was the child of our laundress, who used to bring her to the house on wash days, when I would look after her, play with her, and indulge her for the pleasure of hearing her laugh with delight. She was an enchanting child, with a sweet smile, a pretty face, and hair like spun red gold, tumbling over her head in curls. Children are taken in by appearances, I realize now.

I loved her dearly. Leaving her behind was almost as difficult for me as leaving my beloved city and the sea behind me when I was sent off to be married. When I returned, I inquired after her, half-expecting that she, like so many others, would have died when the plague killed so many of us. I was told that it was not so. She had married and then after a few years had run away to Valencia with a stranger. He had left her, and she had fallen into life on the streets.

I made inquiries after her, sent her passage money home to

Mallorca, and paved the way for her acceptance—in a limited way—back into the community. She returned a few months later with little Josep, then seven. I helped her, of course. She was like a daughter to me—a difficult daughter, but one to whom I owed a mother's care. I employed her, and I found her other employment. I have tried to ignore the signs that from time to time she goes back to her old ways.

In a further effort to help her, I arranged for her son, Josep, to be apprenticed, but after two or three years he ran away from his master. From then on he lived like a wild thing amongst the groups of boys who infest the town. But I believe that Josep has kept in contact with his mother all along, for many people said that they saw our Rubèn, when he should have been in school, running wild down by Sara's house near the seafront and and in other low parts of the City in the company of Sara's son.

I asked Rubèn about this. He confessed that it was true. He said that he had been miserable at school but that he was happy with Josep and Josep's friends. He said that Sara's son had been taken on as an apprentice—how, I do not know—by a master in herbs and medicines, who was teaching him these new skills. They were to leave for Genoa, where such men are highly prized. The herbalist promised Josep fabulous riches from the new skills he was learning. Rubèn deeply envied his friend and wished that he could be apprenticed in a trade that would give him a possibility of rising in the world.

Josep lost his chance to go to Genoa, however. It seems that although he was quick at learning, he was not willing to follow orders. The master quarreled with him and took another young man instead.

Rubèn spent all of last summer with Josep. Days would pass when we scarcely saw him. Faneta and I were distraught with worry. To our great relief, we heard that Josep had left the island. My joy was short-lived, for three days after he left, Faneta and Rubèn fell desperately ill.

Your friend Daniel asked me how they died; I could not bear to speak of it then. I will tell you. They died within an hour of each other, after a day of desperate thirst, agonizing cramps in their limbs, and numbness in their hands and feet. Our physician suspected that a poisonous mushroom had been by accident introduced into a dish of egg and mushroom that they had both eaten, but he was uncertain. In the end, he called it an infectious inflammation of the gut, and nothing more was said. I do not know.

Now that Rubèn is dead, I have no way of knowing anything about either of his friends. I have since then had conversations with Sara about her son and know only that she worries about him falling into the path of danger. But she has also said a few things that make me believe that she still has some way of keeping in contact with him.

I beg you, if you do not need this knowledge, to forget it forever. It would distress me greatly to betray her secrets and mine to no purpose.

"He is dead," said Mordecai. "They were both lying. Neither one of them could possibly be Faneta's child."

"Unless Mistress Perla is lying to protect the boy in some way," said Isaac. "By pretending that he is dead."

"I cannot believe that," said Mordecai. "She is too upright and honest a woman to lie like that." He set the letter down on the table and stared blankly at the window. "The rest of the letter contains some personal messages to me," he added at last, his voice sounding a little uncertain for a moment. "But then there is an odd sort of postscript."

"What is that?" asked Isaac.

"It is in a completely different hand—a neat one, but not that of a professional scribe. It is short. Let me read it to you. 'I have asked my friend, Rubèn's teacher, to finish off this letter for me. When the letter writer had written down my words and read them back to me, he said, with a lack of discretion disturbing in one of his profession, that he had written another letter just the other day for someone he thought I knew. That letter was also to be delivered to Girona, and what a pity it was that they could not have gone in the same package, for then we both could have saved much money. I fear it is Sara of whom he spoke, and that the letter was destined for Josep. Watch out for him, Mordecai. I fear that he is dangerous.'"

"Do you suspect that Sara's son was the young man who first presented himself to you?" asked Isaac. "He could have learned the details of your family's life from Rubèn and from his own mother."

"That cannot be," said Mordecai. "The young man who came to see me could not have been the son of Perla's laundress, who sounds as if she were no more than a whore on the streets of the city there, even though Perla still takes pity on her. He seemed to be so well brought up, almost learned. But there is one thing—if he is Sara's son, he has nothing to do with the poisoned medicines."

"Why is that?"

"Because his body was found a week or so after he disappeared from Sant Feliu."

"But you have already said that you doubted that it was his body," said Isaac. "Many men drown in storms, and a week or so in the sea can wreak many changes in a man's flesh."

"Isaac, Isaac, you can be cruel when you pit your clear mind against mine. I still say that we do not know enough to judge."

"That may well be," said Isaac.

"Can you send me young Daniel as soon as he has breakfasted? I would like to hear what he discovered from his own lips, and to thank him for his efforts. He will not be sorry on his wedding day that he has done me such favors," said Mordecai. "He is a splendid young man. I envy you your prospective son-in-law, Isaac. But do not tell my daughters that."

"I would be delighted," said Isaac, "but he is not here yet. If he was carrying those letters, perhaps he sent them on by a courier when the ship made port, intending to return at a more leisurely pace. Otherwise they came on Thursday by fast galley."

"I find it difficult to believe that Daniel would send the letters on ahead so that he could ride back at his leisure, Isaac," said Mordecai. "And if it is true, I am not sure if I do envy you your son-in-law. Mistress Raquel must be feeling sorely neglected if the joys of the road mean more to him than her lovely smiles."

"At least she knows that he is safely on land again and will be here soon," said Isaac. "If you will excuse me, Mordecai, I must return home."

"I'm afraid that Mistress Perla's letter was more helpful to me than to you, Isaac. I regret it did not contain something that would help young Lucà."

"It may have," said Isaac. "We must see. May I ask you a great favor, Mordecai?"

"Certainly," said his friend. "And what is it?"

"Could you keep to yourself the news that Faneta's son is dead? Just until Daniel gets here and can explain to us exactly what has been happening on the island."

"If you like," said Mordecai. "I cannot see what difference it will make, but I shall do it."

"It will ease my mind," said Isaac.

<hr />

ISAAC hastened back through the *call* to his own house through the quiet of early morning. Here and there a few early rising housewives and busy servant girls were up and bustling about their duties, but most households in the city were just beginning to wake up to the new day.

The physician slowed considerably as he approached the slope to his own gate, to give himself time to make sense of everything he had just heard. "If they both died at the same time," he said softly to himself, "what did they die of? An illness that struck both at once in the same house and left Mistress Perla unaffected? It is possible."

"Master Isaac," said a familiar voice. "There is no need to talk to yourself. His Excellency would be delighted to have a word with you."

"Now, Sergeant Domingo?" asked Isaac, turning quickly in the direction of the voice.

"At this very minute," said the sergeant. "I am sorry that I did not come back last night to speak to you, but I discovered something that was so extraordinarily tantalizing that I carried it back almost at once to His Excellency."

"Can you tell me what it is while we walk to the palace?"

"If you promise to listen to His Excellency's retelling of it as if you had not heard a word of it before."

"That is the least I can do for you, friend. If you will allow me to have one brief word with my daughter, I will hasten to the palace with all the speed I can muster."

"I will wait here," said the sergeant.

Isaac moved rapidly across the courtyard, knocked lightly on the study door and entered. "Raquel?" he whispered. "Are you still here?"

"Oh, Papa," said a groggy voice. "I fell asleep sitting on the floor by the couch. I am so stiff." He heard a rustling of clothing as she struggled to her feet.

"Is Daniel still there?"

"I'm sorry, Papa, but he is," she said. "Nothing has happened," she added quickly. "He has been sleeping so soundly that I could not bear—"

"Don't waste your breath in apologies. I want you to keep him safe and secret in here until my return. Get him some breakfast by all means if I am longer than I expect to be, but let no one—no one at all, not even your mama or Mistress Dolsa—know that he has come back. For his sake and yours, my dear, please do as I ask. I must go now."

"I wish I had known all this yesterday rather than this morning," said Isaac, when the sergeant had finished.

"Why then?" asked the sergeant.

"Because somewhere in all of this, even if you cannot find this Raimon and seize him, there is evidence that might cause Lucà to be spared. As it is, I do not believe it can be done."

"It can be done if His Excellency also believes he might be innocent," said the sergeant. "His Excellency's court does not sit until His Excellency is ready, and it has a way of divining His Excellency's opinions and then deciding that they are very good opinions indeed. Just like His Majesty's court. It is fortunate that they are both, on the whole, just men," said Domingo, in a surprising burst of candor.

"I believe you are right," said Isaac. "You hearten me somewhat."

"I am not sure that this has very much to do with young Lucà's guilt or innocence," said the Bishop, as he finished a summary of the previous night's endeavors, "but it does seem to touch upon them."

"I have another reason for believing that the person we are seeking is this Raimon, Your Excellency," said Isaac, slowly. "And that he is from Mallorca."

"Yes? Are you going to tell us this reason?"

"At once, Your Excellency. The child who was attacked near the bridge came to his senses last night for a short while and remembered one thing about the supposed messenger. He said that the person he grappled with under the bridge sounded like his mother, and used the same words—I took it, Your Excellency, that he meant by that vulgar or irreligious expressions—as she did when she was angry, and he remembered feeling momentarily homesick because of it. His mother was from Mallorca. He also described the thick cloak and hood, and the long, narrow basket slung over his shoulder, that the others had noticed when the poisons were delivered. Each thing by itself is not a great deal, I agree," he said, before anyone could object, "but together they are suggestive."

"But where is he? How did he know that suddenly he had to leave?" asked the Bishop.

"I suspect that is my fault, Your Excellency," said the sergeant. "I went straight from the farmhouse to the notary's and asked Master Jaume any number of questions. He stirred up his assistant, who answered my queries and left again. He could have gone to his bed, or he could have taken a pleasant evening walk to the *finca* to let his friend know that people were asking questions about him."

"How do you know they were friends?" asked Berenguer.

"I don't, Your Excellency," said the sergeant. "But it would explain a great deal."

"It would explain one thing," interrupted Isaac. "I had wondered how Master Lucà could have known that Mistress Magdalena had changed her will in his favor, or that Master Narcís had done the same, or even that Master Mordecai had sent for the notary. I know that rumor flies quickly in this city, but the provisions of wills are not generally known by everyone, unless a man chooses to tell his friends how he has left his possessions. Master Jaume Xavier is famous for being a discreet man—one could even call him stubborn and secretive."

"That is true," said Berenguer and paused. "The person in the best position to know all those things would surely be Master Jaume's clerk. Since he would have copied out all the wills in question."

"And if the two young men were friends," said the sergeant, "this Raimon would be the next most likely to know. Because if Jaume's clerk gossiped over his cups to everyone at the tavern about all the clients who went to visit the notary, their private affairs would now be a matter of public scandal. If Your Excellency would excuse me for a moment, I think I will find out who Master Jaume's clerk's friends are." He stepped out into the hall and could be heard to shout for Gabriel.

"And the clerk would most certainly be unemployed by now," said Berenguer and stopped. "But all this does not convince me that Lucà is innocent. Who else would wish to poison those three people? Who else has a motive for doing so? I have difficulty believing that a man would endanger both his mortal body and his immortal soul by committing a despicable crime for no other reason than to harm someone else," he continued. "Someone whom we do not know that he even knows. And why will Lucà not defend himself?"

"Because we haven't asked him the right questions," said Isaac. "He may know less than we do about much of this. Ask him about Raimon and Joan Cristià."

"The herbalist who died at Cruïlles? That is worth considering," said the Bishop. "Have you had any word of Daniel's return to the city? I am not sure that I can hold the trial back for much longer without questions being asked."

"Who would ask questions, Your Excellency?" asked Isaac in innocent tones.

"Who indeed," said Berenguer, laughing. "But if he does not turn up to be married, Isaac, we shall have to consider this further, and most seriously."

⊹⟫══ ══⟪⊹

ISAAC walked back from the Bishop's palace at a slow pace and in a thoughtful mood. Hiding Daniel from the Bishop's notice was not going to be easy, given the near impossibility of smuggling him out of the city by any orthodox route. Hiding him away from his uncle and aunt would be even more difficult, especially from his Aunt Dolsa, who was fretting about him, and the wedding, and his safety, and Raquel in equal amounts. But hiding him in his own household, away from Judith, would be an awe-inspiring task.

"Don't worry, Papa," Raquel had said with the optimism of youth. "Mama is so wrapped up in Beniamin these days that there are many things she overlooks."

That was not quite true. There were a few things she left to be done by others; there was little she overlooked. But he had contented himself with saying, "Don't underestimate your mother, my dear." One way or another they would keep him from being noticed even by Judith's sharp eyes.

And if keeping Daniel out of the way was one problem, the other was to flush out Raimon, who came and went, apparently to deadly effect, with the speed and silence of a weasel. But perhaps there was one thing that would bring him to the surface.

Isaac turned in at his gate and called for Yusuf.

--+:==== ====:+--

WHEN the market stalls were at their busiest and the streets were filled with housewives, merchants, loungers, apprentices, stray boys, maids, tradesmen stopping for a bite to eat and a cup of wine, Yusuf wandered into the crowd and began to talk. He started at the north end of the city, outside the gates, and by the time he worked his way up the Onyar River to the south end of the city, his little pieces of news had arrived before him. After the fourth person told him the gossip, instead of him having to pass it on, he drifted back into the *call* and Isaac's house.

"It has been done, lord," he said quietly. "By the time everyone sits down to dinner, there won't be a cat or a baby who hasn't heard the news."

"Excellent," said the physician. "Now it is time you returned to your studies."

WORD of the fortune that awaited one of the claimants to the position of son of Mordecai's cousin spread throughout the city like wildfire. Raimon, if that was his name, heard it almost as soon as he slipped inside the north gate and saw an acquaintance. "Don't you wish you were this Rubèn?" asked the acquaintance.

"Why?" he asked. "I work hard enough being me."

"For the money," said the acquaintance.

"What money?" asked Raimon.

"A fortune, as I heard. An absolute fortune. And it was all left to him by his uncle or grandfather or someone like that. Mordecai has it, and he has to give it to him in a week, I think, only he's not sure who he is."

"Where did you hear this?"

"Everyone knows about it. They're going to try that fellow that came into town and pretended to be him, and it came out in the depositions they're taking down now. I think one of the guards or jailers or someone like that heard it and told his wife."

"I never heard of him," said Raimon. "What are they trying him for?"

"Killing some people—patients of his—and then trying to kill Mordecai."

"Look, my friend, I have to deliver some papers for my master, and then why don't we go across the river to a quiet tavern and have a cup of wine? Then you can tell me all about this and all the rest of the gossip. I work so hard I don't get into town very much. I'll meet you over by the meadow in an hour." And they parted, with Raimon walking slowly and rather thoughtfully away from the river.

THE sergeant presented himself to the Bishop as soon as Gabriel had returned with the results of his inquiry. "I sent someone around to each of the taverns, Your Excellency, to try to find out who Master Jaume's clerk spent his free hours with."

"Did he have any success?" asked the Bishop crisply.

"A little. He has never been seen with someone who bears the name Raimon, or who looks like this person, going by the descriptions that we have, Your Excellency."

"That is unfortunate," said Berenguer.

"But he was seen in Mother Benedicta's down by the river once or twice with Lucà. Nowhere else."

"It's the closest tavern to Romeu's house," said the Bishop.

"Yes, Your Excellency, it is. And not one where people usually take much notice of their fellows. Or at least if they do, they don't tell us about it very readily."

"Has this Raimon ever visited Master's Jaume's office?"

"Never after the first time, according to Master Jaume. He does not encourage his clerk to have visitors whether he is working or resting. And he does not acknowledge a friendship with young Raimon."

＋＝＝　＝＝＋

THE next morning, four members of the Bishop's Guard arrived at the house of Romeu the joiner once again.

"What are they doing there this time?" asked the woman who lived across the street.

"Perhaps they're looking for someone else," said her neighbor.

"How many people do you think Romeu can hide in a house that size? Most of it is taken up by his workroom," said the first woman.

"Even his apprentice slept upstairs with the family," said another. "I would never have stood that in my house."

"Do you know what's happening at Romeu's house this morning, Mistress Rebecca?" asked the woman who lived across the street, deferring to the pretty young woman who had stepped outside with her four-year-old son. "Four members of the Guard went in there." They all looked to the newcomer for an answer, for her husband, Nicolas, was a scribe at the cathedral, and she was the daughter of the wise and learned physician Isaac, although as everyone knew, she had been rejected by her family for having married a Christian. The neighbors, however, had often seen the physician visit Mistress Rebecca's house when he was in the neighborhood, even if they didn't speak of it much.

"I expect they are looking for evidence for the trial," said Rebecca, "or they might just be fetching things that he needs. That will be it," she said. "For look—there they go. And they're carrying his things in a bundle. Mistress Regina is going with them, and she's carrying something too—there's been a delay in the trial, and he'll be needing fresh linen and clothes. He's allowed to be clean and neat, you know," she said, with all the conviction of one whose husband was often present during the Bishop's courts. "He hasn't been convicted."

"That's it," said one.

"It's an awfully big bundle just for his clothes," said another.

"Oh, I don't think so," said Rebecca. "When they took him, he was wearing that terrible old tunic he wore when he helped Romeu, and no shirt, I'll be bound. That'll be his good tunic and boots, and a shirt or two."

Everyone nodded and agreed. By the time the guards disappeared from sight, the women were convinced that the nine-year-old boy they had seen carried out of Romeu's house wrapped in a blanket was a long black tunic and a pair of boots.

Carles, Rebecca's son, began to complain of hunger. Rebecca smiled at her neighbors and, sweating profusely with the effort she had just expended, took him back into her house.

＊＝＝ ＝＝＊

ISAAC met the party of six—Tomas, the four guards, and Regina—in the Bishop's palace, where he waited with Raquel. "He should be safe here," said Bernat, who had supervised the arrangements for housing the lad.

"Except that the entire city must know by now where he is," said Berenguer. "You can't carry a child through the streets like that without people noticing."

"It is possible that they did not notice," said Isaac. "I arranged for a slight diversion. It would be much better if the person who struck the boy thought that he had been swept down the river and out to sea."

"What kind of diversion?" asked the Bishop.

"The boy was wrapped in a heavy bedcovering and my daughter Rebecca was posted outside the door. She had express instructions to convince all the onlookers that they were

watching the guards carry a bundle of clothing for Master
Lucà."

"She seemed to be successful, Master Isaac, sir," said one of
the guards. "I carried him over my shoulder like a pack of gear,
but carefully, so as not to hurt his head, and we had no trouble
at all."

PART V

THE TRIAL

EIGHTEEN

una sabor d'agre e dolç amor llança

a taste of bitter and of sweet love throws off

DANIEL awoke to the sounds of a busy household at work. A baby was crying; a voice was sharply scolding someone—a housemaid, perhaps—about work undone. He opened his eyes and blinked. In spite of the apparent activity, the world around him was still engulfed in darkness. He struggled to sit up, became tangled in unfamiliar bedclothes, and froze, panic-stricken for a moment. Nothing made sense, except that there was something familiar about that scolding voice.

"Don't trouble yourself, Mama," said an even more familiar voice. "I'll do it."

The door opened. Sunlight and recollection flooded into the room at the same time. "Raquel," said Daniel, "what am I doing here?"

"Being as quiet as you can," whispered Raquel, opening the heavy shutters and letting fresh air and more light pour in. "I have brought you some breakfast. There's fresh water, and your bundle of linen is over there, on Papa's table. I will be back in a moment. We're cleaning today, and you're not to let anyone know you're here."

"YOU'LL have to ask Papa," said Raquel, when she returned. "I spoke to him for a few moments this morning, when he told me that you were to keep yourself hidden from everyone, even Mama, the twins, and the servants. Including Naomi. Then he rushed off to see the Bishop."

"I find this difficult to believe. Why am I hiding? How long am I to stay hidden?" he asked.

"I'm sure Papa can explain the reason for all this better than I can," she said again, halfway between exasperation and bafflement.

"I cannot stay in your father's study in the dark for an indefinite period of time for no reason," said Daniel. "I shall go mad."

"I shall keep you company," said Raquel. "Don't worry. And you won't be in the dark except at night."

"And how are you going to explain to your mother that you are spending all your time in your father's study?" he asked.

"That's easy. We're cleaning for Passover," she replied. "I promised Mama I would look after this room. I assure you that I am going to find that it is terribly dirty."

IT was not until Friday that Berenguer had free time to concern himself with the details of Lucà's coming trial. "How is the boy?" he asked Isaac.

"He is much better, Your Excellency," said the physician. "He still suffers from the headache from time to time, and is somewhat troubled and much weakened, although I am inclined to believe that the weakness comes largely from a lack of good food while he foraged for himself all that time. He seems cheerful much of the time now, and I suspect that he is becoming restless."

"I shall have him brought here," said the Bishop. "It will be a change for him. And then we shall hear what he has to tell us."

REGINA brought the boy, pushed him gently into the open door, and retreated to wait for him in the corridor. For the occasion, Tomas had been outfitted with a respectable tunic and footwear, along with another clean shirt from some source or other within the extensive world of the cathedral and the Bishop's palace. He looked around him with a mixture of lively interest and awe, and then attempted a bow in the direction of Bernat, whom he mistook for the Bishop.

Berenguer had been standing by the window to observe his entrance. He moved over next to the boy and directed him with a hand on his shoulder into the chair close to his desk. "Let us both sit down, shall we?" he said. "You are Tomas? I am Berenguer, the Bishop. And that person you greeted as you came in is Father Bernat, who will make notes of what you say, because he has a very bad memory, and otherwise would forget the important things you tell us. Master Isaac is here to make sure that we don't work you too hard."

"Yes, sir," said Tomas.

Bernat's scribe, who was sitting unobtrusively on the far side of the Bishop's desk, slipped out of his place and whispered in the boy's ear.

"Yes, Your Excellency," said Tomas.

"You are becoming a polished gentleman already," said Berenguer. "How very quick of you. Now, you told the physician that the man who pushed you out of his way—"

"He hit me, Your Excellency," said Tomas indignantly. "Here, on the arm. I had a bruise from it. And it's still there." He pushed up the sleeve of his tunic to reveal the yellowed skin of an old bruise.

"That's interesting," said Berenguer. "And I think you said that the man who hit you under the bridge reminded you of your mother? Did he sound like a woman?"

"Not exactly," said the boy. "Not like women around here. Not like Regina or Raquel, or the baker's wife who gave me a roll of bread. Twice she did that."

"Then why did she remind you of your mother? Tell me what your mother is like."

"Mostly she's nice," said the boy in a troubled voice. "Then she sings to me, songs she learned in the islands, about the sea and sailors and the winds and the tempests. Sad songs, but pretty. And if you sit on her lap with your ear against her chest you can feel her voice. But that was when I was younger," he added, as if to thrust aside such childish weaknesses.

"Then she has a deep voice," said Berenguer. "Not a high one, like the boys singing in church."

"Not like that," said Tomas, slowly.

"You said that mostly she's nice," said Isaac. "Not all the time, though?"

"No," he said. "She gets cross and angry, especially when she's had too much wine, and then she says terrible things, things like the men from the boats say to each other when they're fighting. Those were the kinds of words that he used, and the voice sounded the same except that he was a different person . . ." His voice trailed away in confusion. "I can't explain it," he said desperately. "It's too hard. But he reminded me of her when she's like that, and I was scared, the way I was scared a few times that she'd take her knife to me, like she did sometimes to those men." Tears stood up in his eyes. "Even though she said she never hurt them much, just enough to make them notice."

"What is he talking about?" asked Berenguer softly.

"I think perhaps it has nothing to do with anything we need to know," replied Isaac just as quietly. "I expect his mother lived among some rough people." He turned back to the boy. "But your mother came from Mallorca," said Isaac. "From the city or out in the country?"

"From the city, I think," said the boy. "My father said he found her by the harbor and brought her home with him as a prize after the battle. But I think he was making a joke."

"I think, Your Excellency, that the boy is becoming weary," said Isaac.

"I would not be surprised," said Berenguer gently. "I just have one more thing to ask of you, Tomas. There should be two men talking to each other out in the corridor. Would you go to the door, which someone will open for you, and listen to them? Then tell me if you recognize either one of them as the man who hit you. Can you do that?"

"Will he see me?"

"No. He won't know you're there," said Berenguer, and he nodded.

The scribe slipped out of his place and opened the door a

crack. Tomas got down from his chair and walked over, looking weary and pale. He stood near the opening and listened.

After a while he turned, looking confused and unhappy. "I think maybe the second man who spoke sounded a little bit like the one under the bridge," he said, "but I'm not sure." Tears started up in his eyes.

"That's all you have to do," said Berenguer. "Mistress Regina will come to fetch you. You have worked hard, Tomas. Thank you. I'm afraid that I must ask you to stay here, in the palace with us, for a little longer. We wouldn't want anything to happen to you."

Bernat went to the door, spoke to someone out in the corridor, and after a brief pause, Regina came into the room.

She looked at Tomas's white face and picked him up like an infant. "I will carry him back," she said accusingly. "He looks very tired."

"Allow me to carry him, mistress," said the scribe, and the three of them left together.

"I'm not sure that we exhausted him to any purpose," said Berenguer. "Do you think he recognized Lucà's voice as that of the man who attacked him?"

"It's difficult to say, Your Excellency," said Bernat cautiously. "He didn't seem certain. I had thought he would be more definite, because it seems to me that the boy has a quick ear, like a musician. I wonder if he can sing," he added thoughtfully.

"You did not consider that to be an identification, Bernat?"

"It seemed very tentative, Your Excellency, although usable."

"By the way," said the Bishop. "How have you explained his presence in the palace?"

"I haven't really had to, in so many words, Your Excellency," said Bernat uneasily. "For some reason, it has got about that he is Your Excellency's nephew, and is ailing and that he was brought here to be treated by Master Isaac."

"A wandering stray? Child, no doubt, of a sailor's whore abandoned by his mother? My nephew?" said Berenguer.

"He doesn't sound like one, Your Excellency," pointed out Bernat. "As I said, he has a quick ear for voices. Another few days and he will sound as if he were raised by the noblest of orders. And what is more important, he is being treated like a little viscount at the moment, and that is what has convinced everyone. I don't think anyone with evil intentions will look for him in one of Your Excellency's guest chambers."

"Which one?"

Bernat told him.

"I should think not," said Berenguer. "The royal princesses have slept in that chamber. This is your doing, Bernat, isn't it? You put him in that chamber and spread the rumor that he was my nephew."

"It may be that something I said was misinterpreted as that," said Bernat diplomatically. "And perhaps I was not as careful to deny the rumor as I could have been."

"Well—he should be safe. Fortunately he doesn't look much like me," Berenguer added cheerfully, "or they'd be lining up at his chamber door to heap little gifts and delicacies on his bed in hopes of currying favor in the diocese." He walked over once more to the window and looked out over the square. "Now, let us see this Lucà. Have him brought in here."

＋‡══ ══‡＋

"TELL us about Raimon," said Berenguer, still standing by the window and looking out.

"Raimon, Your Excellency? I'm afraid I don't understand. I know some people with that name, but I'm not sure which one Your Excellency is referring to."

"Raimon from Mallorca," said Berenguer, "who has an angelic face and fair hair and concocts effective poisons."

"Raimon, Your Excellency?" said Lucà. "And a maker of poisons?" He paused, frowning. "I have known of people who come from my city who are rumored to know how to concoct subtle poisons and their antidotes as well, but none have that name, to my knowledge."

"Then Cristià? Joan Cristià?"

"He is no poisoner, Your Excellency," said Lucà quickly. "Not Joan. No matter what they say. An herbalist, very adept at the art, that is what he is. Some of his concoctions contain small amounts of dangerous poisons, Your Excellency, and he admits that freely, but in the mixtures he makes, and at the dilution that he uses to administer them, the poison heals and strengthens the body instead of destroying it. He is a great artist at what he does."

"What is your connection with him?"

"I met him when I was an apprentice. I admired him greatly and was blinded by his skill, Your Excellency. What he did seemed so important that I wished desperately to be able to do the same, but I think I was too old when I started. I learned a few things from him," he said, "and I traveled with him for a while because he had no assistant or apprentice at the time. I helped him by gathering herbs, trying to learn all their names and their properties. But he was impatient with my slowness, I think, and we fell out. I returned and came here, because one of his acquaintances had spoken of Master Isaac as a great herbalist."

"And why did you claim to be Master Mordecai's kinsman?" asked Isaac.

"I thought I would have a better chance of being acknowledged and welcomed, Master Isaac. I was too clumsy and ignorant to realize what a foolish lie it was."

"When did you return to Catalonia?" asked Bernat suddenly.

"In the spring, father," said Lucà. "Before the war started. I knew there would be a war—"

"You were in Sardinia," said the Bishop.

"Yes, we were, Your Excellency," said Lucà. "In Alghero. Joan Cristià said that we were going to Genoa, but he changed his mind, and we went to Alghero."

"I see. How did you know there would be a war?" asked Berenguer.

"Everyone knew, Your Excellency," said Lucà. "They were making preparations, rumors were flying, and people were taking sides. Joan Cristià said that with all this going on I was more trouble to him than assistance, and so I left."

"How did you get away from the island?" asked Berenguer.

"I found work on a ship to Valencia," he said. "And from there I walked, finding work as I could along the way. I met interesting people, some good, some bad, and much kindness and generosity. It took me near a year to get this far. And look where I am," he added ruefully. "Not that I am complaining,

Your Excellency. God sends such trials to punish us for our misdeeds, even if men mistake the reason for the punishment."

"Then you did not poison Master Narcís Bellfont?"

"No, I did not."

"Nor Mistress Magdalena?"

"No, I did not."

"Nor attempt to poison Master Mordecai?"

"Certainly not, Your Excellency. None of those people. They were all kind to me, and treated me well, like a friend. How could I have harmed any of them? And I swear that the concoction I gave them was one that Joan Cristià taught me for easing severe and cramping pain. He said it was one of the most useful ones he knew, and would make my fortune. Every time I made it, I tried it myself to make sure that it was not too strong. I could not have made a mistake or I would have been the first to die, not the last."

"The boy identified you by your voice," said Berenguer.

"Which boy, Your Excellency?" said Lucà.

"The one by the bridge."

"There are so many boys and they do congregate around the bridges, Your Excellency. It is true that some of them know me, but I don't understand what you mean."

"We'll discuss it later. That is all for now. Your testimony will be presented at your trial, and you will have a chance to say what you wish in your defense or in mitigation of your sentence," said Berenguer with a nod, and Lucà was led away to his place in the Bishop's prison.

Berenguer had scarcely settled down to a stack of documents that needed to be reviewed and signed, when a faint knock on the door interrupted him. "I thought you had issued orders that I was not to be disturbed before dinner, Bernat," he said in a dangerous voice.

"I did, Your Excellency," said the secretary.

"Then what is that?"

"One moment, Your Excellency. I will deal with it." Bernat opened the door and said in his flattest voice—the one that accepted no arguments—"His Excellency is not to be disturbed."

"I know he's there, and I must see him." The door opened wide, and Regina rushed past the astonished Franciscan. "Your Excellency, I must speak to you for just a moment."

"Mistress Regina!" said Berenguer, astonished and alarmed-sounding. "Is the boy worse?"

"No, the boy is fine. Very pleased to have spoken to such an important person as yourself, Your Excellency. But can you tell me if Lucà said anything that could help . . ." Her voice trailed off on the edge of tears. She swallowed. "It is so important to my father. He has come to feel for him almost as if he were his son, and these have been difficult times for him."

"I'm afraid he didn't, Mistress Regina. Although he still maintains that he had nothing to do with those deaths, curiously enough he seems to have given up and to embrace his fate."

"Will you allow me to see him? I am sure there is much that he could tell you if he thought it would help. He is not used to speaking about himself."

HIS Excellency's prison was a section of the lower floor of the palace, near the kitchens and other offices, different mainly in that it had a stout door with a lock between it and the rest of the building. It was not in general crowded; its prisoners over the years had been a motley collection of erring priests, lay persons who had had the bad judgment to commit their crimes on the Church's property, and a few souls whose crimes had crossed over the boundary between the Jewish community's courts and the Christian community's courts, for the Jews tried and punished their own malefactors, as did the Christians.

But wherever they came from, the guests in the Bishop's prison were generally only there for a day or so, awaiting trial. Lucà was therefore something of an exception. Regina had rather expected to find him in shackles, and was surprised to see him seated at a table with the jailer, with a basket between them, covered with a cloth, both of which she knew came from her own kitchen.

"Mistress Regina," said Lucà, reddening as he jumped to his feet. "I had hardly expected to see you here."

"His Excellency has given me permission to come and see you," she said nervously, with a glance at the amiable-looking jailer.

"It is indeed too early for us to dine," said the jailer, rising to his feet as well. "Good day, Mistress Regina. I shall go in search of something to add to the bounty that your father has brought. You will be more comfortable here, I think," he added, "if you wish to visit for a while."

Regina held her breath until she heard the clang of the lock turning over. "I had to come to see you," she said.

"Please, sit down," said Lucà. "I don't know why you felt you had to. As you can see, thanks to your father, I lack for nothing material, and the good man who keeps this prison most kindly keeps me company."

"Why will you not save yourself?" asked Regina. "Why will you sit here, saying nothing, doing nothing except waiting until they hang you?" Tears welled up in her eyes and spilled over. Fiercely, she mopped them up with a kerchief and looked at him, silently demanding an answer.

"Regina, please, don't cry," he said. "I cannot bear it."

"Then talk to me," she said. "Explain to me why you are throwing yourself into the hands of the hangman."

"I'm not." The words burst out of him. "I don't know how to explain myself or defend myself. I haven't done these things, even though it looks as if no one else could have. Mistress Regina, I swear to you, I couldn't have done these things. I don't know how, but how can I prove that? At least while I am here, in prison, no more people have died. Is that not a good thing? And when they hang me—" He stopped. "I know that they will hang me, even though good men like Romeu and Master Isaac are trying to help me, but when they do, perhaps no more will die. At least I will have done that."

"I don't understand it," said Regina. "I don't understand what happened. I don't understand you. Do you want to die here, like this?"

"Mistress Regina, I have done many wrong things in my life—lies, betrayals, cruel acts. I have never betrayed anyone here, I swear, and from the first day I came into this city I found I had lost any taste or skill I had for lying. I have told the truth or been silent. But I have thought much about what was happening to me, and I realize that I am being punished. Clearly the punishment must be just, since God allows it to happen. What else can I think? Now you know. I never wanted to say that to you, because your good opinion meant something to me and to tell you these things and to have you despise me——" He drew in a gasping breath. "To have you despise me is like having a red-hot sword piercing my gut." He stood up and turned away from her, leaning his hand on the cool stone wall. "I had hoped that I could go to my grave having you feel a little sorrow at my passing, and some indignation that an innocent had been wronged. The thought soothed me, but it, too, was a lie to comfort me. It was good that you came today. Good-bye, Mistress."

"You are rather hasty in bidding me farewell, Lucà," said Regina. "I have not decided to go, and without the jailer's return, it seems to me that I cannot leave. The door is locked."

"I am sorry," he said. "I will return to my own cell."

"This door is locked as well," said Regina, "and so you must continue our conversation. You have no choice."

"How can you bear to talk to such a one as I am?" he asked.

"Lucà, for a clever, skilled man, you sometimes seem to lack much comprehension of the world."

"Why do you say that?"

"Why do you say that I despise you? I do not, and never did. I knew you were no expert in herbs—my grandmother concocted more efficacious remedies than you ever did. But you never said you were, you know. Other people said it, and because you wanted to be an herbalist—for some reason that I cannot tell—you let them believe it. But you made people feel better with your two remedies and your kindly nature."

"That is no excuse," he said.

"I am judge now, Lucà, and I say it was not wrong. Now listen to me. Many people tell terrible, wicked lies from time to time, and are still loved and admired by their families and friends. We all betray people from time to time. Whom have you betrayed? Your country? Your king? Tell me what you have done, and I will tell you if you are wicked, and I swear I will keep silent if it was a grave crime. Tell me, by all that's holy, what have you done?"

"You are no priest that I must pour out the poison in my soul to you," he said.

"No. I am a healer, sent to draw the poison out and heal you."

"What is the difference?"

"Don't argue. Tell me."

He pulled his chair closer to hers, sat down, and low-voiced, began to talk.

+‡ ‡+

SOME half hour later, Lucà looked up at Regina for the first time. "I can think of nothing more," he said, and was surprised to notice a smile trembling on her lips, although her eyes were still suspiciously wet with tears.

"That is it? Nothing more than that?" She stood up and walked once around the office, listening to the sounds from the other side of a wooden wall. She came back to him, took him by the hands, and pulled him to his feet. "If that is so," she said very softly, "then every man in the square and every woman in the market should be hanged before nightfall. You have been unkind and thoughtless, but so have all of us. Lucà, you are so good, and so foolish—either that, or I am the stupidest woman in creation."

"Why do you say that?"

"For I love you, Lucà, and if I have to rescue you from the gallows themselves, then I will do it."

When the jailer returned, he walked into the room next to his office, on the palace offices side of the locked door. "Hola, Pere," he said to the man working there on a set of account books. "Just coming in to check on things." He stepped up to wall and applied his eye to a small knothole.

"They're both still there," said Pere, "I can hear their voices."

"I think," said the jailer, "that under the circumstances, I will give them a few minutes more. He's a nice lad."

+‡ ‡+

IT had been Wednesday morning when Daniel awoke to find himself in the physician's study; on Sunday, he was still in the house, exercising surreptitiously in the early morning or after the household went to bed, eating food that Raquel brought in to him at odd hours of the day and night, and spending many hours in low-voiced conversation with his future father-in-law.

"I have an account set down," said Daniel, "that I worked on every day, so that I would not forget details that might be important. I'm afraid that most of it is very trivial, but if you wish, I will go over it and see what else I can find in it."

"That is excellent," said Isaac. "But what I would like you to do is read it to me, day by day."

"Where would you like me to start?"

"In Mallorca," said Isaac. "I think we can pass over your shipboard experiences for the moment."

And so he read, and in many cases reread, until his voice began to get hoarse from the exercise. Raquel darted in and out, watching for people in the courtyard, warning of her mother's impending approach, carrying food and drink, and carrying away bowls and cups and jugs.

Isaac paid little attention to matters that had appeared paramount to Daniel: Mistress Perla, Sara and the attack on his person, the woman down by the tanneries who took his inquiries so ill. On the other hand, he seemed fascinated by details that Daniel had neglected to say much about: the schoolmaster, the cabinetmaker's landlady, the woman and the soldier on the ramparts as they were leaving. "Why did you not mention them before?" he asked when Daniel finally read that passage, with all its fanciful description.

"Because they had nothing to do with anything I had been sent to inquire into."

"Nonetheless, they are interesting in their way," said Isaac. And so the probing of Daniel's experience went on.

◄►═══ ═══◄►

FOR five days, while everyone in the physician's house except the master and his infant son were involved in making the house ready for Passover—sweeping, scrubbing, cooking, cleaning, shaking, and airing—Daniel hid in the physician's study. At last, as afternoon shaded into evening, everyone put on their freshly laundered best garments and gathered for the Passover Seder. Ephraim and Dolsa, even though they were worried and saddened by Daniel's failure to return, joined the physician's family as they had planned before the Mallorca trip had been proposed. The board was laid with the most beautiful linen the house possessed, dishes had been set out, and everyone was prepared to take his place, from the mistress and her guests down to the kitchen lad, when the moment came. Judith cast her sharp eye over the arrangements.

"Jacinta," she said, "we will need an extra place."

"But mistress," said Jacinta indignantly, "I have set the extra place."

"Set another, Jacinta. And Raquel, I think that before I light the candles you might fetch Daniel. It is inhospitable to make him sit alone in your father's study during the festivities."

"Daniel!" said Dolsa. "When did he return?"

"You knew," said Raquel. "Yusuf, go and get him, please. How did you know?"

"My dear, you might be able to hide an extra spoon in this house and I won't notice it—"

"I don't believe that," said Jacinta to the kitchen lad, who giggled.

"But to hide a full-grown man in your father's study and think that I would not notice him—you do me an injustice. Ah, Daniel. I am pleased to see you. I have already seen you, of course, but we haven't had a chance to talk. Let us wait until later, and then we can speak as freely as we wish."

⊹⊱──⊰⊹

HALFWAY through the splendid supper—the best the household could create, through the combined efforts of Naomi, Judith, Jacinta, and Raquel, with the help of the kitchen lad—there was one of those brief lulls that strikes any festive meal. "Now, Isaac," said Judith, "while everyone is present, tell me why you and Raquel found it so necessary to hide Daniel that you tried to keep the news of his return from me and, what is worse, from Dolsa and Ephraim."

Isaac raised his head and turned toward his wife. "You are right. The blame falls on my head, and I am sorry for the suffering it caused," he said. "But I had powerful reasons. The most important was that Daniel was the only person who knew certain truths concerning the deaths of Narcís Bellfont and another man, not from this city, and concerning the attempt upon Mordecai's life. There is someone in this city who would dearly like Daniel to fail to return."

"Who is this person?" asked Ephraim.

"I do not know," said Isaac. "And that is why he is so dangerous. He is no one in this room, that I do know. By a most fortunate stroke of luck, Daniel returned to the city by the south gate in the most unobtrusive manner possible, and passed by our gate first on his way to yours, Mistress Dolsa."

"And he stopped to tell Mistress Raquel that he was back," said Mistress Dolsa. "I would have expected him to do so," she added.

"We invited him in for a little while," said Isaac. "But when he told me, in all innocence of its importance, what it was he knew, I decided that he was in danger of his life, and resolved on keeping him hidden. The fewer people who knew the secret, the more ordinary I thought everyone's behavior would be, and so I kept it a secret with only those who had seen him as he entered knowing that he was here. I reckoned without my Judith's powers of observation. But now that we all know, I can only beg everyone to behave as if he did not exist once you leave this room."

"Before I promise to do that, what were your other reasons?" asked Judith.

"The next most important, I'm afraid, was that I extracted a promise from the Bishop that he would not hold Lucà's trial until Daniel were back and able to testify."

"But he is back, Isaac," said Judith.

"True enough, but he is unable to testify."

"And why not?" asked his wife. "He looks perfectly well to me."

"Because I will not permit him to leave this house," said Isaac, and returned to his plate.

✦━━ ━━✦

"YOUR Excellency, I have received word from my prospective son-in-law, Daniel. He is in Barcelona. He fell ill with a fever, but is recovered—"

"Travel is perilous in more than one sense, Master Isaac,"

said the Bishop. "It has been my experience that it leads to fevers and other disorders of every kind."

"That is very true, Your Excellency. But as Your Excellency is no doubt aware, the feast of the Passover ends in four days, at sundown on Monday. He is spending this time with his acquaintances in Barcelona and will set out on Tuesday morning to return home, with, he says, all the documents and materials that His Excellency requires. He hopes to be in the city before nightfall.

"That is good news," said Berenguer. "For you and for the diocese. This trial—that should have been held a week ago and is even now shamefully late—will take place. I am pleased that young Daniel is well and able to travel. Let me know as soon as he arrives."

"Certainly, Your Excellency."

NINETEEN

Tant és subtils qu'om non la pot vezer

So subtle it is that one cannot see it

IT was Saturday afternoon and the second day of May. Almost the entire city had fallen into a state of blissful indolence. Work was finished, the sun was shining, the breezes were light, and the meadows were filled with flowers.

On the grassy, fragrant slopes, a few young couples sat in the warm sun with wary eyes out for suspicious mothers and angry fathers. Here and there women watched their children play and men strolled along the paths deep in conversation. But if you wanted to chat without your conversation becoming the news of the marketplace, it was easy to find a comfortable place to sit where nothing larger than a field mouse could eavesdrop on you without being noticed.

It was in one of these favored spots that a young man with tumbling gold curls was talking earnestly to a dark young man with a bad complexion and a nervous manner.

"But the Bishop summoned me to the palace and spent much time asking me questions. I don't know what to do. Master Jaume is very angry, and if it weren't for my father, I would have lost my post already."

"Did he ask about me?"

"Yes. He wanted to know everything about you—where you

were, and where you came from, and how I know you."

"And did you know the answers?"

"How could I, Raimon? You never told me where you were going, and I still don't know," he answered sulkily.

"And now you know why. It was to keep you out of trouble. You know, Pau, I think I've only met one or two men who could lie. I can't. If people ask me a question, either I have to tell them the truth, or I just don't answer it. When people lie, they say too much, and they speak too quickly, and they look at you too sincerely. Anyone who's looking for it knows right away. So anything that I knew would be dangerous or difficult for you to know—like the place where I live when things need time to settle themselves a little—anything like that, I haven't told you."

"I don't know how you know so much," said Pau. "How do you find these things out?"

"I watch people," said Raimon. "I was quiet when I was little, and afraid of strangers, so I watched people very carefully. That's how you learn. And then I met some very clever men who told me things like that about lying that I just told you. And I listened."

"But the Bishop thinks I'm lying, and that's what he's told Master Jaume," said Pau.

"Listen to me, Pau. You won't need that post when I come into my money. You know that."

"But why should Master Mordecai give you that fortune? Isn't it supposed to go to his nephew or cousin?"

"Well, yes, it is. But it's a bit complicated. I can't really give you all the details, because it involves another person—the one who's supposed to collect the money. Rubèn. That cousin you were talking about."

"Why would Mordecai's cousin give you the money?" asked Pau stubbornly. "What reason could he have? I mean, it's not natural, is it, just to give away a lot of money like that."

"No, it's not like that at all," said Raimon. "It was a simple ordinary business transaction. He was desperate for money, and knew he was getting this soon, and so I lent it to him. He'll be paying it back any day now, believe me. We've been in touch, and he lives not far from here right now."

"Where did you get that much money?" asked Pau.

"I told you. My parents died," he said.

"When is Mordecai going to pay your friend? I have to know," said Pau.

"When I spoke to him last, he said it would be best to wait until the trial of this false Rubèn was over. Is it?"

"Not yet," said Pau, now sunk in gloom. "I was told that they were waiting for Ephraim's nephew Daniel to return. It seems he's been in Mallorca. They say he made some interesting discoveries while he was there."

"Mallorca? That's a fair distance. When does he return?"

"Monday, I heard," said Pau. "But two of the guards who were drinking at Rodrigue's tavern said it won't be Monday—more likely Tuesday. They were complaining that they'd been sent all over the place looking for witnesses, when all they have to do is wait until Daniel comes back. Then the other witnesses won't be needed. They could have saved themselves a lot of bother."

"I wonder who this Daniel is traveling with," said Raimon idly. "He hates traveling alone—my friend went with him to Sant Feliu de Guíxols last fall to keep him company."

"Don't know," said Pau. "He was supposed to come back with Mordecai's daughter and son-in-law, but didn't. I suppose this time he's coming alone."

⊹═══ ═══⊹

"EVERYTHING is arranged," said Isaac. "His Excellency has given permission, and the captain has organized it. The guard who looks most like you will be dressed in one of your old tunics and cloaks, supplied by your Aunt Dolsa. He will ride slowly into the city along the Barcelona road. There will be a troop far enough behind to hear but not be seen if or when the guard is attacked."

"What if the man you hope to trap knows me?"

"How could he?" said Isaac. "Unless I am very wrong, he arrived by ship from Sardinia in October. His companion, Joan Cristià, left him in Palamós before coming to Cruïlles to die. He seems to have come to Girona after you left for Mallorca."

"Let us hope, Master Isaac," said Daniel soberly, "that you are not wrong."

+‡=== ===‡+

THE bells had rung for compline before the captain of the Bishop's Guard reported back to Berenguer.

"What success did you have?" asked the Bishop.

"None whatsoever, Your Excellency," said the captain. "Our man rode in at the time agreed. Our sharpest-eyed men had been so placed that they could have seen a leaf fluttering unexpectedly anywhere on or off the road. They did this twice, after nones and after vespers, with the same result. It is now pitch dark, Your Excellency, with no hope of a moon for hours. No one could expect a wayfarer to continue home under these conditions. I called them off. It was a good idea, Your Excellency, but I do not think our man, if he exists, thought of it."

"Perhaps not," said Berenguer.

"Do you wish me to continue tomorrow?"

The Bishop waited for a moment and then turned to the captain and smiled. "If it was worth trying today, it would seem foolish to abandon it tomorrow. Start at terce—that will give him time to settle into his hiding place, wherever that is."

+‡=== ===‡+

ISAAC returned late that evening. Judith had been coaxed into going to bed soon after the children, but Yusuf, Daniel, and Raquel were waiting for him in the courtyard. "Did they take him, Master Isaac?" asked Daniel.

"I'm afraid not," said Isaac. "They saw no sign of him. Either he was not there at all, or their false Daniel was not enough to lure him out of his hiding place. They will try again tomorrow morning. Now I am weary and will go to my bed, I think. Is your mother asleep, Raquel?"

"I believe so, Papa," said his daughter.

"Then I bid you all good night," he said, and went over to his study.

Daniel had now been assigned a sleeping chamber of his own in the house, but he seemed reluctant to climb up to it this particular evening. "I am restless," he said to Raquel. "I think I will walk around down here in the cool air before going to my bed. Good night, my dearest," he murmured.

But instead of strolling about in the courtyard, as soon as he was alone, he walked quickly over to the room next to Isaac's study, which had been given over to Yusuf when he first came to the physician's house. He knocked softly. "Yusuf," he called, coming into the room, "are you awake?"

"No," said Yusuf.

"Then wake up," he said, closing the door.

"What is it?" asked Yusuf.

"I need to borrow your mare tomorrow morning, very early."

"Why?"

And Daniel explained.

BEFORE sunrise, Yusuf was at the Bishop's stables, where his mare lived in luxury under the watchful eye of His Excellency's head groom. That august official and his stable boys were accustomed to Yusuf appearing before the sun to exercise his mare and practice his equestrian skills. This particular morning, the routine did not change as far as the stable boy on duty was concerned, except that Yusuf was perhaps a little earlier than usual. He rode, as he always did, out the north gate, and disappeared.

This time, however, he headed east, and by means of a complicated set of narrow, unkempt roads and paths, made a half circuit of the city until he was directly south of the south gate, about a mile or so away from the walls. There he turned in at a path that led to a farmhouse with a large stable block behind it. Daniel walked out of the stable leading a small, neat horse. He mounted and rode down the path to where Yusuf waited.

"I brought us some breakfast," said Yusuf. "It sounded to me as if we might need it. Did anyone notice you leaving?"

"I don't believe so," said Daniel. "The small breach in the walls is still there, and there seemed to be no one awake to notice my taking advantage of it. The mistress here said that the second path on the left would lead us in the right direction. The one with a dead tree halfway up the slope. From it, we will find other paths to take us around to join the main road farther up."

As they turned up the path to the left, Daniel looked back at his traveling companion. "There was no need for you to come with me," he said. "I could have gone by myself, either on your horse or this one."

"I wasn't going to let someone try to kill you while you were riding my horse," said Yusuf indignantly. "I think we should turn up there, around the hill."

"There's someone else out this early," said Daniel. "I can hear hoofbeats behind us on the other side of the river."

"Hurry that beast up, then," said the boy. "We don't want to announce our presence to the whole world."

"I suppose not," said Daniel, and stirred his horse to a canter.

THE Bishop's court was due to start at the hour of terce. A few less important cases were to be heard first, and the clerk had calculated that he would not have to have witnesses gathered together for Lucà's trial for at least an hour after that.

The last of the short cases, a contentious but uncomplicated property dispute, was heard and decided upon to the dissatisfaction of both parties. His Excellency leaned forward to summon the clerk. "Has there been any word?" he asked.

"No, Your Excellency," said the clerk, imperturbable as ever. When the Bishop elected to hold a court, the clerk's mission was to organize the cases and have them heard as efficiently as possible. The presence or absence of witnesses, if he had not had the duty of producing them, was no concern of his.

"Then we must proceed," said Berenguer, and the bustle attendant on the new case was set into motion.

THE first statement from a witness speaking to the accusation had been taken from Master Jaume Xavier, the notary. The clerk read it in a flat and unemotional voice to the three judges, two men learned in canon and civil law and the Bishop. When the clerk came to Mistress Magdalena's candid explanation of why she felt young Lucà deserved her fifty *sous*, it caused a small ripple of laughter, quickly suppressed, from those who had managed to talk, blandish, or bribe their way into the trial, but the rest of his testimony was listened to with gravity by all present.

"Concerning Master Narcís Bellfont, who died of poisoning on the tenth day of April," read the clerk. "Master Narcís sent for me saying that he wished to change his will. He had been informed that his principal beneficiary, his uncle in holy orders, was near death, and was making this change so that his uncle's order would not benefit, explaining to me that the order had treated the old man badly in recent months. According to his previous will, the order would have received the uncle's portion if the uncle had died before him. This new will was a temporary measure, Master Narcís said, because his recovery from his injuries had progressed well enough that he was considering finding himself a wife. When this event took place he would make another new will, but for the time being he wished his fortune to be divided between the diocese of Girona and Master Lucà.

"Concerning Master Mordecai, upon whose life an attempt was made in exactly the same manner on the evening of the eighteenth day of April. Master Mordecai requested that I visit him, sending a message that when I arrived he would explain the matter to be dealt with. In any event, when I arrived, the attempted poisoning had taken place, and Master Mordecai cancelled the appointment.

"All this I swear & etc., Jaume Xavier, Notary of Girona." The clerk laid the deposition before the judges and sat down.

"What further testimony do we have against this accused person?" asked the first judge, who sat at the Bishop's right hand.

"The statement, duly taken and witnessed on the twentieth day of April, of Master Mordecai ben Aaron, Jew of the diocese, in which he states:" said the clerk, "that on the eleventh day of March, near the hour of compline, the person known as Lucà arrived in the *call* at the house of Master Isaac the physician seeking me, and declaring himself to be the only son of my cousin Faneta, born in Seville. I was extremely suspicious, since this was the second time within five months that a young man had arrived claiming to be my cousin Faneta's only son. The young man declared himself only interested in meeting his kinsfolk, pointed out that he was Christian, since his parents had converted long since, and left after partaking of a glass of wine and a little supper in honor of the physician's newborn son.

"All this I swear & etc., Mordecai ben Aaron, Jew of the Diocese."

The clerk handed the document to the three judges. The third, who sat at the Bishop's left hand, leaned forward. "Is Master Mordecai present in the court?"

"I am, your lordship," said Mordecai, rising to his feet.

"Did this young man, the accused, attempt to gain any benefit from you because of this supposed relationship?" he asked.

"None at all, your lordship," said Mordecai. "I spoke to him a few times after that evening, but only because I summoned him to my house."

"Why was that?"

"I was most anxious to discover if he really was Faneta's son, for if he was, then he was the proper beneficiary of a large sum of money and considerable property that I hold in trust, your lordship. This trust expires quite soon, and it will be my duty to wind it up then."

"Did the accused put forward any further arguments to convince you that he was the heir to this fortune?"

"I soon discovered that he knew nothing of the fortune, your lordship. When I asked him about his background, Lucà said that his parents were dead, and that it was others who had convinced him to come to Girona. He said he didn't really believe that he was any kin to me, and certainly did not expect any assistance from me. He said he had been more interested in meeting the physician, whose reputation he had heard of."

"Very odd," murmured the third judge. "Have you made other attempts to verify these claims?" he asked.

"I have," said Mordecai. "I asked Daniel ben Mossé, who was going over to Mallorca on business, to see what he could find out."

"And has that been of any assistance?"

"I do not know, your lordship," said Mordecai. "As far as I know, Daniel has not returned."

The third judge bent his head toward Berenguer. All three began to confer in low voices and then turned back to the court.

"Is there more testimony to be read concerning the crime?" asked the first judge.

The clerk leaned over the table and murmured a few words.

"By all means, let us hear it," said the first judge.

"This is the sworn statement of Anna, housemaid to Master Narcís Bellfont, duly taken and witnessed on the thirteenth day of April, in which she states:" said the clerk, "that on the night of the ninth of April, a Thursday, there was a knocking on the door after I had locked up the house. When I opened up, there was a messenger who said he had come with a new medication for Master Narcís, sent by Master Lucà, the herbalist. When I turned to get money to pay him, he said he had already been paid and left. He was as tall as a man of average stature and moved quickly, like someone young. I couldn't see his face very well, because it was dark and he was wearing a thick cloak and hood, and so I could not tell who he was.

"All this I swear & etc., Anna, housemaid, of Girona."

"Is Mistress Anna here?" asked Berenguer.

"I am, Your Excellency," said Anna from the back of the room.

"Can you tell me what he was carrying the packet in?"

"In one of those baskets, Your Excellency. The long, narrow ones you carry with a strap on your back. He had to reach way down to get it out."

"Thank you," said the Bishop. "And what did you notice about his speech?"

"He sounded as if he came from somewhere else—somewhere foreign, like," she said. "I thought way out in the country toward the coast, maybe, or something like that."

"Good. Now do we have a statement from Master Mordecai's servant who answered the door?"

"It is not a very extensive one," said the clerk disapprovingly.

"We'll hear it anyway," said the first judge, with a glance at the Bishop, who nodded.

The statement began as expected, and at first, differed little from Anna's. The porter had deposed that it was late, the house was locked up, and the night was hellish dark and wet with heavy rain. "I tried to pay him, but he said he'd been paid and left. I didn't notice what he looked like nor how tall he was, nor nothing else about him because of the rain."

"Is the porter here?" asked Berenguer.

Several people pushed him forward. "He is, Your Excellency," said one of them.

"What did he carry the medicine in?" asked Berenguer casually.

"Just like she said, that other one," said the porter. "One of those skinny baskets you can never get nothing out of once you drop it in."

"On a strap?"

"No other way to carry it," he said. Someone from behind gave him a violent poke in the ribs. "Your Excellency."

"Thank you very much," said Berenguer. At that moment a page boy came into the room and hurried up to the judges. He bowed and murmured a message into the Bishop's ear. Berenguer frowned. He looked at the other two judges, and they all three fell into a huddle.

Those in attendance—especially those who were not important enough to have been provided with a place on a bench—were becoming restless, shuffling their feet, holding muted conversations, and then not-so-muted ones, when finally the first judge looked up coldly and the Bishop glared. Silence fell.

"The court would like to hear a statement from the accused next," said the first judge.

The clerk jumped hastily to his feet. "I have his deposition here," he said. "If you wish me to read it."

The first judge nodded.

"This is the statement of Lucà, son of Gabriel and Catarina, deceased, of Mallorca City, taken the thirtieth day of April, 1355, in which he states:" said the clerk, "that I am innocent of the crimes of poisoning Master Narcís Bellfont and attempting to poison to Master Mordecai, Jew of the diocese, in that I did not concoct any mixture that could have brought about their deaths, nor do I know how such a mixture would be concocted, nor did I send either one of them a noxious compound that had been concocted by any other person. All this I swear & etc., Lucà of Mallorca."

"That is all?" asked the third judge.

"That is all," said the clerk.

"I think that we would like to examine the prisoner," said the first judge.

"WHAT were you planning to do now?" asked Yusuf, after their slow and careful circling had brought them back to the highroad, some miles farther from the city than the point where they had started it. They were lying comfortably on their stomachs on a soft patch of grass, partially concealed from the road by a large rock, waiting for something to happen. The sun was riding above the line of hills to their east. Their horses were grazing peacefully on the far side of a small stand of trees. The warmth of the sun, the scent of meadow flowers, and the hum of bees was lulling them into trance-like state. Yusuf untied a large towel and set out the food he had scooped up from the kitchen before leaving.

"I thought I would wait until the guards came by," said Daniel, helping himself to some bread and cheese. "They're supposed to send the one who looks like me on first, with the others following some distance behind. When he's attacked, they'll ride in to rescue him."

"Then we'll have to hope that the attacker's strategy does not depend upon placing an arrow or two in his back," said Yusuf.

"I believe he'll be wearing armor under that cloak," said Daniel. "It sounds uncomfortably hot. But I have a feeling that the attacker knows that it isn't me and will just let him go by. I'll follow a good distance behind the guards."

"And if you're attacked?"

"I'll yell for help," said Daniel. "They'll just be up ahead." Daniel put his hand on Yusuf's shoulder. "There they come," he whispered, looking to the south. "I can hear them."

"No," whispered Yusuf, "there they come." He pointed in the direction of Girona, where a plume of dust rose from the road. "They're riding along the road right by his hiding place. No wonder he knows about the trick."

"You think he's in his hiding place already?"

"Who else came galloping in this direction so early this morning?"

"Of course," said Daniel. "I should have thought of that. I took him for a courier."

"Coming from over there?" said Yusuf. "Not likely."

They both ducked further down behind the rock as the troop of five guards galloped by on their way south. As soon as the dust of their passage settled again, Yusuf rolled over and sat up. "Why did the guards leave it so late?" he said. "Anyone hurrying from Barcelona arrives in the evening, unless he has to spend the night on the road. Then he sets out again at dawn. Our attacker would know that, surely."

"They don't believe he exists," said Daniel flatly. "If he doesn't exist, then it doesn't matter when they carry out this exercise."

"They've stopped, I think," said Yusuf quietly. "Either that, or they're riding all the way to Barcelona. Now they'll rest, water the horses, and eat something, probably. We can close our eyes until the shade of that tree touches us," he added.

"Stop boasting, Yusuf," said Daniel. "You can't predict what they'll do down to the moment like that."

"Perhaps not," said Yusuf. "But I'll lay a wager that it'll take them some time to come back here. The longer they stay out, the less they have to do today. When that shadow reaches the white stone, I'll go and get the horses." He lay back and closed his eyes.

"You don't believe he exists either, do you?"

"No, I don't. I think he is the invention of a boy who hopes to find a new home and a girl who has fallen in love with a nice smile and a pair of strong shoulders," said Yusuf, his eyes still shut. "For who else had such a good chance to poison all those people?"

"No one has been able to find that messenger boy," protested Daniel.

"The city is filled with boys who would keep a secret for someone for years if you paid them a penny," said Yusuf. "Unless you happened to know they were lying, and gave them a *sou* to tell the truth, with guarantees of more to come."

"But you yourself said that he knew nothing of herbs."

"Either that," said the boy, opening one eye, "or he went to a great deal of trouble to convince me that he knew nothing."

"But Master Isaac and Raquel—they both believe . . ."

"Master Isaac is the first person to say that he makes mistakes, that all of us make mistakes. That is why he is so careful. And it is also why he forgives the errors of others so readily. And as for Raquel, have you asked her what she really believes?"

Daniel fell silent.

"I think it is time I fetched the horses," said Yusuf.

——————

THEY stood in the shade of the small grove with the horses and waited for the false Daniel to ride by. It was not a long vigil. He came by at a canter, looking neither to left nor to right, and soon disappeared over a rise to the north.

"He's going terribly fast for someone who hopes to attract an attack," observed Yusuf.

"I noticed that too. I think I will walk," said Daniel, "and lead the horse. There's a good-sized tree branch up there," he added, taking out his knife and hacking it off, then quickly trimming it of its smaller branches. "This will give me something to fend off our phantom attacker with."

"Just a minute," said Yusuf. He took out a kerchief he wore around his neck, folded it and tied it neatly around the mare's front left fetlock.

"Why did you do that?"

"Anyone seeing you will think that you dismounted because the mare is injured. She'll probably hardly notice it. But maybe, if she isn't used to having something wrapped around her fetlock, she'll walk with a slight limp, which will be even more convincing. If it seems to be bothering her," he added in worried tones, "take it off. I didn't tie it tightly."

"You worry more about the horse than about me," said Daniel.

"You can worry about yourself," said Yusuf, and started to lead his bay mare along a path that ran more or less parallel to the road.

"Where are you going?"

"There's a narrow place up ahead with good cover. That's where I'd be if I were an attacker. I thought I'd wait near there. You might need someone else to help you yell for those guards—they seem to be intent on getting home," said Yusuf, with a grin, and disappeared into the woodland.

The troop rode by, Daniel counted to a hundred, paused, and then counted to fifty more. He picked up the mare's reins and urged her toward the road. She curved her head down to inspect the kerchief and then followed along, stepping gingerly on that left forefoot until she reached the road, when she evidently decided that the cloth was nothing but another useless and unnecessary adornment to her person and walked steadily along.

After a quarter of an hour and two gently rising hills, the scenery changed abruptly. The road seemed to narrow drastically, although Daniel realized that it was the roadside that was different. Rough, rocky terrain, filled with trees and thickly growing bushes, rose steeply on the right-hand side of the road, and more gently on the left. It was dark and cool along there, suddenly, and the sound of the mare's hooves on the road seemed muffled and strange. The breeze that had been blowing, now from the east, now from the northeast, died completely in here, as if someone had closed the shutters in an enormous, tree-filled house.

He clutched his makeshift staff tightly in his right hand and looked back and forth, trying to catch a glimpse of telltale movement. Nothing. Even the birds had fallen silent in this oppressive atmosphere. Every once in a while a rustling sound drew his attention. He whirled around, but saw nothing.

It was the steep, hostile landscape to his right that looked the most ominous, and without meaning to, he found himself drifting over toward the easier ground on the left.

At last, after what seemed an eternity in these woods, the road up ahead brightened. One more rise and he would be back in the sunlight once more. He took a deep breath, laughed at himself for his irrational fears, and looked at his horse, who was peering down at her left forefoot again. "Is that bothering you?" he said softly to her, and she shook her bridle impatiently. Taking that to be a "yes," he brought her to a halt, walked around to her left side, and bent over to undo the kerchief.

The mare neighed in alarm and jerked free of Daniel's loose hold on the reins. In the same instant, something the size of a mountain boulder landed on one of his shoulders and carried him to the ground, winded and temporarily unable to speak or move.

Daniel struggled as best he could against the inexplicable weight sliding over his back and his inability to grab a breath.

Then he realized that the weight was alive and moving purposefully. Suddenly, it grasped him by the hair and yanked his head
up. He uttered a cry of surprise and pain and tried to free his
head from those horrible fingers. Out of the corner of his eye, he
saw the glint of a knife blade and stopped moving.

"Drop that knife onto the ground or I'll run you through."
The words echoed strangely, and the voice that said them seemed
to come from somewhere in the distance, but they were the first
comprehensible things to penetrate Daniel's consciousness. The
grip on his hair relaxed, his head fell down to the rocky, dusty
road surface, and he lost all idea of what was going on.

Next the oppressive weight on his back suddenly disappeared, and he stirred, discovering that he was able both to
breathe and to move. "Pick up that knife, will you, Daniel, and
give me a hand here." That was Yusuf, and he sounded annoyed.

He opened his eyes and jumped up. Yusuf, sword in hand,
was standing over a boy of sixteen or seventeen, with reddish
gold curls, a small dark red beard, and a face streaked with
dust. Yusuf had a booted foot stamped down on the boy's wrist,
and his sword point was pressed hard into the boy's throat.

Daniel scooped up the knife. Then he undid the captive's
tunic sash. "Let's tie his hands," he said.

"Why not just kill him?" asked Yusuf.

"Because we need him for proof that he exists," said Daniel.

A few moments later, they had the boy's arms trussed tightly
behind his back, Daniel had found his mare, who had recovered
from the sight of someone hurtling down from a tree branch almost onto her head, and was searching for something appetiz-
ing by the side of the road, and Yusuf had collected his own
and the other's horses.

"Where did you come from?" asked Daniel. "I kept looking
for you, and never saw a glimpse."

"I grew up learning how to hide," said Yusuf. "And it was a
good thing, too. As soon as he saw you wander over to the left
side of the road, he scrambled up a tree with an overhanging
branch and just waited for you to come by. But you weren't

where he expected you to be when he landed, so I guess it all
went wrong."

"The mare saw him before I did," said Daniel. "She neighed
and I jumped, I think."

TWENTY

Tal só com cell que pensa que morrà

I am as one who thinks that he will die

THERE was a pause while the defendant was sent for and brought to the room where the court was being held. Those in attendance were leaning toward each other, exchanging views, shaking their heads grimly as they considered the arrogance of anyone who tried to defend himself against such strong evidence for such horrifying crimes. Everyone was, in short, wrapped cosily in the cloak of self-righteousness and enjoying themselves hugely.

One small group, however, were not enjoying themselves. Seated over in a corner, away from the spectators, were Tomas, Romeu, and Regina, who had come to speak in Lucà's defense. "Why have we not been allowed to say anything, Papa?" asked Regina.

"Maybe we'll have a moment later," said her father, looking sick with concern. "His Excellency knows how these things are done," he added. "We don't want to do anything we shouldn't."

"His Excellency is not thinking of us or of Lucà," said Regina. "His Excellency is thinking of his dinner." In thus, Regina was partly right, but was doing Berenguer of Cruïlles a great injustice. He was thinking of dinner, but in the context of the case. He was saying to the first judge that if they could not get all the witnesses together before dinner, when the crowd dispersed, there would be serious trouble.

"You mustn't say things like that," said Romeu rather desperately, thoroughly cowed by the atmosphere of the court.

"I must, and I will," said Regina. She rose from the bench where she had been seated and, before anyone could stop her, walked quickly up to the table where the judges were still deep in conversation. "Why have those who would bring evidence in his favor not had depositions taken, Your Excellency?" she asked. "That is not justice, to have only the accusers listened to. I beg you to allow those who would defend him to speak up. It is his right to have justice, is it not?" she asked, her cheeks scarlet with the anger that emboldened her.

"My daughter," said Berenguer, "first we wish to hear from Lucà himself." He dropped his voice to close to a whisper. "But what he has been saying until now never seems to help him, so I would not have him speak last." He raised his voice again to its normal level. "Then, in all justice to him, we will hear those who would speak for him, like yourself. I promise you, my daughter, you will be heard. Now, take your seat, for I see that the prisoner is ready to come in."

Lucà was brought in at that moment. He cast a puzzled and unhappy look at Regina and bowed to the presiding judges.

"Do you wish to add anything to the deposition that you made and signed?" asked the first judge.

"If I knew of something to add," said Lucà, "then I would gladly do so, but I do not."

"That being the case," said the first judge, looking down at the document in front of him, "the court has some questions for you. Whether the answers to these questions help your case or not, we cannot know, but they should reveal more of the truth." Having delivered himself of that homily on the purposes of the law, he nodded to his brother on the bench, the third judge, who was studying the material in front of him with a rather worried air.

The reason for the third judge's concern was that—for some reason that he could not fathom—the case seemed to be of great importance to His Excellency. Having come to this conclusion, he was prepared to give this healer—whatever his background and credentials—as much attention as he would grant to a gentleman or even a nobleman. His only difficulty was that the questions His Excellency wished him to ask seemed to have no direct bearing on the case in front of them. "Could you explain why it was that you came to the city of Girona saying that you were a kinsman of Master Mordecai? I understand that the claim is not true."

"It was not the truth, my lord," said Lucà. "And not only was it wrong, but it was also foolish of me to say it. I did so thinking to obtain more work as an herbalist, because I hoped that Master Mordecai would introduce me to people who might want my services."

"Your motive was not admirable," said the third judge, "but it was understandable. How did you come to pick Master Mordecai, rather than any other man of substance in the city?"

"I knew the lad Rubèn, my lord. The real son of Faneta. He was lonely and unhappy, living in Mallorca, and he used to come to the workshop where I was an apprentice—"

"To an herbalist?" asked the first judge.

"No, my lord," said Lucà, turning scarlet. "To a cabinet-maker."

"I knew it," whispered Romeu to his daughter with satisfaction in his voice.

"And he would tell us—"

"Us?" asked the first judge.

"Yes, my lord, me and my master, and sometimes this other boy who was poor and had nowhere to go would come to visit as well. My master was a very kind sort of man. And Rubèn told us tales of his fabulously rich relations in Girona, and how his childless uncle had sent a letter to his mother because he was searching for an heir. But before leaving his money to his nephew, his uncle wanted to meet him. Rubèn was going to have to go to Girona. He said he didn't want to leave us. But, you see, my lord, I wanted to go away when my apprenticeship was over, and the other boy was talking about leaving the island too, so Rubèn was going to wait until then to go to Girona and come into his inheritance. He said that his relations in Girona drank from gold cups and ate with gold spoons, and had windows with colored glass in them like a church, and houses the size of the Almudaina, filled with servants, and slaves, and enormous fountains, and no one had to work."

The vision of their city as a paradise of sloth and a treasure-house of wealth silenced the amazed spectators.

"You must have been surprised when you arrived here," said Berenguer dryly.

"Oh, I never expected it to be like that, Your Excellency," said Lucà. "He was just a boy who loved to tell wonderful stories to impress us."

"Then you didn't expect to inherit this vast fortune?" asked the third judge.

"It isn't mine, my lord," said Lucà. "It's Rubèn's. I just wanted to find work."

The last few statements of the defendant were almost ignored by everyone except the scribes and the judges, for as Lucà was speaking, a clerk appeared through the door in the side of the room that, when courts were held, was usually reserved for the judges and other officials to make their entrances. He walked over to the table where the judges were seated and crouched down behind Berenguer, murmuring a few words to him before turning to go out. Instead of leaving the room directly, however, the clerk walked over to where the witnesses were gathered and tapped the boy Tomas on the shoulder. Tomas rose and followed the clerk out. As soon as Lucà finished speaking, Berenguer glanced over at his fellow judges, nodded, and left as well.

"Now," said the third judge. "I would just like to go over once more your statement concerning your visits to Master Narcís Bellfont."

⊹⊱══⊰ ⊱══⊰⊹

WHEN the clerk, Tomas, and Berenguer came through the door, Daniel and his captive were seated at a table in the antechamber to the room where the court was sitting, their backs to the three who had just come in. Daniel had cleaned himself up as best he could in the short space of time he had been given. The young man who had leaped from the tree branch onto him was scraped and dusty-looking, but he bristled with injured innocence.

The clerk sat down at one end of the table and was joined by a scribe who had been lurking in the shadows. He was followed by the captain of the guards, who sat next to him, prepared to question him.

"You say your name is Raimon?" said the captain.

"It is," said the young man.

"You are the Raimon who worked for the manager of the estates that lie to the northwest of the road to Figueres—"

"I still work for him. I am his clerk and confidential assistant," he replied.

"Is that him?" asked Berenguer very softly to Tomas.

"No," whispered the boy. "That doesn't sound like him. That one sounds like a gentleman, all polite and rich."

"I must return to the court soon," murmured Berenguer, "but after I leave I would like you to stay here where they can't see you and keep listening. The clerk will bring you into the court again when you are wanted there."

"May I ask what is going on?" said Raimon crisply. "I am a respectable citizen who was traveling on a business matter for my master. I had stepped into the woods for a moment out of natural necessity, and when I tried to come to the assistance of a man who was being attacked on a lonely and dangerous stretch of road, I was seized and dragged in here as if I were a criminal."

"Who attacked him?" asked the captain.

"Some madman who jumped down on him from a tree branch. I would think he was trying to steal his horse. I had just rushed in, when an ignorant lad appeared from nowhere waving a sword about—no doubt stolen from someone—and threatened my life. Clearly he had misunderstood the situation."

"We're sorry for that," said the Bishop blandly, stepping forward so that the young man could see that he was there. "There may have been a misunderstanding. But by a curious coincidence we believe that you might be able to help us in identifying the malefactor now on trial. He or his colleagues may even have been involved in the attack at the road, and we are hoping that you have seen him before." Berenguer swept out of the room and returned to his place on the panel of judges.

The captain gave Raimon a sharp nudge. The young man

looked around him warily before standing up to be escorted
into the chamber.

Lucà was still talking, going over in detail every moment of
his treatment of Master Narcís Bellfont, when Raimon, escorted by the captain, came into the courtroom and stopped in
the doorway.

Berenguer raised his hand to stop the flow of his words for a
moment. "Master Raimon," he said in his silkiest tones, "is this
the man who attacked you on the highroad this morning?"

"It is hard to say, Your Excellency," said the young man,
turning sharply away from the prisoner to face the judges, "because I didn't get a clear look at him before I was attacked by
that boy, but it might be."

At the sound of Raimon's voice, Lucà turned his head and
stared in amazement. "Josep," he said, "what are you doing in
Girona? I thought you were with Joan Cristià in Sardinia. He
sent for you—is he here too? Because if he is, your lordships, he
can testify on my behalf. He knows how little I can do, and
that I know nothing about poisons."

Raimon's face turned chalk-white. "I have never seen this
man in my life before."

"That's not true," said Lucà. "This is the boy I was telling
you about," he said earnestly to the judges. "The one who used
to come and listen to Rubèn's stories and tales at my master's
workroom. Please, your lordships, make him tell you where
Joan Cristià is. He will speak for me."

"This man is mistaken," said Raimon. "I have never been in
Mallorca in my life. I am from Valencia."

"That is interesting, Master Raimon," said the third judge. A
flick of malice narrowed his eyes. "I too am from Valencia. Who
is your family? For surely I must know them."

"I've never met this man before," he replied, pointing over
at the prisoner, his voice rising in panic.

"But that's not true," said Lucà. "His name is Josep, not
Raimon. And he used to help sweep up the workroom floor in
return for his dinner, because his mother—"

"You leave my mother out of it," shrieked Josep. "You
worthless bastard son of a whoring mother, you—" And those
were the last of the obscenities that most of the fascinated spec-

tators understood. The rest continued to pour out of his mouth in an increasingly rapid and almost incomprehensible stream.

"Yes, that's him," cried out Tomas in great excitement, from where he stood behind the captain in the doorway. "That's him. That's the man with the hood and the basket who hit me under the bridge that night it was raining so hard. You see?" he asked, stepping forward and looking around the court in triumphant justification. "He does sound just like my mother when he's angry."

Daniel, who was behind him, nodded. "They all speak like that down around the tanneries in Mallorca City." But his voice was lost to everyone except the judges in the general uproar.

"Young man," said the first judge, bending forward to see Tomas more clearly, "are you sure he is the same person who hit you?"

"Yes, my lord," said Tomas, "that's the person who hit me under the bridge, the one with the cloak and the hood and the basket."

"Then he is the messenger who delivered the noxious compounds to Master Narcís and Master Mordecai," said the first judge. "Young man," he said courteously, "who engaged you to deliver those vials?"

"I had nothing to do with any vials," he said, his voice rising higher. "I know nothing of it."

"Most interesting," said the third judge. "We can perhaps go into that later. But who is this Joan Cristià who can speak for the accused? Is he in court?"

A voice penetrated the noise that rose from the excited spectators. "My lords, may I speak to the question that was just raised concerning the identity of Joan Cristià?"

"Come forward, Master Isaac," said the clerk, who had risen in consternation. "There will be silence before their lordships, the judges."

Isaac came forward, his hand on Yusuf's shoulder to guide him. He bowed to the judges. "Your lordships, I had occasion to treat Joan Cristià in his last illness. He died in the castle at Cruïlles, where he had been most hospitably taken in by His Excellency and His Excellency's attendants."

"What was the cause of his death?" asked the third judge.

"Poison, my lord," said Isaac. "He told me as soon as I spoke to him at the castle that he had been poisoned, and that he knew who had poisoned him."

"How could he have known so certainly?" asked the first judge.

"It seems only one person knew how to mix the poison he had swallowed, and only one person had the opportunity to give it to him. That man he described as a faithless apprentice, to whom he had taught the formula for that particular deadly mixture. When he arrived at Cruïlles, he prescribed for himself an antidote to the concoction he had been given. We made it up and gave it to him, but he knew well that it was unlikely to succeed, since too much time had passed between his drinking the mixture while breakfasting and his arrival at the castle."

"In your opinion, Master Isaac," said the third judge, "was his opinion to be relied upon?"

"It was, my lords. He was clearly a man who was expert in all these matters. He knew as the symptoms began to overcome him, what he had unwittingly swallowed. And the manner in which he died, my lords, is important in this court because his symptoms and the course of his death were precisely the same as those I observed while attempting to treat Master Narcís. They were also consistent with the symptoms Master Mordecai suffered from the tiny amount of poison that he took in before he realized that something was wrong and spat the mixture out."

"Do you know what was in this poison?"

"Now I do, to a great degree," said Isaac. "Unfortunately, I did not have that knowledge in time to help Master Narcís. Master Mordecai kept the remainder of the vial that had been delivered to him, and I was able to apply a variety of different tests in order to study it. Most poisons, your lordships, are simple extracts from a single, deadly herb, and have a telltale odor or taste or even feel, when touched by the fingertips, but this was not a common drug, such as you would expect to find. It was, I discovered, a subtle blend of paralytics and spasmodics that to a certain extent would balance each other out. That, I decided, was the principle operating behind the choice of ingredients.

"What would be the purpose of such a mixture, then, if the

contrary elements counteracted each other?" asked the third judge.

"I suspect that the poisoner who developed the recipe was hoping to blend and confuse the initial effects of the various poisons."

"To what possible end?" asked the third judge.

"To mask what was happening, my lord. To use a homely example, my lords, it was similar to a cook adding a sweet fruit and a bitter orange together to a meat dish. The mouth tastes both, but believes them to be one, neither sweet nor bitter."

"Are you saying that a man could not taste that he was ingesting a poison?" asked the third judge. "Because of the mixture?"

"It had a most unpleasant taste even when heavily diluted with water. That taste could be masked with honey and spices, perhaps. But I think the creator of the mixture was more concerned that his victim not know exactly which poisons he had been given, for there are contraries—antidotes—that some suspicious men might keep about them. And also the poisoner didn't wish the victim to realize what was happening until he had a chance to be far away."

"Who was the creator of this diabolical mixture?" asked Berenguer. "Did he say?"

"Without a doubt, Your Excellency, it was Joan Cristià himself," said Isaac. "That was why he was so bitterly angry."

"The man that I sheltered at Cruïlles and to whom we gave a Christian burial there? Life indeed has many strange turns."

"Then it was close to miraculous that Master Mordecai survived," observed the first judge.

"Not at all, my lord. He had been warned of the possibility, and the taste, along with a certain numbness in the mouth, alerted him. But I am quite certain, my lords, that the same hand, following his master's formula, mixed three, or possibly four batches of that poison: the ones that killed Joan Cristià and Narcís Bellfort, the one that endangered Mordecai ben Aaron, and perhaps one that killed Mistress Magdalena."

"Could it have been the accused?" asked the first judge.

"I don't believe so. The person who was with Joan Cristià when he was poisoned was a young man who called himself

Raimon. According to various accounts, this Raimon has reddish gold hair and the face of an angel. I cannot see the young man who has come into the court, but others here can tell if that is a possible description of him."

"May you die in agony and rot in hell, you blind, useless bastard!" screamed Josep.

"That is the curse that Joan Cristià called down upon the head of his destroyer in his final agonies," said the physician.

"He is dead? Joan?" asked Lucà, looking stricken. "Poor Joan Cristià. Whatever you may say of him, he cured many people."

"It sounds as if he killed a good number as well. Or what is worse, provided the means for many others to destroy their rivals and enemies."

"I cannot believe it," said Lucà. "He was such a clever man and generous too. When did he die?"

"It was, I believe, the twenty-third or twenty-fourth day of October, last year, when His Excellency was so very ill," said Isaac.

"You, I believe you said," observed the Bishop, "were wandering through the province, looking for work at that time."

"I wasn't traveling then, Your Excellency," said Lucà, "From St. Michael's Day in September until after All Saints' Day, I was in Vilafranca de Penedés. I was fortunate enough to get work with a cabinetmaker who was hired by the city to make a splendid carved chest for the royal palace there. It will be presented to Her Majesty later this year. I am sure there are people in Vilafranca who will remember me—I boarded with a widow whose name I could give you. A most respectable, honest woman. Unless poor Joan was poisoned nearby, I could not have been where he was to do such a terrible thing."

"He was not poisoned anywhere near Vilafranca de Penedès," said Isaac. "But I believe Your Excellency's sergeant, who made careful inquiries into the death of the man, could testify to these things more readily than I."

"May I speak?" asked another voice from the room.

The clerk murmured something to the judges.

"Certainly, Master Mordecai," said the first judge.

"According to letters that I have received from Mallorca, this Josep is the son of one Sara, who works from time to time in the household of my kinswoman, Perla, mother of my cousin, Faneta. He reminds me very strongly of a young man who called himself Rubèn, who came to me in October, saying that he was the child of my cousin, Faneta. The hair is the same, but he has grown and put on flesh, and now has a beard."

"Then approach, Master Mordecai, and look more carefully at him."

Mordecai made his way through the crowd and walked up to Josep. "Well, Josep," he said. "It is you. No longer calling yourself Rubèn. I thought so. It takes more than a little beard to confuse me."

"I've never met you before," said Josep. "For which I am heartily thankful."

"What kind of poison did you use to kill my cousin, Faneta, and her poor son?" asked Mordecai softly. "Perla described their deaths in a way that leaves no doubt in my mind that they were poisoned, but how did you do it after you had left the island? Did it take days to kill them? Or did your mother give it to them? That was why you had to kill Master Daniel, wasn't it? Before he could tell anyone that Faneta and Rubèn were dead. Because you believed all that about golden cups and spoons, and your friend's family possessing wealth beyond the dreams of avarice."

"Get me away from these people!" shouted Josep, struggling with the guards who held him tightly. "You can't make me listen to them."

Berenguer waved a dismissive hand, and the guards left with Josep. "Mistress Regina," said the Bishop as calmly as if nothing untoward had happened. "You wished to make a statement in defense of Master Lucà?"

"I wished to say that Master Lucà could not have delivered the poison vials and also that he could not have brewed the poison without my knowing."

"We would be pleased to have you explain," said the first judge.

And in a clear, steady voice, Regina laid out her evidence.

"And Master Romeu," said Berenguer, "you can speak to your knowledge of the movements of the accused man?"

Romeu, hesitant at first, but gaining confidence as the judges listened gravely, pointed out that in his spare time, Lucà was in Romeu's workroom, helping him, and that he was never absent without Romeu knowing exactly where he was and what he was doing. Once or twice, he had gone to a local tavern, but Romeu had gone with him. And since they did not like to leave Mistress Regina alone, that practice had stopped almost before it started.

The spectators, by now in a state of confusion, listened to the reassuring solemn tones of their neighbors and nodded in agreement. They had never thought such a pleasant young man could have done such terrible things, they murmured to each other, not at all disappointed, since there seemed to be some other wicked soul—and such a pretty boy, too—to despise for his evil ways. And the distinct promise of a hanging in the near future.

Berenguer gathered together his court with a glance. The first judge spoke to the clerk, the clerk discharged the prisoner, and everyone left the room. Or almost everyone.

Standing at the back were Romeu, Regina, and Tomas. Not far from them were Isaac, Raquel, Daniel, and Yusuf.

The bells rang for midday. As the sound of the last bell died away against the answering hills, Raquel took her father's hand. "You must go and speak to Lucà, Papa," she said. "He looks so alone."

"Are Regina and Romeu still here?" asked Isaac.

"Yes," said Raquel. "I was going to go over to see her—"

"No, Raquel. Leave them to each other. It is much kinder. And we have much that has to be done, my dear. Should we not go home?"

"What is to be done?" asked Daniel. "This day seems to have had its fill already of things accomplished."

"Oh, Daniel," said Raquel. "Have you forgotten that tomorrow you are to be wed? You must move back to your own house now that the world knows you have returned. You will know it then—there is hardly room for a cat in your house, much less a man right now, with all the cooking and baking and such going on."

"Of course I have not forgotten," said Daniel indignantly. "After waiting all this time, I am not likely to. Come with me, Yusuf, and explain to me how you managed not to appear in the Bishop's court."

"His Excellency thought it would not look quite right," said Yusuf. "And it seems I was not needed."

✢═══ ═══✢

LUCÀ stood where he had been left when the court departed and looked around the almost empty chamber like a lost, bewildered soul. Regina flicked her veil away from her face and walked quickly across the empty space between them. "It's time we went home now, Lucà," she said. "You mustn't keep us waiting too long. I left mutton braising on the fire this morning, and it must be looked to."

"Home?" said Lucà. "I thought I would be dead by now."

Regina took him by the hand and led him over to where her father was standing with the boy.

"This is Tomas," said Regina. "He found the person who killed Master Narcís. You're coming home now, too, Tomas."

"Aren't I sick any more?" he asked.

"Now that they have found that man," said Romeu, "you aren't sick." Without a further word, he took Lucà by the elbow and steered him toward the door that led to the entrance to the palace. They stepped into the bright May sun, strolled across the square, and went down the hill toward the gate.

"Now, Lucà, tell me," said Romeu, paying no attention to the stares of the passing townspeople, "what kind of cabinetry did your master specialize in? As you have seen, I have more work than I can handle, and it seems to me that we could work well together. It is time that Tomas here learned a trade as well."

TWENTY-ONE

Junt és lo temps que mon goig és complet

Come has the time that my pleasure is complete

EARLY in the morning of Raquel's wedding day, a page boy arrived at Isaac's gate with a summons from the Bishop. Without a qualm, he called for Yusuf and left, stepping gratefully into the cool quiet of the palace. They followed the page boy, not to the Bishop's study, but to one of the smaller rooms on the ground floor. The boy knocked; the door opened at once.

"Master Isaac," said Berenguer. "I thank you for your swift response. Before we begin our business, we must finish this little conversation we're having with Master Jaume's clerk, Pau. Perhaps you will join us."

"Certainly, Your Excellency," said Isaac, and sat down.

"Young Pau, here, is telling us everything he knows about Josep, he says. Only he says he knows very little."

"That's true, Your Excellency," said Pau. The physician could smell the fear and panic that dripped in the sweat from the young man's body. "He told me if I didn't know how to find him, or where he was living, then I couldn't get tangled in lies and get in trouble."

"He was wrong, wasn't he?" said the captain of the guard. "Because now you're getting into worse trouble than you can imagine."

"I knew I'd lose my position if Master Jaume found out I was helping him, with letters and such," said Pau.

"It's not just your position you stand to lose, lad," said the captain. "Your friend will be hanged before the week is out, I expect, and so what you have to consider is whether you want to be a loyal friend and be hanged with him."

"Hanged!" said Pau, his voice rising to a squeak. "I never did anything wrong but get him his letters. And there weren't many. Only two."

"Who were these letters from?" asked Berenguer.

"His mother, that's all. And she's a poor widow who can't afford to send letters, so they went to Barcelona with a friend and then they came whenever we—whenever Master Jaume had documents that had to be sent up here."

"A poor widow, is she?" said the Bishop. "There are other ways to describe her, I suspect, but that will do. So he came in and picked them up?"

"Well," said Pau, "he didn't, actually. I took them out to him. There was someone in the city he knew and he didn't want to see him again, because they'd quarreled."

"So you walked out to the *finca* and delivered them?"

"Once. Or we met on the hillside just beyond the bridge."

"And that was where you told him about all the wills that Master Jaume drew up," said the captain.

"No, I didn't," he said indignantly. "I only told him about Mistress Magdalena's, because I thought it was funny what she said in her will, and he said if he were Lucà he'd be tempted to slip a little henbane in the next batch of stomach medicine he gave her, and we laughed about that, because of course he'd never have done it."

"And then she died."

"But everyone knew how sick she was," said Pau. "She just died, that's all."

"And then you told him about Master Narcís," said the captain. It wasn't a question. It was a statement, cold and brutal.

"I didn't tell him," said Pau. "It just came out when I was talking about something else. I didn't mean to say it, and he promised he wouldn't tell anyone what I'd told him. But he said that he'd bet me sixpence that something would happen to Master Narcís. And when it did, he collected the money and told me that any man who puts someone in his will like that— leaving money to a man who knows how to mix poisons—deserves what he gets, especially if he tells him."

"What do you mean, if he tells him?" asked Berenguer.

"He must have, mustn't he?" said Pau. "How else would he know? I didn't tell Master Lucà. Raimon said I must have, but I never did. Everyone thought I was telling everybody about what was in people's wills—His Excellency accused me of lying, and told Master Jaume that I must have told people about those wills, because how else would they find out. But Raimon said I wasn't to worry, because when he came into his money he'd share it with me, and I'd be rich, too."

"What money?" asked the captain. "I didn't know that your friend was going to come into some money."

"Yes, he was," said Pau. "He loaned money to that Rubèn, who was going to inherit the money that Master Mordecai was keeping for him. And that was true, because the documents were in our records and I found them. It was a prodigious amount of money," he said, his eyes widening. "More than—"

"Pau," said Berenguer. "You are doing it again. There are eight people in this room, and you are about to tell us all confidential information most of us have no right to hear."

"Oh," said Pau. "Well, as soon as Master Mordecai gave Rubèn the money, Rubèn was going to give most of it to Raimon, because he owed it to him. They grew up together and were always great friends. And then we'd both be rich. He had a lot of things to do then because the money was coming in, and so he stopped working for a while to concentrate on it."

"Where was he when he stopped working to concentrate?" asked Berenguer.

"At the *finca*," said Pau. "Mostly. The housekeeper and the mistress, they're always ready to hide him someplace if someone came looking for him. Everyone likes him, Your Excellency. You see? He's never done anything."

"Take him away," said Berenguer. "And would someone try to explain to him what his friend has done? I cannot stand to see such sweet ignorance in a modern world."

When the others had left, Isaac turned to his patient. "Are you well, Your Excellency?"

"I am, Master Isaac. And I am mightily relieved to have young Master Lucà tried and not to have had the obligation of turning him over to the civil authorities to be hanged. Because in spite of logic and evidence, I had trouble believing he could have poisoned anything—not even a rat."

"I expect Mistress Regina is also relieved," said Isaac.

"Indeed. And Romeu, who is taking him into the business. Apparently, whatever skills he had or didn't have as an herbalist, he's very good with wood. And Romeu asked if he could take the lad as an apprentice, since little Tomas seems to have no kin—not even me."

"I had heard that rumor, Your Excellency, and hoped that you did not find it too distressing."

"It seemed useful, and so I took no steps to contradict it," said Berenguer. "He's a nice lad, for all that his mother might not have been as good as she could be. But he will live that down. Many a rich and powerful man in this kingdom has already done that," he added, with the laugh of one whose ancestry was ancient, impeccable, and well attested to.

"Will you be trying Josep?" asked Isaac.

"I have turned him over to the city," said the Bishop. "I wish no more of this troubling business, and they will make short work of it."

"It is troubling, Your Excellency," said Isaac. "It disturbs me that the deaths occurred after I had sent Daniel to Mallorca to find out who Rubèn was. Almost as if I had precipitated them."

"Isaac, my friend, it must be thinking of your daughter's wedding that clouds your mind. The deaths started when Josep returned to the city," said Berenguer.

"But it took us time to act," said Isaac stubbornly.

"Not at all. Consider. First a sick old lady dies and then an invalid. The wills roused our suspicions, even if we pursued the wrong scent. We were led astray by the evil of the young man's motives and his wanton disregard for the lives of others."

"True, Your Excellency. He dreamed of eating from gold and dressing in silk," said Isaac. "And the power of a young man's dreams can be frightening."

"The captain asked him why he concocted such an elaborate plan to involve young Lucà," said Berenguer.

"What did he say, Your Excellency?"

"Nothing," said the Bishop. "He laughed. He laughed because he almost made us hang an innocent man. An old friend."

"I think that he saw him more as a rival than a friend, Your Excellency," said Isaac. "And he needed someone for you to hang for Mordecai's death. He was determined to inherit, and knew Mordecai would make inquiries sooner or later. He was not going to let him live long enough to discover that Rubèn was dead."

"And, of course, Lucà knew who he was. So it had to be Lucà," said the Bishop. "But I find the deaths on Mallorca as troubling as any part of this, and yet I doubt that there is anything that I can do about them."

"If Josep's mother did indeed poison Faneta and Rubèn," said Isaac, "it would be difficult to find proof of it. And if she did, it would have been at the instigation of her son."

"That carries mother love too far for my tastes, my friend. But I fear in this case we must leave her punishment to heaven."

⊹〉═══ ═══〈⊹

ONCE the evening began to spread its shadows over the *call*, the women gathered in the courtyard to escort Raquel to the synagogue to be married. After a whole day spent in marriage preparations, she put on her embroidered silk shift, and then a silk gown of tawny gold trimmed with green. Over it she slipped a surcoat of green silk embroidered with gold thread. Her veil fell almost to her feet, covering her perfumed hair.

"Mama," she said. "I feel strange. Not like me at all. How can I possibly do anything dressed like this?"

"You look unbelievably beautiful, my love," said her mother. "And no one expects you to do anything but blush and smile, dance a little, and walk very carefully in all that silk. I swear you are even more beautiful than I was as a bride, and everyone said that I was the greatest beauty they had ever seen." She sighed.

"You still are, Mama," said Raquel. "It can be almost annoying at times."

"I haven't your height," said her mother, with that cool judgment she applied to such questions. "Come now," she said, "it's time."

AFTER the wedding, one sharp-eared little boy insisted that when Daniel was standing near his bride, veiled as he had never seen her before, he whispered, "I won't marry you wrapped up like that unless you promise your name is Raquel."

To which she replied, "Rip off the veil and look."

"Now I know," he said. "No one else could say that."

AND after hours of merriment and feasting and dancing and songs, religious, sentimental, and alas, also bawdy, the bride was carried off to Daniel's house to be bedded.

Isaac was sitting beside Ephraim when Mordecai joined them. "Isaac," he said. "I have come into a house."

"Which house is that?" asked Isaac.

"It is next to yours. Indeed, it even shares a wall with you. It would be a simple thing to put a door into that wall and have the two houses join."

"Mordecai, unless my Judith starts to present me with another son every year, I don't think we need another house, although it is a good, well-built one."

"*You* don't need it," said Mordecai, "but Daniel and Raquel could use a house, especially one joined to her father's house. Raquel's dowry would buy them the house."

"Raquel's dowry is not quite that substantial," said Isaac.

"The house is not as expensive as you may think, Isaac. I know the size of Raquel's dowry, and I know it will cover the cost of the house, with some left over."

"Mordecai, that is too extravagant a wedding present even for my Raquel. And no one knows better than I how much she deserves."

"Think of all they suffered on my behalf when I sent Daniel

to Mallorca, where he was forced to stay with Maimó and sleep in silken sheets and eat like a prince every night," said Mordecai. "Someone has to acknowledge his sacrifice."

"Were they really silken sheets?" asked Ephraim.

"They should have been," said Mordecai.

BUT in the chamber prepared for them, Raquel and Daniel were not thinking of houses, or family, or dowries at all.

"My beloved is mine," murmured Raquel in a voice husky with desire. "And I was beginning to think it would never happen," she added with a giggle. "Blow out those candles and come here, Daniel."

"Never," he said. "Our bedchamber will always be filled with wax candles—for they reveal your beauty with their light."

"You're going to be an expensive husband."

AFTERWORD

"I received a letter from Perla," said Mordecai, sitting down in the shade of the fruit trees in Isaac's courtyard.

"And is she well?" asked Isaac.

"Disturbed, but well," said Mordecai. "May I read some of it to you, my friend? I would like your opinion before I answer it."

"Certainly," said Isaac. "I would be most interested."

"She says, 'Your news troubled me, for I fear my silence allowed Josep to harm that unfortunate man,' although," added Mordecai, "if Perla knew the entire tale, she would not have said that. I told her only of the murder of Master Narcís. I think it was a misplaced kindness on my part."

"Possibly," said Isaac. "But I understand your reasons."

"The letter continues, 'and Sara would have been spared much sorrow. I mourned for the sweet boy I had known and loved, but poor Sara was distraught with grief on learning the news of his trial and death. At least her suffering was short-lived.'"

"Short-lived?" said Isaac, surprised.

"Yes," said Mordecai. "'Not a week after we received the news, Sara's body was found at the foot of the ramparts. No one knows whether she threw herself over in despair, or tripped by accident—for she smelled strongly of wine, alas—or was hurled over by intention. No matter which it was, no one is going to stir himself to look into the death of a laundress, and so I am left alone to mourn the beautiful Sara I used to know.

"'Mostly I am disturbed because before your letter arrived, she begged me for an enormous sum of money—a thousand *sous*—saying that she needed it to pay back a loan from a friend who had become threatening. She swore that it was only for a short time, for she had every expectation of receiving more than that from Josep, who was doing very well in his new employment. I had given her various sums over the years, none of them repaid, and this time I refused. It was too much, and I feared it would go straight to Josep. Now I wonder if she did owe the money and was being threatened by the lender. She had some rough friends, who could well have taken such a crude vengeance.

"'No matter how I look at the affair, I see that I have been wrong. If you could be so generous as to write to me, I would find it a great comfort.' And that is all she says of Josep and Sara. What do you think?"

"What do I think, Mordecai? I think that the thousand *sous* bought a laundress's son passage back and forth from Mallorca and other places. How he afforded all that travel had puzzled me."

"It must also have bought him the clothing that was suitable for a gentleman of some quality," said Mordecai.

"No doubt," said Isaac. "But mostly I believe that the Lord has spared all of us from seeking retribution from a foolish and wicked woman. And if I were you, Mordecai, I would send Mistress Perla a gentle and kindly reply."

AUTHOR'S NOTE

ALL the chapter headings are from the works of the
Valencian poet,
Ausiàs March, c. 1397–1459,
translated by Harry Roe, 2002.